Hot Summer Loving

Seduction, passion and blazing heat…

By Request

Praise for three bestselling authors –
Jacqueline Baird, Miranda Lee
and Sandra Field

About A MOST PASSIONATE REVENGE:
'Jacqueline Baird pens a delicious tale with
fabulous characters, an explosive conflict
and thrilling scenes.'
—*Romantic Times*

About AUNT LUCY'S LOVER:
'[A] spicy tale of sensual romance set against a
lush, tropical backdrop.'
—*Romantic Times*

About Sandra Field:
'Sandra Field pens a phenomenal love story.'
—*Romantic Times*

Hot Summer Loving

A MOST PASSIONATE REVENGE
by
Jacqueline Baird

AUNT LUCY'S LOVER
by
Miranda Lee

REMARRIED IN HASTE
by
Sandra Field

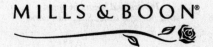

MILLS & BOON®

*MILLS & BOON and MILLS & BOON with the Rose Device
are registered trademarks of the publisher.
Harlequin Mills & Boon Limited,
Eton House, 18-24 Paradise Road, Richmond, Surrey, TW9 1SR*

HOT SUMMER LOVING © by Harlequin Enterprises II B.V., 2004

A Most Passionate Revenge, Aunt Lucy's Lover and
Remarried in Haste were first published in Great Britain by
Harlequin Mills & Boon Limited in separate, single volumes.

A Most Passionate Revenge © Jacqueline Baird 2000
Aunt Lucy's Lover © Miranda Lee 1996
Remarried in Haste © Sandra Field 1998

ISBN 0 263 84073 5

05-0804

*Printed and bound in Spain
by Litografia Rosés S.A., Barcelona*

Jacqueline Baird began writing as a hobby when her family objected to the smell of her oil painting, and immediately became hooked on the romantic genre. She loves travelling and worked her way around the world from Europe to the Americas and Australia, returning to marry her teenage sweetheart. She lives in Ponteland, Northumbria, the county of her birth, and has two teenage sons. She enjoys playing badminton, and spends most weekends with husband Jim, sailing their Gp.14 around Derwent Reservoir.

A MOST PASSIONATE REVENGE

by
Jacqueline Baird

A MOST PASSIONATE
REVENGE

group of the club and doing likewise in the corner of the room. Their last Date was to attend a dinner party for recently engaged couple, at a nearby country house hotel, arranged so the two families could meet. Xavier was a reluctant guest.

'Your trouble is that you have never been in love,' Teresa's comment interrupted his thoughts.

'But I have been married,' Xavier drawled mockingly. 'And I can assure you Teresa, very few people in this world find the kind of relationship you call 'love' so satisfying.'

'Rubbish, you're just a hopeless cynic,' she answered spiritedly. 'Anyway, it's always so different and varied...

CHAPTER ONE

'THE BOY is only twenty-four years old; that's far too young to marry. Jamie is your son; surely you can talk him out of it?' Xavier demanded, with a cynical twist to his sensual mouth as he glanced down at his sister, Teresa, lounging on the sofa. He knew from personal experience his older sister was perfectly capable of controlling her son, if she wanted to. *¡Dios!* She'd certainly controlled Xavier when their mother had died when he was only eight. Ten years older than him she'd taken on the role of mother and had been stricter than the mother they'd lost. Much as he loved his sister, he had heaved a sigh of relief when at the age of twenty-four Teresa had met and fallen in love with David Easterby. The Englishman had been visiting their ranch some miles east of Seville to purchase a pure Spanish-Andaluz horse, for his stables in Yorkshire.

The rest was history, Xavier mused. Twenty-five years on their only child wanted to get married. The reason for his trip to the farm and racing stables in the heart of the Yorkshire Dales was to attend a dinner party for the engaged couple, at a nearby country house hotel, arranged so the two families could meet. Xavier was a reluctant guest…

'Your trouble is that you have never been in love.' Teresa's comment interrupted his thoughts.

'But I have been married,' Xavier drawled mockingly. 'And I can assure you Teresa, very few people in this world find the kind of partnership you and David share.'

'Rubbish, you're just a hopeless cynic,' his sister responded bluntly. 'Anyway it's Jamie's decision and David

5

and I support him unconditionally. They will be here any minute, so please keep your opinions to yourself, and try to be civil to his fiancée Ann, and her parents.'

'Not to mention the spinster cousin,' Xavier prompted with the sardonic arch of one ebony brow. He'd been disconcerted to learn on his arrival three hours earlier that not only were the parents and the fiancée staying for the weekend, but also a female cousin. 'I'm warning you, Teresa; if you have any notion of pairing me off with the lady—forget it!'

'As if I would dare!' Teresa said archly, her dark eyes sweeping over his six feet four frame and comparing it with her own very average build. Her brother was a formidable man in every respect; wealthy, powerful and with a spectacularly handsome profile, night black hair, and hooded chestnut brown eyes that appeared almost golden when he was amused or excited. As a young man, women had fallen at his feet like ninepins and he'd taken full advantage of the fact. But for the past few years the gold was rarely evident in his gaze. His eyes were cold and hard, and he rarely smiled. 'I doubt anyone would dare challenge you anymore, Xavier, about anything,' Teresa added a flicker of compassion in her brown eyes.

Wincing at the unwanted pity he saw in his sister's face, Xavier gave her an exasperated glance then turned and crossed the elegant yet comfortable living room. After all it was none of his business. If his nephew wanted to get married at a ridiculously young age why should he try to stop him? He stood in the large bow of the window and gazed out over the gravelled drive and parkland beyond, without really seeing it. His thoughts were on his father, Don Pablo Ortega Valdespino. At seventy-nine and with a weak heart he was too ill to travel to England and so he'd insisted on Xavier representing him at the engagement party.

Xavier and his father rarely saw eye to eye on anything, and Jamie's forthcoming betrothal had been no exception. It was only when Don Pablo had begun berating him for not producing children of his own to carry on the family name that Xavier had given in, and agreed to be his father's representative for the weekend. He disliked house parties unless they were in his own home with a few carefully chosen friends. In fact it must be almost nine years since he'd spent a weekend out of Spain on anything other than business. Xavier supposed it was time to face up to the fact that he'd become jaded. His work was his life, with an occasional visit to his mistress to take care of his physical needs, and thinking back it must be over five months since he'd even done that....

The sound of a car caught his attention, and he stared through the window with some interest at the two vehicles coming up the drive. He recognised the first one as the large four-wheel drive that belonged to Jamie. He should, he'd bought it for the boy as a twenty-first birthday present. But it was the second that grabbed his attention. It was a classic racing green E-Type Jaguar of the nineteen sixties. The exaggerated long elegant bonnet and wire wheels were unmistakable and with the bodywork gleaming in the afternoon sun, it was immaculate; a delight to any dedicated car buff, and Xavier did love cars.

His nephew, Jamie, bounced out of the first vehicle, and opened the rear door, allowing a middle-aged couple to alight. Xavier glanced briefly at the man and the woman, and at the pretty brunette who'd appeared at Jamie's side, the bride-to-be presumably. But it was the second car that held his attention. The weekend might not be lost after all, with a bit of luck he could talk cars to a real enthusiast.

The owner of the E-Type Jaguar was obviously a person after his own heart.

Xavier tensed. His hooded dark eyes—usually so cold—suddenly flared with a brilliant light, as the driver alighted and rubbed a microscopic speck of dust from the front wing. It was a woman, and *what* a woman! Tall, long-legged, Titian hair scraped back from her face and tied at her nape with a red silk scarf. She turned towards the boot of the car and he saw the tumble of curls reached halfway down her elegant back. The voices floated up on the cool spring air and Xavier's dark brows drew together in a thunderous frown.

'Where on earth did this old wreck of a car come from, Rose? It can't possibly be environmentally-friendly!' Jamie demanded, but amusement danced in his eyes and his arm was firmly fixed around the waist of his fiancée, which softened his scathing comments.

The driver slammed the trunk closed, and with a week-end case in one hand she tilted back her head, and glanced across at the young couple. 'Watch it, boyoh! Any one who insults Bertram insults *moi!* He's the love of my life and far more dependable than any man.' Brilliant green eyes sparkled with amusement, and a lush mouth curved in a broad smile as the stunning woman strode over to the young couple.

'And for your information, Jamie, it came from my father; it was his pride and joy, and is probably worth twice as much as that monster motor you drive.'

'She's right. It's a classic and highly sought after,' the older grey-haired man cut in and turned to the woman. 'A bit of a coincidence meeting on the road like that! I hope you didn't drive too fast, Rosalyn dear.'

'Yes it was quite a coincidence. I recognised Jamie's car just outside of Richmond, but then I had the dubious pleasure of being picked up by these two at the airport last week. And no, Uncle Alex, I never broke the speed limit all the way here,' she laughed.

Xavier hardly heard the conversation. The instant tightening in his groin had been a stunning affirmation of the woman's beauty. '¡Dios mío!' he exclaimed under his breath. He'd never reacted this strongly to a woman in over a decade. He was shocked but not surprised. He'd just been thinking it was a long time since he'd visited his mistress!

He took a step back and half concealed by the velvet drapes at the window, he watched, his tall broad-shouldered frame rigid with tension. His dark eyes narrowed intently on the red-haired laughing woman and in that instant his decision was made. He was going to have her. He was going to crush those pouting sensual lips beneath his own. He was going to strip that delicious body naked and bury himself in her womanhood over and over again. A devilish light of challenge burned in his deep brown eyes; he felt more vitally alive than he had in years. The weekend promised to be an experience he would never forget, and neither would the laughing woman, he vowed. He felt like punching his nephew simply because she bestowed a smile upon the young man.

He saw her glance up at the window and suddenly realising what he was doing, he shoved his hands deep into the pockets of his black jeans. Her fate was sealed but now was not the time, not yet… He needed a game plan, and at the moment his hands were shaking and his brain was clouded by testosterone, just like a hormonal teenager.

He spun around. 'Your guests have arrived, Teresa,' he said with not a hint of the turmoil in his mind showing in his hard expressionless face. 'I'm going for a walk; I'll meet them at dinner.' And, not waiting for a response, he strode across the room through the adjoining conservatory and out into the side garden of the house.

A SMILE lingering around her lips, Rose glanced up at the house. Built with small red bricks, and mellowed with time it looked friendly and welcoming. The graceful bay windows were surrounded with a profusion of climbing plants. The fresh bright green leaves of a Virginia creeper half covered the walls and intermingled with the small pink flowers of a rampant clematis. The weekend was looking better already. She smoothed her green cashmere sweater down over her slim hips, and tightening her grip on her weekend case she moved forward, then stopped and hesitated for a second before walking on.

Then she shivered; all the hair on her body leaped to attention and she had the inexplicable feeling that someone's eyes were following her every move. She glanced back up at the rambling building and for some reason it no longer seemed so friendly. Don't be stupid, she told herself, and quickened her pace to catch up with the others, heading for the front door.

The director of the overseas medical relief agency for whom she'd worked for the past three years had warned her that she badly needed a rest. She was becoming far too involved with her young patients, and was suffering from emotional fatigue. For these reasons he'd insisted she return to England for an extended three-month holiday, saying that otherwise she would crack up. She hadn't wanted to believe him but maybe he was right. If she was going to imagine that eyes were following her everywhere, she really needed the break!

The front door was opened wide, and Rose forgot her fears as she was swept up in a flurry of introductions. Jamie's mother, Teresa, was a small dark-haired, very attractive woman, somewhere in her forties. His father David was tall with grey hair and looked a good few years older than his wife.

Milling around in the large hall the conversation was typical: the weather, and the journey down. Rose glanced at her Aunt Jean and Uncle Alex, and was happy to see they seemed to be relaxed. Her cousin, Ann, was clasped to Jamie's side, as if he was frightened she would run away, and the glances the two youngsters shared told the world they were madly in love.

'My father was unable to travel all the way to Yorkshire from our family home in Seville because of ill health, but hopefully he will be better by the wedding in September,' Teresa explained, before offering to show them to their rooms.

Seville! Rose's heart missed a beat. 'You're Spanish! But you don't sound it—' she blurted, and colour surged up her face as the conversation stopped and everyone looked at her. Teresa laughed and broke the awkward moment.

'My husband is always telling me I sound more Yorkshire than he does, but I have lived here twenty-five years so it is hardly surprising.'

Not to Teresa maybe, but it was a hell of a shock to Rose and five minutes later as she followed everyone upstairs, she was still worrying. Uncle Alex and Aunt Jean disappeared into a bedroom suite at the front of the house, with Ann next door, and Rose continued along the hall with Teresa. Her hostess indicated a closed door with a wave of her hand.

'This is my brother's bedroom. He arrived this morning but he has gone for a walk on the moors. You will meet him at dinner.' Teresa led her to the next door. 'This is your room.'

Mechanically Rose made the right response and walked

into the bedroom. A brother! The news, coupled with the earlier mention of Seville sent alarm bells ringing in her mind. She shrugged her slender shoulders dismissing the chilling thought. There must be a million or more people in Seville. The odds on it being the only other Sevilliano she'd met must be astronomical.

Still, no one had said anything about a brother... But then to be honest she'd hardly spoken to Ann in the past week. The young couple had picked her up at the airport, driven her to her own flat in Islington, north London, dropped the bombshell of their engagement, told her to attend this celebration dinner at the weekend and then they'd taken off the next day. The two telephone conversations Rose had had with her Aunt Jean in Richmond, had been about the arrangements for the party, and if the truth be known, Rose had slept for much of the past week.

Glancing around the comfortable bedroom, Rose was tempted to drop down on the queen-sized bed and sleep again. But mindful of Teresa's instruction to come down for cocktails at seven, she unpacked her weekend case instead, placing her underwear in the top drawer of a lovely old pine chest, and the rest of her clothes in the matching wardrobe. Rose glanced around the room. It really was lovely; the pine furniture was genuinely old, and the sprigged wallpaper and matching drapes and duvet, were charming. She investigated a door to one side and found a neat little shower room with vanity basin and toilet.

Stripping off her clothes, she stepped into the shower stall and turned on the taps. The warm spray caressed her body and she sighed with relief. When she'd arrived back in England last week, Ann had informed her almost straight away that she was engaged. Rose had wondered if her cousin was too young at twenty-one. Plus she'd felt guilty because Rose had been indirectly responsible for the couple meeting. She'd rented out her apartment in London to students for the past three years, allowing Ann to stay rent free. Jamie and another student, Mike, had shared the three-bedroomed flat with Ann. Jamie and Ann had been drawn together when they realised they only lived a few miles apart in Yorkshire.

Everything was going to be fine, Rose told herself as the hot jets of water eased the tension from her taut muscles and relaxed her mind.

Twenty minutes later, Rose closed the bedroom door behind her, and hurried along down the stairs. The sitting room door was slightly ajar and she could hear the sound of chatter and laughter. Drawing a deep breath she pushed open the door and entered.

'Last as usual, Rosalyn! But you look as lovely as ever.' Her Uncle Alex was standing by the fireplace, a smile on his face, and Rose started to cross the room towards him. But then it happened...

Teresa moved from the entrance to the conservatory. 'You know everyone Rosalyn, except my brother. Please, allow me to introduce you to Xavier.'

At the sound of the man's name Rose's step faltered. It could not be! Such an outrageous coincidence just wasn't possible. Nervously she smoothed her damp palms down over her slim hips and almost in slow motion she turned towards Teresa, and the man beside her exiting the conservatory beside the hostess. Fate could not be so cruel, she told herself, but with a terrible sense of inevitability about it, she slowly tilted back her head to look up at the man.

'My brother Xavier Valdespino, and this is Ann's cousin, Dr. Rosalyn May.'

She barely heard the introduction but she did not need to...

Xavier Valdespino gazed down at her, his dark face

shadowed by the evening sunlight shining through the conservatory behind him. He stepped forward, his bronzed features set in a mask of social politeness.

'It is a pleasure to meet you. Dr….' His deep voice hesitated a moment. 'Rosalyn May.'

He reached out and took her hand in his. Numb with shock Rose let him and felt the strength of his long fingers close around hers. Panic flared briefly in her wide green eyes as they met his but his golden-brown eyes smiled coolly down at her without the slightest hint of recognition in his gaze.

'How do you do,' she murmured politely. But her heart was pounding like jungle drums in her chest. Seeing him again after a decade was an experience that needed all her self-control. His tall, broad-shouldered presence exuded the same aura of vibrant masculinity which she'd recognised and succumbed to at their first meeting. Only years of discipline in controlling her emotions enabled her to behave with the modicum of social necessity.

'Better for having met you.' And, before Rose realised what he intended, his head bowed and he raised her hand to plant firm warm lips on the back of her hand. In any other man it would have been over the top but somehow from this man it seemed perfectly natural.

Electric sensation sizzled through her flesh and she tugged her hand away, her mouth opening and closing without a sound.

'And may I say; I concur completely with your Uncle, you do look lovely.' Dark eyes swept down from the flame of her hair, and lingered on her face then her green silk dress and finally on the long length of her legs, before returning to her face.

She felt the colour rise in her cheeks, and with it her temper. Her thick-lashed green eyes swept over his tall frame with the same studied intensity. He was powerfully built with not an ounce of superfluous flesh on the long lean length of his body. Clothed in an immaculately tailored black dinner suit, with a white silk dress shirt, and black bow tie, he looked exactly what he was: a hugely successful business tycoon, who financed his own formula-one racing team as a hobby. Now he was acting like the womanizer she knew he was, never mind the fact he was married!

'Thank you,' she said calmly recovering from the horrendous shock of being presented to a man she had not seen for ten years and had hoped never to see again in this lifetime.

Then she noticed what shock had made her miss at first glance. The incredibly handsome face was not quite as she remembered. A deep scar curved in a sickle shape from his ear to his jaw on one side of his face, marring the perfect olive-skinned complexion. Her professional interest aroused, she realised he'd obviously had a skin graft sometime ago, possibly for a burn, as the skin encircled by the scar was paler and continued down beneath the collar of his shirt.

'I believe I am to be your partner for the evening, Rosalyn. I may call you Rosalyn?' One superbly arched dark brow lifted in query. 'Unless you prefer another name?' he prompted smoothly.

'Another name! Well, most people call me Rose, apart from my Aunt and Uncle, but I have no preference,' Rose answered cagily, her green eyes narrowing on his hard unyielding face. Had he recognised her after all? She couldn't be sure, she'd been a teenager when they'd met; she'd been much slimmer with short straight hair a couple of shades darker than it was now; the African sun over the past three years had lightened it quite a lot. Whereas he'd been already a mature man of twenty-nine and the intervening years had hardly changed him at all, except for the scar.

'With your permission I will call you Rosalyn. It's such a very feminine name—it suits you,' his deep voice opined throatily.

He'd lost none of his charm, that was for sure, Rose acknowledged. Thankfully he did not seem to know who she was. Then why would he? As far as he was concerned she'd been little more than a one-night stand, one among thousands. She was flattering herself to imagine he would remember her, let alone the name she'd used for the brief time she'd been a model.

'Whatever you prefer,' Rose said casually, all too aware of his intense male scrutiny. His dark eyes roamed over her body, lingering on her physical attributes in turn. She felt as though he had mentally stripped her naked, but she was almost sure it was not memory prompting his interest but simply a purely male reaction to a halfway attractive woman.

'Now Uncle Xavier, no hogging my soon-to-be-cousin; the poor girl might die of thirst!' Jamie appeared suddenly at her side holding out a crystal flute filled to the brim with sparkling Dom Perignon. 'Champagne, Rose?'

Glad of the interruption, Rose turned slightly and took the proffered glass with a smile.

'A toast,' Jamie offered with a broad grin, and glancing around the room he lifted his glass. 'To Ann and I, as nobody else seems to be going to do it.'

In the congratulations and laughter that followed, Rose took the opportunity to slip across the room to her Aunt Jean, but she had the uncanny feeling that a pair of dark assessing eyes were following her every move. Maybe she should have admitted to him that they'd met before, and they could have talked as old friends. No—they had never been friends. But lovers, yes!

The memory made her wince. Pain like a red-hot needle pierced her heart for a second, and she couldn't stop herself glancing back at the man who'd caused it. The softly curling raven hair was longer now, with silver wings curving around his ears. The fine lines around his eyes, and the deep grooves on either side of his sinfully sexy mouth were deeper, but he was still the most staggeringly attractive man she'd ever seen. A pity his nature was anything but attractive... At that moment his dark head lifted from a conversation with his brother-in-law, and his piercing eyes clashed with hers. She watched as he moved towards her. A bit like a rabbit caught in the headlights of a car, she was helpless to look away. What on earth was happening to her? She was long past this kind of nonsense. But to her chagrin when he reached her, he glanced past her to say something to her Aunt and Uncle.

'Alex, Jean, David informs me the taxis have arrived so if you are ready we can leave.' Only then did he look at Rose. 'Us four are to share one car, Rosalyn, if that's all right with you?'

'Yes, of course.' What else could she say?

'You're sure? he asked with slow deliberation. 'I got the distinct impression you couldn't get away from me fast enough,' he drawled mockingly, his eyes still holding hers. 'I hope I was wrong.'

Rose could feel the angry colour rising in her cheeks, but she swallowed down a scathing retort and got slowly to her feet. 'You were,' she replied lightly. 'Shall we go? I'm starving.'

Once again, more blatantly this time, his gaze ran the length of her shapely body, and then rested on the classic oval of her face. 'I know the feeling.' Curving a large hand around her elbow he added, 'My hunger is rising by the minute.'

She cast him a swift wary glance beneath the thick veil of her lashes. She knew by the suggestive tone of his voice that he was being deliberately provocative. The very last thing she wanted was to spend an evening in Xavier's company, and she almost groaned out loud when she realised, never mind the evening, it was perfectly possible she would have to spend all weekend with him. She was not due to depart until Monday morning with her Aunt and Uncle, as she was going to stay with them for a week or two. Her other suitcase was still in her car along with a pile of books she had been promising herself to read for years.

'When are you returning to Spain?' she blurted without thinking as he led her out of the house and to the waiting limousine. The warmth of his hand on her bare arm reminding her of feelings she'd thought were long forgotten.

'You're not very flattering to a man's ego, Rosalyn. We've only just met and you seem to have a great desire to see me depart,' he drawled and she could see the mockery in his dark eyes as he met her gaze.

'No, really, I was only making polite conversation,' she denied flatly.

'Forgive me, I am not well versed on the social niceties of the English.' His dark head bent and he murmured in her ear, 'Perhaps you can teach me.' He promptly released her, and stood back to allow her Aunt and Uncle to get in the car first.

Thank heaven the journey to the hotel was only ten minutes Rose thought angrily. She cast a sideways glance at the man seated beside her. He was talking quite easily to her Aunt and Uncle, while she was tense with the effort to hold herself away from the long body so close to her own. His shoulder and thigh lightly brushed hers every so often as the chauffeur negotiated the twists and turns of the narrow Yorkshire lanes. But Xavier was obviously not concerned by the physical contact—instead his expression remained coolly aloof.

'Rosalyn was in Spain once.' Aunt Jean's comment impinged on Rose's distracted thoughts.

'On holiday,' Rose cut in quickly. No way did she want her aunt mentioning she'd once been a model. It might just jog the arrogant devil's memory.

'So you've visited my country, Rosalyn? Where did you stay?' She could see no hint of anything but polite query in the expression that met hers, and she chastised herself for overreacting. The man did not know her from Adam.

'Oh I stayed in Barcelona; a wonderful city,' she responded coolly.

'I agree with you. I used to visit Barcelona every year for the Grand Prix racing. But I have not been for some years.'

Rose gave him a considering look. Except for a slight narrowing of his heavy-lidded dark eyes, his expression remained one of polite interest, but for a second she wondered if it was overly polite—as though he was concealing something. She sure as hell would not want to play poker with the man, she thought dryly.

'You used to race cars?' Alex cut in enthusiastically.

'No. I used to support a team, as a hobby.' Xavier aimed his response at Alex. 'But unfortunately other commitments took over and I no longer have the time. But I still love cars and have quite a collection at home.'

'Have you seen Rosalyn's car? It's a beauty.'

Xavier turned back to Rose. 'Yes, I saw it in the drive—an E-type Jaguar.' His dark eyes caught and held hers. 'Rather a fast car for a lady, I would have thought.'

'Rather a chauvinistic statement for the twenty-first century, I would have thought,' Rose shot back with feeling. Male chauvinism of any kind was absolute anathema to her.

'You are not one of those rampant feminists who believe a man is only good for one thing, are you?'

There was no mistaking the cynical amusement in his tone. 'And if I am?' she asked curtly.

'It has always been my opinion that beautiful women should be protected, pampered and adored by the male of the species, after all it was what they were put on earth for, that and having babies,' he replied with slow deliberation. 'It is such a waste when a woman looks like an angel but has the mind of a steel trap.' His hand lifted and casually caught a single wayward curl of red hair and tucked it behind her ear. 'A loose strand.'

Loose strand be blowed! Rose's green eyes blazed with outrage, angry colour rising in her face. He was deliberately winding her up and she could sense the amusement lurking beneath his cool gaze. 'Better than no mind at all, like some men I have met,' she returned furiously, oddly disturbed by the touch of his long finger on her cheek.

'It was meant as a joke,' Xavier said dryly. 'And perhaps I thought it would be amusing to discover if you had a temper to match your hair.'

CHAPTER TWO

ROSE GLARED at Xavier, and jerked her head back. 'If you'd spent the last few years in the trouble spots of the world, like I've been, most recently Africa, and had to repair the damage done to young girls by a male chauvinistic society, you would not find the subject so amusing. Girls with their bodies mangled by a badly done circumcision, simply because it is the custom. Or had to watch a fourteen-year-old die in childbirth having been repeatedly raped until she was pregnant and then married off to her rapist. Officially against the law, but a male tradition and so the law turns a blind eye. People like you disgust me,' she declared emphatically.

Xavier, his mouth twisting wryly at the way Rose was looking at him said quietly, 'I seem to have upset you, and that was not my intention. I apologise most sincerely.'

Alex intervened, 'I shouldn't worry about it, Xavier. She has a quick temper. It was your bad luck you touched on a subject that is a particular hobby-horse of hers. She'll get over it.'

'Do you mind, Uncle? I can speak for myself,' Rose cut in, ignoring Xavier's apology. She hated injustice of any kind but particularly against children. And deep down she realised the way Xavier had behaved towards her when she'd been barely nineteen and little more than a child herself still made her burn with rage and resentment. She'd thought she'd put the past behind her, but seeing Xavier again had brought back a lot of bitter memories. And he, damn him, did not even recognise her!

The hotel they were going to for dinner was one Rose knew well. As a child she'd spent most of her school holidays with her Aunt and Uncle in the Yorkshire town of Richmond, and dined at the place frequently.

Teresa sat at one end of the rectangular table, while her husband David sat at the other end. Seeing her Aunt Jean and Uncle Alex sit down, Rose hastily grabbed the seat next to them. No way did she want to end up next to Xavier. She picked up the linen napkin provided, and spread it on her lap heaving a silent sigh of relief. But her relief was short-lived when she looked up and discovered her nemesis was sitting directly opposite her with Ann then Jamie next to him.

Her startled gaze collided with Xavier's and for a second Rose imagined she saw something dark and sinister flicker in the depths of his eyes. Quickly she hid behind the menu the waiter had handed her. But she couldn't concentrate on the list of dishes on offer. Instead she was intensely aware of the hard cynical man sitting opposite to her. A dozen questions spun around in her mind. What joke of fate had led Ann to meet his nephew Jamie—in Rose's own flat for heaven's sake? And why was Xavier here alone? She knew for an absolute fact he was married, so where was his wife? Did he have children? she wondered. The thought made her heart miss a beat.

She glanced sideways at her uncle. Her aunt and uncle and Ann were her only family since the death of her parents in a plane crash when she was seventeen. And once Ann was married to Jamie where did that leave her? She could not contemplate a life that included Xavier as part of her family. Weddings, birthdays, christenings with the arrogant Xavier Valdespino in attendance, her mind boggled at the thought. She would never be able to keep up the pretence of not knowing him. In fact she'd severe doubts as to whether she would be able to last the weekend, without telling the man exactly what she thought of him. He was a callous, rotten, devious, chauvinistic pig of a man, and she hated him with a depth of passion that was alien to her usual caring nature. She wasn't proud of it, but she couldn't help it.

'Have you decided what you want to eat, Rosalyn?' His deep melodious voice drawling her full name cut into her musings. 'Or shall I choose for you?'

His audacity at suggesting he should order for her grated on her over-sensitive nerves and lowering the menu, her stormy eyes scanned his ruggedly handsome face. On any other man the scar would have appeared ugly but on Xavier it gave him a rakish piratical air, and highlighted the perfection of his bone structure. She knew he was deliberately baiting her with his offer to choose.

She dropped the menu on the table. 'I don't need your help. I will have the melon followed by a prawn salad.'

'Watching your figure?' one dark brow arched quizzically. 'There's really no need—you're quite exquisitely proportioned already. As I am sure many men must have told you before me,' he opined smoothly.

He'd lost none of his legendary charm; the gleam of appreciation in his dark eyes was precise enough to show interest, but not enough to offend. Oh, he was good! Rose thought, but two could play at that game.

'You flatter me, Señor Valdespino,' she said coyly fluttering her eyelashes at him.

His mouth twisted. 'Xavier, please. And I do not flatter. You are a beautiful woman in every way,' he added after a deliberate pause, subjecting her to a more detailed scrutiny, his eyes lingering on the curve of her breasts exposed by the neckline of her dress, then ever so slowly back to her face. 'Perfection that it would be a crime to spoil by a foolish desire to slim.'

His crack about dieting was frighteningly familiar. He'd said the same thing the night they'd spent together. Rose's green eyes narrowed warily on his tanned face, but his expression gave nothing away, and forcing herself to meet his cynical gaze she responded, 'Oh, I never slim, I simply fancy the salad, and I bet you're going to order the steak?' Widening her eyes to their fullest extent she added in mock surprise, 'Oh! Maybe not, I forgot you are all bull.' She wanted to add a four-letter word beginning with 'S,' but bit her tongue in time.

'Rosalyn,' Aunt Jean admonished. 'What a thing to say.'

Completely absorbed in her exchange with Xavier, Rose hadn't realised everyone else had stopped talking. But the laughter in Ann's and Jamie's eyes, told her they'd heard.

'What?' Rose queried with a swift glance around the table at her companions. Casually shrugging her shoulders, she continued, 'I simply meant that Xavier is Spanish. As I understand it, they eat a lot of bull meat in Spain, what with all the bullfights they have.' She played the innocent for all she was worth. And was relieved to see her Aunt and Uncle bought it, but one glance at Xavier's face told her he was not fooled. A hard smile twisted his sensuous lips; he knew she'd intended to insult him.

'Such an instant rapport between two virtual strangers is truly amazing. You read my mind, Rosalyn.' There was a faint hint of cynicism to the words Rose could not fail to recognise.

'I will have the smoked salmon starter, and I *am* going to have the steak, and I really do not mind if it is your cow meat, even though the rest of Europe saw fit to ban it for some considerable time. I am sure it will be just as tasty as Spanish bull.'

Sarcastic devil… But she was saved from having to respond by the waiter arriving to take their order.

Champagne was delivered to the table, and the meal took on a festive glow as David toasted the happy couple, and everyone joined in. The first course arrived and Rose resolved to keep her head down and only speak when spoken to, but it was not that simple.

Jamie, high on love and maybe a little too much champagne, insisted on drinking a toast to everyone—including Rose. 'If it hadn't been for you letting out your London home I may never have met Ann.'

'I only hope you don't live to regret it,' Rose said with a grin. 'I know my cousin of old; she can be quite a handful! I remember the time when she was ten and she talked me into following the local hunt on a couple of donkeys Uncle Alex kept at the time. I wouldn't care but I was nearly eighteen and not even in favour of blood sports!'

'Now that I would have liked to see.' Xavier leaned forward slightly, pushing his empty plate to one side, his face on a level with Rose's. 'Do you enjoy riding, Rosalyn?' he asked with a bland smile.

Boldly she held his gaze, and she knew his question had nothing to do with blood sports. The golden gleam of a primitive predatory male sparkled in his eyes, the black pupils dilated ever so slightly. But she also sensed beneath the surface charm of his smile a supreme arrogance that was distinctly threatening. This man was used to getting any woman he wanted with out expending too much effort at all.

'I used to when I visited my Aunt and Uncle,' she confirmed lightly, ignoring the challenge in his eyes and answering him factually. 'But for the past few years I've not really had the opportunity. Unless of course you consider sitting on a camel in the Kalahari Desert, but I doubt very much if that would appeal to a man of your—sophisticated status.'

'I could be tempted if you were to accompany me,' Xavier responded his voice deepening seductively. 'A beautiful woman is a great incentive to perform well.'

Rose eyed him quizzically; there was something not quite right. Even when he was flirting with her, there was a certain aloofness about him that was at odds with the compliments he was handing out. But she wasn't about to waste her time analysing the man. She wanted nothing to do with him.

'You're wasting your time, Señor Valdespino.'

'Oh, I don't think so. After all, the night is still young.' He leaned back in his chair and indicated to the wine waiter, and ordered more champagne. Then glancing back at her he added, 'A few more bottles of champagne and who knows what might happen, Rosalyn, darling.' He'd drawled the endearment teasingly.

The whole company greeted his comment with genuine laughter, and he grinned, his lips curling back over brilliant white teeth. But only Rose noticed the smile didn't reach his eyes.

'I doubt if your wife would find your comment so amusing,' she snapped back.

'And what makes you think I have a wife?' Xavier queried silkily, and raising his glass to his lips he took a long drink before returning the glass to the table. Leaning back in his seat he observed her beneath hooded eyelids.

Rose was all too aware of the sudden silence that had greeted her statement and the sudden tension in the man opposite. She realised she'd almost revealed she knew him, or at least knew a lot about him. Thinking quickly she tried to hide her blunder by blaming his earlier chauvinistic attitude.

'Well a man of your age with your views…' One delicate eyebrow arched cynically. 'I took it for granted you would be married with three or four children at your feet and probably a pregnant wife at home.'

'Your perception is really quite remarkable. One would almost think we had met before.'

Rose stiffened. He had recognised her! But he continued, his voice as unyielding as his expression. 'Yes, I have been married, but no children I'm afraid, and my wife died two years ago.'

'I am sorry,' she mumbled, her face going scarlet. Rose wanted the ground to open and swallow her. Her dislike for the man had led her into being deliberately rude. But Ann jumping to her feet saved her from any further embarrassment.

'Excuse me, but I must visit the rest room,' Ann said quite loudly. 'Come with me, Rose.'

Rose grasped the chance to escape and pushing back her chair she walked around the table and out of the dining room with her cousin.

'My God, Rose, what are you trying to do?' Ann said urgently, dragging her by the arm across the elegant lobby and into the powder room. 'End my engagement before it has begun?'

'I don't know what you mean,' Rose dismissed, glancing around the mirrored walls and finally down at Ann, immediately perturbed by the agitation in her pretty face.

'Oh! For heaven's sake, Rose! Xavier Valdespino is to all intents and purposes the head of the family. His father Don Pablo Ortega Valdespino is retired and very ill. So if Xavier decided against my marrying Jamie, that's it… I know Jamie loves me, but it is his uncle who pays his allowance and his college fees and he still has a year to do. This dinner was supposed to unite our two families, and you've done nothing but insult Xavier since you met him. What is the matter with you? He's a charming, polite man. A bit old, but not bad-looking if you discount the scar. Is that it, his scar?' Ann's puzzled brown eyes fixed on her cousin. 'You're a doctor! I can't believe you would let a thing like that influence your opinion of him.'

'No, no, of course not,' Rose denied adamantly, mortified that Ann should even think such a thing. 'But I never realised how important it was to you and Jamie that his uncle approved. David and Teresa must be quite wealthy in their own right, surely? The farm is vast and then there are the racing stables. Don't you think you're putting too much importance on the opinion of an Uncle?' she queried bluntly.

Ann grimaced, 'It is obvious you've been far too long abroad, and too involved in your career; you don't realise what is happening in the rest of the world. For the past few years British farmers have been going out of business by the dozen. Mad Cow Disease and the European ban on beef exports have finished off hundreds. The racing stables pay their way but only just, according to Jamie. If it weren't for his uncle's help the farm would have gone to the wall. So for heaven's sake try and be nice to Xavier or you will wreck everything. We are counting on him giving us the money for Jamie to set up in his own practice as a Vet in two or three years' time.'

'I never realised,' Rose said slowly, frowning at her cousin. She'd lost touch with Ann over the years she realised guiltily. The young girl who'd followed her around as a child had grown up into a confident young woman who knew exactly what she wanted from life. Rose sighed. 'You're right, I have probably been away too long. I have forgotten how to behave.' She excused her behaviour. 'But from now on I will be sweetness and light with Señor

Xavier Valdespino, I promise.' She glanced at her reflection in the mirrored wall, smoothed a few errant curls back from her brow, and straightened her shoulders. 'He will have no reason to complain I assure you, Ann.'

'That's more like it,' Ann grinned and glanced appreciatively at the reflection of the tall elegant woman beside her. 'The supermodel is back.'

'Don't mention I was a model,' Rose returned quickly.

'Why ever not? You will have him eating out of your hand. I can see he fancies you.'

'No,' she protested. 'I mean it, Ann. Not one word about modelling.'

'Okay,' Ann said easily. 'But you have to keep your side of the bargain; no more snide remarks. Be nice to the man.' Her cousin chuckled softly. 'And hey, even a dedicated career girl like you must see he is quite a catch. A bit of a cold fish admittedly, but wealthy, sophisticated and single, what more could you want?'

A *cold fish* was going a bit far but Rose knew what Ann meant. Xavier had the poised and watchful air of a man who was in the family scene, but yet not quite part of it. Detached, somehow above it. As for the rest at one time Rose inwardly acknowledged she would have agreed with Ann, but not anymore. 'You know, cousin mine,' she said slipping her arm through Ann's and walking back towards the dining room. 'I have just realised you have quite a mercenary little streak in your otherwise perfect nature.'

'No. But I love Jamie with all my heart, and I am simply being practical.'

There was no answer to that and Rose did not attempt to make one.

'We were beginning to wonder if you'd got lost,' Jamie said as the two women returned to their places at the table.

'Your youth is showing, Jamie,' Xavier remarked. 'We

older men know from experience,' he exchanged looks with Alex and David, 'Ladies always go to the rest room in twos as if it were an annexe to Noah's Ark, and when they get there, they have a good gossip, and pick the men in their lives to bits while us poor men are left waiting for hours.'

His comment was greeted by laughter and the conversation became general.

Rose ate the food put in front of her without really tasting it, and tried her damnedest not to look at Xavier, but for some reason her eyes were constantly drawn to his hard face. He was a brilliant conversationalist, and the topics discussed ranged from the state of the stock market to the state of David's racehorses. The main course was cleared away and the dessert ordered and eaten when the conversation got around to the next race meeting at York the following weekend, and somehow then on to travel.

'Your Aunt tells me you have been abroad for three years,' Xavier said, the first direct comment he had made to Rose in over an hour. 'You must have had some interesting experiences.'

Mindful of her promise to Ann, Rose forced herself to smile. 'A few, but mostly it was work and more work. There is a dreadful shortage of doctors in almost all the African states, especially in the rural areas. People in the west are so used to simply making a phone call and an ambulance arriving, we forget a lot of the world is not so fortunate.' Warming to her subject her face glowed with an inner fervour, that fascinated the man watching her, something she was totally unaware of.

Jean cut into the conversation. 'Really Rose, do you have to?'

'But it is shaming to all of us, Aunt Jean,' her green eyes flashed at her aunt. 'That in the twenty-first century there are still many places in the world where a woman will walk for days with a sick child simply to get to a clinic, never mind a hospital.'

'Rose. Not tonight, you know what your superior said: three months rest and relaxation,' her aunt reminded her.

'That does not prevent me from having an opinion,' she began to argue, and stopped abruptly, at the sight of Ann's frowning face across the table.

'You're on an extended holiday,' Xavier prompted filling the sudden pause in the conversation. His dark eyes narrowed intently on her beautiful face. 'I did not realise.'

'No reason why you should.' Rose lifted her eyes to his, and took a swift involuntary breath. Something flickered in the brilliant gaze something dark and vaguely dangerous. 'After all we've only just met,' she lied.

Quite unbidden into her mind sprang the sudden erotic image of his tall, powerful bronzed body, totally naked, sprawled on black satin sheets, and her stomach clenched in fierce sexual response. Her reaction stunned her. She'd tried sex once again two years ago, and decided it was definitely overrated and had not had a vaguely sensual experience since, so why now? Perhaps because her anger at Xavier Valdespino was tempered by pity for the man on hearing his wife had died. Suddenly she was seeing him simply as a very virile man.

She tore her gaze away from his, her eyes dropping to his strong jaw, the vicious scar and the hint of hardness in his chiselled mouth. But that was a mistake. Involuntarily, her tongue slipped out between her teeth and licked her bottom lip as if the taste of him still lingered a decade later. She swallowed hard. Oh, be sensible, she told herself, and for a second she closed her eyes, to dispel the haunting images of the past. When she opened them again. It took her a moment to realise Xavier was still talking to her.

'You must come with Ann and Jamie tomorrow, I insist.'

Rose shook her head in confusion, her green gaze fixing warily on the man opposite. What was he talking about? Go where with Jamie and Ann?

'That is a great idea,' Ann joined the conversation. 'I was thinking I would be outnumbered by men and with no one to shop with.'

'You must come, Rose, anything to save me from shopping,' Jamie laughingly agreed.

'Yes, it will do you the world of good.' Aunt Jean was all for it.

But *what?* Bemused, Rose glanced around the smiling faces; everyone seemed to be in favour of her going out with Jamie and Ann tomorrow. Maybe a day in Harrogate or Leeds, shopping…? She looked at Ann's smiling face, the anticipation in her brown eyes, and mindful of her promise to her cousin. She said, 'Yes, okay, where exactly is it that we are going?'

'To my home in Spain,' Xavier offered smoothly. Rising to his feet he pushed back his chair. 'And now we have that settled, I believe the coffee is served in the lounge. And no doubt these two youngsters want to get down to the disco and meet their friends.'

'Wait a minute I can't go to Spain!' Rose jumped to her feet. 'I thought you meant a day in Leeds to shop, or something.' She was babbling, she knew. What had she agreed to? In the general exodus she glanced frantically around, and they all stopped. Suddenly seven pairs of eyes were fixed on her with varying degrees of amusement.

'Of course you can,' Aunt Jean said. 'It will be much more fun for you than staying with Alex and I. Do you have your passport with you?'

'Yes, but…'

'Good, then it's no problem,' Jean stated emphatically.

'But I can't just swan off to Spain, I mean.' Rose cast a

swift glance at Xavier, but there was no help there. His dark eyes gleamed with devilish amusement as he watched her dig herself deeper. 'Well, your grandfather is ill, Jamie,' she appealed to the younger man. 'He won't want to entertain a stranger in his house.'

'Actually the opposite is true,' Teresa said firmly. 'My father is of the old school; very traditional. To be honest he was not very happy about Ann staying at the hacienda on her own with Jamie before they are married without a chaperone present.'

'A chaperone!' Rose repeated incredulously. Was the man still living in the Dark Ages or what? 'You must be joking!' But no one was laughing…

'My sister is correct,' Xavier drawled, his cool gaze captured and held her flashing green eyes, as he calmly responded, 'It is our custom for an older female relative to act as a chaperone for the young bride-to-be. You would be doing Teresa and I a great favour and giving our father peace of mind while he is so ill.'

'Xavier is right,' Ann said moving to stand beside Rose and laying a hand on her arm. 'Please say you will come; I don't want to upset Jamie's grandfather before I am even married.'

Rose's mouth worked but no sound came out. Her furious expression narrowed on Xavier's bland face. The swine was enjoying this, and she felt like some aging spinster maiden aunt. She looked back down at Ann, and saw the worry behind her brown eyes.

'Yes. Okay,' she capitulated, she could not do much else. But how on earth she was going to put up with living in the same house as Xavier Valdespino she had no idea.

'Great. See you downstairs, later,' Ann gave her a hug. 'It will be fun to have you with us in Spain.' And with a wink she walked off.

'Allow me to escort you to the lounge,' Xavier offered with a hand in the small of her back. 'You look rather dazed. Too much champagne, perhaps?'

He was laughing at her; she could hear it in his voice. The arrogant devil knew damn well that she did not want to go to Spain. How in heaven's name had she landed herself in such a mess?

'Put like that how can I refuse?' Rose replied dryly. But with his large hand spread across the small of her back, the warmth of his touch sending quivers of awareness down her spine, it took every speck of willpower she possessed to control. She knew in the interest of self-preservation she should have refused. His intimidating height, and powerful body so close to her own set every one of her senses on full alert as they crossed into the lounge.

It was with an inward sigh of relief that she felt his hand fall from her back. Rose glanced at the three sofas arranged around a low coffee table and moved to join her Uncle Alex on one of them, smoothing the soft fabric of her dress down over her hips with palms that were slightly damp. Xavier chose to sit opposite with his sister, and Aunt Jean and David occupied the third sofa. Coffee was served, and the conversation revolved around the Spanish home of the Valdespino's. Apparently the ranch was some miles from Seville, in the high plains of the interior, but the family kept a town house in Seville as well.

'I can promise you will not be bored,' Xavier said serenely, his dark eyes lazily roaming over her beautiful face. 'My father is at present in the town house, mainly so he can be near the hospital if the need arises while I am not there. Hopefully you and Ann will have the opportunity to see a little of the city, and then depending on what my father's doctor thinks, we will all go back to the ranch.'

'It sounds very nice,' Rose said agreeably, just managing

to keep a note of mockery from her voice. Who was she kidding; the thought of spending a week in his company sounded like the holiday from hell! What was more, she was sure he knew exactly how she felt! For the past half hour she'd watched him perform. The suave sophisticated business man had led the conversation skilfully. Never once paying more attention to Rose than he did to her Aunt or his sister. But there was something... Beneath his cool, confident surface she caught glimpses of something primitive, a gleam in his dark eyes when they deigned to rest on her that was anything but cool.

Maybe she was being paranoid, transferring her own banked-down anger onto him. Shaking her head she got to her feet as the receptionist arrived to inform them the cars were waiting.

For a few moments Teresa was deep in conversation with Xavier in their native language. Rose took the opportunity to move to her Aunt Jean and murmur, 'Not the ordeal you imagined, I think it all went off very well.'

'Exceptionally well,' a deep husky voice cut in.

Rose spun around to find Xavier standing so close he was invading her personal space and instinctively she splayed her hand across his chest in self-defence. 'I didn't see you.' She could feel the heat of his body, the steady beat of his heart through the fine silk of his shirt and she pulled her hand back, her fingers burning as though she had touched hot coals. 'You shouldn't creep up on people like that.'

'"Creep up,"' he parroted, mockery gleaming in the depths of his eyes. 'No one has ever accused me of being a creep before. I think your superior is quite right, you are far too nervous, you do need a change.'

'Exactly,' Aunt Jean agreed. 'Now you run along with Xavier to the disco, and let your hair down, you have been far too serious for far too long, Rosalyn. But you will check on Ann and Jamie for us won't you?'

Which was why ten minutes later Rose found herself at the entrance to a noisy basement club with strobelights flashing and a strong male hand pressing at the base of her spine urging her forward.

'You can't possibly want to stay here.' Glancing up at her companion and catching a glimpse of such icy derision in his black eyes she instinctively recoiled from his guiding hand.

'Sorry, I can't hear you.' Without warning he reached out and pulled her into his arms, his dark head bent towards her and his mouth moved against the soft curve of her ear. 'I gather you are past such simple amusement, Rosalyn. But one dance, a swift check on the youngsters and our duty to their parents will be achieved and we can leave. Agreed?'

With the warmth of his breath in her ear her heart jumped and breathlessly she mouthed her agreement. It was her bad luck the DJ chose that moment to play a ballad. Xavier held her fast with one strong hand between her shoulder blades the other encircling her tiny waist to settle low on her hip. Too low for decency, Rose thought. But it got worse; with her breasts flattened against his broad chest, he moved her to the rhythm of the music with an underlying sensuality that aroused a swift pang of response she tried her utmost to ignore.

Her tension ratio shot up to astronomical heights. Every cell in her body clamouring to surrender to the magnetic pull of his devastatingly powerful masculinity. She should get away now, common sense told her. Xavier Valdespino was a very dangerous man. But contrarily she was offended at the implication she was too old to enjoy a disco.

So when the music changed, and with his black eyes

dancing, he said huskily, 'Can you Salsa?' Stupidly she said 'yes'…

He should have looked foolish; he was much older than any other male in the room. Instead he looked like every woman's fantasy.

'Way to go, uncle!' Jamie's voice echoed above the music, and Rose glanced briefly at the young couple that had appeared next to them on the dance floor.

But her eyes were quickly drawn back to the man holding her. Xavier's large body moved with a sinuous grace, and a sensual awareness that was as erotic as it was arousing. Cynically, Rose recognised it was the dichotomy between the aloof, strong-willed powerful male, and the red-hot sexuality he exuded without even trying that made every woman in the place cast him blatant sideways glances.

Whether it was the champagne she had drunk or simply the angry frustration that had simmered inside her since meeting the man, Rose did not know, but the brush of his long body against her own was a tantalising challenge she could not resist and she threw herself uninhibitedly into the dance.

When the music ended, he hauled her close against the hard heat of his body and she was lost. She felt the hard pressure of his arousal against her belly, and knew then that he was equally affected, she watched as his dark head lowered towards her. He was going to kiss her. Her lips parted invitingly. But abruptly he straightened up his strong hands curved around her shoulders and casually he stepped back. His dark eyes sweeping down over her from head to toe, his expression coldly remote…

CHAPTER THREE

CONFUSED, Rose stared dazedly up at his face. A ray of strobe lighting illuminated his features, and for an instant he looked like the devil himself.

'Thank you. You dance well,' he said with practised politeness, his hands dropping from her shoulders.

'Thank you,' she mumbled, her face burning with embarrassment. What was happening to her? How could she have been so stupid as to think a man like Xavier Valdespino was going to kiss her in the middle of a crowded dance floor? Had she taken leave of her senses or what? Averting her face she took a step backwards. 'So do you,' she tagged on, because it was all she could think of, and, face it, she told herself, it was the truth. The man had all the moves and a body to die for, and she should know…

'Come, I think we have done our duty. The young couple are well able to take care of themselves and I need a long cool drink.' Taking her arm he led her towards the exit and back upstairs, to the relative quiet of the cocktail lounge. It said something about Rose's confused emotions that she let him.

He ordered two lemonades from a passing waiter, and then urged Rose to sit down on a long sofa. 'Too much champagne and dancing we are liable to dehydrate,' he commented blandly lowering his long body down beside her.

She turned her head slightly forcing herself to meet his dark eyes. 'I do know that. I am a doctor,' she said, irked by the fact that she was hot, her hair escaping from its former neat style into curling disarray, while Xavier looked remarkably cool and in control. Even his damned bow tie had not moved, she thought bitterly.

The waiter arrived with their drinks and Rose hastily grabbed the glass and drained it in a second. Her companion did the same.

'I needed that,' she admitted placing the glass back on the table.

'*Sí,*' Xavier agreed after he finished his, lounging back against the arm of the sofa. A respectable space between them, he studied her from beneath hooded lids.

'A very English Doctor who dances like a Latin!' His dark brows rose in mock astonishment and he smiled. 'Tell me your secret? Where did you learn to Salsa?'

It was an innocuous question, and Rose grasped the chance to indulge in a normal conversation. Hoping it would diffuse the sexual tension that had consumed her for the past hour, though seeing Xavier's interested but arrogantly aloof expression told her he had suffered from no such affliction.

'In Africa,' she said honestly and paused for a moment, happy memories making her green eyes sparkle with reminiscent humour.

'And,' he prompted.

'Dominic, an archaeologist from Buenos Aries ended up at our hospital in Somalia. Apparently he'd been travelling privately when he was robbed and was lucky to escape with his life. No money, no clothes, a black eye and a cracked skull, but bizarrely he'd managed to hang on to a CD of Salsa music. He played the CD night and day on the music centre at the residence. By the time he left three months later I could dance the Salsa, the Tango and the Samba. He was a very good singer as well,' Rose offered with a smile. The lemonade had cooled her down, and the night was almost over—Xavier had ordered the car along with the drinks. She could afford to be friendly and let her guard down.

She'd no idea how tempting she looked to the man watching her. His dark profile clenched, and he looked at her with black eyes glinting beneath thick curling lashes. Tendrils of long red hair swirled around the perfect oval of her face, the neckline of her green gown had slipped a little and exposed more of one firm creamy breast than was absolutely decent. With her body turned towards him and her long shapely legs crossed, an expanse of smooth thigh, was begging to be stroked by a male hand, and she appeared completely unaware of the fact.

'He went back to Brazil and the last I heard from him, he was somewhere in the high Andes looking for some sacrificial burial ground,' Rose added a tinge of sadness shadowing her glorious green eyes. Dominic had fallen in love with her, and on one memorable night she'd ended up in his bed. It had been a mistake, and almost spoilt a great friendship.

'A burial ground seems the best place for him,' Xavier drawled sardonically.

'Why do you say that?' Rose asked in genuine surprise. 'He is a nice man; you would probably like him.' And as she said it she realised it was true. Dominic was the same type of man as Xavier, though without Xavier's ruthless streak. With a flash of insight, she admitted to herself that was probably why Dominic had been the only man to tempt her into bed in ten years. He had reminded her of Xavier! Dominic, bless him had realised her emotions were not involved and had graciously withdrawn from his pursuit of her.

'If you say so,' Xavier said showing his teeth. He gave a curt nod to someone behind Rose and got to his feet. 'It appears our cab has arrived.' He stretched out an imperious hand towards her and something about his stance, the gleaming hooded eyes told her not to argue, and she placed her hand in his.

But he did not need to jerk her to her feet quite so violently Rose thought, almost tripping over on her high-heeled shoes. But with one derisory glance at her lovely face he tightened his hold on her hand and dashed her through the reception and out into the cool night air.

'What's the hurry?' She couldn't help commenting, a slight shiver running down her spine, but whether it was the cold air, or the effect of his large hand enfolding her own, she didn't know.

'Get in the car,' Xavier said coldly, dropping her hand. 'It's been a long day and an even longer night, and I for one have had enough. I will be glad to get home tomorrow. With you and Jamie and Ann of course.'

Why did she think the last sentence had been tacked on as an afterthought? Rose grimaced as she climbed into the car. Xavier Valdespino had come to Yorkshire out of duty. He'd played his part with smooth sophistication, and charm, and he couldn't wait to get away. Rose had nothing to worry about, she would spend a week in Seville with Jamie and Ann. Xavier Valdespino would no doubt be the perfect host. But as for remembering a stupid young girl he'd once spent a night with ten years ago, she had nothing to fear, nothing at all…

On returning to the house she refused Xavier's terse offer of a nightcap and went straight to bed. An hour later she was still wide awake. It was no use; she was never going to get to sleep, and with a defeated sigh she opened her eyes, and let her memory stray back to the past. Maybe if she faced her demons, to be more exact one demon— Xavier, she might finally find the sleep she craved.

*   *   *

THE HEAVY BEAT of the music signalled her entrance on to the catwalk. Head held high, she sauntered down the runway wearing a wisp of silk. Tiny spaghetti straps over her slender shoulders made no pretence of supporting the bodice that plunged almost to her navel and a hemline that struggled to cover her behind. Her beautiful face was expressionless, her dark red hair cut in a short bob and ruthlessly straightened. Her wide emerald eyes were heavily lined with kohl; the waif look was in…. For Rose it was no hardship to achieve.

At sixteen she'd been spotted at the Birmingham Clothes Show and asked if she would like to be a model. Five feet eight and as thin as a reed she was just the type the model agency was looking for.

Her parents, both doctors, had discussed the offer with her and finally agreed to her modelling, but only in the school holidays. Her modelling name was simply ''Maylyn,'' a play on her own name Rosalyn May, because as her father had pointed out, if she eventually wanted to be taken seriously as a doctor, it would be better not to use her real name.

Glancing around the glittering audience Maylyn was totally oblivious to the enthusiastic applause. Tonight her mind was consumed with the technicalities of moving house next week, and when she was going to get all her packing done. After the tragic death of her parents a year past January on a mercy mission in Central Africa when their plane had crashed killing all on board, Rose had found herself alone except for Peggy, the au pair who'd looked after her since she was two. After talking it over with her Aunt Jean and Uncle Alex, the only family she had left, it was decided Rose would stay in the family home in London with Peggy until she finished her A-level exams. She'd passed with straight As last summer although she'd been weighed down with grief. She'd been accepted by University College London to read medicine, but decided to defer for a year and concentrate on her modelling with the idea of making enough money to see her through medical school.

Last Christmas Peggy announced she was getting married in a few months, and so Rose had put the large family house up for sale and decided to buy an apartment a couple of streets away. Ironically the death of her parents had resulted in her losing a lot more weight, and her career as a model had really taken off, so money was not a problem.

Which was why she was in Barcelona taking part in a few charity fashion shows held in conjunction with the Spanish Grand Prix in the month of May. Personally she would rather be in England with her Aunt and family in Yorkshire celebrating her birthday. She was nineteen today, but looking around the glittering crowd she felt more like ninety. But not for much longer she consoled herself.

Maylyn the model, working on autopilot reached the end of the catwalk and with a swing of her hips she spun around. The tiny slip of grey silk that passed for a designer gown, flared seductively around her thighs and she had the traitorous thought that no woman in her right mind would be seen in public in the thing. But then after tomorrow neither would she. Completely unconsciously she smiled at the thought. Next week a new apartment and a long holiday, then come September, she'd be a student once again. Sauntering back towards the stage she felt the hair on the back of her neck stand on end, along with a frisson of excitement as shocking as it was unexpected. Her eyes widened and she was suddenly aware of a tall, magnetically handsome man standing to one side, his dark eyes fixed on hers with a glittering intensity, his firm mouth curved in a sensual smile.

Oh hell! He thought she was smiling at him! He'd been at the show yesterday and Maylyn had hardly been able to keep her eyes off him. He had appeared backstage after the show and spoken to her.

'Maylyn, I have been longing to meet you. You were brilliant out there tonight.'

With the arrogance of youth and intelligence Maylyn had avoided all the pitfalls that assailed other models. She did not smoke, and she had yet to meet a man who could persuade her into bed. But one look at the dark stranger, and she had lost herself entirely in eyes as warm as hot chocolate. She felt a laser-sharp stirring in her blood and her cheeks flared scarlet. She could not drag her gaze away and in that moment all her preconceived notions of love and morality vanished in a puff of smoke. Deep down inside some instinct warned her this man was dangerous, but she ignored it. Smiling up at him—he was well over six feet—she said, 'Thank you,' in a voice that was decidedly husky.

He offered her a cigarette, but when she refused, he'd said he could get her something stronger. She knew drugs abounded in the modelling world, but she had nothing to do with them. Bitterly disillusioned and imagining he was a drug dealer she'd slapped his face and walked away... Remembering where she was and what she was supposed to be doing she dragged her gaze away from the handsome devil and completed the parade.

'YOU WERE NOT supposed to smile,' the very angry Spanish designer who had hired her snapped at her as soon as she got backstage. 'And I think you are putting on weight.'

Maylyn looked at the small, dark, effeminate man, and smiled again. A designer's ploy for keeping models in line was to tell them they were getting fat but she no longer cared. 'Sorry, Sergio,' she grinned. 'I could not help my-self.'

'You are impossible Maylyn; beautiful but impossible,' Sergio declared. 'For once in your life try and do as you are told. Keep that gown on and get around the front and mingle. The party is about to start, and everyone who is any one in Spain is here as well as every racing driver in the world and their backers.'

'Do I have to?' Maylyn groaned.

'If you want to be paid. Yes.'

Taking a glass of champagne she had no intention of drinking from a passing waiter, Maylyn edged her way through the press of bodies. She responded to the countless calls of her name with a brief smile and a nod of her head. Finally she found what she was looking for; a quiet corner behind a large potted palm and leaned against the wall. She slipped one foot out of a ridiculously high-heeled shoe, and sighed with relief. With a bit of luck she could escape in a minute back to her hotel, and glancing warily around, she upended the glass of champagne into the potted palm.

'I saw that. How cruel—you destroy an innocent plant as easily as you destroyed my hope yesterday.'

She dropped the glass into the pot in surprise and turned her head, astonished to see sliding behind the other side of the palm was the tall dark man who had grabbed her attention earlier on the catwalk.

She blushed to the roots of her hair. 'I didn't mean... I wasn't...' she stammered helplessly, her heartbeat quickening as she stared at him. He was even more devastating than she remembered. He had the face of a fallen angel, she thought fancifully. He was incredibly handsome, with the olive-skinned complexion of the Mediterranean male. Perfectly arched black brows rose over deep brown eyes that glinted with a touch of gold. He had a not-quite-straight nose with slightly flaring nostrils, and high cheekbones that most women would kill for. Add a wide sensual mouth, and he was too attractive to be true. Maylyn was tall but he towered over her by a good eight inches. His broad shoulders strained against the fine cotton of an obviously tailor-made shirt, a carved leather belt rode low on his hips supporting cream pleated trousers. He was casually dressed, but she recognised the designer label.

He leaned back against the wall beside her, crossing one long leg over the other at the ankle revealing the finest hand-tooled leather loafers. 'Only joking Maylyn. I simply wanted a chance to set the record straight. I am not a drug dealer, as you seemed to imagine yesterday, I was only trying to ascertain you were not on drugs. I'm afraid my cynicism where models are concerned was showing, and I apologise.'

Maylyn believed him, on second acquaintance he looked far too distinguished to be a drug dealer. 'That's all right,' she said dryly, she knew only too well the public conception of models and drugs.

'I can assure you I work honestly for my living, and I would really like to talk to you again without getting my face slapped,' he smiled and she forgot every doubt she had harboured about the man.

She was totally captivated by his dark good looks, and the rush of relief, the *frisson* of excitement she felt made her lips curve in a perfect smile. 'So long as it is only talk, fire away,' she responded cheekily.

'Well I did have something else in mind as well,' he drawled throatily.

With a real sense of disappointment Maylyn straightened up and slipped her foot back in her shoe. She had lost count of the times handsome older men had come on to her in the past year. She had hoped this one might be different, but obviously not. 'You've got the wrong girl,' she said quietly.

'No.' He caught her arm as she would have moved away. 'Please. I only meant I have not eaten yet this evening, and I would be honoured if you would have dinner with me.'

'I don't even know your name,' Maylyn prompted, sorely tempted to accept his dinner invitation. The man's fingers around her bare arm, set off a tingling sensation in her whole body, the like of which she had never experienced in her life before. His dark soulful eyes seemed to pierce right through the model mask she wore and reach out to the girl beneath, and she was inclined to believe him.

'No.' One dark brow arched sardonically. 'I assumed you knew who…' He stopped in midsentence, his gaze narrowing cynically on her face, and what he read in her youthful open countenance seemed to make him change his mind. 'Allow me to introduce myself, Xavier Valdespino. I am twenty-nine years old and I'm single. Also, I'm Spanish; *Sevillano* to be exact. At present I live in Barcelona to attend the racing.'

His deep melodious slightly accented voice flowed over Maylyn like a caress. He was also quite spectacularly physically beautiful, she thought he might have added quite honestly. And in that moment she decided to throw caution to the winds and except his invitation. After all it was her birthday…

She held out her hand. 'Maylyn, I am nineteen, and I am single. Also, I am English, and I am in Barcelona for the fashion shows.' She repeated his method of introduction, her full lips parting over her pearly white teeth in a relieved smile.

'Does this mean you will have dinner with me?' Her small hand was engulfed in his much larger one, and his other hand fell from her arm to encircle her waist. She felt the electric shock right through to the soles of her feet, but his laughing eyes grinning down at her blinded her to the danger.

'Yes,' she agreed, mesmerised by the glory of his smile.

'I shall never look at a potted palm without thinking of you,' Xavier remarked as he urged her out of the room.

'I've had better compliments,' Maylyn giggled glancing up at him through her thick lashes.

'But none so genuine I can assure you,' Xavier said quite seriously. Their eyes met and fused, innocent green and worldly chocolate, and for a moment the crowd and the noise vanished, and the world stood still.

'Maylyn,' Xavier murmured, lifting one long finger he traced her cheek and jawbone. 'A lovely name for a lovely girl.'

Her stomach curled a spark of heat igniting in her belly, and flaring down to a more intimate part of her anatomy. She was shocked but trapped by the look in his eyes, and slightly afraid. She did not know what was happening to her, she only knew it was momentous. Maylyn opened her mouth, intent on defusing the tension that surrounded them like a force field. But he placed his finger firmly over her parted lips.

'No, don't say anything, there is no need.' His golden gaze swept down the length of her firm young body, and to her chagrin she felt her breasts swell, her nipples tighten to rigid peaks pressing against the scrap of grey silk. She had difficulty breathing, her heart pounded in her chest, and helplessly she stared up at him.

'I know,' he told her, and his hand firmed around her tiny waist pulling her close against him. His dark eyes burned down into hers, and she knew he was going to kiss her. But a man addressed Xavier in his native tongue and the moment was gone… His arrogant head tilted towards the other man and he responded quickly with a smile.

Then he was urging her through the crowd. He was stopped countless times, by various people, and replied to a dozen greetings, but as most were in Spanish Maylyn did not understand a word. It was only as they approached the exit Maylyn remembered where she was and what she was wearing.

'Wait. I must get changed.'

'You look perfect the way you are,' Xavier drawled huskily against her ear.

'But it is not my gown,' she broke free from his hold and took a deep steadying breath.

'Maylyn, there you are. I thought I told you to mingle.' Sergio appeared at her side. 'Is that too much for you to do?' he demanded fussily. 'I want everyone to see this design.' His hands waved either side of her body. 'I have high hopes of selling a slight variation to the mass market, so for heaven's sake darling, mingle.'

'She is mingling. With me.' Xavier's long arm circled her waist once more, giving Sergio a hard glance as he did so. 'As for the gown. Bill me. I am taking Maylyn to dinner.'

'Now wait a minute.' Nobody bought Maylyn clothes and certainly not a man she hardly knew. The man might enchant her but she was not a complete idiot.

'I did not realise you were with Señor Valdespino darling. Keep the gown, and go, go, go.' Sergio was almost pushing her out of the door. 'Enjoy the meal and don't forget. Tomorrow noon, a private show for royalty.' And turning his attention to Xavier he added, 'I do need her at twelve tomorrow.'

Before she knew what had hit her Maylyn was in a lethal

long black sports car with Xavier at the steering wheel, speeding through the streets of Barcelona.

'I meant what I said about getting changed.' She finally found her voice. 'I have no intention of appearing in public in this dress,' she stated emphatically ' It is not my style at all.'

'No problem.' Xavier glanced sideways at her mutinous face, his dark eyes brimming with laughter. 'I have the perfect solution. We will eat at my place.'

'But, but…' she spluttered at a loss for words. She could hardly object after declaring she did not want to be seen in the damn dress.

A large strong hand curved over her knee. 'Don't worry Maylyn, you are safe with me. I promise.'

Rose stirred restlessly on the bed. It was the first promise Xavier had made her all those years ago, and it was as false as the one that followed. With the wisdom of hindsight she realised, Xavier had caught her at a crucial point of change in her life.

After over a year of grieving for her parents and working almost like an automaton, she had just about recovered. The family home was sold, and she was in the process of buying her own apartment. Peggy, her childhood nanny, was leaving to get married and Rose was ready to enter the real adult world, not the fantasy of the modelling world. She was looking forward to going to university and studying for the career she had really wanted. High on confidence, she had walked down the catwalk that night and for the first time in over a year a spontaneous smile had curved her full lips. That had been her big mistake…

Watching the light of dawn shoot rays of light across the night sky Rose admitted to herself. The granddaddy of them all—the biggest mistake of all time, was what happened next. Groaning she rolled over on the bed and buried her head in the pillow, trying to hold back the final memory. But it was no good, parts of that night had haunted her dreams for years, and if she was honest, they had coloured how she looked at the male of the species ever since. It was way past time she got over it and moved on. Eventually she wanted a husband and a family of her own. Was she going to let a stupid one-night stand blight her life for ever? Xavier who had caused her trauma did not even remember her. Face it, she told herself staunchly. He hadn't been that good. Had he?

CHAPTER FOUR

MAYLYN STOOD in the middle of the large room and wondered what on earth she was doing here. The floor was polished wood and the window was the length of one wall; the view beyond a stunning picture of Barcelona at night. Looking around she realised the furniture was minimal, two stark-white hide sofas and a black marble coffee table. There was an elegant marble fireplace, the only object on it a small silver photo frame. She crossed the room and glanced at the photo. It was Xavier with his arm linked shoulder-height with another man, and a pretty dark haired girl between them. They were all laughing and the girl had a huge ring on her finger.

'Friends of yours?' she queried, trying to make conversation.

'Yes, good friends.' Xavier smiled.

'You have a lovely home,' she blurted, his smile adding to her nervous state.

'You think so?' Xavier looked dispassionately around the room, his glance coming back to rest on her taut figure. He caught her wary gaze with his own, and added, 'Don't look so frightened. I am not about to leap on you.' And taking her by the arm he turned her around to face him. 'I invited you to dinner, that is all.'

'You can cook?' she asked sceptically, regaining the thin veneer of sophistication her modelling career had taught her, while trying to ignore the closeness of his vibrantly male body, and the racing of her own heart.

'But of course. I am a man of many talents.' With a

shrug of his shoulders and hands palm up spread wide, Maylyn fell a little deeper under his spell.

'I believe you,' she said her eyes sweeping over his tall frame her imagination running riot at the thought of his other talents.

'How does a real Spanish omelette and salad, washed down with a fine bottle of white wine sound to you?' he asked a satisfied smile twisting his wide mouth telling her he knew exactly what she had been thinking.

'Very nice thank you,' she responded primly, and he burst out laughing.

'You're priceless, Maylyn!' His laughing eyes beamed down into hers, his hand curling around her upper arm. 'Come on, you can make the salad,' and he led her into the kitchen.

For the next fifteen minutes they worked happily together, and if Maylyn caught her breath as he brushed passed her in the small space she tried to ignore her reaction. But later, when she was sitting opposite him at the small breakfast table with a plate of food in front of her, and he filled her glass with wine, she was struck with a terrible feeling of inadequacy. She had never been alone with a man in his home before, and the enormity of what she was doing suddenly hit her. A strange man and in a foreign country, she had never behaved so recklessly in her life. But one look at his incredibly handsome face, the breadth of his shoulders, and the strength of his arms bronzed and lightly dusted with black hair, she lost every jot of common sense she possessed.

'A toast to my beautiful Maylyn.'

Picking up her glass she gazed at him, he was so devastatingly attractive he made her heart ache.

Slowly lifting the wineglass to his lips Xavier took a sip, his dark eyes lazily scanning the flimsy bit of silk over her breasts. Maylyn took a hasty swallow of the fine wine but she had no control over her body's reaction, her breasts swelling, her nipples straining against the fine fabric almost painfully. Abruptly she put the glass down and made to fold her arms self-consciously across her chest, shocked by what he could do to her with one appreciative glance. But Xavier caught her hand across the table.

'No, Maylyn. Don't be embarrassed.' Holding her eyes with his he added, 'It is the same for me. Only the table protects my embarrassment,' he said with a wry grin.

Her mouth fell open in shock when rather belatedly she registered what he meant. 'Oh my,' she exclaimed like some Victorian virgin, her face turning beetroot red.

Xavier flung his head back and laughed out loud. 'Such innocence, I don't believe it. But you were right about that dress, Maylyn. The gown is strictly for the eyes of a lover and no other man. Now eat up before the food gets cold.'

He was older, more experienced, he could joke about his body's reaction. Maylyn could not. She ate two mouthfuls of food, and then pushed the rest around with her fork. She hardly dared to look at him, because when she did she could barely breathe.

'What is the matter Maylyn? The omelette not to your liking?' Xavier asked with concern.

Her head jerked up and she tried to smile. 'Yes, it's perfect, but I seem to have lost my appetite.'

'You're a model. It is your work this I understand. But you are also a perfectly beautiful girl, Maylyn.' His brilliant dark eyes held hers. 'Perfection that would be a crime to spoil by a foolish desire to slim.' He told her firmly, 'Now eat.' And she did.

Xavier put her at ease by talking about his passion for cars, and she gathered he worked at the racetrack. Soon they were chatting like old friends. She told him some of the funny things that had happened to her as a model, and he reciprocated by telling her his father ran a farm in Southern Spain. He made her laugh as he described his one disastrous attempt to be a Toreador in the bullring in Seville and falling off his horse.

He laughed with her, and she forgot it was her birthday, forgot everything but the sheer animal magnetism of the man. But it was *more,* she thought as they exchanged confidences. They talked about everything and nothing until Xavier pointed out he had never sat over two hours on a hard kitchen chair in his life and suggested they moved to the sitting room.

Later relaxed sitting beside him on a plush sofa in the living room, she drank the coffee he had made, and cast a sidelong glance at his handsome profile. Suddenly she was overcome by a restlessness that brought hot colour to her cheeks. The meal was over, the coffee almost finished. It was time she made a move to leave. He had behaved as a perfect gentleman. It was Maylyn who was having trouble keeping her hands off him. She didn't know what had come over her, she'd met dozens of handsome men in her working life but none had ever affected her the way Xavier did.

Sprawled beside her on the sofa, his long legs stretched out before him with nonchalant ease, he looked relaxed and sinfully sexy. Her fascinated gaze lingered on his legs, and she guessed by the musculature of his thighs that he was a much better rider than he had implied. Heat surged up under her skin at where her wayward thoughts were leading her, and hastily she raised her eyes. But that was not a lot better; her glance lingered on his chest, the top few buttons of his shirt were undone, offering her a brief glimpse of silky black body hair, and she had an almost overwhelming urge to reach out and slide her hand beneath his shirt. Was the hair soft or wiry? Mortified at where her erotic thoughts were leading her she jumped to her feet.

'I'd better leave now,' she said, her voice tellingly husky, as she nervously tried to tug the hem of her dress down. 'It's getting late, and I have to work tomorrow.' She chanced a glance down at him and was stunned by the blaze of golden fire in his dark eyes. He reached up and caught her hand, and before she knew what had happened he had pulled her down onto his lap. 'Not without a goodnight kiss, surely.'

'Please, you will spoil the dress.' Maylyn said the first thing that came into her head. 'It has to go back.' She knew she sounded like an idiot, but with his arm firmly around her waist, her bottom fitted snugly in his lap and his other lean brown hand clasping her naked shoulder, she felt as helpless as a kitten.

'No, consider it a present.' His strong hand trailed teasingly around the nape of her neck bringing her face ever nearer to his, and she was paralysed by the sudden fierce burst of excitement arrowing through her body. His long fingers raked up through her hair, and he urged her head towards him, slowly as though not to frighten her. But the brilliance of his eyes told a different story.

'I can't accept.' Whether it was the dress or his kiss she was refusing she did not know.

'Call it a birthday present.' His sensual mouth brushed lightly over her lips. 'My sweet Maylyn.'

A brilliant smile made her eyes sparkle, and she leaned away from him slightly. 'How on earth did you know today was my birthday?' she asked, diverted from the perilous situation she was in for a moment.

A deep throaty chuckle greeted her remark. 'I didn't. We are so well attuned to each other it must be ESP!' Wrapping both his arms around her he gave her a big hug. 'Happy birthday my lovely, But why didn't you tell me? An omelette is hardly a great celebration, I would have taken you out if I had known,' Xavier said with easy grace. 'But what about your friends, your parents, didn't they want to share the day with you?'

Maylyn's lustrous green eyes blurred with moisture. He really was a nice man, so caring. 'My parents died almost eighteen months ago.'

'Oh you poor thing.' This time when his dark head bent, his lips captured hers in a long sweet drugging kiss, a kiss of comfort and compassion. Her soft mouth opened to the subtle pressure of his lips, and with a sudden husky groan Xavier spun her around beneath him on the sofa, his lips never leaving hers.

Maylyn did not know what had hit her. One minute she felt secure and comforted in his arms and the next she was flung into a maelstrom of sensations she did not fully comprehend. Pinned beneath his long hard body, his large hands cradling her face his lips moved demandingly over hers, his tongue plunging into her mouth, devouring the sweetness within with a hungry passion that made her head spin. Her slender arms wrapped around him, her lithe young body strained against him, he played on her senses like no drug ever invented.

Her agile fingers slid up over his broad shoulders to tangle ecstatically in his silky black hair. She felt as if she'd never been kissed before until this moment, and it was like a lightning flash, a revelation. This was what she was born for. Instinctively she responded with an urgency, a hunger that had been waiting a lifetime to escape. She shuddered with the force of her passion; she did not simply surrender to Xavier's potent masculine demands, she exulted in it and demanded in return.

Finally Xavier lifted his head, his dark eyes clashed with

her molten green, as they both fought to recover their breath. Tenderly his hand slid from her face to her shoulder, one fine strap of her dress was trailed down her arm, and he leaned back to stare down at the swollen hardness of a perfect creamy breast.

'You are exquisite,' he grated, and gently he cupped her breast, his thumb trailing across the rosy pink nipple, his eyes following the progress of his thumb in rapt fascination as the tip rose to a hard aching peak beneath his expert caress.

Maylyn trembled, her eyes fixed in blind adoration on his strong lean face, her small hands tugged at his hair, urging his mouth back down to hers. Her whole being burned with wild excitement, the musky male scent of him filling her nostrils, and she ached for the taste of him.

'Not here, Maylyn,' Xavier rasped, and swinging her up into his arms he carried her though to a bedroom.

She might have resisted, but any hope of sanity returning was lost as his mouth sought hers once more. Then she was lying on a bed, and Xavier was leaning over her, his dark eyes gleaming golden shards of blazing desire, as he slipped the dress from her shoulders, exposing her high firm breasts totally to his view.

'¡Dios you are perfect.' In seconds he had dispensed with his shirt and trousers, and joined her on the bed.

But not before Maylyn had been seduced all over again by the beauty of his naked body. Her shy but fascinated gaze roamed over every inch of him, from his wide shoulders to the broad muscular chest liberally sprinkled with black hair. Excitement bubbled in her veins like the finest champagne, her curiousity forcing her to look lower to where the essence of his manhood stood blatantly erect between hard tanned thighs.

She gulped and then he was leaning over her, his strong

hands divesting her of her dress and trailing on down the length of her legs, removing her briefs, and her shoes in one deft movement. Naked on the bed, completely exposed to his fiercely glittering gaze she gasped out loud, as slowly he dragged the tips of his long fingers sensually back up her legs sending shock waves through her sensitised flesh that made her shake with a hunger as undeniable as breathing.

'Xavier,' she moaned his name.

'I love the way you say my name,' he rasped, his hand caressing her hip, the indentation of her waist and over her breast to her throat. He raised up supporting himself on one elbow, his wide shoulders leaning over her, then his dark head bent down and his mouth found hers once more. They kissed with a wild primitive passion that made the blood sing in her veins. His hand swept over her body, his agile fingers rolling her burgeoning nipples, first one and then the other and then caressing lower over her flat stomach to the soft curls at the juncture of her thighs.

No man had ever touched her so intimately before and for a second a semblance of sanity surfaced, but it was extinguished as his head dipped to a rigid straining nipple and suckled the bud into the heat of his mouth. She gasped out loud, her body trembling in pleasure that was almost pain, and then he soothed with his tongue, sending her heartbeat hammering against the wall of her chest.

Maylyn didn't know such feelings, such cravings, existed until now. She reached for him, her hands curving around his wide shoulders, stroking down his broad back and 'round to his chest. She discovered the hair she had wondered about earlier was soft and curly, and she was fascinated by the pebble-like male nipple buried in the silky down. His body fascinated her. He fascinated her, and all the time she felt as if she was on fire, her skin burned. She could not control her response; indeed she did not want to, as the sensual expertise of his hands and his mouth led her ever and ever deeper under his spell.

Xavier reared over and crushed her swollen lips once more under his, as his fingers traced along her slender thigh and sought the moist heat of her tender flesh, while his tongue plundered her mouth with a primitive rhythm her body ached to follow.

'Please…' Maylyn gasped wildly. She looked up into his face distorted by passion, the skin pulled taut across high cheekbones and the dark eyes turned to black pools of sheer hunger, and she knew it was for her.

'¡Dios! You don't have to ask,' Xavier growled as he rose over her and surged hot and hard into her pliant body.

For a moment he froze as he registered the resistance and her muffled cry, but her hands clasped around his back, she kissed the satin skin of his shoulder, and then cried out with pleasure as he surged back into the hot silken warmth of her.

Maylyn discovered the true meaning of sensuality. Her body knew instinctively how to respond arching into him, meeting every thrust of his loins with a throbbing fiery pleasure that had her fingernails digging into his back. Higher and higher she flew soaring into the unknown, her heart thundering, her greedy hands holding him fiercely, terrified he would stop, and deny her craving for the ecstasy she knew was waiting just over the horizon.

Then it happened; her body convulsed in wave upon wave of scorching release as he surged into her one last time. The sound she could hear was her own cry as she felt his magnificent body shudder in an explosive climax.

Xavier collapsed on top of her, his head resting in the curve of her neck, and she lifted a trembling hand and smoothed the dark sweat-damp hair of his head, loving the way he rested against her, loving the heat of his hard body over her. Loving him...

Xavier sighed and rolled onto his back and sliding an arm under her waist he scooped her up so she was splayed half over his broad chest. 'I was the first.' He swept the damp tendrils of hair from her brow, his dark eyes searching her lovely face flushed with the rosy glow of passion fulfilled. 'Why did you not tell me, Maylyn?'

'Does it matter?' she asked levering herself up so she could rest her arms across his chest and look down into his darkly handsome face. 'It had to happen sometime,' she tried to smile, but ended up nervously biting her lip. She had no idea how to behave in this situation; and a hysterical laugh bubbled to the surface.

'Maylyn, it is not funny, if I had known I would have been more gentle, slower.'

'Sorry,' she said in a flat voice. 'As you have gathered I am not used to this sort of thing.'

Xavier groaned, and lifting his hand he smoothed the hair down the back of her head in a tender gesture. 'And you think I am?' he murmured, brushing the top of her head with his lips. 'Well, I have a confession to make—I am not. This was a first for me as well. I have never had a virgin lover in my life, and as for being sorry,' he tilted her chin up to look into her huge green eyes. 'I'm not sorry, Maylyn. I'm delighted, ecstatic over the moon. You are mine, and only mine now and forever, and in a minute I will prove it to you all over again.' His lips parted in a slow sensual smile, his dark eyes dancing with devilment that made her heart expand in her chest with love.

Daringly she reached down and planted a light kiss on his nose. 'Later. I need to go to the bathroom.'

'So prosaic,' he grinned. 'I'll come with you.'

'No,' she struggled out of his hold, and sat up. She might

have lost her virginity but she had not lost all her inhibitions.

'It's over there.' He indicated a door set in the wall opposite with a wave of his hand, his dark eyes lit with amusement catching hers. 'But remember you are mine and soon you will share everything with me, including the bathroom.'

'Promises, promises,' Maylyn teased. Swinging her legs over the side of the bed and finally glancing around the room that had witnessed her gigantic step into womanhood. She spluttered, she chuckled, then laughed out loud. Pulling the top sheet off the bed and wrapping it around her, she surveyed the totally naked Xavier sprawled on the bed. 'Black satin sheets, Xavier! How naff can you get!' she mocked him light-heartedly and still chuckling she walked across the room and into the bathroom.

When she returned to the bedroom having washed all her make-up off and tried to comb her hair, she stopped just inside the door. Xavier was lying on his back, his eyes closed, his mighty chest rising and falling with a steady beat, his arms outstretched, his magnificent bronzed body completely defenceless somehow, and she was hit with such an overpowering feeling of love, she could hardly breathe.

'Come to bed, Maylyn I can feel you standing there,' Xavier said softly without even opening his eyes.

'How did you know I was here?' she asked crossing to the bed and letting the satin sheet fall from her body.

'You're the other half of me.' His eyes opened and captured hers, and the golden warmth in his eyes dazzled her. His gaze slid slowly over her slim naked figure, and then back to her freshly scrubbed face, an arrested expression on his handsome face. 'I knew you were beautiful, but without your model make-up, you are too exquisite for words. Come join me,' and he held out his hand.

Trustingly she put her hand in his, and he pulled her down into his arms, and kissed her long and lazily, his tongue laving her lips and the innermost secrets of her mouth, and slowly they began the dance of love all over again.

A DISTANT RINGING of a telephone woke Maylyn from a deep dreamless sleep. Stirring she moved but found she could not get far as a strong male arm pinned her to the bed. For a second she was disorientated, then memory returned. 'Xavier, the phone,' she said, pulling at the arm holding her, praying she would see the same love in his eyes this morning as she had seen countless times through the night. Nervously she watched her breath trapped in her throat.

'Maylyn.' He said her name softly, his voice deep and husky with sleep, and his arm tightened fractionally around her. Then quickly his eyes flashed open, and a broad beaming smile illuminated his whole face when he saw her watching him. 'So it wasn't a dream.'

Her fear vanished like snow on a fire. 'No and neither is that telephone,' she told him, an answering smile curving her love-swollen lips. He pressed a quick kiss on her mouth, and leaning over to the bedside table he picked up the offending instrument. Maylyn lay back down and studied him through half-closed eyes. He was so gorgeous; she wanted to pinch herself to make sure what had happened last night was really true. Xavier loved her; he wanted her to stay with him. He'd asked her to stop modelling, and she had happily agreed because she was going to anyway, but before she could explain, he'd pulled her back down in his arms and made wonderful love to her. But it didn't matter. Nothing mattered this morning except their feelings for each other. As she watched his face darkened, his black brows drew together in a ferocious frown and suddenly he looked much older and much tougher, and an inexplicable tendril of fear slithered down Maylyn's spine.

He slammed the telephone down and swung his long legs over the side of the bed.

'What's the matter?' she asked reaching out a hand to his broad back. He twisted around as if just realising she was there.

A wry smile curved his firm lips. 'Sorry, darling but I have to go to the racetrack, I don't know how long I will be.' His deep brown eyes lingered on her young face flushed with sleep. 'My birthday girl,' and smoothing her hair back from her brow he added, 'It is only six-thirty, go back to sleep. I will leave you a key for the apartment on the kitchen table and a card with the address.' His dark head lowered and he kissed her quickly, the bristles on his jaw scraping the fine skin of her face. 'If I get back quickly I will stop by your show. Your last show,' he said with some satisfaction. 'Or ring you at your hotel, and collect you.' And, heading for the bathroom he added, 'But if I don't call you by five, pack your clothes from the hotel and come back here and wait for me. Okay?' He vanished into the bathroom.

Maylyn pulled the black satin sheet up over her naked body and sighed dreamily, and in minutes was fast asleep again. She never saw Xavier walk back into the bedroom, and smile tenderly down at her. But she did stir slightly in her sleep, as she felt a kiss as light as a gossamer wing brush her softly parted lips, and in her dreams she imagined she heard a man's voice saying, I love you.

Maylyn studied her reflection in the mirror above the vanity basin in Xavier's bathroom, and grinned. She looked different, her face held a new knowledge and her softly swollen mouth was a dead giveaway, but she did not care! She was in love. 'Xavier!' She wanted to shout his name from the rooftop, her very own Prince Charming. Instead, humming happily to herself she headed for the kitchen. She had time for a cup of coffee before calling a cab to take her back to the hotel.

Filling a cup with coffee she cradled it in her two hands, and breathed in the wonderful aroma, and sighed, a sigh of complete sybaritic delight. She'd never been so aware of her senses. Everything in her world had taken on a clearer sharper image. A delicious languor invaded her whole body, there were a few sore places, but they only reinforced the ecstasy of last night.

She glanced at the small key on the table resting on the address card. The key shone gold in the morning sun, the key to the rest of her life... A glorious golden future stretched before her with Xavier, her lover. She had only known him two days but she had no doubts, he was her soul mate. She picked up the card and pushed it in her purse and palmed the key. She heard the sound of birdsong from outside, above the noise of the traffic. Every sound was more acute; when she heard the sound of a door opening she shot out of her seat. Xavier was back.

Hurrying through into the living room, her eyes sparkling with anticipation lighted on the man coming in the door. She opened her mouth to speak and stopped dead. It was a complete stranger... He was medium height, heavily built, and quite attractive with black curly hair. He was wearing jeans and a white sweatshirt and carried a holdall in one hand, which he dropped at his feet, and on straightening, his narrowed eyes raked her from head to toe. Then he said something in Spanish, which sounded suspiciously like a curse.

'What are you doing here?' she demanded suddenly realising the danger of her situation.

'My English is not great, but I am Sebastian Guarda,' he introduced himself. 'I live here.'

'But you can't, this is Xavier's home.'

'Ah, Xavier,' he shook his dark head and moved across to sit down on the sofa, letting his head fall back and closing his eyes. 'Xavier is sharing the apartment with me for the week of the Grand Prix, and it is not his home, whatever he told you.' Opening his eyes he fixed Maylyn with a mocking glance. 'Where is he? Still in bed and got you making coffee hmmm?'

'No, he has gone to work,' she told him then wished she had kept her mouth shut, it was not a good idea letting him know she was alone in the apartment.

'Work!' and then he laughed. 'I suppose that is as good an excuse as any. Look little lady I am very tired, I have been travelling for hours, I want a coffee, and to sleep. Xavier and I usually share everything,' and with a crude glance up at her he added, 'But on this occasion you look beat, and I certainly am. So why don't you just leave.'

Maylyn blanched as the import of his words struck home. 'That's disgusting, and I don't believe you for a minute. Xavier loves me. He, he, wants me to stay,' she stammered, and as she spoke, she realised how feeble she sounded.

A snort of derision greeted her comment, but then as if realising she was serious the man sat up, 'He told you this.'

'Yes, he is meeting me when he has finished work at the racetrack.' Xavier had promised. Maylyn refused to believe he had lied. She did not want to believe it… But a tiny cynical voice whispered in her head, *What did she really know about Xavier?* Except he was a great lover, and suddenly she recognised the man. 'You're the man in the photo on the mantelpiece.'

'Yes, and Xavier Valdespino does not work, not as you and I know it,' Sebastian Guarda told her with a sardonic arch of one brow in her direction. 'His money backs a formula-one racing team, a hobby for a very wealthy man. He owns a merchant bank, and has homes in Seville, Madrid, and Buenos Aries, where he also owns vast amounts of land.'

She felt as though she had been punched in the stomach. Feeling the key in her palm she produced it like a talisman. 'But he gave me the key to the apartment.' She opened her palm, her mind reeling with shock.

For a long moment Sebastian Guarda looked at the key, frowning. 'He gave you a key,' he drawled softly, and raising cynical eyes to Maylyn's pale face he added, 'And of course you've tried it in the lock little girl?' The mockery in his tone was unmistakable.

Maylyn wanted to shrivel up and die there and then. It was her worst nightmare come true. Stupidly she looked at the key in her hand and she realised it would never have entered her head to try it before she left.

'Xavier keeps a bunch of keys it is a favourite ploy of his to get rid of his one-night stands without any fuss. I should know—he is my best friend and engaged to my sister. But if you don't believe me go ahead and try it.'

'Engaged to your sister!' Maylyn whispered. With dawning horror she realised the picture in the frame she had asked Xavier about last night was of him and his fiancée. Nausea clawed at her stomach, and she swayed slightly, it could not be true, her mind screamed.

Suddenly the man was at her side holding her arm. 'Are you all right?—you look pale.' His dark eyes slid over her scantily clad form and back to the pale face devoid of make-up. 'Come and sit down, you've had a shock. ' And meekly Maylyn let him lead her to the sofa.

'Allow me to apologise for my countryman. I am sorry. I did not realise, you are much younger than the women he usually takes to bed.'

Sebastian Guarda was kind. He slid a comforting arm around her shoulders, and tried to let her down gently. 'You have seen the photo on the mantelpiece, it was taken three months ago. Need I say more?'

'But your sister... Don't you mind? I mean... Well, you know Xavier is being unfaithful?'

His laughter cut across her stumbling question. 'Xavier's family is one of the oldest in Seville, his ancestors were a mixture of Moorish and Spanish. He is a traditionalist, his fiancée must be a virgin on her wedding night, so until his marriage he is not being unfaithful, simply fulfilling his male urge with a variety of willing women. It means nothing to him, and Catia understands this. Though sometimes, as now, I am ashamed of his behaviour. I can see you are not the worldly type, so once again I am sorry.'

Numb with shock and horror, Maylyn could not speak. Sebastian ordered her a cab and ten minutes later she was on her way back to her hotel.

Sergio the designer was delighted with her performance at the noon fashion show, and he told her so backstage. 'Marvellous, Maylyn. Exactly the pathos I was looking for.'

Her great green eyes filled with tears, and she blinked furiously. 'I'm glad someone is satisfied,' she said in a voice that wobbled.

'Oh my God! Valdespino, you've fallen for him, you poor thing,' Sergio's arm curved around her shoulder, his expression filled with compassion on her pale face. 'I should have warned you, rumour has it he is engaged to a suitable young girl, although he is a notorious womaniser. But to give him his due, he is very generous with the ladies in his life. Look on the bright side, one of his staff contacted me this morning, and arranged to pay for the dress, so you are now a proud owner of a fabulous Sergio original.'

Listening to Sergio, any faint lingering hope that it might all be a terrible mistake, and Xavier would arrive at the show, or perhaps contact her at her hotel, died a death. He'd bought her for the cost of a dress. If she had not disliked the dress before, she hated it now.

Back in her hotel room, Maylyn called the airport, and was lucky to get a seat on a holiday charter flight leaving at four-thirty that evening. Hastily she flung her clothes in a suitcase. Tears streaming down her cheeks she tore the dress to shreds and shoved it in the waste bin. Whether the tears were for a broken heart or simply pure rage at her own stupidity in believing in love at first sight, she did not dare to analyse. She had behaved like a naive young fool and fallen for Xavier's lies. Never again, she vowed, and called a cab.

Replacing the receiver, she picked up her purse, checking she had her passport. Her glance lingered on the printed card—Sebastian Guarda and the address and telephone number of the apartment. Proof if more proof were needed that Xavier had lied—he had not even given her his own phone number. The phone rang and she picked it up again.

'Maylyn, what are you playing at? You left the key,' Xavier's angry voice echoed down the line.

'I don't need the key or you. Goodbye.' and she hung up on him. The telephone was ringing again as she picked up her suitcase and left.

CHAPTER FIVE

ROSE WOKE UP to the sound of a door slamming. Blinking sleepily she began to sit up and only then realised by the strange decor she was not at home. She rubbed her eyes with her knuckles. Had yesterday really happened? Xavier Valdespino was going to be related to her family—it did not bear thinking about. She groaned out loud and was tempted to slide back down under the covers.

'Sorry Rose, but you have to get up.' Ann approached the bed carrying a mug of coffee in one hand.

'What time is it?' Rose muttered, viewing her pretty cousin with bleary vision.

'Eleven-thirty. Drink this and hurry up and get ready, we are leaving soon.' She placed the china mug on the bedside table.

'Eleven-thirty.' Rose yelped. 'Why didn't you wake me?' swinging her legs over the side of the bed she sat up, and reached for the steaming cup of coffee.

'Because Xavier reminded us your boss had sent you back to England to rest, and insisted we leave you to sleep. I think you have made a conquest there!' Ann grinned down at her. 'So thank him, not me,' and with that she left.

Standing under the shower Rose groaned in mortification. A houseguest that stayed in bed till almost lunchtime, and it was all that dreadful man's fault. Stepping out of the shower she quickly rubbed herself dry with a soft towel, and back in the bedroom, she slipped on a clean bra and briefs. Shoving her arms into a short-sleeved blue polo shirt, she pulled on a pair of grey chinos and slipped a snakeskin belt through the loops of the pants fastening it firmly around her slim waist.

Vigorously brushing her long hair back from her face, she mused on the anomaly of the snakeskin belt. It had been a present from a tribe in Botswana where she'd run a clinic for a while and she felt no guilt wearing it. But she would not dream of wearing a fur coat. Hypocrite, she told herself with a grin as she walked out of the bedroom and down the stairs, the lingering traces of her smile making her green eyes sparkle.

'Good morning, Rosalyn. I trust you slept well,' Xavier drawled, his long-legged frame leaning against the drawing room door watching her descent.

Her head held high, her eyes flicked quickly over him. He was dressed in black jeans and a black polo shirt. He looked like a superb male specimen, arrogance in every line of his large frame. 'Yes thank you,' she said stiffly, refusing to be intimidated by his overwhelming masculine presence. 'But you could have woken me up.' She was still seething at the information Ann had imparted. It had been his decision to leave her to rest.

'Now there is an invitation almost impossible to refuse,' he sounded amused 'I must remember that the next time you sleep late.'

Realising what she had said, Rose felt a hot tide of colour sweep up her face, and dashing past him she fled to the back of the house and the safety of the kitchen with the sound of his husky chuckle ringing in her ears. The man was impossible, her mind was made up—she was not going anywhere with him.

Ann, Jean and Teresa were in the kitchen and as soon as Rose entered, a large plate of eggs and bacon was placed on the table and she was told to sit down and eat as they were leaving in half an hour.

Between forking the food into her mouth she tried to tell them she was not going to Spain. 'It's the twenty-first century, nobody has a chaperone nowadays.'

'Please Rose stop wasting time,' Ann snapped. 'Xavier has already called his pilot twice and put back the flight time. East Midlands Airport is incredibly busy this time of year with holiday charter flights all over the Mediterranean. If we miss the next take-off slot, that is it until tomorrow.'

In the process of swallowing a mouthful of the egg, Rose almost choked. He had his own plane, but then why not, he had everything else, she thought bitterly.

'Have you packed?' Ann demanded.

'Yes, no.' Rose muttered. 'My weekend things are upstairs and the rest are in the car.' The E-type—it was a lifeline. 'But I can't leave Bertram,' she declared triumphantly.

A movement in the doorway jerked her head around. Silently, somehow making the large farmhouse kitchen suddenly seem small Xavier walked into the room with Uncle Alex trailing behind him. But it was Xavier who held her attention. He stilled, tension in every line of his body, his lashes dropping very low masking his expression.

'Surely your boyfriend can live on memories for a week in support of your family,' Xavier prompted, his voice deep and with a note in it that hinted of strong emotions rigidly kept under control by sheer strength of will. 'I had to,' he added in a roughened undertone.

She caught his last comment just before the sound of Ann and Alex's laughter filled the room. Obviously he was referring to living on memories of his late wife; he must have loved her a lot, Rose realised and dismissed the pang of hurt she felt as indigestion. Dropping her fork she pushed her plate away. She almost felt sorry for him.

Alex tapped Xavier on the back. 'No, old man, you have

it all wrong.' His laughter faded to a chuckle. 'Rosalyn doesn't have a boyfriend. She is far too involved in serving the masses,' he said still chuckling. 'Bertram is her car.' And turning to Rose, he added, 'There is no need to worry about the car. I will look after it for you. Jean and I will keep it until you return. In fact you will be doing me a favour. I can't wait to get behind the wheel again. Your Dad used to let me drive it sometimes, we had such fun.'

Uncle Alex's reference to her father, and the unmistakable wistful smile he bestowed on her, convinced Rose she had no choice. 'I'll go get my bag and the key,' she surrendered gracefully and rising to her feet she glanced at Xavier as she made to walk past him.

'Good girl,' he said with a brief smile that had driven the tension from his striking features. 'And I promise you will have an interesting holiday.'

She almost smiled back, but common sense prevailed. She needed another promise from the powerful Xavier Valdespino like a hole in the head, and where did he get off calling her a girl, the patronising prig, Rose thought dryly, and escaped back to the privacy of her bedroom.

The fact that her heart was beating rather fast she put down to running upstairs; not for a second was she going to admit it was because Xavier had smiled at her. Her decision made she wasted no time packing her few belongings and dashed back downstairs and outside. Hurrying over to her car she opened the boot and curved her hand around the handle of her suitcase.

'Allow me,' a large masculine hand took the suitcase from her grasp, and swung it out and onto the ground.

Rose's glance flew up to meet dark enigmatic eyes. 'I am not helpless.'

'Did I suggest you were?' he demanded with an arrogant arch of one black brow. 'Any woman, who calls a magnif-

icent piece of machinery like this ''Bertram'' would have
to be reasonably self-confident. It is not the easiest car to
drive or maintain.' Ignoring her, his eyes lit up with genuine appreciation of the long low-slung sports car, and
slowly he strolled around it.

Rose hid a wry smile. In a choice between the E-type
and herself, as far as Xavier was concerned the car won
hands down. She had nothing to worry about from the man.

Relaxing slightly, she handed the keys to her uncle, and
he went whistling off happily to where the rest of the family
stood at the door, while Xavier arrived back at her side.

'The popular myth is that men like sports cars because
they are a kind of phallic extension of themselves. It suddenly occurred to me the same could be said for a woman
like you, Rosalyn,' he declared with dark eyes that blazed
with blatant sexual awareness that shocked Rose even as
her stomach clenched in response.

'What?' she exclaimed, captured by the raw magnetism
of his gaze. He'd changed in a second from cool sophisti-
cate to something much more threatening to her equilib-
rium. A wide charismatic smile curved his sensuous mouth
that made her heart squeeze in her breast. She tore her eyes
away from his, appalled by the sudden rush of heat to her
cheeks.

'Admit it. Bertram has to be a real turn-on for you.'

She had just convinced herself he had no interest in her
as a woman, and now this… He was doing it deliberately,
trying to get a rise out of her she knew. But no way was
she going there. 'You're mad,' she said curtly, but she was
too embarrassed to look at him, and heaved a sigh of relief
when Jamie called out to them to get in his car.

Rose wrinkled her nose up disapprovingly as she sat
down in the aircraft seat and fastened her safety belt. Xavier
was at the front of the plane in conversation with the pilot.

Jamie and Ann were wrapped up in each other as usual. And Rose was frowning at the pure luxury evident in the private Jet. After the poverty she had seen it was some how slightly disgraceful that one man should own so much.

'Penny for your thoughts,' Xavier appeared sinking down into the seat beside her. his shoulder only inches from her own.

Glancing sideways at his handsome profile and with the slight brush of his hard thigh against hers, she was maddeningly aware of her own weak willed body's heated response to him. A million pounds was not enough to divulge her true thoughts she thought despairingly. Why did this one man have such an electric effect on her? It wasn't fair. But then not much in life was. So she told him her view on conspicuous consumption as the easy way out.

Surprisingly the flight passed quickly as they got into an argument on the distribution of wealth. Xavier was a highly intelligent articulate man and Rose realised she was actually enjoying pitting her wits against his. In the heat of the argument about the western banks wiping out the debt of all the Third World countries, an idea Rose espoused, and Xavier as a Banker did not, her convictions got the better of her temper and she called him a *typical greedy capitalist power-hungry control freak* and Jamie intervened.

'Pack it in, Rose, he is winding you up. He donates to a host of charities, and supports dozens of African students, and heaven knows what else!'

Shamefaced, Rose lifted wary eyes to Xavier's. 'Is that right?'

'Guilty as charged,' Xavier murmured, his mobile mouth twitching in the briefest of smiles. 'But you do rise to the bait so easily Rosalyn, I could not resist.'

Rose swallowed hard. It was her own fault for running

off at the mouth. 'Then I am sorry for calling you what I did.'

Xavier stared steadily back at her, his dark eyes unfathomable, not a revealing muscle moving on his strongly chiselled features. 'Your apology is premature. You were at least half right. I am a hungry control freak,' he admitted in a deep-voiced cynical drawl that left Rose feeling vaguely threatened. Why? She had no idea...

The captain's voice at that moment sounded over the intercom, and her attention was diverted. They were about to land.

LATER ROSE would wonder how she could have been so stupid, but when the airport formalities had been completed, she made no demure when Xavier informed her Jamie and Ann would be travelling in the waiting limousine to his home. She and Xavier would follow on in his Ferrari, conveniently parked at the airport. The excuse there was not enough room for all the luggage sounded plausible.

But once she was seated in his low-slung sports car, with Xavier's long body only inches away from her, she began to wonder on the advisability of being alone with him. She shot him a sideways glance as he manoeuvred the car out of the airport and onto the main road. 'I might have guessed you would drive a Ferrari,' she said to break the tension growing in the silence.

'You know me so well.' His dark gaze flicked to her and back to the road, and immediately she realised she had almost put her foot in it again.

'Well you liked my car so,' she shrugged her shoulders, 'Obviously you are the sports car type.'

'Correct, I have quite a collection of veteran models. They are in storage outside the city. I'll show them to you one day,' he said conversationally. 'But for every day driving, I love my red Ferrari.'

'Why red? A bit blinding in the sun I would have thought,' she asked composedly, because she was keeping such a tight rein on herself. Enclosed with Xavier in the close confines of the car was having a disastrous effect on her senses. She couldn't help but be aware of his strong fingers curved around the steering wheel, or the movement of muscle and sinew in his long legs as he steered the car through the frantic traffic.

'I'm a traditionalist. A Ferrari can only be red in my book.'

Without comment Rose turned her head to look out of the window. He'd reaffirmed what she already knew. She'd found out the hard way at nineteen from his friend Sebastian exactly how traditional Xavier was, and why she should feel depressed at the thought she didn't know. Xavier meant nothing to her. The reason she was sitting beside him in the car was simply another tradition—to act as chaperone to her cousin.

Suddenly Xavier cursed and the car swerved violently to avoid a white van cutting in front of them. 'My God,' Rose exclaimed. 'We could have been killed!' Then she noticed the speeding traffic.

'Welcome to Seville, Rosalyn! The drivers are noted as being the most chaotic in Spain,' he drawled laconically.

'I believe you,' she responded dryly, and after a few minutes of watching the traffic she added, 'Almost every car on the road has a dent in it.'

'Not mine,' Xavier said arrogantly.

'No one would dare,' she murmured under her breath, as the car stopped at some traffic lights.

But he heard and turning his dark head, hard black eyes

narrowing with some fierce emotion captured hers, 'Are you afraid of me Rosalyn?'

'No,' she said with curt authority. She was a mature adult woman, her days of being intimidated by the male of the species were long since over.

'Perhaps you should be,' he said quietly as he changed gear and drove on into the centre of the city.

For a second Rosalyn wondered what he meant, then all her attention was captivated by her surroundings. The roads were narrow and twisting, some had canvas blinds looped from the buildings on one side of the road to the other. Xavier explained they were to shade the public from the fierce heat of the summer sun and if she liked he would take her on a quick tour of the city. She agreed and very quickly realised Xavier was very well informed about the history of his hometown.

He pointed out the famous Gothic Cathedral, Santa Maria de la Sede that had taken a hundred and two years to built. It was actually in the Guinness book of records as having the third largest interior in the world. She watched in fascination as he indicated the Giralda tower, Seville's Moorish minaret, standing alongside the church soaring over old Seville, a magnificent reminder of the city's Moorish history. She glanced at Xavier; his hawklike nose and smouldering dark eyes and jet-black hair, seemed somehow more pronounced now he was back on his home turf. She shuddered slightly, and looked out of the car window.

'I never knew a river ran through the middle of Seville,' she exclaimed in astonishment, as she realised the road they were on was following a wide green waterway.

'The Guadalquivir is a famous river, but strictly speaking what you are looking at is the Canal de Alfonso XIII. The river was diverted at the beginning of the twentieth century to prevent the flooding of the city, enabling the city to continue as a port.'

'But it is miles inland!' That much she knew, her geography wasn't that bad.

A husky chuckle greeted her comment. 'The river has always been a famous waterway, a great inland port. Queen Isabelle chose it because it is so far inland and therefore safer from the English and a few other enemies. Christopher Columbus set sail from here to discover America.' He gave her a quick grin. 'There is an enormous statue of him in the cathedral, supposedly his tomb, one of five dotted around Europe.'

Rose was captivated by the architecture, and the truly Spanish feel of the city. When the car turned off the road and through a huge stone archway and halted in a cobbled courtyard Rose gasped in amazement. It was like no town house she'd ever seen before. Probably built in the nineteenth century, there was a huge wall with garaging and stables set into it which enclosed the courtyard on three sides, with the house on the other. A sweeping semicircle of steps led up to huge iron-banded oak doors that were opened wide. A small dark man was standing stiffly to attention to one side, obviously waiting their arrival. Xavier slid out of the car and she watched as he walked around the front and opened the passenger door for her.

'Welcome to my home, Rosalyn.'

Rose swung her long legs out of the low-slung car with more haste than grace. She glanced up at him and surprised him surveying her with a very masculine appreciation. Her heart jumped and she stood up quickly, her fingernails curling into her palms to combat the sudden fluctuation in her pulse.

'It looks lovely,' she said blandly and stiffened when his large hand curved around her upper arm and he urged her up the stone steps. He said a few words in Spanish to the manservant and then introduced her. 'Max' was apparently the butler come-chauffeur and his wife Marta was the cook.

After the heat outside the interior of the house was refreshingly cool, and incredibly impressive. A mixture of Spanish and Arabic, the floor of the huge hall was a brilliant mosaic, the domed roof a testament to the skill of the craftsmen who had so painstakingly built it. Graceful pillars along each side were covered in very Moorish blue *azul* tiles that dazzled the eye. Behind the columns were the shadowed entrance doors to the reception rooms, and a very Spanish magnificent wood-carved staircase was the centre point.

'My father is resting now, you will meet him at dinner. I will show you to your room.' Without relinquishing her arm Xavier led her across the vast expanse of hall to the staircase.

Suddenly Ann and Jamie appeared at the top of the stairs. 'We are going to explore. See you at seven,' Jamie said brightly descending the stairs.

'Isn't this place fantastic?' Ann cried at Rose as they shot past.

Rose swivelled around. 'Wait.' She was wasting her time they had vanished. 'So much for being a chaperone,' she muttered.

Xavier's lean fingers gripped her arm rather more tightly. 'Oh, I'm sure I can find some way of occupying your time beneficially,' he murmured smoothly urging her to the top of the stairs and along a wide-galleried landing. He swept her along another corridor and past two doors before stopping outside the third. 'Marta has given you the corner suite. I hope it meets with your approval.' And opening the door he ushered her inside.

'My word!' Rose exclaimed. She'd never seen anything

like it. A huge gold canopied circular bed stood in the centre of the room, the heavy silk drapes ribboned in blue. Four elegantly arched windows were set in two of the walls, and walking around she gasped in amazement at the view. One side looked out over the housetops, and to the Giralda tower in the distance. The other had a spectacular view of the river. The furnishings were all blue and gold. An exquisite scrolled writing desk was set between two of the windows, a satin-covered wood-framed antique sofa, was opposite a matching chair, and a low table equally as beautiful divided them.

Slowly she turned around. Xavier had moved and was now standing next to the enormous bed.

'The bed came from a Sheikh's harem. Do you like it?' he asked with supreme casualness, a strange golden challenge in his dark eyes.

'Like it. What's not too like?' she exclaimed, her fascinated gaze flying around everywhere. 'I have seen whole families live in a tent not as big as the bed.'

Xavier chuckled. 'Over here is the bathroom and dressing room that leads to a sitting room that can also be entered from the hall.' Striding across the room he opened another door set in the windowless wall. Rose followed, and gasped out loud.

The walls were lined in thinly veined white marble. A gilt-framed door led into what must be the dressing room Rose surmised, and all the accompanying features were in gold. A double shower, vanity basin bidet, but the *pièce de résistance* was a huge sunken circular pure white marble whirlpool bath.

'Decadent, is the word that springs to mind,' she said dryly stepping back into the bedroom, and finding Xavier was right behind her.

His strong elegant hands fell on her shoulders. She tried

to shrug him off; she did not want him touching her but his fingers bit into her flesh as he slowly turned her around to face him.

'It suits you, a decadent room for a decadent lady... "Maylyn."'

For a split second she was convinced she heard wrong. Her stunned green gaze lifted up to his. His dark eyes glinted ruthless with contempt and there was a menace about the hard mouth and the immobility of his striking features that told her she had not. The colour drained from her face, she could not breathe. He knew—he had known all along she was Maylyn. He'd remembered her. He'd been playing with her all weekend like a sleek black panther waiting to pounce and now he was watching to see how she would react.

After her brief disastrous relationship with him ten years ago, she'd learned the hard way how to disguise her feelings. Years of study at medical school and more years spent looking after the sick and dying, she was adept at blocking out her emotions, in fact it was almost a necessary skill for a doctor.

'The only decadent person here is you,' Rose said stonily. Tearing her gaze away from his she glanced at their surroundings. 'And somewhat melodramatic if you recognised me, why didn't you say so?' She took a step back and broke free from his hold, but only because he let her she realised shakily.

'I could ask you the same question.' Xavier drawled cynically, 'But I know the answer, I could read it in your face when Teresa introduced us. You were as white as a sheet and absolutely horrified.' He stared at her grimly. 'What was the problem, frightened I would reveal the serious dedicated doctor was once a model with a penchant for one-night stands?'

Rose could not answer him. For the past twenty-four hours she'd been living in fear of his remembering who she was. No not fear, in a state of nervous tension, and now he had she was speechless.

'I was watching from the window when you arrived. I thought I recognised you, your hair threw me for a moment, from short and straight to long and curly, and a few shades lighter. But the years have been kind to you. If anything you are more stunningly beautiful than you were at nineteen, and your figure.' His dark eyes slid to her high firm breasts, clearly outlined by the soft knit shirt, and back to her face. 'You have filled out in a subtle but voluptuous way.'

She'd been a late developer Rose could have told him bitterly, as the memories came flooding back of the first few months after he had left her. Her breasts were fuller but her waist was still as tiny. When she gave her shape any thought nowadays it was usually to bemoan her rather luscious curves. 'You mean I am fat,' she said bluntly.

'No.' Xavier curved a large hand quite blatantly around her breast, sending a fierce current of sexual awareness through her.

'Keep your hands to yourself,' she gasped and knocked his hand away, the atmosphere suddenly raw with tension.

Xavier laughed softly. 'So defensive.' His dark eyes flicked down to her shirtfront, where her nipple was clearly defined against the soft knit garment. Then back to her face, his teeth gleaming in a sudden menacing smile. 'When we both know I could have you mindless in a minute. Once I gave you a taste for sex you leaped straight into bed with the next man you met. You can't help yourself.'

The injustice of his comment made her blood boil. 'Why you—' Sheer fury had her hand swinging wildly towards his face, but he caught her wrist and held it in a grip of steel and forced it behind her back, bringing her body into close contact with his long lean length.

'No, my lovely, I am not appearing at dinner with your mark on my face, one is quite enough,' he said dryly. 'But you and I have to talk.'

She closed her eyes and counted to ten under her breath. She was not going to demean herself by arguing about morals or lack of them with the arrogant swine. He did not have any... And if she allowed herself to challenge him over their past association, she knew it would be courting disaster. She would end up howling at him like a banshee. The hurt went too deep.

Slowly, painfully she achieved a semblance of self-control, and opening her eyes she flicked a glance at his hard face. 'If you want to talk, talk. But personally I don't think we have anything to say to each other. We met once a long time ago, but we have both moved on.' She was proud of her ability to control her temper, even though her insides were trembling held firmly against his hard body. She did not know what his game was, but she had a nasty feeling it would not be anything she liked.

He shrugged slightly, his powerful shoulders lifting beneath the smooth black shirt, his austerely handsome face once more devoid of expression.

'As you say it was a long time ago, and the past is just the past. It is the present that concerns me.'

'What do you want?' her mouth was dry.

Slowly his eyes drifted over her, assessing eyes that betrayed not a flicker of warmth. But it did not stop her skin heating where those eyes touched. His mouth twisted in a cruel little smile that terrified her. Belatedly she lifted her free hand and shoved against his chest and began to struggle in earnest, but she was too late as his mouth fastened with deadly accuracy over hers.

She'd been kissed in the intervening years, but nothing to compare with this. He forced apart her tightly closed lips with a ruthless brutality that shocked and yet aroused her. Xavier had lost none of his skill, subtly easing the pressure until the kiss became a battle, a drugging torment that she had to fight with every fibre of her being to resist. A silent moan died in her throat as she felt herself sinking into a sea of sensuality that drained any semblance of resistance from her mind.

Sensing his victory Xavier carefully eased her away from him, and then she knew what real fear was. How could her body have betrayed her so quickly and so completely? She did not dare contemplate… 'I think you'd better go now….' she said refusing to look at him.

His hand cupped her chin and tilted her head back. His hard eyes lingered on her softly swollen lips with a slight trace of satisfaction in their depths. 'What do I want, you ask?' he drawled mockingly. 'You know… What every man that looks at you wants. But I want a little more.'

'You're disgusting, and I hate you.' Her voice was flat and toneless. 'And what ever crazy idea you have has nothing to do with me.' When he had called her decadent implied she had slept with dozens of men, he'd insulted her. Yet *he* was a notorious womaniser. He had some nerve.

'It has everything to do with you. I want you to be my wife,' he told her casually, with no more emotion than if he had been asking what time of day it was.

Her mouth fell open, her eyes felt as if they were out on stalks, as she stared at him completely stunned. 'You're kidding or you're mental,' she grated.

'No, just logical. My father is ill; he has not long left on this world. His last few months will be much easier if he knows I am married.'

'Not to me.' She shook her head in negation, dislodging

his hand from her chin. She was no longer a silly love-struck teenager, she was a mature intelligent woman, and it did not take an Einstein to see Xavier was hoping to use her again, as he had once before.

'That is a shame. I thought your cousin and Jamie made such a nice couple.' Startled green eyes were riveted to his austere features, seeing the mocking twist of his sensuous lips. 'But a little subtle persuasion from me and Jamie and Ann will no longer be getting married in September. No, I think Jamie will decide to wait until he has finished college, and in the meantime, I will make sure he gets a taste of *la vida loca*. He has spent a long time studying—I think he will enjoy the crazy lifestyle for a while. Pity about your cousin, but no doubt she will find some other man to love.'

'You, you…' She could not find a name vile enough to call him. 'You would actually try to break up their rela-tionship?' she exclaimed, the depths he would sink to to get what he wanted was unbelievable. But then thinking clearly she added, 'No, they love each other. They won't let you.' She stood her ground. What kind of fool did he take her for?

'If you want to take the risk with your cousin's happi-ness, then fine.' One dark brow arched in sardonic mock-ery. 'But both you and I know young love is notoriously fickle.'

If Jamie were anything like his Uncle Xavier then Ann would be better off without him. Rose was just about to say as much, when she remembered her conversation with Ann last night at the dinner party and blurted, 'You pay his allowance.'

'I do.' Xavier said succinctly. 'The decision is yours. You agree to marry me, and Jamie keeps his allowance, suitably increased to accommodate his soon-to-be-married state. Something I am sure your cousin will appreciate. Otherwise…' Another shrug of his broad shoulders as much as to say, Who cares? Certainly not the black-haired, black-hearted man staring at Rose with cold cynical eyes.

CHAPTER SIX

'BUT WHY ME?' she asked almost silently, her intelligent brain racing. It did not make sense. Xavier was the kind of man who could get any woman he chose. He certainly didn't need to blackmail a woman into marrying him. 'You said yourself you're a traditionalist, so why not ask some young Spanish girl? I'm sure there must be dozens who would leap at the chance to become your wife.'

'I tried that the first time. This time I want a mature wife with her own interests, so she will not impinge on mine. A woman who knows the score. I want a mutually beneficial arrangement with no sentimental strings attached. A woman to warm my bed, without pretending to warm my heart. Knowing you as I do, that makes you the perfect candidate.'

He did not know her at all, except once in the biblical sense, and yet he had no compunction in labelling her a woman of little or no sexual morals, he had suggested as much several times. Why, she did not know. But it hurt, and the fact made her angry, angry with herself but furious with him. Her glance flew up to his face, a humourless cynical smile curved the corners of his lips registering a supreme masculine confidence in her capitulation.

His blatant declaration, his casual arrogance fed her rage. 'Go to hell! And take your asinine proposal with you.' She would not dignify it with an answer but beneath her anger there was a growing sense of fear.

He laughed harshly. 'I may go to hell, as you so elegantly put it, but believe me, lady, I am taking you with me. You

88

owe me, and I always collect on my debts.' He was close, too close…

'I owe you?' she exclaimed incredulously, this man who'd caused her more pain and heartache than she would have thought possible had the nerve to suggest she owed him! He was mad he had to be…

Xavier's mouth curled in a smile and her blood ran cold. 'You'd better believe it,' he drawled, the threat implicit in his tone. 'Sebastian told me all about your meeting and how you fell into his arms before you walked out on me. So save the innocent act, it won't work twice.'

'He tried to comfort me.' Unwittingly she was admitting that she had been in Sebastian's arms, but she didn't realise it, she was too angry. 'At least Sebastian was honest, and told me the truth,' she said furiously, her eyes wide with bitter contempt. 'Which is more than can be said for you. You with your hide-bound traditions, and the morals of an alley cat. God help your poor wife, she must have had a life of hell.' She knew as soon as she said it she had gone too far.

His eyes filled with icy anger. 'My late wife is no concern of yours. But as my future wife you would do well to learn some manners.'

'In your dreams,' she flung at him and shivered at the cold implacability in his saturnine features.

'Think about it, Rosalyn,' His hands closed painfully over her shoulders. 'And I'm sure you will agree,' he drawled pulling her so close she could smell the faint musky aroma of his cologne, and her traitorous skin heated where he touched. Paralysed by shock and something more elemental she watched as his head lowered. His mouth was hard and possessive, almost savage, as savage as the fire that flamed through her at his kiss.

She fought to stay passive beneath the onslaught, her

hands clenched into fists at her side, and she would have won, but his mouth lightened on hers his lips brushing gently from the upper to her lower lip, his tongue teasing and tasting until her mouth opened eagerly for him. It was like coming home after ten long arid years. She heard his ragged intake of breath, her body softening against him, and with a husky moan she wound her arms around his neck.

When he took his mouth from hers, and lifted her hands from his nape she cringed at her weak-willed surrender. His hands dropped back to her shoulders and gently he put her away watching through half-closed eyes as the shaming colour flooded her face. 'As I thought; some things never change. I'll be back at seven for your answer, and to escort you to dinner.' He smiled knowingly. 'Perhaps you would like to have a chat with Ann first, I have no doubt she will be all for our liaison.'

The colour drained from her face, taking all the warmth from it. Humiliatingly she knew he was right on both counts. With one kiss she fell victim to his sensual mastery, and Ann was determined to marry Jamie. She watched with frustrated wide stormy eyes as Xavier walked towards the door.

He turned to face her, the cynical aloof mask slipping to reveal a dark intense anger. 'And don't make the mistake of underestimating me this time, Rosalyn. I mean every word I say. I have never been more serious in my life.' And with that parting shot he left, closing the door quietly behind him.

Rose had no idea how long she stood staring at the door. The gentleness with which he closed it was far more threatening than any angry departure, her mind in chaos. She had no doubt he intended to carry out his threat to destroy Ann and Jamie's engagement. But worse she knew he could do it. She liked Jamie and she knew he loved Ann, but he was young. How many twenty-four-year-old young men would be able to resist the temptations a sophisticated man of the world like Xavier could provide? It would not take long for Xavier to drive a wedge between the young couple, and with the added threat of withdrawing funding if the couple did not wait to marry left Xavier holding all the power.

She gazed around the sumptuous room and wanted to weep. In fact tears did glaze her eyes, and brutally she brushed them away. At one time Xavier's proposal of marriage would have been a dream come true. But not anymore...

She had gone that route once before. A month after returning to England ten years ago she had discovered she was pregnant. As she was supposed to have been going on holiday it was easy to hide it from her Aunt. But alone, and desperately lonely, nearly three months into her pregnancy she had swallowed her pride and telephoned the apartment in Barcelona. Sebastian had answered and agreed to tell Xavier she wanted to speak to him urgently, though she had not given the reason. Sebastian had called her back half an hour later with the news, Xavier was getting married the following week and as far as "Maylyn" was concerned he had nothing to say to her. Sebastian was under direct orders not to give her Xavier's private home address or telephone number. She began to bleed the same day and suffered a miscarriage that night. She blamed shock and betrayal for the loss of her precious baby, and a decade later the pain still lingered.

Her green eyes hardened. Recalling the past was not going to solve her problem. Rose stalked into the bathroom, a quick look into the dressing room told her someone had unpacked for her. Turning the water on in the whirlpool bath, she stripped off her clothes, and twisting her long hair up into a pleat she secured it with a few pins. She stepped down into the quickly filling bath. A few moments later she turned off the tap, and let her head fall back against the padded rest set into the side of the white marble, and willed her troubles to vanish.

But it was not that easy. Recalling her altercation with Xavier on the plane, she remembered him admitting she was half right, he was a *hungry control freak.* He had not been kidding… Looking back on the past twenty-four hours she could not believe how easily she had been manoeuvred into the position she now found herself in. Xavier was a clever devious bastard, but calling him names did not solve her problem. Slowly she stood up and stepped out of the bath, pulling a fluffy white towel off the towel rail she wrapped it around her body, and shivered. The trouble was there was no solution with the memory of Ann's face pleading with her to be nice to the man still fresh in her mind. She could see no way out, unless she played him at his own game and behaved as ruthlessly as he did!

With a new determination in her step, and her wide full mouth held in a tight line, she dried herself down. In the dressing room she selected black bra and briefs, from a drawer, and then going to the bank of closets, she withdrew a black dress, from the meagre selection of clothes she'd brought with her. A wry smile twisted her lips. Black was very appropriate.

Ten minutes later she walked back into the bedroom and froze. Xavier was standing by a window dressed in a white dinner jacket, dark trousers, a white dress shirt and red bow tie. He looked staggeringly handsome, but she stared at his dark harshly etched profile with unconcealed loathing. 'It is customary to knock.'

'I did,' Xavier pointed out turning around to face her. His eyes swept over her, his gaze enigmatic. She'd left her hair loose to fall down her back in thick red curls. Her dress was wild silk with a halter neck, leaving her shoulders and back bare, while covering her front to her throat, where a band of black beading formed a choker around her neck. The skirt was slightly A-line and ended a few inches above her knees. On her feet she wore low-heeled black mules, exposing her delicately painted toenails. The same colour garnished her fingernails, and her full lips, were coated with a matching lipstick. She had utilised all her old modelling skills on her make-up, a tinted moisturiser for a skin that needed little assistance to glow with health. A blend of eye shadows enhanced her large green eyes and the subtle application of a dark brow eyeliner, plus two coat of mascara to her curling lashes and she was ready to do battle.

'Is the black supposed to tell me something, other than you are a very sexy woman?' Xavier drawled mockingly. In a few strides he had covered the space between them.

'It seemed appropriate for a chaperone.' Rose was equally as mocking. 'Shall we go?' And she was about to walk past him to the door, but he stopped her with a hand on her arm.

'Not so fast. I want your answer. You will marry me?' She had been praying for a miracle and hoping their previous conversation was an apparition on his part, but no such luck...

'Look, Xavier.' She tried for the reasonable approach when really she felt like spitting in his face. 'I can understand you want to make your father happy, but I don't want to get married. I'm a doctor, I have a career.

'An out-of-work doctor at the moment,' Xavier looked amused, 'Sorry Rosalyn but your objections are futile. You still want me, I knew it the moment I spoke to you at Teresa's. You looked at me with wide eyes and the tiny pulse in your throat.' He lifted a finger and placed it over the exact spot. 'Yes, this one was racing just as it is now. I also need a wife. "Yes" is the only answer I am prepared to accept.'

Anger hot and hurtful flashed in her eyes as they rested on his dark face but she fought to control it. She had a plan, it went against her better nature, but he'd left her no option, and it was certainly better than marrying a man she despised.

'I am not a whore to climb into the bed of any man who asks,' she said quietly. 'And I am certainly not going to marry you. But if you insist I will be your mistress for the length of my vacation on condition you do not interfere between Jamie and Ann.'

If she fell pregnant in that time, she would have a child to replace the one she had lost. She was nearing thirty and very conscious of her biological clock ticking. She longed for a child, and she had the money to support a baby for a year or two, and as a doctor, she should have no trouble getting another job. It would mean losing contact with her Aunt and Uncle but that would be inevitable anyway when Ann was married into Xavier's family. But on the plus side she would have her own child to love.

'I don't need a mistress, I already have one.' Xavier said almost indifferently. 'I need a wife. Yes or no.'

The sheer naked gall of the man took her breath away. She didn't know whether to laugh or cry. She'd been wrestling with her inner demons wondering what it would be like to have Xavier as her lover once more, planning to have his child without telling him. Served him right she'd thought. She'd imagined he wanted her back in his bed. Now she discovered his mistress already filled the position…

'Let me get this straight.' Carefully she felt her way through her confused thoughts. 'You mean I play the part of your wife to keep your father happy, nothing more.' She glanced at him then and his dark eyes gave nothing away. 'While your mistress takes care of your other needs.'

'Something like that,' he drawled laconically, his hand dropping from her arm.

She stared at him long and hard. 'Why don't you marry your mistress?'

One dark brow arched sardonically. 'You are not that naïve, Rosalyn. A man does not marry his mistress. As a compatriot of yours once said, it only creates a vacancy.'

Why she should be surprised at his callous comment she did not know. He'd kissed her into surrendering to him simply to prove his masculine supremacy over her, while she'd been deluding herself that he actually wanted her. More fool her! He hadn't wanted her at nineteen, how much less likely he would be bowled over by her charms when she was a decade older… His mistress was probably some absolutely stunning young woman who was quite prepared to earn her living flat on her back.

'You agree.' His deep voice cut into her thoughts, she glanced at him, he was flicking back the sleeve of his jacket studying the fine gold Rolex circling his strong wrist with some impatience.

'When would the wedding take place?' she asked, still not convinced, but unable to think of any alternative that would not leave Ann broken-hearted.

'Two maybe three weeks' time. Tonight you will behave towards me in the same friendly way you do with Ann and Jamie. In the next few days we will foster the belief in us being a couple by exchanging the occasional kiss and caress. My father will see the possibility, and by the end of next week I will make the announcement of our wedding. You can leave all the technicalities to me.'

'Do I have a choice?' Rose asked dryly.

His eyes like steel raked her mercilessly. 'Not if you care for Ann's happiness as you would have me believe. But then you are rather good at pretending emotion you don't really feel.'

A bitter smile twisted her full lips. To have a man like Xavier question the sincerity of her beliefs and emotions was ironic to say the least. 'Okay I agree,' she said flatly.

A large hand settled at the base of her spine. 'Sensible lady,' he intoned with a trace of what sounded like smug satisfaction to Rose, as he urged her out of the room and together they walked down the wide staircase.

Rose sidestepped away from his controlling hand as they approached the entrance to the salon. She had agreed to his blackmail, but she was not yet ready to behave as some starry-eyed doting female. She was too angry.

Head held high she swept past Xavier and into the large elegant room. 'Ann, Jamie,' she nodded to the young couple happily lounging side by side on a long brocade sofa. Rose's gaze was drawn to the man rising to his feet from the depths of a high winged-back chair. He picked up an ivory-handled walking cane, and stepped towards her. He had been tall but age and illness had stooped his once broad shoulders. His black dinner suit hung loosely on his thin frame, and the bow tie at the collar of a frilled white shirt that belonged to a bygone age was unable to disguise the slenderness of his neck. One glance told Rose this man was very ill and it was only superb good manners that had got him to his feet as she'd entered the room.

Immediately she crossed towards him stretching out a slim elegant hand.

'You must be Don Pablo Valdespino.' Thank goodness she remembered the name, she congratulated herself. 'Jamie's grandfather, and I am Dr Rosalyn May, Ann's cousin and her chaperone for a week.'

The dull brown eyes set in a face lined and ravaged with pain, suddenly sparkled. 'Excuse me my dear but you are far too young and beautiful to be a chaperone. In fact the mamas would be in fear of you stealing the fiancée.' He chuckled. 'Isn't that so, son?'

Rose was suddenly conscious that Xavier had moved to stand by her side. She glanced at him, and discovered a smile for his father of such tenderness on his usually aloof features that she was left in no doubt he loved him. Much as she hated the thought of being coerced into marriage, suddenly she could understand Xavier's reasoning. She liked the old man.

'You might quite possibly be right father,' Xavier responded. 'But please sit down, and let me get our guests a drink.' And crossing to a drinks trolley he asked Rose, 'What will you have?'

'A dry sherry please,' she responded smoothly but without taking her eyes off the old man.

Don Pablo sat back down in the chair, and glanced up at Rose. 'You are a doctor, but like no other doctor I have seen before, and believe me I have seen dozens over the years. If any one of them had looked like you I am sure I would have been cured immediately.'

'You, sir, are a flatterer!' Rose said with a smile.

'It is all I can do now,' the old man returned with an outrageous wink, and Rose laughed out loud.

'He's a terrible flirt; don't encourage him,' Xavier drawled, handing her a crystal glass filled with amber liquid. She took it from him her fingers brushing lightly against his sending an unwelcome tingle of pleasure through her whole body.

Lifting the glass to her lips she took a sip of the sherry, the liquid warmth of it moistening her suddenly dry mouth. She had to get over this stupid reaction to Xavier's slightest touch, she told herself firmly. He'd made it abundantly clear he only wanted a wife to please his father. Keeping that thought uppermost in her mind she joined in the general conversation with determined good humour.

Max announced that dinner was served and they all moved to the dining room. Rose glanced around, slightly awed by the elegance and wealth on display. The wall hangings and drapes were from another era. The dining table, large enough to seat twenty, was set with the finest porcelain china framed by silver cutlery, and the wine and water goblets were made of the best crystal.

Don Pablo took his seat at the head of the table and indicated Ann should sit on his right with Rose on his left. Jamie sat next to Ann, which left Xavier at Rose's side.

Rose picked up one of the glasses, and was stunned to see the monogram of the family, a scrolled V engraved on the side. How the other half live, she thought once again.

Xavier's dark head bent towards her, his lips very close to her ear, 'They have been in the family for generations,' he murmured reading her mind and at the same time initiating an intimacy between them for the benefit of his father.

'They are very beautiful,' she responded lightly, carefully replacing the glass on the table. She would be terrified to drink out of the thing now in case she dropped it. Not trusting herself to look at Xavier she asked Ann what she thought of Seville.

Everything went smoothly. A young maid helped Max serve the food and wine. A fresh green and nut salad was followed by tender fillets of beef cooked Andalucian style with olive oil and tomatoes, peppers, garlic and onions.

Don Pablo was a witty man with a great knowledge of local history, and a perfect host. The conversation never flagged until Max entered as they were finishing dessert, and informed Xavier there was a telephone call for him. Xavier rose to his feet, and his father stopped him with one word.

Father and son spoke in rapid-fire Spanish, the exchange obviously getting more and more heated by the second, until Xavier said 'Excuse me,' and walked out.

'I apologise for my son's lack of manners,' Don Pablo said with quiet dignity, breaking the lengthening silence, his sallow skin tinged with red.

'Don't worry,' Rose jumped in, she did not like to see the old man upset. 'It is only a phone call. You have a very beautiful home Don Pablo. It must have an interesting history,' she deliberately changed the subject. But it was the worst thing she could have said...

'Yes. The Valdespino family home has been on this spot for five hundred years, the house has changed but always Valdespinos have owned it. Now unfortunately it looks as if the Valdespino name will die out.'

Xavier returned just as his father spoke, he gave the old man a filthy look. 'Please excuse me, I am afraid I have to go out for a while.' He addressed his words to Ann and Jamie, barely sparing Rose a glance, and said something violently in Spanish to his father and walked out.

'You see what I mean,' Don Pablo said with a jerk of his head towards the door his son exited, his dark eyes glinting feverishly. 'It's becoming more and more obvious to me, my son is not going to provide me with an heir. His first night home and he deserts our guests...' Suddenly as if realising he had said too much he stopped, and rang for Max.

'I am sorry I am afraid I must leave you young ones now.' Allowing the manservant to help him out of the chair, he added, 'I am very tired, but please enjoy your evening,' and he departed.

'Phew…talk about drama,' Ann said with a chuckle.

Jamie joined in. 'Forget it. I've seen it all before. My Uncle and Grandfather are always arguing, they are too much alike to live together.'

Personally Rose wondered if any one on the planet could live with Xavier—he was so damn sure of himself; so autocratic he could make a saint curse, never mind his poor father. 'You speak Spanish Jamie, what were they arguing about?' she asked, intrigued by the fiery outburst.

Jamie grinned. 'Grandfather was furious because Uncle Xavier has taken off to visit his mistress. That was who called him.'

Ann gave Jamie a playful punch. 'You better not take after your uncle or I will throttle you.'

Rose knew the feeling, she would happily strangle Xavier herself. But watching the young couple Rose realised she had made the right decision in agreeing to marry the man. Jamie loved Ann and she was not going to be responsible for allowing a reptile like Xavier to destroy the young couple.

After coffee, Rose said goodnight and went upstairs to bed with a splitting headache. It had been a hell of a day… It was okay for Xavier, he was probably comfortably in the arms of his mistress by now… But for Rose there was no comfort as she prepared for bed. Her mind spun like a windmill in a gale. Having met Don Pablo she could see why Xavier wanted the marriage to take place. But God help her! How could she live with a man as a friend when he only had to touch her to send her up in flames?

Dressed in white shortie pyjamas, she prowled restlessly around the huge bedroom, she was too strung up to sleep. She felt a bit like a bird in a golden cage. She supposed that technically, she should have stayed downstairs with the young couple; after all she was their chaperone. What a joke! Xavier had simply conned her into coming to Spain.

She stopped by the window and looked down into the courtyard, as she watched a car swing through the entrance archway, a car she recognised. Xavier was back early from his assignation with this mistress. He stepped out of the car, his dark head tilting back as he looked directly at the window where she stood as if he sensed her presence. Quickly she stepped back, but not before she saw he was minus his jacket and tie.

It was not really early she accepted. After all, how long did it take to make love? He'd been gone two hours. Rose told herself she was relieved he had a mistress, ignoring the hollow feeling in the pit of her stomach. It confirmed what Xavier had said. He wanted a wife who would not interfere in his life, a wife who had her own interests. In time she would take up her career again. Having met Don Pablo it saddened her to admit the man would probably not last the three months she had holiday. Think positively she told herself; by marrying Xavier she could make at least three people happy: Ann, Jamie and Don Pablo. How bad could it be? A long holiday in Spain. And it wasn't as if she would have to sleep with Xavier, and closing her eyes she tried to sleep.

She shifted restlessly trying to relax but her muscles were inexplicably tense. Images danced behind her closed lids. Xavier all bronzed naked strength splayed across a bed, his masculine potency a promise of erotic sexual delights she remembered all too well. The image made her groan, her body hot with frustration and burying her head in the pillow she prayed for sleep.

The next morning, the sound of voices led her to the breakfast room. Xavier, looking uncompromisingly masculine, smiled at Rose as she walked in.

'Good morning, Rosalyn, you look delightful today.' His glittering gaze skimmed over her shapely form with blatant male appreciation. Braless, she was wearing a simple brightly printed red cotton sheath dress, with narrow shoulder straps and a skirt that ended mid-thigh, and sandals on her feet. It was too hot for anything more.

Obviously the open courtship had begun, Rose thought cynically, but mindful of her promise she said, 'Why, thank you, Xavier,' though she almost choked on his name.

'My pleasure. I am only sorry I can't spend the morning with you.' And turning to Ann and Jamie who were already seated at the breakfast table he added, 'And you two of course,' making it obvious where his interest lay. Rose bristled with resentment the mockery in his tone told her he could sense her underlining anger and was amused by it. 'The three of you spend the morning exploring the city but make sure you are back by one. We are leaving for the Hacienda after lunch.'

Which was why Rose was now melting under the midday sun, and completely lost. Seville was a fascinating city; the old town a chaotic jumble of narrow streets that Ann and Jamie had promptly disappeared into, leaving Rose standing in a street lined in orange trees, wondering where she was and more to the point where they were? She'd searched for them for over an hour and she was now hot, thirsty and thoroughly fed up. Striding down yet another narrow street she plodded on until eventually spying a lone woman sitting outside a small pavement café. Rose decided to do the same, and sank gratefully down on a none too clean white plastic chair. A rather rough-looking man appeared and she ordered a coffee and a glass of water.

Her thirst quenched she looked idly around and suddenly realised the streets had become even narrower, and a general air of decay permeated the ancient buildings. A man, a complete stranger stopped and spoke to her. She smiled inanely not having the slightest idea what he was talking about, but when he reached for her arm, she jumped to her feet, and shrugged him off. Time to leave, and she was not waiting for the waiter. She dashed into the dimly lit café and approached the counter to pay her bill, and opened her purse.

How could she have been so stupid? She had a few English pounds with her all coins, but no Spanish pesetas. She tried to give the proprietor a credit card and he made it abundantly clear he didn't take them. She tried to suggest he wait while she found a cash dispenser, and withdrew some Spanish currency, but he wasn't letting her out of his café. He raged at her in his native tongue and the only word she recognised was *Policía,* and she knew it meant police. The situation was becoming threatening.

She hated to do it, but in desperation she finally mentioned Xavier Valdespino, Don Pablo and by gesture asked him to telephone them. The proprietor looked her up and down, and repeated 'Xavier Valdespino' and pointed at her, 'Name.'

'Doctor Rosalyn May,' she heaved a sigh of relief as she watched him pick up the telephone from the counter.

A rapid conversation in Spanish followed and a few minutes later the change was amazing, the man smiled and handed her the receiver.

'What the hell do you think you are doing, Rosalyn?' Xavier roared down the telephone. 'And where are Ann and Jamie?'

'I lost them,' she snapped, not appreciating being yelled at.

'¡Dios mío!' You are not safe to be let out. Sit down, and wait for me. Do not move do not speak to any one

else. The proprietor will provide you with whatever you want. Understand…?'

'Yes,' she agreed meekly. She did not have a choice.

'Now put the owner back on.'

She could not get rid of the telephone fast enough. A minute later the proprietor had urged her back outside, the seat was wiped down, before she was almost forced into it. A bottle of wine appeared, and a sparkling clean glass. A soft drink was mentioned and to her horror the proprietor sat down beside her. She felt as if she was under guard.

A deep sigh of relief escaped her as a red Ferrari hurtled down the street ten minutes later. It stopped with a squeal of tyres outside the café, effectively blocking the narrow road. The beginning of a smile twitched Rose's lips as the car door was flung open and Xavier stepped out. Her smile vanished at the expression on his face and her eyes lowered. He was wearing tailored cream trousers and a short-sleeved sage green shirt open at the neck to reveal the beginning of curly black body hair.

'Rosalyn,' he said her name, and reluctantly she lifted her eyes to his. The expression in his made her tremble. Furious did not begin to describe him…

CHAPTER SEVEN

IN TWO STRIDES he was beside her; his eyes flashed with rage, and a muscle jerked in his cheek. 'What the hell do you think you are doing?' he grated furiously.

'I...' was as far as she got.

'Shut up.' Ignoring her completely he spoke at some length to the proprietor finally giving him a bundle of notes with what looked like very bad grace to Rose's eyes, and only then did he deign to look at her again.

'Are you are all right?' Xavier demanded harshly, his eyes raking over her slender frame with analytical thoroughness.

She shrugged 'Fine, apart from getting lost and almost melting in the heat.'

'You're lucky that's all that happened to you,' he drawled cynically, and grabbing her by her upper arm he hauled her to her feet. 'We're leaving.'

Rose gave the proprietor what she hoped was a grateful smile, but inside she was shaking. Xavier was towering over her like a hawk preparing for the kill, his hard face expressionless, but his narrowed eyes were like shards of black ice piercing into her.

His car was holding up the traffic and in the midst of the cacophony of angrily shouted comments and car horns, she was unceremoniously bundled into the passenger seat and the door slammed on her. Xavier slid in behind the wheel, started the engine and the car shot off.

Glancing sideways at his hard profile, she searched for something to say, her eyes dropped down to the open neck of his shirt, and she was surprised to see the scarring that curved his jaw carried on down over his collarbone. She'd never noticed before and then she realised, in spite of the heat she'd not seen him with an open-necked shirt on all weekend.

'How did you get the scar?' The words were out of her mouth before she could stop them.

'*Por Dios!*' Xavier's voice sounded explosively loud in the close confines of the car. 'You like living dangerously,' he said tersely his rage barely contained. 'You know very well, and if you value your life you will shut up until we are home.'

Know? She hadn't the slightest idea. She'd only asked to break the tense silence in the damned car. 'Sorry I spoke,' she mumbled, the sight of his white knuckles on the steering wheel telling her he was still livid.

They drove in tense silence through the narrow streets. Rose felt her nerves stretch like violin strings almost to breaking point. The car screeched to a halt at the entrance to the town house, and once again she was dragged out and frog-marched up the steps and into the cool interior.

'Look.' Rose stopped in the middle of the hall. She was fed up of being treated like a recalcitrant schoolgirl. 'It's not my fault I had to call you because I had no Spanish money. If you had not dragged me to Spain with a few hours' notice…'

His fingers tightened around her bare arm, his dark eyes became coldly remote on her mutinous face. 'In my study,' he ordered between clenched teeth, and a moment later she was in a book-lined room and the door closed and locked firmly behind her.

'So I got lost, it's no big deal,' she tried to diffuse the situation but his hand simply tightened around her arm, and he spun her around to face him.

'Lost in the red light district,' he drawled contemptuously. 'Or like water you found your own level.' His voice was low and dangerous, and she was still reeling at his mention of the red light district when he added, 'What happened? Did the man who approached you not appeal?'

'How did you know someone spoke to me?' she asked diverted for a second from his icy anger.

'The proprietor took great delight in telling me, and demanded I pay for the time you spent soliciting from his bar,' he answered with stark cynicism.

The colour drained from Rose's cheeks 'You paid, it really was a red light…?' She ground to a halt and stared at him, searching the harshly etched angles of his face for some sign that this was a joke. 'No, you must be mistaken, I chose that café because there was a lady already sitting there by herself, so…' She stopped appalled by her own stupidity. 'You mean,' she gasped…

'Exactly the lady was waiting for business. A percentage of her fees go to the café owner for allowing her the use of the table and the same applied to you.'

'Oh my God!' Rose could not help it, her full lips twitched and she started to chuckle. 'You mean he thought I was on the game?' she spluttered, and burst out laughing. The great Xavier Valdespino having to pay for time at a prostitute's table was hilarious. No wonder he was furious.

'Amuse you, does it?' he snarled. 'I wonder if you would find it so funny if the man had not taken *No* for an answer,' and in a deft movement his hand dropped to close around her waist, hauling her hard against his large muscular body. His head lowered and he kissed her. 'What could you do?' he muttered against her lips and as she opened her mouth to protest he stopped her with another kiss.

His mouth was hard and urgent, his tongue delving into the moist interior of hers with devastating results. Her heart roaring in her ears she fought to deny Xavier's sensual demand. His hand moved to curve her buttocks pulling her hips into the cradle of his, making her shockingly aware of the hard force of his desire. While his other hand slid beneath the bodice of her dress, dragging the shoulder strap down her arm, to palm the fullness of her breast, his thumb flicking across the pouting nipple.

Her mature adult rational mind told her to resist, it was pure male animal aggression, but her body behaved with the same urgent need as it had at nineteen. Her slender arms reached up and wound around his neck, and she moved against him, trembling with a yearning, a need she had no thought to deny. She gasped as he lifted his head, and deliberately caressed her breast again. 'Don't,' she moaned shuddering with sensual pleasure.

'Is that the best you can do?' He gave a twisted ironic smile, his hand sweeping from her breast to encircle her throat tipping her head back on the slender column of her neck.

'Try again Rosalyn.'

'I can't,' she murmured, bowing her head, her arms falling from his neck to hang loosely at her side. The imp of truth that had been nudging at her consciousness for the past three days had finally made itself heard. Was she in love with him? She didn't know, but he was the only man she'd ever met who could tear down all her defences with a touch, the only man to make her feel this way. The familiar male scent of him, his hard-muscled body enfolding her had called out to every nerve and cell in her body in a primitive recognition she was helpless to deny. Ten years or a hundred, her body would recognise his to her dying day. The realisation appalled her...

He stopped. 'You can't.' Slipping the strap of her dress back onto her shoulder he set her free. 'You really are a slave to your senses.' He looked amused. 'Well I can see as my wife I am going to have to keep a very close guard on you.'

Anger hot and instant broke through her moment of weakness. 'I can look after myself, Xavier. I have done for some considerable time.' He thought her little better than a whore. Where he'd got that idea from she did not know, but she was not about to disillusion him. Let him think she was a push-over for any man. It was preferable to Xavier knowing it was his touch alone that turned her to mush. 'I suggest you stick to your mistress, and leave me alone.'

He watched her with merciless eyes, she looked away. 'I don't think I will need a mistress,' he drawled cynically. 'Your response just now tells me you are going to be quite enough for me.' Quite calmly he added, 'At least for a while.'

Rose's head shot up at the sheer naked arrogance of his comment. Never mind the fact that she knew he was lying—he'd been with his mistress last night. The thought made her green eyes blaze with anger. But whatever she would have said was stopped in her throat by a knock on the study door and Jamie's voice asking. 'Uncle Xavier, can I speak to you?'

Xavier brushed past her and unlocked the door. 'And I want to speak to you,' he snapped as Jamie walked into the study.

The younger man glanced at his uncle and then at Rose, his eyes widening with the dawning light of knowledge. Her hair was a mess and her swollen lips were a dead give-away.

'Well, well, so you found Rose,' Jamie prompted glancing at Xavier with a broad grin splitting his face. 'Or did the pair of you plan to spend the morning together the same as Ann and I?' he chuckled.

Xavier reached for Rose and took her arm in a firm grip. 'Go to your room, and pack. Leave Jamie to me.' She noticed his voice held the ominous softness of rage tightly leashed, as he pushed her out of the door.

The door had barely closed when she heard the harsh implacable tone of Xavier's voice lancing into Jamie. She almost felt sorry for the young man. But not half as sorry as she felt for herself. Realising she still lusted after a tyrant like Xavier was soul destroying. It hit at her basic confidence in herself as a woman. She, who over the years had been a champion for woman's rights. Who as a doctor had despaired of women who meekly stayed with men who ruled them, now found she was in very much the same position. To be a slave to one's senses was not something she dared to contemplate.

A very subdued Rose was the last to enter the dining room for lunch. Xavier immediately leaped to his feet and pulled out a chair for her, and Don Pablo attempted to rise to his feet his innate good manners allowing him to do no less.

'Please, I am late,' Rose said sitting down. 'There is no need.'

'Courtesy to a lady was a necessity to a gentleman in my time,' Don Pablo opined, and sank back into his seat with a dry look at the still seated Jamie. 'Though the young seem to forget.'

'That is not all they forget,' Xavier remarked sitting down in the chair next to Rose with a dark look at Jamie.

Obviously the young couple were still in his black books for leaving her to her own devices this morning, Rose mused as she took a sip of the wine instantly provided by the hovering Max.

'I don't know what you're griping about Uncle Xavier,

it seems to me we did you a favour. You got to play knight errant to a beautiful woman,' Jamie said cheekily.

Unfortunately Don Pablo insisted on an explanation and to Rose's horror Jamie recounted her folly of the morning in lurid detail amid much amusement. Don Pablo's wrinkled face creased in a broad smile, his old eyes twinkling on Rose's face and then he said something in Spanish that made Xavier and Jamie look at her, and they all burst out laughing.

Rose felt the colour surge up her face, she didn't appreciate being the butt of male humour, especially when she hadn't understood what had been said. 'What did you have to tell Jamie for?' she demanded in an angry aside to Xavier.

'Unusually my anger got the better of me, and I told him in no uncertain terms, my opinion of a man who would leave a woman unprotected and the unfortunate consequences of such a dereliction of duty,' he informed her in a low tone, and sat watching her an oblique smile curving the corners of his mouth. 'How was I to know he would repeat it?' With a shrug of his broad shoulders he added, 'Forgive me.'

Aware Don Pablo was watching the exchange with interest she took another gulp of wine, and replied sweetly. 'Yes, of course.'

Lunch was horrendous. Xavier threw himself into the role of would-be suitor with a skill and ardour that left her speechless. His cold dark eyes suddenly turned warm and slumberous every time he looked at her while Rose alternated between blushing scarlet and cold fury. When she felt a large warm hand stroke her thigh under the table, she almost jumped out of her skin. It was only by a massive strength of will she resisted flinging the contents of her glass in his wickedly grinning face.

*   *   *

'IT'S A BEAUTIFUL HOUSE, and the lake is like a mirage,' Rose remarked to Ann later that evening sitting at the back of the long single-storied building, on a circular bench that surrounded a huge jacaranda tree on a wide terrace. Below was another terrace and another and then the waters of a gem of a small lake lapped against the shore. The journey to the hacienda had been accomplished with no trouble. To Rose's relief she had travelled in the large specially appointed people carrier with Don Pablo, Max and his wife, and Ann. Xavier and Jamie had used the Ferrari.

'Yes, nice for a rest, but a bit quiet for me,' Ann murmured. 'Jamie reckons there isn't a decent shop or anything much within miles.'

'Poor you,' Rose mocked lightly, beginning to relax a little for the first time in three days.

Jamie and Xavier were in the front courtyard playing football with some of the staff. Don Pablo had retired for the night tired from the journey—he was going to eat in his room. Consequently dinner was to be served at the more Andalucian time of ten.

Ann leaned forward slightly, her pretty face wearing an expression of some seriousness. 'Poor me,' she repeated. 'I don't think I have anything to worry about Rose. But you could be in imminent danger of getting hurt. I know I told you to be nice to Xavier, but well… I've seen the way he looks at you, and Jamie told me he caught the pair of you locked in the study doing heaven knows what. I know you're older than I am, and have seen more of the world, but you've never really bothered with men before. After years spent abroad in the desert or whatever, you could be vulnerable to a man like Xavier.'

'It's all right. I know what I am doing,' Rose said softly, immeasurably touched by Ann's concern. Thank heaven for the darkness, she thought as her eyes filled with tears. But

Ann's concern only confirmed what she already knew. Rose had to go along with whatever Xavier wanted. She slipped an arm around her cousin and squeezed, Ann cared about her, and would probably have done the same for her. 'I am a big girl you know, and not so naive as you seem to think.'

Ann grinned. 'Thank heaven for that. Jamie and I almost had an argument over it. He said you could look after yourself. But I said any man who has a mistress should not be flirting with other women, I mean Xavier is a widower, so why not bring his girlfriend home? It doesn't make sense.'

Rose chuckled suddenly feeling rather old. Ann was not as worldly as she thought, and she gave the girl another hug, before glancing at her wristwatch. She rose to her feet. 'Come on, its almost dinner time.'

Xavier was the perfect host over dinner. Without Don Pablo's presence, the meal took on a less formal air. It could not do much else with Jamie and Ann so open and happy in their love for each other.

Champagne was served; according to Xavier a tradition they upheld every time they returned to the country after staying in Seville. Yet another tradition Rose scowled. For a man who liked fast cars and fast women, and was perceived by the world at large as one of the most successful dynamic businessmen around, it was amazing his personal morality was a throw-back to the Moors and given half a chance the harem…

'To young love,' Xavier smiled with lazy humour and lifted a flute of champagne to Jamie and Ann. 'Long may it flourish.' But when his glance slid to Rose she saw the lazy humour was tinged with an explicit warning just for her.

Twisting her lips in what she hoped was a benign smile she joined in the toast, 'To Ann and Jamie.' Lifting her glass she took a long swallow. But she'd got Xavier's silent message. The romance would only flourish if she did as he wanted. Rose ate little and blamed her lack of appetite on the heat, but in reality it was more to do with Xavier's intimidating presence. Her stomach was tied up in knots with tension.

Xavier was at his most solicitous, his dark eyes warm and intimate whenever they rested on her, which was pretty much all the time. It became increasingly difficult for her to retain an aura of friendly interest, and when he let his fingers trail down the length of her bare arm, she could not prevent a slight trembling in the hand that hastily lifted the glass of champagne to her mouth. She allowed Xavier to refill her glass without keeping count, and by the time the meal reached the coffee stage the wine had helped dull her senses as well as an inexplicable ache in her heart.

'Excuse us, we are going for a walk,' Jamie was the first to rise from the table with Ann at his side.

Feeling amazingly floaty and slightly euphoric Rose grinned, 'Oh no you don't—I am the chaperone remember.' Standing up she swayed slightly. 'I'm coming with you.'

'No way,' Xavier chuckled, and getting to his feet he put a restraining hand on her arm. 'Leave the lovebirds alone, Rosalyn, and allow me to escort you to your room.'

'This from the man who demanded I come to Spain as a chaperone!' Rose glanced sideways at him. 'You've changed your tune,' she prompted belligerently.

'No, simply bowing to the inevitable, as will you,' Xavier drawled evenly, as he slowly turned her to face him. His close proximity, his hand on her arm, sent butterflies in her stomach fluttering like mad. He tilted her chin slightly with one long finger, his dark eyes narrowed on her lovely face. Even in her less than sober state Rose recognized the hint of warning in the inky depths of his irises.

Suddenly weariness hit her, and she barely raised a smile

when Jamie escorted Ann out of the room with the laughing comment, 'I trust you Uncle Xavier to look after Rose— she looks a bit the worse for wear.'

'Cheeky devil!' Rose mumbled. 'It must run in the family.' But she made no demur as Xavier slipped an arm around her shoulder.

'Bed for you, Rosalyn.' Faint alarm flickered over her expressive features before she successfully masked it. Xavier smiled grimly, 'On your own…for now.'

The next morning Rose woke with a splitting headache and a hazy memory of gentle hands divesting her of her clothes and lying her gently on a large bed, cool cotton sheet being carefully placed over her body, and the fleeting touch of warm lips on her brow.

'Oh, no!' she groaned, she had a very low tolerance to alcohol and usually stuck to one or two glasses of wine at most. Woefully, she struggled out of bed, made her way to the *en suite* shower room and stood beneath a freezing spray until she felt halfway normal. She dried her hair haphazardly with the wall-mounted hair dryer and left the bathroom.

Back in the bedroom she dressed quickly in white shorts and a blue cropped top. She opened the French windows that led out onto a wide terrace and let in the full force of the morning sun. For a second she was blinded by the light, and blasted by the heat. Slowly her eyes adjusted and she drew in a deep breath of the heady fresh air.

Her bedroom was on the back of the house that faced out over the terraced gardens and to the lake beyond. As she watched a flock of wading birds rose from the water and circled in formation before heading off to the distant hills. She sighed and wished she could join them, before turning back into the room. She sat down on the side of the bed and proceeded to try and brush the tangles out of her hair. She really should get it cut, she thought for the umpteenth time, when a knock sounded on her bedroom door.

'Come in.' It was probably Ann coming to tell her what a fool she had made of herself, she grimaced. 'Don't say anything I know…' She turned slightly and her mouth fell open. It was not Ann, but Xavier…

He walked towards her a silver tray bearing a pot of coffee, milk jug, sugar bowl, and two cups in his large hands. He should have looked servile, but the opposite was true. He looked as if he was lord of the universe, the sun gleaming on the silver in his thick black hair, and glancing off his perfectly sculptured features like a bronzed god, she thought fancifully. She couldn't help it; her eyes lingered on the breadth of his shoulders and the musculature of his wide chest perfectly outlined by a clinging black T-shirt. A shirt that was tucked into the waistband of very old denim shorts, the faded patches drawing attention to his masculine attributes with a devastating effect on her libido.

Her pulse beat a crazy rhythm throughout her body, and as her glance slid down over his long legs she almost groaned. She dragged her eyes away from the tanned muscular limbs with the lightest dusting of dark hair, and ran her tongue over suddenly dry lips. 'What do you want?'

It had not been a sensible comment to make. He placed the tray on the bedside table and stood looking down at her, his chiselled features as hard as stone, while a savage sensual smile played around his mouth. He projected a raw virility that was as electrifying as it was mesmerising to Rose and she could not prevent a swift indrawn breath or the involuntary tremble in her hand that had the brush dropping from her fingers. She recovered quickly enough and when she would have picked up the brush he beat her to it.

'Oh, I think you know,' he said, his smile deepening as he leaned forward and ran a casual insulting hand from the curve of her jaw down the long elegant length of her throat and then 'round to the nape of her neck his fingers tightening on the smooth skin.

His touch burned like fire, and yet his grip was not painful. Looking up into his dark eyes she held her gaze steady. 'Can I have my hairbrush please?' and waited.

'So cool.' He raised his brows, and straightened up, his eyes resting thoughtfully on her proud face. 'Perhaps that's best for now. Pour the coffee, and I'll attend to your hair.' She wanted to object, but he sat down beside her and gently ran the brush down the long tangle of her hair. 'Your hair is magnificent, like rich red wine with the occasional glint of gold.'

'Too much sun; it dries it out and streaks it.' She was babbling she knew. But with his hand on her shoulder holding her steady while his other gently drew the brush through her hair, she was so intensely aware of his scent, the heat of him, she wanted to lean back against the hard wall of his chest, and for a second she almost did.

'That's enough,' she said between her teeth, jerking forward and wincing as the action pulled her hair.

He laughed and cupping the back of her head he turned her face towards him, 'Enough is not a word I can ever see myself using in relation to you, Rosalyn.' He bent and kissed her.

The pressure of his mouth and the sudden heated response that arced through her completely overwhelmed her common sense. A slight pressure of his hand on her shoulder and she was tumbled down onto the bed, his large body following her down, never breaking the kiss. One long leg nudged hers apart, and he settled between her thighs, and all the while the kiss went on. His teeth nipped her lower lip, and then soothed with the sensual lick of his tongue. His lips teased and toyed with her mouth, nipping, brushing and thrusting deep, until Rose helplessly succumbed to the controlled hunger of his passion.

His hand slid from her head and stroked down her throat creating ripples of sensation burning through her body. His knowing fingers pressed lightly on the tiny pulse that throbbed there, as though testing her reaction. She felt the smile against her lips, and then she gasped as his hand snaked lower to rest over the smooth curve of her breast.

Waves of sensation crashed through her control, and she curled her feet around his lower legs, her back arching her body thrusting against the hard, hot, heat of his arousal. She wanted him. She wanted him to cure the burning fiery ache in her loins.

His fingers gripped the bottom of the cropped top she was wearing and pushed it up over her breasts, and then those same fingers plucked the straining peak of one breast with delicate expertise before moving to the other.

He raised his head, he was smiling, a flame of pure male satisfaction gleaming in his dark eyes, and something more, a devilish desire, a promise of sensual delight to come.

Sensuality had long since overcome sense, and she wanted him naked. Feverishly Rose's trembling hand pulled at his T-shirt, her fingers burrowing beneath to the flat plane of his stomach. Her hand stroked up over his ribcage and she heard him catch his breath on a ragged groan. Then suddenly he reared back, and stood up…

'No.'

No, what did he mean 'no.' Rose lay on the bed and stared up at him. He was tucking his shirt firmly back in his shorts, but her dazed gaze took in the fact he was still highly aroused.

'Straighten yourself up, and I'll pour the coffee.'

Struggling to a sitting position, Rose pulled her top down over her aching breasts, fierce colour scalding her face. She should have called a halt as soon as he touched her. It was humiliating to realise she had no defence against the man. While he was a supremely sophisticated devil, with a wealth of experience in the sexual stakes, and able to turn the pressure on and off at will.

Stubborn determination got her to her feet, the colour fleeing her skin leaving her unnaturally pale. 'Don't bother, it will be cold by now,' she said lightly, matching him for sophistication and headed for the door. 'I'll get a fresh cup in the kitchen.'

'Good idea,' he said softly, striding past her and courteously opening the bedroom door.

Rose walked past him, her gaze carefully averted from his dark mocking eyes. Then suddenly she was brought to an abrupt halt as Xavier grabbed her wrist. 'Let go…'

He cut in, 'Wait Rosalyn, your hair.' Reaching out he brushed a thick swathe of hair from her face. 'It's a bit of a give-away—I suggest you do something with it before meeting the rest of the household.'

But his warning was too late, and disaster struck…

CHAPTER EIGHT

AS THEY STOOD in the entrance to the bedroom, Don Pablo was not six feet away sitting in a wheelchair with Max behind him guiding it down the corridor. Taking one amazed look at Rose, with her hair in tangled disarray falling over her shoulders, and then at his son who had one hand gripping her waist, and the other in her hair, Don Pablo jumped to the obvious conclusion.

For a dying man he bellowed like a bull: 'Xavier! You dare to seduce a girl—a guest in our house!' His face red with anger he reverted to his native tongue and raged at his son in a tirade of abuse that appeared to be liberally sprinkled with curses even to Rose's untutored ears.

Her professional persona took over. Worried at what the anger would do to the state of the old man's health, Rose intervened. 'Please Don Pablo, don't excite yourself,' she tried to placate him. 'It isn't…' Was as far as she got as long fingers dug into the flesh of her waist, and she bit down a yelp of pain.

'Leave it to me,' Xavier cut in firmly. Leave what to him? Rose shot him a scathing glance, couldn't the unfeeling swine see how he had upset his father, but he avoided her eyes, and continued, 'What Rose was about to say, father, was: *"it isn't as bad as it appears."* Because she has done me the great honour of consenting to be my wife.'

Appalled, Rose stared at him. She opened her mouth to deny it, but the increased pressure from the hand at her waist combined with the implacable set to his impressive features, stopped the words in her throat.

Don Pablo's startled glance slid between his son and Rose a couple of times, finally resting on Rose's now scarlet face. 'My dear, dear girl I am delighted,' he said with genuine emotion, his lined face lit with a wondrous smile. Glancing down at the old man Rose saw his eyes were wet with tears of joy. 'I never thought I would live to see this day.' He reached a frail hand out towards her. 'Come give me a kiss.'

She flicked a blistering look at Xavier, his lips quirked in a challenging smile daring her to deny the old man. She bit her lip. What choice did she have? Now or next week wasn't going to make much difference. Turning her attention back to Don Pablo, she took hold of the hand he was offering, and bowing her head she pressed a swift kiss on his wrinkled cheek. Bowing to the inevitable sprang to mind...

'Now that wasn't *too* painful,' Xavier drawled mockingly, after Max and his father had departed in great haste for the nearest telephone to spread the news.

'If you take your fingers out of my waist I might agree.' The deed was done; there was no point in arguing, but his large hand idly massaging her flesh was a different proposition. Her pulse beat an erratic rhythm through her body, she pulled away, fighting to control her treacherous senses. 'I still need a coffee.'

'You also need a ring.'

'I don't need a ring.' She was still arguing the point five minutes later standing in the middle of his study, a steaming cup of coffee in her hand provided by the maid on Xavier's instructions. Rose studied him as he withdrew something from the wall safe, her gaze slipping furtively to his firm male buttocks and long tanned muscular legs. Xavier wearing shorts should be banned as detrimental to the health of the female population, Rose groaned.

Without warning he spun around, and caught her staring, and in one lithe stride he was beside her. His dark eyes gleamed with sardonic humour, 'The ring and the wedding first I think.' He knew exactly what she'd been thinking.

In an attempt to regain control of her wayward thoughts Rose slowly drained the contents of her coffee cup, and then placed it down on a convenient table. 'Look Xavier, let's get one thing straight. This is an arranged marriage, nothing more. I... I.' she stuttered and lost her nerve. 'I don't want any repetition of what happened earlier between us.' In other words no sex.

'You will get no argument from me.' His eyes were dark, enigmatic, yet with a brief glint of something else less easy to define. Anyone but Xavier, and she would have thought it was wariness as though he was not quite so confident as he appeared. 'This was my mother's ring, and I want you to wear it.'

Her eyes flashed to the open ring box in his hand, and lingered on the magnificent square-cut emerald surrounded by diamonds nestling in the ruby velvet. Her chin lifted fractionally as she boldly raised her eyes to his. It was exquisite, but she was not going to tell him that. 'Did your wife like it?' she demanded bluntly.

'My late wife chose her own ring,' he responded silkily. 'You have no choice,' and catching her hand slipped the ring on to the third finger of her left hand. 'A perfect fit, my father will be pleased.'

Anger bubbled up inside her. He was right again, damn him! She had no choice. Rose glanced at the jewel on her finger, and she knew she was not prepared to force the issue. 'All right, I will wear it for your father's sake, and it will add weight to the pretence I suppose,' she conceded grudgingly.

'So docile Rosalyn,' he gave her an ironic grin. 'I wonder how long you can stay that way.' Before she'd guessed his intention his arms imprisoned her and he kissed her.

Rose was so furious she could barely breathe when he finally let her go. 'What did you do that for? There is no one here to see us.'

'If you pardon the cliché—because you look so beautiful when you're angry.' His grin was an open taunt at her mutinous expression.

'We will never make it to the wedding,' she flung incautiously, her angry green eyes roaming over his splendid muscled frame that held more than a hint of ruthless power. A power she could not help trying to defy. 'Someone is bound to twig.'

'Twig.' His dark brows rose quizzically. 'Twig, as in tree?'

For once she'd stumped him... no pun intended, she thought smiling inwardly and murmured, 'Yes.'

'Ah! You think the family will find us wooden,' he surmised.

Something about the way he spoke with a trace of accent and his arrogant conclusion made her lips twitch. She tried to smother the laughter that bubbled in her throat, but it broke free, and she laughed out loud.

'I am glad I amuse. The sound of your laughter is a delightful change from the frowning countenance you usually present to me.' Xavier smiled, his dark eyes crinkling at the corners in a cheerful happy grin that made him look a decade younger, and touched her heart. 'How about we saddle up a couple of horses and I will show you something of your new home, while you are in the mood to enjoy it.'

After changing into a pair of cream chinos, Rose met

Xavier in the hall. He'd also changed his shorts for hip-hugging black trousers, and with a broad-brimmed hat held by a cord around his throat he looked devastatingly attractive and slightly dangerous. Rose wondered how it was possible to hate the man, and yet be so vitally totally aware of him that it bordered on pain, at one and the same time.

'You need a hat.' Xavier produced a broad-brimmed cream hat from the hall table and unceremoniously plonked it on her head. 'Your skin is too pale for our midsummer heat.' Then, picking up a square package from the same table he added. 'For our lunch.'

The stable block and barns were a short walk down to the right of the Hacienda. A wizened little man appeared leading a gentle-looking chestnut mare. Xavier waited while she mounted, and assured she was safe. Then the little man led out an evil-eyed black stallion and Xavier placed the package in its saddlebag.

Rose watched as Xavier mounted with lithe grace. Man and beast made a perfect pair, she thought and wished the same could be said of her, as the mare meekly followed the stallion.

Out of the stable yard and paddock, Xavier halted and turned in the saddle, his dark eyes gleaming in the sunlight. His gaze swept from the top of her head down over her elegant torso to her long legs gripping the body of the horse.

'You look good mounted; you really can ride,' he drawled with a devilish lift of one eyebrow. 'Let's go.' Flashing her a blatant roguish grin, he spun around and with the lightest pressure of his muscular thighs he urged his horse into a gallop.

The years rolled back and for a moment she was reminded of the much younger Xavier she'd first met, and her heart lurched in her chest. The transformation from domineering arrogant tycoon to a dare devil cowboy was so unexpected Rose grinned and gave her horse a gentle nudge with her heel and followed.

It was a brilliant clear day. The sun shimmered in a hot haze, turning the surface of the lake into a sparkling diamond blaze that dazzled the eye. Her spirits lifted as they galloped across the hard earth, and later when they dismounted and secured the horse's reins around the branch of a tree, they shared a picnic prepared by Marta.

Rose looked around with wide-eyed appreciation. 'This is a beautiful part of the country,' she murmured idly. Replete with wine and food she sat with the trunk of a tree for a backrest, feeling about as relaxed as it was possible to be in Xavier's intimidating company. 'I am amazed you ever want to leave here.' In the distance she could see acres of olive groves intercepting the rolling acres of sun-baked earth. Surprisingly, there was a section devoted to sunflowers, reminiscent of France, another where cattle grazed and the far horizon was a rugged mountainous outline.

Xavier sprawled on the grass beside her; his head propped on one hand he looked up at her. 'I very rarely do, and then only on business. With modern technology I can oversee the bank and most of my other interests from home.'

'I see.' She didn't at all, he was a renowned playboy, or at least he was when she'd known him. She frowned, maybe his great love for his late wife cured him, but she doubted it.

His eyes were keen and searching on her lovely face. 'I get the impression you don't believe me.' His free hand fell apparently casually over her thigh. 'Am I right?'

She felt the imprint of his every finger through the fabric of her chinos, his closeness, the unique male scent, the powerful intoxicating heat from his body touched an answering chord in her. It was so hard to fight the quick flare of desire his touch evoked, and suddenly the relaxed lazy atmosphere of the past few hours dissolved into an electric tension.

Her analytical mind told her it was simply a natural chemical reaction between a virile man and a fertile woman. But her common sense told her that to give in to the basic urges of the flesh with Xavier was a route to hell: that would destroy her.

Rose scrambled to her feet. 'Believe you? In your dreams!' she snorted inelegantly. 'What I feel or think is of no importance to you, never was.' Her stormy green eyes flicked over his long muscular body sprawled in the grass, and in a voice tinged with a bitterness she couldn't quite disguise she added, 'We have a business arrangement and before I walk down the aisle with you I want it in writing: a legal contract that you will make adequate provision for Jamie and Ann, or there is no deal.'

His face was taut, his black eyes flashed with a devilish light, before long lashes lowered masking his expression, and he sprang to his feet. 'But of course, I would expect no less from you.' Gathering up the remains of the picnic he strolled to where the horses were tethered, angry tension oozing from every pore. He stuffed the remains of their lunch in the saddlebag. 'Shall we go?' And without waiting for her answer he swung up into the saddle. He stared down at her, his expression set, his cutting gaze contemptuous.

TWO WEEKS LATER, Rose stood in front of the long mirror in her bedroom. She decided she might look like a bride, with her red hair swept up in a mass of curls, and framed with a coronet of flowers. Her dress—smooth ivory satin sculptured to fit her tall elegant figure—emphasised her slender waist, and hugged her hips. Classic in its simplicity, the skirt slid sleekly over thigh and leg, to end at feet clad in satin slippers. But she felt nothing remotely like a bride should on her wedding day, there was a wary resignation in the green eyes that stared back at her.

'You look beautiful,' Anne remarked. 'I can hardly wait for my wedding.'

Rose glanced at Ann. She looked as pretty as a picture wearing the same style dress in palest green. 'So do you,' Rose said softly.

Uncle Alex rapped hard on the half-open door. 'Come on, time to go.'

Ann pressed a beautiful posy of flowers into Rose's hand. 'See you at the church,' and walked off to share a car with Aunt Jean for the journey.

Alex took Rose's arm and led her out to the waiting bridal car. 'You look beautiful *lass*. Your parents would have been so proud of you today,' he murmured.

Rose felt like crying as her uncle handed her into the car and slid in beside her. Since the fatal morning when Xavier had told his father they were going to marry, and the angry ending to their picnic later the same day, she'd seen little of her prospective groom. The same night at dinner she'd sat and smiled and accepted the congratulations of everyone. The following day there had been one sticky moment when Rose and Ann were relaxing by the swimming pool. Ann had queried Rose's lightening-fast engagement. Rose had managed to persuade her cousin she'd fallen in love, and with the arrival of Jamie and Xavier at the poolside Ann had dropped the subject.

Chewing her bottom lip, Rose reflected on Xavier's behaviour that day, he'd made harmless conversation, while quite blatantly allowing his gaze to roam appreciatively over her bikini-clad form. The heat had been intense, but when Jamie had suggested they play a game of water polo in the pool Xavier had smiled grimly and flatly refused to join them.

In fact from that day Rose had barely seen Xavier alone. If she'd been harbouring a secret wish that he meant their marriage to be real it was well and truly squashed. He appeared briefly at breakfast, and then promptly disappeared. He reappeared at dinner and acted the part of the perfect host and fiancé well enough to fool everyone. Her one consolation at the predicament she found herself in was Don Pablo. His happiness was a joy to behold; it had given the old man a new lease of life.

Rose had not the heart to disillusion him; instead she'd been engulfed in a wild flurry of activity. The following weekend had been taken up without Xavier on a brief trip to England by private jet of course, returning with Ann and Jamie's parents. Teresa had taken over the organisation of the wedding. There were trips to Seville shopping, beauty parlours, the works, and even if Rose had wanted to speak to Xavier alone she never got the chance.

It didn't take a genius to work out he was avoiding her. Once the engagement had been made public he'd not so much as kissed her apart from the occasional peck on the cheek in front of the family. The conclusion was obvious; she was to be exactly what he'd stated in the beginning, a socially acceptable wife to satisfy his father. His basic masculine needs were already perfectly catered for by his mistress. Rose told herself she didn't care, and almost believed it…

Her Uncle Alex's hand squeezing hers brought her out of her reverie. They'd arrived. The church was situated at the other side of the lake in the tiny hamlet of Valdespino, the home of the workers on the ranch that was a short drive from the main house.

Too short for Rose… She felt her heart begin to pound

and if she hadn't had her uncle's arm to cling to she doubted she would make it up the few steps to the church door.

Her eyes took a moment to adjust to the dark interior of the church and when they did she caught her breath. Tall, broad-shouldered and looking incredibly handsome in an elegant pearl grey suit, Xavier was standing at the foot of the altar, watching every step she took. Her nervous gaze clashed with black eyes that suddenly blazed with a golden fire of triumphant possession that threatened to engulf her. Rose almost turned and ran...

Xavier stepped forward, and grasped her hand. She felt an inexplicable shiver race through her and froze on the spot. His dark eyes narrowed as if her hesitation angered him, and he drew her closer towards him as the priest offered a greeting and the service began.

Afterwards she remembered little of the ceremony, only the overwhelming presence of the tall brooding man by her side. The wedding ring felt like a cold hard seal of possession on her finger, and surprisingly she was given a ring to place on Xavier's finger. When the priest intoned the words, 'You may kiss the bride,' she had barely succeeded in suppressing a shudder when Xavier had taken full advantage and folded her in his arms and lowered his proud head to claim her lips with his own.

Flushed and furious, she looked up into his powerful dark face when he finally let her go, their eyes warring for a second. He didn't have to make it so convincing—a brief touch would have conformed to tradition.

'My wife,' he smiled and she trembled as he tucked her hand proprietarily under his arm and led her back down the aisle.

The mandatory photographs were taken and Rose heaved a sigh of relief as she sank gratefully into the back seat of the bridal car. A short respite before facing everyone again at the reception at the Hacienda.

'That went very well I think,' Xavier remarked sliding in beside her, his long body too close for comfort. 'And you look very beautiful my darling wife,' he opined turning towards her and trailing his glance over her slender figure with an arrogance that was as shocking as it was blatant. 'Quite virginal,' he mocked.

He knew damn fine she was no virgin, and why. 'The dress was your sister's idea, not mine,' she snapped. She must have been mad to marry the man, she thought bitterly as she met the direct gaze of his ice-black eyes. There was no tenderness in his glance, only the cold cynicism of a man studying a newly acquired possession and considering its worth. 'Personally I would have preferred black,' she said bluntly and was aware of his anger, but didn't care. She felt oddly hurt that he could make a mockery of the marriage within minutes of leaving the church. But then it was not a real marriage she firmly reminded herself.

The meal and the speeches over the Hacienda echoed with the sounds of music and laughter, the champagne flowed freely and the guests were spread out over the house and gardens. Rose smiled until her face ached, and finally she felt a blessed numbness taking over her.

Xavier's arm was firmly around her waist where it had been for most of the afternoon, he turned her fully into his arms. And lowering his head he brushed the words against her cheek. 'It's time we left for our honeymoon, Rosalyn.' His dark eyes challenged her. 'Do you want me to help you change?'

'You're joking!' And catching sight of Ann near by she added, 'That's what a bridesmaid is for!' and she grasped the girl.

While Rose was getting changed, Ann, full of enthusiasm

and quite a bit of champagne gave Rose the confirmation that Xavier had fulfilled his side of the bargain. 'Your new husband is brilliant—Jamie and I are thrilled to bits at the allowance he has arranged for us.'

'You told me, yesterday,' Rose tried to stop her. She didn't need to hear yet again how wonderful Xavier was but Ann continued to give the exact arrangement in minute detail.

Straightening the narrow straps of the designer linen sun-dress in a rich terra cotta, Rose picked up the matching jacket, and her purse. She'd removed the flowers from her hair, and swept it into a smooth French pleat, and felt slightly more in control. But she was almost relieved to leave. Ann's good humour was too much to bear.

Xavier was waiting for her in the hall, his frame straightening perceptibly at her approach. His dark gaze drifted down over her in an explicit sexual survey, his mobile mouth curving in a smile as he eyed the long length of her legs with obvious appreciation. It was an act for the guests, Rose told herself firmly, but it did not stop her pulse beating in her throat, and by the time she got to his side her nerves were as taut as a bow string.

'Very nice,' he murmured looping an arm around her slender shoulders and urging her across the crowded room to where his father sat surrounded by his family. Don Pablo and Teresa kissed Rose, as did Jean, Alex, Jamie and Ann. It was Ann she clung to for a moment. The young girl must never know this was all for her benefit.

The red Ferrari purred down the long drive and out onto the main road. Xavier put his foot down on the accelerator and the car surged forward in a burst of speed that threw Rose back against the seat.

'Why the rush?' she demanded.

'Hmmm,' he snorted and shot her a brief glance before returning his attention to the road. 'I'm frustrated.'

She shot him a startled glance. If he thought he was relieving his sexual frustration with her he had another think coming. 'Now wait a minute....'

'A frustrated-racing driver,' he drawled mockingly.

Embarrassed Rose closed her eyes and pretended to sleep, the effect of countless sleepless nights caught up with her and surprisingly she did.

'Rosalyn,' the husky murmur played with her dreams.

'Yes,' she sighed opening her eyes. Deep slumberous green clashed with ebony, and she couldn't prevent a swift indrawn breath. Xavier was leaning over her, his chiselled features hard as stone and something raw and savage in the depths of his eyes. His lashes drooped hiding any sign of emotion and he smiled a frightening little smile.

'We have arrived,' he said and his arm stretched across her body, his fingers unclipping her seat belt.

Rose was shaken by an awareness so intense that her hand involuntarily lifted towards his compelling face. Just in time she realised what she was doing and forced her traitorous senses back under control. She completed the gesture by running her hand over one side of her hair with what she hoped was casual ease. 'So I see.'

A man she'd never seen before appeared at the side of the car and opened the door. As she climbed out Xavier appeared at her side and made the introduction.

'Rosalyn, this is Franco—my, how do you say, Butler?'

Intrigued Rose asked, 'Then what is Max?'

'Max and Marta are my father's constant attendants. Where he goes, they go. Franco is in charge of this house; he was on holiday when you were here last.'

Walking across the massive elegant hall with Xavier a

step ahead of her and Franco leading the way carrying her suitcase, Rose had the irrepressible urge to giggle.

Marching in a single file across the vast expanse of mosaic flooring she was reminded of a comic filmstrip of the three Egyptians. She bit down hard on her bottom lip to stop the laughter breaking forth. For a couple on their wedding night it was so formal it was ridiculous.

'Something amusing you?' Xavier asked, halting and taking her arm and forcing her to face him. His touch burned like fire and she glanced at his long tanned fingers against her skin, and all amusement vanished.

She lifted her eyes to his, and saw the dangerous challenge in his smile. 'No, no nothing at all.' Where was the humour in a loveless marriage? 'But I could use a drink.' This from a girl who hardly ever drank said something for the nervous tension consuming her.

He raised his brows his eyes resting thoughtfully on her taut face. 'I think we both could. Franco has provided a cold meal in the dining room, and the champagne is on ice. Shall we?'

It was polite and civilised. Rose ate a few mouthfuls of cold meat but she couldn't have said what it was, forcing the food down a dry throat. She sipped very sparingly at a glass of champagne, determined to keep her wits about her, and all the time she felt the tension building to stifling proportions.

They exchanged meaningless platitudes. The wedding had gone well. Teresa looked well. The weather had been brilliant. Rose tried to keep up a polite conversation but Xavier's replies became more and more monosyllabic making it obvious he had no desire to comply with the social niceties. Instead he sat in a brooding silence that completely unnerved Rose, until she finally pushed back her chair and got to her feet.

'Going somewhere?' His brilliant dark gaze narrowed on her face and he stared at her for long tense seconds. The line of his jaw was taut, then he picked up his wineglass and casually took a drink as though he could not give a damn...

Rose stiffened. 'I've had enough,' and she was not just talking about the food. It was obvious the wedding was over, mission accomplished as far as Xavier was concerned. What more was there to say? 'I thought I might unpack; it's been a long day and I'm rather tired.'

'As you please,' he said smoothly. 'I believe Franco has put you in your old room.'

So that was it... He couldn't have made it plainer if he'd written it in to the marriage contract. 'Goodnight,' Rose intoned flatly and walked out of the room. Xavier did not try to stop her.

She climbed into the big gold canopied bed, some half an hour later having showered and donned the only nightie she could find, a confection in satin and lace—obviously Ann's choice. As wedding nights go she thought dryly, it was a bit of a let-down. Lying on her back she watched the silver rays of the moon shimmer and move across the ceiling. It was too hot for a cover, but out of habit she pulled the sheet up to her neck and closed her eyes,

Soon she was drifting in a kind of stupor, half asleep and half wakening. The gossamer light brush of sensuous lips against her mouth, the wonderful sensation of being enfolded in a warm protective cocoon made her sigh with pleasure. She wriggled into the heated warmth, her tongue slipping out to taste the shape and texture of the intriguing lips. Languorously she opened her eyes but saw nothing, the blackness was complete. She was dreaming. Lifting her slender arms she reached for her phantom lover, her hands curving around a hard male back, her fingers stroking over the soft silk of... She froze...

Her eyes adjusting to the darkness, she realised the dark shape was all too real. 'Xavier.' He was wearing pyjamas...

'Who else, my lovely Rosalyn.' The fiery glint in his black eyes was all too discernible. As was the hard tension of his body arching over her.

The arms that had been reaching for him instinctively tried to push him away, one hand tangling in the open pyjama jacket the other spreading over his naked hair-roughened chest. His skin felt like fire, and with remarkable ease he captured her hands in his, his body crushing hers.

'Yes, my wife,' he grated.

'What do you think you are doing?' Rose demanded in a voice that lacked conviction even to her own ears. But in the inky blackness with the scent and weight and feel of his magnificent body overpowering her she was once again plunged into the spell of his dark male sorcery, as she had been years ago.

A husky chuckle and hard warm lips covering hers was her answer.

Rose tried. She did try to resist... Closing her eyes, she willed herself to feel no emotion, but with her eyes shut it only strengthened all her other senses. She opened her mouth to deny him, and taking the advantage she so carelessly offered, his tongue sought the heated warmth of her mouth. She felt the heavy beat of his heart against her chest, the heat and rigid power of his arousal against her thigh and the devastating sensuality of his hungry lips made her senses whirl. His touch instigated an answering hunger within her that she was powerless to deny, her tongue slipping into his mouth to duel with his in a hot moist passionate kiss.

Xavier's lips finally left hers to seek the slender curve

of her throat while his free hand swept down over the satin covering her breast, taking the fabric with it. His mouth lingered on the pulse beating wildly in her neck as his hand found the creamy smoothness of her breast, the tender peak swelling with pulsing desire. She groaned a low guttural sound, as he discovered its twin and rolled the hardening peak between thumb and finger. A multitude of exquisite sensations exploded inside her, she flexed her wrists aching to touch him, to make him feel a fraction of what she felt.

His grip tightened. 'Rosalyn,' he rasped lifting his head, his black eyes gleaming down into hers. 'This is the way it has to be the first time.' With ruthless efficiency he ripped the nightgown from her body the shoulder straps giving way with a single tug from his hand.

Her heart bounded in her ears and she silently cursed the darkness that prevented her seeing his magnificent body clearly, even as her mind told her she should demand he stop.

'*¡Dios!* I have dreamed of this.' His huskily voiced words feathered over the soft curve of her cheek. His sensuous lips bit gently on her own, and his hand caressed a feather-light pattern down over her breasts, and lower his fingers splaying out over her stomach.

Rose was caught up in a desire so intense nothing else mattered. Her tongue greedily sought his, and when he broke the kiss, for a second she felt bereft. But then he lowered his mouth to her breasts to taste and tease each straining peak.

Her whole body seemed to pulsate with fiery pleasure, as sensation after sensation washed over her, his hand slid lower, the heel of his palm pressing on the soft curling hairs at the apex of her thighs, as his long fingers discovered the hot damp core of her.

Her body arched involuntarily to his caressing touch as

he explored every inch of her with hand and mouth in a shockingly sensual intimacy. She threw her head back, her wrist straining in his pinioning hand as great shudders of shattering sensual delight crashed through her in wave after wave. She cried out and his mouth stifled the cry, as his hand curved under her bottom, and lifted her to take the penetrating thrust of his manhood.

'Xavier.' His name escaped on a groan as he held her motionless, then slowly he began to move, filling her body, as he filled her heart and mind. A deep throbbing ache built and built until she thought she could stand no more, and then she was caught up in the pounding rhythmic passion of his total possession, and she cried out his name as they reached the savagely wild all-consuming climax together.

It was some time before she was aware of her surroundings, her naked body held beneath the heavy weight of his strong masculine frame, the steady thud of his heart against her breast and the rasp of his breathing the only sound in the darkened room. What had she done? Keeled over like a stupid teenager at his first kiss, she castigated herself.

'My sweet sensuous Rosalyn, you have not changed,' Xavier mocked huskily, as he nuzzled into the curve of her throat, and finally he let her go.

Flexing her fingers, she lowered her hands to his shoulders, intending to push him away. Deeply ashamed at her helpless surrender to him, and it seemed somehow worse when she realised, he was still wearing a pyjama jacket!

CHAPTER NINE

ROSE LET HER ARMS FALL to her sides, her hands were free, but she knew now her body would never be free of its slavish desire for Xavier. She refused to call it love. When Xavier finally rolled away from her she lay for a long time staring into the darkness, consumed with shame at how easily he'd made her frighteningly aware of her own sensuality yet again.

'You're remarkably quiet Rosalyn,' Xavier's husky comment broke the silence. He turned on his side, his shadowed outline looming over her, a glint of pure male satisfaction in his eyes. One long finger traced the bow of her lips. 'You surprised me, you were so hungry for it. If I didn't know better I'd say it was some considerable time since you had sex.'

From the dizzy heights of ecstasy to brutal reality, Rose did the only thing she could. She hid her shattered emotions beneath a cool sophistication. 'What is there to say. You're a great lover, but then hundreds of women must have told you so, after all you've had plenty of practice,' she opined sarcastically. 'Pity you're not so hot on keeping a promise.'

'You're straying into dangerous territory,' Xavier said coldly 'I have not forgotten or forgiven the way you ran out on me after our first liaison.'

Her attempt at sophistication vanished at his hurtful reminder. 'Neither have I, nor have I forgotten how you blackmailed me into this marriage with the promise it would be platonic,' she hissed at him, all the anger and

138

humiliation she'd suffered at his hands rising like bile in her throat. 'You're a lying swine and I hate you.'

'I never promised a platonic marriage; you heard what you wanted to hear,' he retaliated curtly. 'As for hate. I'd have it any day to false avowals of love. Your hate makes you melt in my arms, and cry out for my possession. You tell me who is the bigger liar?'

Something in his eyes made her shiver and she shoved hard at his chest. But he merely laughed a harsh cruel sound and then he lowered his head to her breast. Finding the soft tip, with unerring accuracy and licking it with his tongue before taking it into his mouth.

'No, no...' Rose cried, her hands reaching for his head and tangling in the thickness of his hair as she tried to pull him away.

'Is it hate that makes your breast swell to my touch?' he asked mockingly, while his hand moved in a sensual caress down her naked length. He raised his head and the brilliant blaze of his eyes scorched into hers, as he claimed her mouth with a searing passion that seemed to burn to her soul.

Despite her best effort to deny him, she could not prevent the shudder of pleasure that betrayed her. Her hands found the opening of his pyjama jacket and moved hungrily across the warm, hair-roughened chest towards the broad shoulders, where the hard muscles rippled beneath her caressing fingers. And she didn't care that her capitulation proved how humiliatingly easily he could arouse her, because he groaned against her mouth, his body hard and tense with an urgency he could not hide, and she realised it was the same for him as she slipped the jacket from his shoulders.

They made love in a wild fury of passion. Xavier grasped her hands and dragged them low down over his firm buttocks, and she explored the smooth male flesh, trailing her fingers over the hard sweep of muscle from hip to thigh, and 'round to the rigid heat of his manhood.

'*¡Dios sí,*' he groaned as she caressed the long length of him with tactile delight. 'Ah! Rosalyn what you do to me,' he rasped and tearing her hands from his body he turned her beneath him and thrust into the silken centre of her. The pounding rhythm of his great body driving her to new heights of exquisite pleasure that left her totally exhausted and utterly fulfilled.

Xavier pulled her into the hard curve of his side. He reached to push back the damp strands of hair from her brow then nuzzling her ear husked something in Spanish. Rose sighed and turned fully into his arms, burying her head against his broad chest where she could hear the throbbing rhythmic beat of his heart and there she slept.

When Rose awoke, she was completely disorientated. The room was still dark, and the weight of a man's arm was flung across her stomach. Realisation dawned and with it came the shameful knowledge of how easy she'd fallen into Xavier's arms again. She stretched and flexed her limbs aching in places she had never ached before, and tried to ease out from beneath his restraining arm.

Xavier muttered something in his sleep but he didn't wake up. He stirred restlessly and rolled over onto his back and she was free. She slipped along the bed, and froze as someone knocked on the door, calling Xavier's name.

The door opened sending a swathe of light across the room quickly followed by the light being switched on and the smiling figure of Franco walking sedately towards the bed carrying a coffee tray.

Three things happened at once. Rose lay back and made a grab for the sheet to cover herself, suddenly realising she was naked. Xavier opened his eyes and sat up in bed. 'What the hell?' and Rose glancing up was presented with the sight of his broad back.

'Oh, my God!' Flowing like a river from under his arm a massive scar flooded down the side of his once beautifully bronzed body to cover half of his back 'What happened to you?' she asked unevenly. It didn't take a doctor to see he'd been very badly burned at some time. Some attempt had been made at plastic surgery but the scarring was unmistakable. The agony it must have caused him made her want to weep.

Xavier's voice cracked out, sharp as a whip. 'Get out Franco.' And not waiting to see he was obeyed Xavier turned his head and stared down at where she lay. She'd no idea how beautiful she looked, with a cloud of red hair laced through with gold shimmering across the pillow, her wide mouth swollen with his kisses, and her green eyes warm and compassionate on his handsome face. But he did not want her pity, it was too little, too late.

'What did you expect from a car crash? A neat little scar?' He drawled cynically. 'You're a doctor, surely you can recognise the effect of burning oil.'

Wriggling up into a sitting position, she impulsively reached out her hand to his back, her slender fingers tracing over the puckered flesh. 'I never knew, I'm sorry,' she offered quietly. Suddenly a lot of little things made sense. His refusal to join them all in the pool at the Hacienda. Last night she'd gone to bed with moonlight shining in the window. Xavier must have closed the heavy drapes blocking out any light before joining her in bed. The Pyjamas!

His gaze lanced through her. 'You knew all right.' Shrugging off her hand he was out of the bed, totally unconcerned by his naked state, his eyes glittering hard as they flicked over her. 'You have the face of an angel and you lie like the devil.'

Rose was horrified by his revelation and confused. It was not the first time he'd called her a liar, but why she had no idea, and she stared at him silently, her eyes wide and tinged with a puzzled compassion. Perhaps his accident had been in the newspapers, and he assumed everyone knew. In her capacity as a doctor she was aware it was not unusual for someone who had suffered a serious accident to be a little paranoid about it.

'I don't need or want your sympathy,' Xavier declared harshly, glimpsing the compassion in her gaze and angered by it. 'Your body is all I want, and as I proved quite spectacularly last night you wanted mine, so don't bother denying it.'

Incredible as it was to believe Rose realised Xavier, her powerful arrogant husband, was vulnerable in one respect. He'd deliberately kept his body hidden from her eyes, and recalling their lovemaking, he had even skilfully manoeuvred her hands so she had touched just about everywhere else but his back.

What had happened? No, she amended, *who* had been cruel enough to reject him because of his scars, his dead wife maybe? Rose didn't know but her heart bled for him, and she felt like strangling the person who had been so insensitive. It was in that moment that she realised that she loved him, probably always had.

Her hand tightened on the sheet. Loved him hopelessly for the rest of her life, probably for all eternity. Emotion choked her and she swallowed hard lowering her lashes to mask her expression from him. 'I wasn't going to,' she finally responded feeling her way.

His mouth curved in a cynical twist. 'Though you would rather not have to look at me. But no matter, you know what they say—all cats are grey in the night.'

Rose was appalled when she heard what he said, and

forgetting she was naked she sprang out of bed and stood barely a foot away from him. 'That's a horrible thing to say. I…' She bit down hard on her bottom lip horrified she had almost confessed she loved him… Wary green eyes flew to his face, and she blushed scarlet.

He was studying her nude body with obvious appreciation, his brows drawing together in a faint frown, at the few darkening bruises on the soft flesh of her uptilted breasts. 'Did I hurt you?' he asked huskily.

She wanted to say yes, a strange mixture of love and resentment stirring in her, but she could not lie to him. 'No,' she murmured, a certain pride in her body and his obvious delight in it caused her to stand a little straighter.

'Good,' he murmured but he had already forgotten the question as he glanced lower to the apex of her thighs, and on down the long length of her legs.

Rose in her turn could not resist appreciating his body, the scar from his face angled down over one shoulder and under his arm but she barely registered it. His chest was broad, liberally covered with black curling hairs that arrowed down past a narrow waist and taut lean hips. Long muscular legs flexed.

Her whole body blushed when she saw the very masculine reaction to her blatant scrutiny of his naked state, and her confidence deserted her. 'I need a shower,' and spinning on her heel she fled into the bathroom, his husky chuckle following her.

Pulling on white lace briefs, she'd taken from one of the drawers in the dressing room, she deftly slipped on the matching bra. Someone had unpacked her clothes, probably one of the maids she mused. Showered and almost dressed she felt more in control of her wayward emotions. Opening a wardrobe door she withdrew a hanger holding a green cotton dress. In seconds she'd pulled it over her head, and smoothed the skirt down over her hips. She could hear water running; and, realising she must have left a tap on, she walked back through into the bathroom and stopped. Through the glass of the shower door was the unmistakable figure of Xavier, water cascading down over his magnificent body, his proud head thrown back, his eyes closed.

She was staring again! She blinked and hastily shot back into the bedroom, her glance dropping to the rumpled bed and quickly away again. She did not need to be reminded it was the scene of her downfall. Spying the coffee Franco had provided, she poured herself a cup. She crossed to the window and flung back the heavy drapes. It was another brilliant sunny day, but her thoughts were anything but sunny. Sipping the coffee she grimaced in distaste; it was almost cold, but she needed the jolt of caffeine to try and bring some order to her befuddled brain. Draining the cup, she spun around. She had to get out of here, but halfway across the room she stopped, her head lifting sharply as Xavier strolled out of the bathroom.

His black hair was plastered to his head, and he was naked apart from a towel slung low around his hips. She gulped. 'Bad enough you invade my bedroom but at least you could use your own bathroom,' she snapped. Only then did she notice the clothes he was carrying.

He frowned at her. '*That is* our bathroom.' He dropped the clothes on the rumpled bed.

'Just a minute, you said this was my bedroom.' After her sojourn in the shower and some heavy thinking Rose had acknowledged that much as she loved Xavier, it did not make their marriage any better. He was still a devious devil, he had a mistress but it did not stop him climbing into Rose's bed, plus ten years ago he had used her quite abominably, however much he tried to pretend to the contrary. He'd married his fiancée, proof enough for any woman that he'd used her and Rose was not an idiot. She loved him but she was not going to be any man's doormat. She had too much pride, she deserved better.

He paused in the process of unfolding a pair of boxer shorts. 'This gold room *is* the master suite Rosalyn,' he said with sardonic humour. He then proceeded to drop the towel from his hips and step into the navy silk shorts.

'But the first night I was here you told me it was a guest bedroom.' Her eyes flashed angrily, their gleaming jade depths reflecting her inner turmoil.

'But nothing Rosalyn. It pleased me to have you in here from the day you arrived, because I had every intention of marrying you.'

His deep lazy drawl sent an icy chill feathering across the surface of her skin. To guess he had plotted to get her to Spain was bad enough, to have him confirm it was chilling. Her startled gaze locked with his.

'I vowed ten years ago that vengeance would be mine, and one day, I would have you again. You dropped out of sight, but from the minute I saw you step out of your E-Type Jaguar at Teresa's your fate was sealed.' And with a shrug of his broad shoulders he added, 'And I succeeded, *querida;* easier than I could have hoped.' He gave her a chilling smile, the endearment said in mockery.

For a long moment his confession left her totally speechless, he'd married her for some twisted revenge... Rose couldn't believe it. If any one had just cause for revenge it was her not him! She wanted to knock the sardonic smile of his face; instead she fought for control and won. 'But why?' she demanded, she needed to know. 'What did I ever do to hurt you?'

'Oh, you didn't hurt me. As I recall your last words ten years ago were *"I don't need the key or you. Goodbye,"* and hung up on...'

'And that's *it?*' she interrupted incredulously. 'Because I dumped you?' Anger made her voice rise an octave. He'd turned her life upside down simply because she'd dented his colossal pride by hanging up on him. The chauvinistic pig was used to women hanging on to his every word, and did not appreciate being jilted. What blasted arrogance! She fumed, 'Or maybe you expected more for the price of a dress?' she raged. Obviously he had not thought he had got his money's worth from one night. 'You're despicable.'

'Maybe.' His eyes flared and his facial muscles tightened into a mask of controlled anger. 'But you're here and you're my wife. Tradition was upheld, virtually every Valdespino bride has spent her wedding night in the harem bed,' he gestured to the bed with a nod of his dark head. 'It's considered to be a fertility symbol. Though in your case it probably does not apply. Protection against pregnancy must be a way of life for you.'

She opened her mouth to deny his claim and closed it. His scathing comment reminded her of her own pregnancy and the tragic outcome. Pain knotted her stomach as though a knife was being twisted in her gut. How could she love this man? She'd actually thought he was vulnerable, but he didn't care a jot about her. For a man who'd gone to great lengths to hide his body from her twenty-four hours ago, he'd certainly had a swift change of heart, she thought bitterly. If it was possible he appeared even more handsome wearing only boxer shorts, his intensely masculine frame exuding an innate sexuality that was lethal in its potency. He was so damnably attractive a million scars could never obliterate the virile power of the man. She watched him pick up a pair of beige chinos from where he'd left them on the bed, step into them, and pull the zip. Then he slipped on a short-sleeved white shirt, fasten the buttons, and tucked the tail into his trousers, before clasping the buckle of a sleek hide belt at his waist.

'Have you finished?'

She was suddenly conscious she had been staring again. 'No I have not.' Her chin took on a defensive tilt, and she held his knowing gaze. 'And as for you and your hide-bound traditions, they certainly didn't do your first wife much good, because you don't have any children.' Reminded of his betrayal she lashed out at him any way she could. 'Or should I say none that are legitimate.' The memory of his mistresses adding to her hurt anger.

In two lithe strides he was beside her. She was tempted to move back a few steps, shivering at the ice-cold eyes boring into hers, but she refused to give in to the feeling of intimidation that his large body towering over her pro-voked.

'You did not know my late wife, and you will not men-tion her again.' His hard dark face was expressionless, but only a fool would fail to detect the steel beneath silky smoothness of his voice. 'Understand?'

Rose was beginning to. His sainted wife was loved, and yet it hadn't stopped him betraying the poor girl with Rose all those years ago, and suddenly all the fury, the resent-ment, the hurt she'd been harbouring for years overflowed.

'Oh! I understand all right. The same way you never mentioned you were engaged to her ten years ago when you tricked me into bed with you. You haven't changed a bit; still the manipulative devil you always were,' she snapped furiously, only to find her shoulders gripped in fingers of steel.

'That's where you're wrong, Rosalyn. I am no longer a fool for a pretty face,' he said fixing her with a piercing glance that sent a sliver of fear down her spine. 'Nor was I betrothed to another woman when I met you. That is a pretence you've invented to salve your guilty conscious for running out on me.'

'Don't insult my intelligence,' she protested hotly. 'I saw the photograph on the mantelpiece, and Sebastian—'

'You will not mention his name in my presence.' He cut her off, and she was struck dumb by the violence in his tone. His hands bit deeper into the soft flesh of her upper arms. 'I will not have you maligning my friend to feed your guilty conscience.'

'*My* guilty conscience?' Rose exclaimed, her hands clenching at her sides.

'I've been patient with you. I have demanded no explanation for your past actions.'

Her temper flared red hot, her eyes flashing 'You've got a bloody nerve,' she swore. 'Or a damned convenient memory.'

Xavier went peculiarly white around the mouth. 'Don't drive me too far Rosalyn,' he warned savagely. 'I have kept my temper, and played the gentleman but not anymore.'

'You a gentleman, don't make me laugh,' she spat scathingly. 'You've done nothing but manipulate me and push me around from the day we met.'

'Enough,' he said, and there was something so savagely contemptuous in his expression that Rose tried to step back. Amazingly Xavier let her, his hands falling from her shoulders.

'Arguing over the past is a futile exercise, Rosalyn. You are my wife.' Then with a level look at her proud angry face he said with a return to his usual cold aloof composure. 'And as such you will endeavour to behave with suitable decorum. Swearing is out, and I am quite prepared to draw a veil over the past and call a truce.'

He sounded like he was addressing a board meeting… She opened her mouth to rage at him. She was sick of being taken for a mug by the arrogant devil, but stopped, biting down hard on her bottom lip.

He stood a foot away, the top button unfastened on his immaculate white shirt. 'I will not question you on your past lovers, Dominic and the rest, and you will grant me the same accord,' he drawled, his sensuous lips twisting in an ironic curve that did not quite make it as a smile.

Guilty colour washed over her face and she fought it back. She'd done nothing to be ashamed of. Dominic had been a kind sensitive man and a good friend. But it had not worked. He'd told her afterwards. *"You're a one-man woman and unfortunately for me I am not the lucky man."* But how had Xavier guessed about Dominic? She'd only mentioned the man once.

His astuteness was amazing, but one look at his hawkish features, the sheer steel-like strength of character the handsome face did not quite disguise, she conceded Xavier was far too astute for her to waste her time trying to defy him. Why not enjoy what he was prepared to give her without hankering for more. Last night she'd lost herself in a physical ecstasy she'd given up hope of ever experiencing again. The fact she loved him and he didn't was not that important, she'd reached the age of twenty-nine, a bit too old to wish for heart and flowers, she told herself wryly.

'By your silence I take it you agree,' Xavier prompted with a sardonic arch of one dark brow. 'Face it Rosalyn we are both mature enough to realise the futility of such confessions. You have an English phrase, no? "It is water under the bridge." Agreed?'

'Agreed,' Rose said quietly, 'But with one proviso.' She lifted fearless green eyes to his. 'I demand absolute fidelity from you.' He didn't love her but given time he might learn to, but not if she had to share him with his mistress. She was not a complete fool…

She'd surprised him. His expression flared with some brilliant emotion, and he took a step towards her. 'But of course you have my word, *querida*,' Xavier drawled, a gleam of humour in his dark eyes. 'But understand I demand no less from you.' His hand reached out to her and she took a swift step back.

'Wait. Haven't you forgotten something?' Rose said curtly 'Or should I say someone.' She watched as his dark eyes drew together in a puzzled frown. 'The mistress you mentioned when you so eloquently proposed to me,' she reminded him sarcastically.

Xavier grimaced. 'I am almost forty, and I've been alone for some years. It would be foolish to deny I have kept a mistress in the past, but not now. Last night with you was the first time I had made love to a woman in six months or more.' And before she guessed his intent his hand curved around her nape, and his mouth covered hers in a long hard kiss, her belated attempt to break free was useless as his other arm circled her waist and drew her close in against him. When he finally lifted his head her eyes were filled with anger and pain.

'This isn't going to work, Xavier,' she told him bluntly. 'I will not live with a liar.'

'Are you referring to me?' he asked incredulously, tension sizzling in the air as they faced each. 'Nobody, but nobody has ever doubted my word. How you...'

'Stop.' Rose held up her hand palm to his face. 'Dinner, the first night in Seville, a telephone call. Jogging your memory?' she prompted sarcastically.

Without comment Xavier strolled towards the door, and Rose's gaze followed him taking in the tense set of his wide shoulders. He spun on his heel, and she noted the flush of guilty colour emphasising his high cheekbones. 'Who told you? Not my father.'

'Jamie joked about it after your father retired for the night.'

'He would!' he opined in a flat chilling voice coming to stand in front of her. 'But he obviously did not give you the whole story.' Rose wasn't sure she wanted to hear it anymore and she tried desperately to mask her confused feelings looking somewhere over his shoulder as he continued. 'I am not in the habit of explaining my actions to anyone, least of all a woman.'

Bravely she raised her eyes to his and said bluntly, 'I'm not any woman, I am your wife.'

His eyes rested almost thoughtfully on her taut face. 'Yes, you are right.' His lashes drooped, hiding any sign of emotion in his dark eyes. 'Cast your mind back, Rosalyn. There was a telephone call for me at dinner, and my father was furious *before* I answered it. He was furious because the lady in question had telephoned here quite a few times over the last few months, and also while I was in England. As my father succinctly pointed out, a good mistress should be seen occasionally but not heard, and certainly not in one's own home.'

'My God, that is archaic!' Rose exclaimed in disgust.

'Maybe but true. I took the telephone call, and decided to put an end to it immediately. After all I had you.'

His supreme arrogance took her breath away. 'What did you do—pay her off?'

'Something like that, suffice it to say it is over, finished, and the lady in question was very satisfied.'

Rose's eyebrows drew together in a quick frown he must have slept with her for the last time.

'In the monetary sense, not the sexual,' Xavier drawled mockingly, accurately reading her mind 'You have no reason to doubt my word or my fidelity.' A dangerous smile curved his hard mouth, his hand reaching out to trace the line of her jaw before, bending down his lips covering hers in a gentle strangely evocative kiss.

She could believe him, or not as she wished, and with the taste of him on her mouth, she was so intensely aware of him. It was no contest.

'Make up your mind, Rosalyn,' he prompted huskily. 'Because it is almost noon and I am dying of hunger.'

Involuntarily her glance flicked to the bed and back to his face.

'That as well.' One dark brow arched eloquently. 'But right now for food.' And at that precise moment a distinct grumbling noise came from his stomach. He grinned slightly shamefacedly. 'I was so nervous yesterday I hardly ate a thing all day.'

His confession made him seem so much more human, and she grinned back. 'Let's eat.'

'Can you cook?' Xavier asked, preceding her to the door and holding it open.

'What if I say, "no"? Is it grounds for a divorce?' she questioned snaking past him, with a provocative toss of her head, suddenly feeling light-hearted for the first time in weeks.

Just as suddenly a large arm slipped around her waist halting her progress along the hall. 'No, Rosalyn. There will be no divorce.' Xavier held her still his eyes watchful and incredibly dark 'Ever. I want you to be the mother of my children.'

Her heart missed a beat. Had he guessed she was pregnant when she had tried to contact him? Could he really be so cruelly insensitive? Her eyes were wide, unblinking as she searched his features for a visible sign that would give her an answer, but there was none.

'Think about it.' Xavier reached out and pushed a stray tendril of hair back behind her ear, his lips curling in a slow wry smile. 'As for the cooking. I will do it. Franco always goes to eleven o'clock mass on Sunday and has the rest of the day off.'

'Ah, now I understand, you expect me to slave over a hot stove,' she teased, while wryly acknowledging it was the easier option. Much as she loved him there would always be a barrier between the two of them. Some subjects and people were not open for discussion.

CHAPTER TEN

BREAKFAST. Brunch. Whatever…was a convivial meal. Much to Rose's astonishment the kitchen was large and very modern, not the least in keeping with the rest of the house, and just as he had been on their very first night together Xavier was a very good cook.

'The ham and scrambled egg were perfect,' she offered, forking the last few crumbs into her mouth, and glancing across the width of the stainless-steel table, to where Xavier was sitting watching her obvious delight with some satisfaction.

'Then let me surprise you again. Go and grab your bag and a bikini and we will go away for a few days.'

'Away! Where?' she asked, astonishment widening her green eyes.

'I have a villa in Marbella. It's little more than a couple of hours away by car, and on the coast it will be a degree or two cooler than here.'

'But why? We only arrived last night, and Franco has just unpacked all my clothes. It will take me ages to pack again.'

Dark brown eyes gleaming with amusement met hers. 'Really Rosalyn, one can buy anything in Marbella; it is the jet-set capital of Europe.' One eyebrow slanted mockingly. 'Unless of course you want me to come upstairs and help you, but I have a feeling it might delay our departure indefinitely.'

He looked a very civilised, sophisticated man Rose thought as her breasts pushed against the confines of her bra in tingling awareness. He was obviously quite used to exchanging sensual innuendoes over the breakfast table with the current lady in his life. She wondered if he knew how tempting his casual sexual offer sounded to her.

'Decision time, Rosalyn.'

The sound of his faintly teasing drawl jolted her into action. She pushed back her chair and stood up. 'Give me ten minutes.'

The villa was built on a terrace into the hillside high above Marbella and to Rose's surprise it was quite new. Approached by a tree-lined steep winding drive, it seemed to be perched on a ledge of the cliff.

'This is fantastic,' Rose said sliding out of the car and glancing around. There was no garden as such. Xavier had parked the car in front of a garage door underneath the main building. Wide wooden steps led up to a thirty-foot-wide deck that surrounded three sides of the house, with enormous long supports sunk forty feet or so down the hill. 'Dangerous but fantastic,' she added as Xavier moved to her side carrying the little luggage they'd brought in one hand.

'Life is dangerous. We take what we can when we can,' Xavier opined cynically, his dark eyes skimming over with brooding intensity.

Now what had she done, she wondered following his long-legged figure through the door into a cool tiled foyer.

Two doors opened off the hall. Xavier flung one open and remarked, 'The kitchen,' and then strode past her to disappear through the other one.

Once more she trailed after him. This was becoming a habit, she thought dryly, eyeing the taut line of his wide shoulders, as he swept across the vast expanse of the room to a door at the far side.

Deliberately she stopped and looked around, her mouth

falling open in stunned amazement. A wall of glass opened out onto the deck, and the view was unbelievable. She slid open the glass doors and stepped outside. What feat of engineering had made it possible she did not know, but there was a rectangular swimming pool, and a couple of meters away a hot tub. She crossed to the far side of the deck and leaned her arms against the protective rail and stared... The panoramic view captured and held the eye. The gleaming white buildings of Marbella, the enormous marina and then the clear blue of the sea stretching to the distant horizon.

'A bustling town is not perhaps the first choice for a honeymoon,' Xavier's deep voice was behind her and she spun around. 'But with my father's health, or lack of it, I should say, I do not want to leave the country at present.'

'I understand,' she murmured, her gaze meshed with his, and suddenly the rail behind her seemed too fragile. His dark saturnine features swam before her eyes. He was like some dark avenging eagle and this house was his eyrie and she was trapped. She felt dizzy, she stepped towards him, and his arms curved around her.

'What is it?' he asked his dark brows drawing together in a frown. 'Rosalyn?'

Shaking her head to dispel the image, she forced a smile to her lips. 'Nothing; just the heat. I think I will have a swim.'

'Good idea. I have a few calls to make and then I might join you.'

There was only the one bedroom, a vast room that opened off a small internal hall from the living room. The same wall of glass and the same view, but with a luxurious *en suite*. Quickly she stripped off her clothes and pulled on a black bikini. Swiftly twisting her hair into a long plait she opened the glass door and walked back out onto the deck. Xavier had gone.

She slid into the pool, the cool water soothing her over-heated flesh. The trouble was she thought sadly, she was always overheating around her powerful husband irrespective of the temperature, and she did not know what to do about it. She forged through the water length after length and tried to make some sense of her confused thoughts. She knew her own nature far too well. Whatever she did, she always did with one hundred percent commitment. As a model she was the best she could be. With medicine she made exactly the same total commitment. Floating over onto her back she remembered her boss's words when he told her to go home and rest. *'Your parents were a wonderful couple and always responded to an emergency anywhere in the world when requested but they had you and each other, a family. You are an intelligent, beautiful woman and a good doctor, always concerned for the less fortunate in the world, but you are always alone. It is time you considered your own needs, perhaps even make a home of your own.'*

Rose closed her eyes, her arms spread wide in the water, flicking her fingers occasionally to keep afloat. She was married to the man she loved. She could already be pregnant. Did it matter that Xavier had married her for some stupid notion of vengeance probably because she was the first or only woman ever to walk out on him? The male ego was a very fragile thing she mused. But he was the best, in fact the only chance she had of ever having a family of her own. He had already said divorce was not an option. What was she beating herself up over? Her complaint was emotional not practical. The reality was she was married to an extremely wealthy man, relaxing in a swimming pool in a luxury villa…

Then she was drowning… Two large hands grabbed her waist and pulled her under the water, in a tangle of arms and legs she fought her way to the surface. Blinking water out of her eyes. 'What did you do that for?' she spluttered, frantically grasping his broad shoulders to stop herself going under again.

He did not answer, his hands grasped her waist and he dragged her hard against his large body, and simply covered her mouth with his own, parting her lips with a deliberate sensuality that she instantly succumbed to and returned.

'I've been watching you for the past ten minutes, and you're driving me mad.' His lips trailed down to her throat and he sucked the fiercely pounding pulse he found there, and then he raised his head, his dark eyes dilated to black. 'I want you...now.'

With water streaming off his bronzed body he climbed out of the pool, pulling Rose by the hand after him. She did not have time to think. He spun her back into his arms, his mouth hungry on hers, his hands stripping off the two bits of cotton she wore. He shucked off his shorts and dropping to his knees he laid her down on the deck caressing with hand and mouth every curve and crevice, until she cried out her need. His black eyes shadowed with lust and hunger bored into hers as he took her mouth again and at the same time took her willing body.

It was fast and furious and totally annihilating. Rose thought she had fainted from the exquisite pleasure. Slowly she opened her eyes, and was staring up at clear blue sky, she turned her head slightly. Xavier was lying beside her flat on his stomach, shudders still moving his wide shoulders. The scarring on his back glistened in the sun, and she reached a tentative hand towards him, stroking over the jagged flesh.

'Are you all right?' she murmured breathlessly her hand

splaying over the scar as he turned on his side. His glance flicked to where her hand rested and then to her face.

'That should be my line,' he laughed without humour. 'I lost control. A first for me.' Getting to his feet he swept her up in his arms again. 'The scar does not bother you?'

'No I've seen thousands worse, but what are you doing...' she asked breathlessly

'Penance for falling on you.' Strangely he seemed shaken, and cradling her in his arms carried her into the house. Rose glanced up through the thick curl of her lashes, and saw that his expression was rueful and nowhere near as arrogant as he normally was.

'What kind of penance?' she prompted feeling oddly protected and at peace in the comfort of his arms. Then she realised they were in the bathroom.

He set her on her feet in the shower stall and stepped in with her and turned on the overhead spray. With gentle hands he washed every inch of her body, and she returned the favour. They made it to the bed, but only just...

ROSE OPENED HER EYES, it was dark, and sitting up in bed she glanced towards the window. The house was so high that from the bed the only view was the sky. It was like living in the clouds the land of the mythological Gods she thought fancifully.

'Rosalyn.' Xavier stirred beside her and abruptly sat up. 'You're still here?' His hand clasped around her forearm.

She glanced at him surprised by the roughness of his tone. 'Of course I was just thinking how peaceful and quiet it is.' She felt his grip on her arm slacken, and his warm breath tease a few stray tendrils of her hair as he curved his arm around her shoulders and pulled her back against him.

'I'm glad you approve,' Xavier murmured, his lips seeking the elegant curve of her throat. But this time it was Rose's tummy that rumbled.

'No more of that until you feed me,' she teased pushing him away.

In a remarkably short space of time they were in the car and travelling down into the town. Xavier parked the car, and taking her hand helped her out.

'It's only a short walk to the restaurant,' he offered slipping a casual arm around her shoulders, and guiding her through the throng of people.

Rose's head was spinning like a top. Marbella was a beautiful brash town heaving with tourists, all devoted to conspicuous consumption. As they strolled past the Marina Rose's eyes were out on stalks.

'My God you could pay off the debt of every Third World country with the cash that has been spent on these yachts alone,' she exclaimed glancing up at Xavier.

His eyes gleamed with amusement 'Damn!' he wiped his brow with the heel of his hand. 'I forgot your radical views on the distribution of wealth. This is the last place I should have brought you.'

'You're right there. I feel considerably under-dressed or do I mean over-dressed. I've never seen so many gorgeous girls in one place.' Her eyes followed on particular long-legged blonde wearing a pellmet for a skirt, and a bra. Xavier's husky chuckle drew her eyes back to his. 'It's not funny I only have this one frock with me.'

'Don't worry *querida*. Tomorrow we will go shopping. But we have arrived.' Dropping his arm to her waist he guided her into the restaurant.

The décor was elegant and expensive Rose noted as they were shown to their table, and it needed only a glance to realise the patrons were among the best dressed and wealthiest around; she grimaced at her own simple green shift dress.

'You are the most beautiful woman in the place,' Xavier drawled, accurately reading her thoughts. 'So relax. Shall I order for you?'

'Yes, please.' She gave him a grateful smile for the compliment, and decided to enjoy what was on offer. The food was perfect, the wine chilled and by the time they reached the coffee stage Rose was feeling mellow and completely relaxed. Then a stunning petite dark-haired beauty stopped at their table and spoke in Spanish to Xavier for a good five minutes.

The woman's flawless figure was encased in a red satin designer gown. Diamonds sparkled at her throat and ears, but the smile she turned on Xavier just before she left, outshone them all. Rose felt a familiar stab of pain in the region of her stomach. She was no competition against the glamorous sophisticates in her husband's life. Basically she did not want to be, she recognised with a pensive smile.

'What are you thinking?' Xavier demanded.

Rose cast him a startled glance. 'I was wondering who your lady friend was. You never introduced me.'

'Isabelle is not my friend, she was a friend of my late wife.' Rose's eyes searched his dark face quizzically. It was an odd thing to say; surely any friend of his wife's would also be his. 'So tell me Rosalyn, when did you decide to become a doctor and go to medical school?'

It was such an abrupt change of subject Rose answered without thinking. 'My parents were doctors and I always intended to follow in their foot steps. I started university the September I was nine…nineteen.' She hesitated, the past was a taboo subject…

But his voice was level and light, totally at odds with the anger she could see in his eyes. 'So when we first met you knew you were going to university in the autumn, you had no intention of continuing as a model.'

'No… I mean, yes.' He smiled and it made her nervous. 'Yes, I knew I was going to university, I took a gap year to model. But I thought we were not supposed to mention the past—your instruction.'

Xavier got to his feet, threw some money on the table, and taking her hand helped her to her feet. 'You're right but I was curious. Forget it and let's go.'

After five days of sun, sea and sex, Rose stood in front of the mirror, and put the finishing touches to her make-up. A quick flick of a mascara brush and the subtle look she had been seeking was achieved. She slipped into the exquisite black designer dress, one of the many items of clothing Xavier had insisted she purchase over the past few days, and did a twirl. A fine halter strap supported the low-cut, softly draped neckline, cut away to dip to her waist at the back, the long skirt skimming her slim hips to taper down to floor length, the black gossamer knit fabric high-lighted with a subtle weaving of satin threads. Matching black high-heeled sandals completed the outfit, and she stood back from the mirror very satisfied with her sophis-ticated image, and walked out onto the deck.

'You're ready,' Xavier drawled, leaning against the safety rail his firm lips curved in a smile.

'Yes.' Her eyes swept over his tall lithe frame, her heart jolting. He looked devastatingly attractive clad in an im-maculately tailored dinner suit.

'You look good enough to eat,' he murmured, his dark eyes appraising the elegant picture she presented, and moved towards her.

'Not on your life,' she held up a defensive hand guessing his intention by the deepening gleam in his dark eyes. 'It has taken me ages to get ready, you're not mussing me up again.'

Xavier chuckled. 'You have a one-track mind, wife. I only wanted to give you this,' and from his jacket pocket he withdrew a velvet box and opening it he took out the most magnificent diamond and emerald necklace Rose had ever seen. Stepping behind her he fixed the shimmering jewels around her neck.

The movement of her hand was involuntary as she reached up and trailed her fingers over the cold stones. 'For me?' she murmured, seeing her reflection in the glass door. With her long hair swept up in curls on the top of her head, the necklace was revealed in all its glory. Her eyes flew to Xavier's. 'It is beautiful. But it must have cost a fortune.'

A faint smile tugged at the corners of his mouth. 'And you are beautiful, too, Rosalyn, and it is a wedding present so please, no dissertation on world poverty. We have not got time.'

The party was being held in a private villa by one of the wealthiest customers of the Valdespino bank. Once it had got around that Xavier was in town there had been dozens of invitations, verbal and written. But tonight was the only one he'd accepted, and tomorrow they were returning to the Hacienda.

It was an elegant affair, with about a hundred guests invited to share a buffet meal, and dance. Rose soon realised she was the talking point of the evening, the great Xavier Valdespino's new wife. She said as much to him when after supper he took her in his arms and held fast against his strong body they moved in perfect unison around the dance floor.

Xavier's dark eyes gleamed down into hers, 'It's not the fact you are my wife, but the fact you are the most beautiful, sexiest lady here. The women are green with envy and the men want to bed you,' he drawled with dry cynicism. His hand snaked up her spine and hugged her for a second as the music stopped playing.

The host of the party, a squat dark-headed man in his sixties, approached with his wife, and spoke to Xavier. Then in heavily accented English, he asked, 'Do you mind Rosalyn? I have need to steal your husband for a moment, my wife will accompany you.'

She smiled her agreement glancing up at Xavier. 'Business before pleasure, hmm?'

'Not for long I assure you,' he responded huskily, the sensual promise in those dark eyes was impossible to miss, and she watched him stroll off with the ghost of a smile playing around her lips.

Their marriage was going better than she could have ever hoped a week ago, a contented sigh escaped. The cold aloof Xavier that had insisted she marry him had given way to a warm humorous, sexy man. He might not love her yet, but she was pretty sure it would not be long before he did.

The poor hostess tried to make conversation with Rose but as neither of them spoke each other's language it was heavy going until some one else caught the hostess's attention. Rose heaved a sigh of relief and slipped quietly into the crowd.

'Well, if it isn't Xavier's new wife.' Rose spun 'round quickly, her glance colliding with the bitter brown eyes of Isabelle, the woman from the restaurant.

'Good evening,' Rose said politely.

'Not very good for you—Xavier has deserted you already? Get used to it he does that with all his women.' The malice in the other woman's eyes made Rose cringe, and backing away, she bumped into someone.

Grateful for the excuse she turned around and said, 'I am terribly sorry.'

The man was shorter than her, but attractive with laughter gleaming in his eyes. 'Don't apologise, dance with me.'

She was about to refuse when she recognised him. 'Sebastian.'

'Yes,' and wrapping his arm around her waist he led her into the crowd of dancers. 'It pains my Spanish soul to admit, lovely lady, that I do not remember your name.'

A gleam of mischief sparked in Rose's eyes. He did not recognise her. 'Rosalyn. Doctor Rosalyn May.'

'Ah yes! I remember you now, how could I have forgotten?' His hand tightened on her waist as they executed a swift turn. 'So tell me Rosalyn what have you been doing since last we met?' he asked smoothly.

The liar, he did not know her from Adam... Rose wanted to burst out laughing. 'Well let me see,' she murmured, her hand on his shoulder sliding down his arm so she could lean back a little and look directly into his tanned face. 'I got married a week ago.'

'My heart is broken—you should have waited for me. But at least let me kiss the bride.' Before she guessed his intent he puckered up and planted a big sloppy kiss on her cheek. 'Who is the lucky man and I will kill him.' He played the part of wounded suitor to the hilt, his cheeky eyes glittering with fun.

She couldn't stop herself from giggling. 'Sebastian you don't remember me at all. Maylyn, ten years ago,' she prompted. 'Now Mrs—'

She never got to finish the sentence. Sebastian's hands fell from her waist and, for a second she glimpsed a look of sheer terror in his eyes, before he was smiling at someone behind her. Abruptly she was jerked back against a hard body, and twisting her head she looked up into the angry face of Xavier.

'Now my wife. Sebastian.' He wasn't looking at Rose, all his attention was on the other man.

'My heartiest congratulations, old friend. I hope you will both be very happy. I am only sorry I missed the wedding.'

'Well I did not think it was worth calling you back from Buenos Aries before you completed the job. In fact I did not expect you back so soon. How did it go?' The conversation continued in Spanish.

Sebastian must still work for Xavier, she mused, and they were obviously the best of friends, as they both completely ignored her. She lifted her hand to cover Xavier's at her waist. He did not seen to know it but he was squeezing the breath out of her. Her finger slipped under his but he simply squeezed her hand and lifting it to his mouth kissed her fingertips.

'Say goodnight to Sebastian, Rosalyn *querida;* we are leaving.'

Rose looked up at Xavier. Noting the indomitable façade—the polite social smile that gave nothing away. She glanced back at Sebastian. 'Goodnight. It was nice meeting you again.' And it was, she realised as Xavier, still holding her hand, led her through the crowd to the exit. Sebastian had been kind to her when she'd needed it. But as Xavier had said the past was gone, it was all water under the bridge. They could all be friends.

A valet appeared with the car. Xavier took the key and bundling Rose into the passenger seat he slid behind the wheel, and started the engine. The car took off like a bat out of hell.

'Where is the fire?' Rose murmured casting a brief glance at his granite profile.

'Shut up,' he said curtly not taking his eyes from the road.

Which was just as well, Rose thought as the car careered

'round a corner on two wheels. She was beginning to get frightened, and she placed a conciliatory hand on his thigh. 'What happened? Our Host renege on his loan payments or something?' she tried to tease.

He knocked her hand off his thigh and shot her a glance, his face stony. 'Or something.'

'Oh.' She nodded, her gaze intent on his face, his mouth was tight, the hawk-like profile rigid with tension, and then the car took another curve, and she was flung against the passenger door. She stopped worrying about Xavier, her heart in her throat as she glimpsed the sheer drop from the side of the road. She was more concerned about getting home in one piece. It was a journey of pure terror.

The car screeched to a halt inches from the garage door, and Rose leaped out. 'You drove up here like a lunatic. What were you trying to do, kill us both?' It was the relief at standing on firm ground again that made her yell.

Xavier walked around the car and took her arm in a firm grip, almost dragging her up the steps to the door. 'Get in the house before I throw you off the deck,' he said tightly, then pushed her through the hall and into the living room, switching on the light and closing the door behind him as he came after her.

Rose looked at his face and backed away from him. 'What is it, what's the matter?' she whispered, seeing the fierce burning anger in his eyes.

'You dare to ask me that?' Xavier grated lessening the distance between them.

Rose backed away, her green eyes wide and fearful, but she was too slow, his hands reached out, grasping her shoulders, one hand tangling in her hair and jerking her head back viciously. 'One look at Sebastian and you could not help yourself, you were in his arms and kissing him.'

She shook her head. 'No, no, you've got it wrong, Xavier. It wasn't like that.'

'Don't lie to me, damn you,' he roared, his dark eyes leaping with violence.

'I'm not lying to you,' she gasped. He lifted his hand and Rose trembled, closing her eyes waiting for the blow.

'*¡Dios mío!* What you drive me to.'

Slowly she opened her eyes his arm was arrested in mid-air, his fingers curling in a fist. He looked appalled, and as she watched his hand fell to his side, but his other hand still bit into the flesh of her shoulder.

The transformation from wild fury to ice-cold contempt was frightening to watch. His mouth curved in a chilling smile his dark eyes hard as jet. 'No, I can't blame you. I knew what you were when I married you. The first time we met you left my bed and went straight to Sebastian's. You would have done the same thing tonight if you'd had the chance,' he grated, his lips drawn back against his teeth in a sneer and suddenly he released her with a force that made her stagger.

She raised her head and stared unwaveringly for a moment into his cold accusing eyes. Incredibly he actually believed she'd slept with Sebastian! Finally she understood Xavier's snide comments on her morals and she was rigid with rage. 'I have met Sebastian once before. In *his* flat the morning after you and I made love, the flat you conveniently let me think was your home.'

'I did leave you the key for it, have you forgotten?' he prompted in a maddening drawl.

'How could I. Sebastian told me you kept a bunch to hand out to your lady friends but they didn't fit any known lock,' she said angrily. 'He also told me you were engaged to his sister, and you made a habit of using his apartment for one-night stands, not wanting to sully the honour of your innocent fiancée, an acceptable tradition apparently, in your world.'

He shook his black head slowly in negation. 'I am not so easily fooled. The other day you told me you saw a photograph of my supposed fiancée, now you say Sebastian told you. To be a good liar Rosalyn you need a good memory,' he opined with icy cynicism 'Obviously yours is seriously impaired. Only the other week when I told you I was going to marry you, you admitted you had slept with Sebastian. Something else you have conveniently forgotten?'

Horrified at his assumption she frantically cast her mind back to the day he'd demanded she marry him. At the time she'd been stunned by his proposition but thinking back Xavier had said something about her leaving his bed and falling straight into Sebastian's arms. But it had never entered her head Xavier actually thought she'd had sex with the man.

'I have never ever slept with Sebastian,' she declared adamantly. 'I would not have dreamt of doing such a thing, surely you of all people must know that.' He had been her first lover; he had to know she was telling the truth. 'You *must* believe me.' But one look at his hard mocking eyes told her he did not, and she wondered why she even bothered trying to explain. 'Sebastian did put his arm around me, but on the sofa in the living room.' Xavier's snort of disbelief was audible, and Rose felt like thumping him to knock some sense into his arrogant head. 'And only because he was comforting me after explaining what a louse you were.'

'And that was when you both discovered that you had a sudden passion for each other.'

'Don't be ridiculous.' Rose was suddenly furious and fed up with the whole thing. 'As far as I'm concerned you deceived and deserted me,' she said bitterly, and spun around and began heading for the bedroom, anywhere out of his sight, before she burst into tears. The evening that had started so well was now in tatters.

His hand snaked out and caught her wrist spinning her around to face him. 'Sebastian told me, Rosalyn, and he does not lie. The same as he told me when he telephoned you at your hotel to tell you I had been in a crash, and you informed him you weren't interested.' His lips curved derisively. 'Where was the caring girl then? The girl who is now a *doctor!*' he drawled sarcastically

'You were in an accident the day I left?' she asked, her green eyes widening with horror. 'I never knew.'

'Never cared you mean.'

'No, no, you are wrong. I never spoke to Sebastian after I left the apartment. I left the hotel for the airport after hanging up on you; I was back in England the same night for heaven's sake! Sebastian could not have phoned me even if he wanted to. I honestly never knew you'd been in an accident,' Rose said fiercely 'What ever you think or Sebastian told you, I did not know.' She recalled the flicker of terror in Sebastian's eyes tonight when he finally discovered who she was, and with a flash of blinding clarity the truth dawned. Sebastian had been protecting his sister's interests ten years ago. 'Sebastian lied to you, Xavier.'

'And you expect me to believe you,' he drawled mockingly. His fingers tightening around her wrist in an iron grip. 'I have known Sebastian for years, he's a life-long friend, he would not lie to me.'

'He did,' she contradicted flatly. 'Sebastian never phoned me and I never slept with him,' she tried one last time.

Xavier gave her a caustic cynical smile 'Says you…'

His mocking sarcasm was the final straw. Deeply hurt at his total lack of trust in her, she said in a tight voice. 'Believe what you like.' She shrugged tiredly. 'What difference does it make, you will anyway. Now if you don't mind, let go of my wrist. I'm going to bed.'

'Yes.' He released her wrist, and gave a humourless laugh. 'The best place for a woman like you. Don't worry Rosalyn, whether I believe you or not is immaterial, we are married. I am quite prepared to forget the past and have a go at making the best of what we have got.' And suiting action to his words, his hands enclosed her waist, and drew her towards him.

Rose gave a stifled gasp before his hard mouth covered hers in a blistering ruthless kiss, that only ended when he had her complete capitulation.

Alone in the bedroom, Rose undressed, her green eyes hazed with moisture as she removed the necklace he'd given her a few hours earlier from her throat. From ecstasy to tragedy in one night she thought sadly. But without trust their relationship had no chance none at all. Xavier was never going to believe her above his friend. Then the sickening realisation hit her. If Sebastian had lied to Xavier, it followed he might have lied to her. If she had tried the key that fatal day, if she had spoken to Xavier when he called her at the hotel, asked him outright if he was engaged, if she had trusted him... If was the loneliest word in the English language, and the tears streamed down her cheeks.

It was ten years too late. Xavier was never going to love her as she dreamed of being loved. How long could she stand a marriage based on just physical passion? She climbed into bed and buried her face in the pillow and let the tears fall. She wept as she had never wept since the loss of her baby, and finally, all cried out, she fell into a sleep of utter exhaustion.

CHAPTER ELEVEN

ROSE, her vision blurring with tears stepped forward and dropped a handful of earth on the coffin. Don Pablo had been her salvation over the last five weeks and now he was dead and they were burying him.

On return from her so-called honeymoon they'd moved into the master suite at the Hacienda and Xavier had treated her in the same manner as he had before they married: playing the attentive husband in front of people, but avoiding her all day if he could. It was only at night in the wide bed that his phenomenal control slipped, and he gave in to the passion they ignited in each other. But it was not love…and for the past three weeks it had been nothing at all as they'd occupied separate bedrooms.

Rose had spent most of her time with Don Pablo, caring for him, and in return he had been teaching her Spanish. Two weeks after they'd returned to the Hacienda, Xavier had gone to Seville for a few days leaving her with his father. Don Pablo had taken a turn for the worse and Doctor Cervantes had asked Rose if she would administer the morphine and take charge of the old man's pain control. On his return from Seville, Xavier had used it as an excuse to occupy a separate bedroom. Telling her he did not want to disturb the little sleep she got while looking after his father. Personally Rose believed it was because he'd taken up with his mistress again, but she'd never asked him.

Instead she'd got to know and love Don Pablo. He'd delighted her with stories of Xavier's childhood, and the night before he died he'd made her promise she would not leave his son. He'd sensed all was not right between them.

A sad smile curved her mouth, as she brushed a tear from her cheek with a trembling hand. She was going to miss the old man. But she had the satisfaction of knowing he had died at peace with her secret revealed to him.

She turned away from the grave and walked back to stand beside Xavier. But there was no supporting arm from her husband. He stood rigid, his emotions held in check, his dark eyes cold as the Arctic waste as they flicked briefly over her, and then returned to contemplate the soil-splattered coffin nestled in the dry earth. Then everyone was moving back to the waiting cars and the drive back from the church to the house.

Circulating among the guests an hour later, Rose was surprised that Don Pablo had so many friends and was held in such high regard that members of the government were in attendance. Glancing around the crowd she checked everything seemed to be in order. Tables laden with food were set out in the courtyard. The champagne flowed freely, all at Don Pablo's specific request. He'd not wanted his friends to weep for him.

A movement to her left drew her attention and turning her head her glance rested on her husband. Xavier stood tall and sombre in a severe black suit, and as she watched his dark head bent towards Isabelle, who was dressed in a tiny slip of a black dress that exposed most of her chest and eighty percent of her legs. She was crying and clinging to Xavier's arm.

A bitter smile curved Rose's mouth. She had thought Xavier had taken up with his mistress again, but perhaps she was wrong, perhaps it was Isabelle if today's display was anything to go by. Suddenly Xavier's head lifted and his dark eyes caught her staring. She raised her brows, her

eyes running over him with contempt she did not bother
trying to disguise. She saw his mouth tighten in an angry
white line. Well, what did he expect? Flirting at his father's
funeral. Spinning on her heel she made tracks for the back
of the house.

She needed to think, and the relative quiet of the long
terraced garden that led down to the lake was the ideal
place. She sat down on a strategically placed wooden seat,
which had been a favourite of Don Pablo's and stared out
over the shimmering blue water. The heat was not quite so
intense, with the lush vegetation cascading over from the
terrace above providing some shade. She sighed, and
smoothed the skirt of her black linen dress down over her
knees. She bent her head back, closed her eyes, and slowly
rotated her head on her shoulders, trying to ease the tension
at the top of her spine. It had been a stressful few weeks.
The thought made her groan in disgust. That must be the
biggest understatement ever...

'May I join you?'

She opened her eyes. 'Sebastian.' She didn't want to
speak to the man, but good manners forced her response.
'If you like.'

He smiled rather warily and moved to sit down beside
her, and suddenly something in Rose snapped. She was sick
and tired of being polite, playing the part required of her.
She was losing her own integrity in the farcical situation
of secrets and lies and she'd had enough. She jumped to
her feet.

'Yes, I damn well do mind.' She turned on Sebastian,
her green eyes clashing angrily with his. 'How dare you
tell Xavier all those lies about me? What gave you the right
to play God with other people's lives?'

Sebastian flinched. 'So he's told you.'

'What do you expect? He's my husband,' she said

briskly curbing her temper. For her own satisfaction she needed to know exactly what Sebastian had or had not done ten years ago. 'You actually told him I slept with you. How could you?'

'I know. I know and I'm sorry. But you were a stranger to me, and Xavier and I had been friends since childhood, plus he's my employer. I never thought the two of you would meet again.'

At least he had the grace to look ashamed, Rose thought. 'But why?' she asked.

'Can't you guess?' he said wryly. 'You're a stunningly beautiful woman, the minute I saw you in the apartment I knew you were different from all the rest of the girls in Xavier's life, and you were a serious threat. I loved my sister Catia, and she'd wanted Xavier for years.'

'You said they were engaged. You told me she was a virgin, it was tradition. Xavier was honouring her innocence.' With hindsight she realised how dumb it sounded.

A harsh laugh escaped him. 'I wished they were. Catia had slept with Xavier years before, but he'd never taken her seriously, mainly because he was not the first or the last. That week in Barcelona she was hoping to get him back; he was unattached at the time. I was going to help her. But when you walked into the room and showed me that door key I knew I had to get rid of you so I made up the story about him having a bunch to give out to his lady friends. I took a chance you'd be too embarrassed to try, and I won.'

She shook her head in disgust. 'And Xavier's car crash?'

'He crashed on the way to your hotel. I was in the car with him trying to persuade him not to bother. I told him you'd left the key, and had simply said "Thanks and goodbye." He didn't believe me, and then it did not matter because a drunk driver on the wrong side of the road drove into him. Funnily enough Xavier's car was hardly damaged but he got burned pulling the other man out of his car.'

'Oh my God,' Rose whispered. 'And when he came 'round you let Xavier think I knew about his accident but did not want to see him.'

'Yes, the last thing Xavier told me was to call you at the hotel before he lost consciousness.'

'And did you?'

'Yes I did and they told me you had already checked out.' A slight noise in the bushes made Sebastian's head turn. 'What was that?'

'Nothing,' Rose said impatiently. 'So what did you do?'

'I told Xavier you weren't interested.' Sebastian shrugged his broad shoulders. 'You'd believed my story and gone, and Xavier was in hospital for weeks, with Catia playing the devoted girlfriend. It was only three months later when you called me and asked to speak to him that I panicked. He was fit, and talking about contacting you to confront you. I told him he was wasting his time, you were not worth the effort, and to finally convince him I reluctantly admitted I'd made love to you the morning after him.' Rose stared at him with horror filled eyes. The depths of his deception appalled her.

'You have to understand,' he grabbed her arm. 'I had to do it to protect my sister. Xavier was Catia's last chance. There were rumours people were beginning to talk about her.'

'So when I called you, and you rang me back and told me Xavier was getting married the next week, that was a lie as well?' Rose prompted flatly.

'Yes. But after I had told him I had slept with you he did not seem to care anymore, and a couple of months later he married Catia anyway.'

Briefly she closed her eyes. So many lies, the life of a

child and all for what? Glancing back at Sebastian's dark troubled face she asked bitterly. 'Why are you telling me now ten years too late? It can't be your conscience bothering you. You obviously don't have one.'

'I'd like to know the answer to that myself.'

Rose spun around and glanced up in shock at Xavier's thunderous countenance. 'Xavier, what are you doing here?'

He shot her a furious glance, a muscle jerking in his cheek, 'Get back to the house and take care of our guests. I'll take care of this.'

Rose was about to refuse, she looked from one man to the other, Sebastian's expression was defiant, Xavier's face was murderous. They were like two stags at bay, or two chauvinist pigs she thought cynically, who between them had almost destroyed her life once. Rose's stomach curled in disgust at what she'd heard, and with a hardness she had not known she was capable of, she decided to let them destroy each other. What did she care? And with a shrug of her slender shoulders, she brushed past the pair of them, and made her way back to the house.

She took a glass of champagne from a passing waiter, and downed it one go, anger and resentment sizzling inside her. But her rage gave her the strength to mingle with the guests and accept the condolences of Don Pablo's many friends.

'Rosalyn, my dear,' Doctor Cervantes stopped her. 'I'm leaving now, but I could not go without expressing my gratitude once more. Don Pablo was a very lucky man to have you to look after him, and he knew it. Although this is a sad day, Don Pablo would have appreciated it. God rest his Soul. You have done him proud.'

Rose smiled at the old man, who was a little bit the worse

for drink but his sentiment was genuine. 'Thank you, and thank you for coming.'

'No, thank you. I am getting old, too old to run a full-time practice. Later you and I must talk. I need a partner, someone young. Your grasp of the Spanish language is phenomenal under Don Pablo's tutelage, so think about it.'

'I will,' she assured him, flattered by his offer, and wished him goodnight.

The next hour saw most of the guests depart. Rose caught a glimpse of Xavier tall and aloof above the heads of the crowd, but he avoided her eyes. His harsh features were set in a brooding impenetrable mask that most people probably thought was grief, but Rose was not so sure. Her anger had cooled somewhat and the more she thought about Sebastian's revelations the more a tiny seed of hope grew in her heart. If she and Xavier talked honestly and openly with each other, perhaps their marriage could be saved. Then she saw her husband wishing Isabelle goodnight, and she castigated herself for being a naive fool. Nothing had changed... She watched him kiss the woman on both cheeks, and then straighten up and look around. Xavier's dark eyes clashed with Rose's, and she watched him approach with a dull ache in her heart.

'Rosalyn,' he took her elbow. 'It is time we said goodnight to our guests.'

She shrugged his hand off her arm. 'You mean now that Isabelle, your lady friend has left,' she drawled sarcastically.

His black eyes narrowed on her angry face. 'She is not now and never has been my girlfriend as I have told you before,' he said tightly. 'Now will you take my arm and behave as my wife until the last guest has left in deference to my father's memory.'

Put like that she could not refuse, and she stood in the

spacious hall, supremely conscious of the closeness of his tall virile body at her side, the light touch of his hand on her bare arm, until the last goodbye was said. Then she abruptly pulled away and turned to face Xavier to ask the question that had been preying on her mind for the past two hours.

'What happened to Sebastian?'

Xavier stared at her, his face rigid. 'He left and is no longer any concern of yours.'

'I see, and that's all you are going to say?' she asked. He was so coldly controlled and then she noted his hands were curled into fists at his sides, the knuckles of one hand white with strain, but on the other red raw.

'You didn't hit him?' she exclaimed.

'No, I grazed my hand on a wall.' Without looking at her he added, 'Now if you will excuse me it has been a hard day and I still have things to sort out.' And he almost knocked her down in his haste to get past her.

Rose watched the back of his black head, the taut set of his shoulders, as he disappeared into the study and slammed the door behind him, leaving her alone. He knew the truth now, he knew Sebastian had lied to them both and yet he had still walked away from her... He didn't care... Never had...

Face it, she thought bitterly, Xavier did not want her, the passion had burnt out. He hadn't touched her in three weeks. He had vanished most days only returning in the evening to sit with his father, and leaving when Rose entered the sickroom. She saw again his affectionate farewell kiss to Isabelle in her mind's eye. What did it matter whether it was his mistress or Isabelle who he was spending his time with? Xavier had promised her fidelity, and broken the promise.

Rose blinked away the tears that threatened to fall and

glanced around the now empty hall. It was the end of an era she thought sadly. No more Don Pablo and possibly no more Rosalyn Valdespino. She wished she could go back to Dr. May and forget the last few months had ever happened. But life was never that simple. What was a deathbed promise worth? Did one broken promise justify breaking another?

Deeply troubled she wandered through into the kitchen. Max was about to leave for the night and he tried to smile at her as she wished him goodnight, but his face was ravaged by grief. Rose sank down onto a hard-backed chair and leaned her arms on the table, her head drooping. She was so tired and emotionally drained she doubted she had the strength to make it to bed, and she certainly did not have the strength to challenge her husband. She had no idea how long she sat there, but eventually with a heavy sigh and after wiping a few stray tears from her eyes, she headed back to the hall, and then she heard it.

The howl was like the cry of some animal in pain, followed by what sounded like the shattering of glass. It was coming from the study. Without thinking she crossed the hall and pushed open the study door.

Xavier was slumped on the black leather sofa, his head in his hands, his great shoulders shaking. On the terrazzo floor was a discarded jacket and tie and the shattered remains of a bottle, and small pool of amber liquid. The persuasive scent of brandy hung in the air and on the sofa table stood an empty glass.

'Xavier,' she murmured. His iron control had finally cracked and she rushed to sit down on the sofa beside him, and put a consoling arm around his shoulders.

He threw back his head, and turned wet dark brown eyes on her. 'Rosalyn you are still here. Is my torment never to end?' he groaned, pushing unsteady fingers through his tousled black hair.

'Shh… I know. It is all right to grieve, your father was a wonderful man,' she murmured soothingly, her heart full of compassion for this arrogant, usually invulnerable man, brought low by his father's death.

His hand lifted to push back a stray curl from her forehead. 'Your sympathy unmans me,' he said in a roughened tone, his long fingers grasping her chin and tilting her face up to his. 'And I can't lie to you. The death of my father is not my torment. You are,' he declared hoarsely. 'How can you bring yourself to speak to me after the way I have behaved? You must hate me.'

'I'm a doctor, I care for people.' She tried to be flippant but her voice shook as emotion almost choked her. 'And I could never hate you,' was as far as she dared go in revealing her true feelings. She watched him breathe again, watched his dark eyes roam over her face her hair her slender body and back to her face.

Xavier looked long and hard at her, the tension building in the air between them, his hand tightened imperceptibly on her chin. 'But can you ever learn to love me?' he asked hoarsely, and she was stunned into silence by the fear and loneliness she glimpsed in his eyes, knowing the same emotions haunted her.

'No, of course you can't,' he said leaping to his feet. He spun around to stare down at her. 'I forfeited the right to ask when I believed the lies Sebastian fed me,' he grated bitterly. 'When I blackmailed you into marrying me. ¡Dios! I'm amazed you're still here. I was convinced you would take off the minute the funeral was over and the last guest departed. I shut myself in here intending to get drunk so I would not have to see you go.' His strained mouth curved in wry grimace 'I couldn't even get that right. I dropped the bottle.'

Slowly Rose got to her feet, and laid her hand on his arm. 'Do you want me to go?' she asked, feeling her way, her fingers unconsciously stroking his bare forearm.

He looked at her pale hand on his tanned flesh 'No.' She watched the strong cord of his throat move convulsively as he swallowed, 'No. No damn it, I love you, I always have.' Rose heard the words she'd longed to hear and hope blazed in her heart. 'For ten long lonely years, through a sham of a marriage to a woman I did not love and should never have married. And now I have found you again, it is too late—I love you far too much to keep you here against your will.'

She tensed. 'And who would you put in my place, Isabelle or your mistress?' she had to ask, she'd been torn apart the last few weeks imagining him in another woman's arms.

Wild eyes captured hers. 'Never. No one on this earth can take your place Rosalyn. You must know that, you must feel it when I am with you, lost in you, loving you.'

'But for the past few weeks...'

Xavier cut in, 'I have suffered the torture of the damned—burning for you, aching for you, and not daring to touch you. My father adored you, he told me so the night before I went to Seville. He was so happy for me, because I had finally found the perfect woman. In the short time he knew you, he recognised your inner goodness, your caring and compassionate nature, your honesty, and in his mind you were almost a saint. A dying man could see what I refused to see. After our wedding I felt the lowest of the low, not fit to be the dirt beneath your feet because I knew he was right. I didn't need to hear Sebastian confess to his lies, I already knew the things I accused you of could not possibly be true, and I felt such overwhelming love for you and at the same time a terrible guilt. I ran off to Seville for a few days because I could not face what I had done to you.'

'Oh, Xavier,' Rose whispered.

'No, let me finish. When I returned, and watched you with my father, talking, soothing him, caring for him. I was filled with such self-loathing I didn't dare touch you or tell you how much I loved you. I didn't deserve you, but I was terrified you would run away again.'

He would not look her in the eye, but he had said he loved her. She was not going to let him get away with playing the noble man. 'You don't see me running,' she murmured throatily. 'Unless it is to the bedroom.'

His dark head shot back and his dulled eyes, glinting with a golden light, clashed with hers. 'Rosalyn I am putting my heart on the line here, don't joke,' he said tautly, his mouth twisting in a shadowy smile as he admitted, 'I can't bear it.'

Slipping her arm around his neck she leaned into the hard warmth of his body and tipped back her head, her eyes gleaming with a look as old as Eve. 'No joke: I love you.'

Two strong arms wrapped round her like steel bands. 'I don't believe it, but I'm not letting you change your mind. I need you desperately, Rosalyn. I need the sweet solace of your touch tonight. I need to lose myself in the passion of your body, and if this is all a dream I don't care,' he declared raggedly, and took her mouth with a hard raw hunger that spoke for itself.

Then cradling her in his arms they reached the bedroom, and he set her on her feet and quickly freed the buttons down the front of her dress. Her hands were just as mobile, and in seconds they were naked on the bed. His mouth sought her lips, his tongue plunged into the moist dark heat of her mouth with a hungry desperation. Rose wound her arms lovingly around his neck, it seemed like a lifetime since he'd kissed her, and this time when she said, 'I love you' he believed her. After drowning in grief and loss all day, it was a confirmation of love and the continuity of life, a pinnacle of pleasure for the body and a healing balm to the soul.

'What really happened to Sebastian?' she asked a long time later as she lay in his arms, languorous in the aftermath of their lovemaking. She lifted his damaged hand to her mouth and kissed the raw knuckles.

'I think you know,' he drawled mockingly. 'I saw you leave the house and I watched Sebastian follow you. I followed him and heard everything he said to you. I was on the terrace above and I wanted to kill him. He lied to both of us. When I think of the years we have wasted…' Xavier tightened his arms around her and he rubbed his chin against the top of her head. 'But I restrained myself to one punch, and we will never see him again.'

'He is your friend,' Rose murmured. 'And he was looking after his sister.'

'He was my friend.' Xavier said trenchantly. 'But some things in life are unforgivable.' He turned her in his arms, and caught her chin, a wry smile slanting his lips, 'Though I have not asked your forgiveness for my despicable behaviour.' The thought made him frown. 'In fact it was all my fault,' he swore angrily. 'I knew I should have looked for you.'

'You had a terrible accident, and yet according to Sebastian you were still going to. That is good enough for me, you're forgiven, and anyway it as much my fault. I should not have believed the lies he told either.'

'You were only nineteen. I was years older and should have known better,' he said, a rueful smile replacing the frown. 'Only one thing puzzles me. What made you ring Sebastian three months after you had left?'

Rose had been dreading the question but she could not avoid it. Her green eyes shadowed with pain. 'I discovered I was pregnant a month after I returned to England. I had my apartment and enough money, and I told myself I would be fine as a single mother. Aunt Jean thought I was on a holiday so I had no need to tell anyone. But I knew you had a right to know, and as the weeks went by I began to get more and more depressed on my own, and finally I rang the number on the card you gave me and spoke to Sebastian. I did not tell him I was pregnant, simply that it was urgent I speak to you, though I think he might have guessed. Anyway he called me back and said you did not want to speak to me, and you were getting married the next week.' Rose stopped and glanced up at Xavier his handsome face was expressionless.

'Go on.'

Suddenly she realised he thought she'd got rid of their child. 'I be…began to bleed that same day,' she stammered. She still found it terribly upsetting to talk about. 'I was rushed into hospital that night and suffered a miscarriage; stress or shock, or perhaps it was just not meant to be…'

'No. ¡Dios! No.' Xavier cried out. 'If I'd known that I would have killed the bastard.'

'It's all right.' Her hands lifted to cradle his hard cheekbones 'It was a long time ago and over now.'

'No, it is not.' Her heart bled for the anguish in his face. 'You don't understand I was married for eight years, we rarely made love, but for some reason Catia never conceived. Maybe my chances of fathering a child are slim, and now you tell me we lost one. The one argument between my father and I was my failure to provide an heir.'

'Well, if your father is looking down on us now,' Rose

said gently smoothing the frown lines across his broad brow with her fingers, 'He will have a broad grin on his loveable old face. Maybe I should have told you first but I told your father the night before he died, and it made him very happy. I'm pregnant.'

'You're carrying my child.' Xavier's voice was deep and rough, his stunned glance sweeping down over the length of her naked body. One hand roamed possessively down over her breast and settled on the flat plain of her stomach, his dark eyes shinning with an adoring glow. 'You're sure? When—'

Rose grinned. 'I am a doctor, and the Valdespino tradition of the harem bed is still working.'

'The first night,' he said. 'Both times.' And a smile of pure masculine complacency split his dark face. She had her handsome arrogant husband back.

Reaching up Rose threaded her fingers through his hair; glad she'd banished the doubt about fatherhood from his mind. She pulled his head down to her waiting lips. 'Want to play Doctor and Nurse?'

'With me as the nurse,' he said drolly.

'Xavier there are male nurses, your chauvinism is rising again.'

'It's not the only thing,' he growled and his husky chuckle and the kiss that followed was long and tender, tinged with regret, forgiveness asked, forgiveness granted, and a soaring passionate promise for the future.

Miranda Lee is Australian, living near Sydney. Born and raised in the bush, she was boarding-school-educated and briefly pursued a career in classical music, before moving to Sydney and embracing the world of computers. Happily married, with three daughters, she began writing when family commitments kept her at home. She likes to create stories that are believable, modern, fast-paced and sexy. Her interests include meaty sagas, doing word puzzles, gambling and going to the movies.

AUNT LUCY'S LOVER
by
Miranda Lee

CHAPTER ONE

'YOUR Aunt Lucy has left you everything.'

Jessica stared at the solicitor across his leather-topped desk. 'Everything?' she repeated blankly, her normally sharp brain a little fuzzy with shock.

She was still getting over the news of Aunt Lucy's death. Of inoperable cancer, three weeks earlier.

When she'd protested over not being told at the time, the solicitor informed her this was because no one had known of her existence till her aunt's will had been found a couple of days ago.

Jessica had not known of her Aunt Lucy's existence, either, till the woman herself had shown up at the Sydney Grand a couple of months back and asked to speak to the hotel's public relations manager, who was none other than Jessica herself.

It had been an awkward meeting. Jessica had been stunned when the woman abruptly announced she was her mother's older sister. Jessica's mother had always claimed she was a foundling, with no known relatives.

Aunt Lucy had seemed a little stunned herself by the sight of her niece. She'd stared and stared at her, as though she'd been confronted by a ghost. When Jessica was called away to a problem with one of the guests, she'd left the tongue-tied woman in her office with the promise to return shortly. There were so many questions

Jessica had wanted to ask. My God, her head had been whirling with them.

But when she'd returned fifteen minutes later, her Aunt Lucy had disappeared.

The memory of the woman's distressed face had tormented Jessica ever since. As had the many questions her aunt's brief and mysterious visit had caused. Why had her mother lied to her? Why hadn't her aunt waited for her to come back? And why had she stared at her so strangely, as though her physical appearance offended her?

Jessica had tried tracing her aunt, but without success. She'd almost got to the stage where she was prepared to hire a private investigator. Only this last week, she'd started searching for one in the yellow pages.

As sad as her Aunt Lucy's death was, at least now she might find some answers to her many questions. To which was added the puzzle of why her aunt had made her—a niece she'd only met once—her one and only heir!

'I can see you're startled by this legacy, Miss Rawlins,' the solicitor said. 'But Mrs. Hardcourt's will is quite clear.'

'*Mrs*. Hardcourt?' Jessica immediately picked up on the title. 'My aunt was married, then?'

No wonder she hadn't been able to trace her. She'd tried Woods, which had been her mother's maiden name.

'She was a widow. For some considerable years, I gather. She had no children of her own. Your mother was her only sibling. Their parents passed away many years back.'

Jessica's heart sank. There went her hope of grandparents, or other aunts and uncles, or even cousins. So she still had no living family who wanted anything to do with her. Her own father—plus his parents and relatives—had abandoned all contact after her mother divorced him.

Not that Jessica had ever really known them. She'd only been three at the time of her parents' divorce, and it had been a bitter parting, one her mother refused to speak of afterwards.

When Jessica had notified her father by telephone of her mother's death eight years ago—he still lived in Sydney—he hadn't even had the decency to attend the funeral.

Jessica's heart turned over as she thought of that wretched day. It had been raining, with no one at the graveside except herself, the priest and the undertakers. Her mother had had no close friends, having been an agoraphobic and an alcoholic for as long as Jessica could remember. She'd died, of liver and kidney failure, at the age of thirty-eight.

Jessica wondered anew what had been behind her mother's self-loathing and misery. She'd thought it was her failed marriage. Now she wasn't so sure.

So many questions about her mother's and her own life, unanswered...

Jessica looked up at the patiently waiting solicitor, her expression curious and thoughtful.

'Surely my aunt's husband must have had some relatives,' she speculated. 'Why didn't she leave them something? Why leave everything to me?'

The solicitor shrugged. 'I'm afraid I don't know the answer to that. She doesn't mention any in-laws in her will. Neither have any come forward. You are her sole legal heir, and might I say her estate is quite considerable.'

Jessica was taken aback. She'd been picturing a small

house perhaps, in a country town. Somehow, Aunt Lucy had looked country. Jessica hadn't envisaged any great fortune. 'How considerable is considerable?' she asked, feeling the first stirring of excitement.

One of Jessica's primary goals in life had been to make herself financially secure. Being poor all her young life had left its mark. When little more than a child, she had vowed never to be poor once she was old enough to support herself. After her mother's death, she'd worked damned hard to put herself into a position where she had a well-paid job with considerable job security.

Though no job was entirely secure in this day and age, she conceded.

'Firstly, there is the property,' the solicitor began enthusiastically. 'It consists of several acres of prime real estate overlooking the Pacific, and a grand old heritage home, which your aunt had been running as a guesthouse for many years. There is no mortgage, and the house itself is reputedly well-furnished with solid pieces, many of them valuable antiques.'

'Goodness!' Jessica exclaimed. 'I had no idea!'

'So I can see. I am also pleased to inform you that even after all legal fees and funeral expenses are paid for, your aunt's bank balance will still be slightly in excess of five hundred thousand dollars.'

Jessica gasped. 'Half a million dollars!' She could hardly believe her ears. 'So where *is* this property? You mentioned an acreage. And a view of the Pacific Ocean. I presume it's along the east coast somewhere, then?'

The solicitor looked surprised. 'You mean you don't know where your aunt lived?'

'No, I told you. I hardly knew her. We only met the once.'

'I see. You're in for another surprise then. Your Aunt Lucy lived on Norfolk Island.'

'Norfolk Island!'

'Yes.'

'Good Lord.' Jessica had never been to Norfolk Island, but she knew where it was. Out in the Pacific Ocean off the east coast of Australia. It was a popular holiday destination for honeymooners and the middle-aged to elderly, the sort of pretty but peaceful place where the most exciting activity available was looking through the ruins of an old convict gaol. One of the staff at the hotel had spent a week there last year and left a tourist brochure lying around. Jessica recalled glancing at it and thinking she'd be bored to tears at a place like that.

Jessica liked to keep busy. And she liked lots of people around her; another mark, perhaps, of her wretched childhood when she'd had no friends, as well as no money. You didn't bring friends home to a drunken mother, and if you had no money, you couldn't afford to go out.

The inner Sydney area was Jessica's type of place. She thrived on the hustle and bustle of city life, the bright lights and the continuous undercurrent of throbbing life. When she wasn't working, there was always some place to go, something to do. Dining out and discos. The theatre. The ballet. Movies. Concerts.

Jessica couldn't imagine living anywhere else, certainly not on a small Pacific island whose only bright lights were the stars in the sky!

'I presume you'd like to go and see your inheritance for yourself?' the solicitor asked.

Jessica gnawed at her bottom lip. Well, of course she would. But she really didn't have the time right now. Her job was very demanding, and February was still a busy month for hotels in Sydney.

Still, how could she pass up the opportunity to find out the truth about her roots? And where better to start than where her aunt lived? It was clear the solicitor didn't know very much.

Jessica mulled over her work situation. She *was* due her annual holidays, having slaved for over a year in her present position without a break. Surely they could spare her for a week or two. She would demand compassionate leave if the boss made a fuss.

'Yes, I *would* like to see it,' she said, making up her mind with her usual decisiveness. 'I should be able to arrange to have the property put up for sale while I'm there, too, shouldn't I?'

The solicitor seemed startled. 'You mean you don't want to live there yourself?'

'Heavens, no. My life is here, in Sydney.'

'You do realise that people with permanent residency on Norfolk Island don't pay any income tax,' he said dryly.

Jessica had forgotten about that. It was a tempting thought—especially now, with her income about to soar—but such a consideration was still not enough for her to give up a career she'd slaved for and a lifestyle she enjoyed. What on earth would she do on Norfolk Island?

'You could take over the running of your aunt's guesthouse,' the solicitor said, as though reading her mind. 'You'd have no trouble securing a permit to stay under your circumstances.'

Jessica wrinkled her nose. She'd spent a year in hotel housekeeping while working her way up in her career, and had hated it. She knew exactly what running a guesthouse would entail, and it was not what she wanted to do with her life.

'That's not for me, I'm afraid. No, I'll be selling up and investing the money.'

'I see. Er, how long were you planning on staying on the island?'

'A fortnight at the most,' Jessica said crisply. 'I can't spare more time than that.'

'Hm, I think you'll have to, Miss Rawlins. You see, there is a small but rather odd condition attached to your inheriting your aunt's estate.'

'Really? You didn't mention anything earlier.'

'I was presuming you'd want to live there permanently. Most people would jump at the chance. Since you don't, then within a reasonable time of your being notified of your aunt's death, you have to take up residence in her home on the island and live there for at least one month.'

'A month! But that's ridiculous. I can't afford a month!'

'I'm afraid you'll have to, if you wish to inherit. Your aunt's wishes are clear. Provisions have even been made in the will to pay for the purchase of your airline ticket, in case you couldn't afford one. Oh, and there's another small condition. During this month, you are to allow a certain Mr. Slade to remain living in the same room he has occupied for the last three years, free of charge.'

'How very peculiar! What happens if I don't comply?'

'Then the estate goes to the aforementioned Mr. Slade, whom Mrs. Hardcourt describes in her will as having been a loyal and loving companion to her over these past three years.'

Jessica frowned. Was loyal and loving companion a euphemism for lover? She remembered her aunt as having been a handsome woman, with a good figure for her age. Although obviously in her fifties, it was not inconceivable she'd been having an intimate physical relationship with a man.

'It was this Mr. Slade who found the will,' the solicitor said. 'It had apparently slipped down behind a drawer. He's been living in and looking after the house and grounds since your aunt's death.'

'Not to mention searching for a will, which he obviously knew existed,' Jessica pointed out dryly. For some reason, she didn't like the sound of this Mr. Slade. Or was it just the complication of that odd condition she didn't like? 'I wonder why my aunt didn't just leave everything to him in the first place, if they were so close?'

'I really couldn't say.'

'No, of course not,' Jessica murmured. The only way she was going to find out anything was to go there herself. But for a whole month? How was she going to wangle that without risking her job?

'This Mr. Slade,' she said, her mind ticking over. 'What do you know about him?'

'Very little. I did speak to him briefly on the telephone yesterday.'

'And?'

'He sounded surprisingly…young.'

'*Young?*' Jessica repeated, startled.

'It was just an impression. Some quite elderly people have young-sounding telephone voices.'

Jessica nodded. That was so true. The owner of the Sydney Grand was well into his sixties but sounded much younger on the telephone.

'There's a flight leaving for Norfolk Island next Sunday morning at seven,' the solicitor informed her. 'If you like, I can call the airline right now and see if they have a spare seat. If you go now, you'll only have to stay four weeks to satisfy your aunt's will. February this year only has twenty-eight days.'

So it had. But four weeks away from the hotel at this time of the year? Her boss would be most put out. Still, what alternative did she have?

'All right,' Jessica agreed.

Now that her mind was made up, she was quite eager to be on her way, her female curiosity more than a little piqued. She wanted to see the place for herself. And the island. And the mysterious Mr. Slade.

Actually, she felt a bit guilty about him. If he'd genuinely loved her aunt and nursed her during her last days, surely he deserved more for his devotion than one month's free board. Jessica decided that if he proved to have been a genuine friend to her aunt and was in any way hard up for money, she would give him a cash legacy. It was the least she could do.

'Would you like the telephone number of your aunt's house?' the solicitor asked once his call to the airline had been successfully completed. 'That way you can call this Mr. Slade yourself and arrange for him to pick you up at the airport when you arrive.'

'All right,' Jessica agreed again. It would be interesting to see how young he sounded to *her*. Maybe the solicitor thought fifty was young. He was nearing sixty himself.

He jotted down her aunt's number on the back of one of his business cards and handed it over to Jessica, who slipped it into her handbag.

'Don't hesitate to call me if you need any help,' he said, standing up when she did so.

Jessica shook his extended hand. 'Thank you,' she said. 'I will.'

As she turned and walked out of the office, the sudden

thought came that her life was never going to be the same again. Suddenly, she was a rich woman, an heiress.

Strange. The realisation was vaguely unsettling. Jessica decided then and there not to tell anyone at work, or even any of her friends. Aside from the jealousy it might inspire, people treated you differently when you were rich, especially the opposite sex.

Of course, there were a couple of people who already knew of her new financial status. That couldn't be helped. But the solicitor was hardly going to present a problem in her day-to-day life. He wasn't likely to make a play for her, either.

Which left only Mr. Slade.

Jessica almost laughed at the instant tightening in her stomach. Now she was being fanciful. Logically, Mr. Slade had to at least be in his fifties. Neither was he likely to be too enamoured with the woman who'd robbed him of a sizeable inheritance. He might very well resent her.

Suddenly, the month she had to spend on Norfolk Island in the same house as Mr. Slade loomed as very awkward, indeed.

Well, that was just too bad, Jessica thought fatalistically. She had every right to go there, and every right to find out what she could about her own and her mother's past!

CHAPTER TWO

JESSICA'S watch said nine-thirty as she unlocked the front door of her flat. Her sigh was a little weary as she stepped inside and switched on the lights. She'd stayed extra late at the hotel tonight, getting things organised so that her PA could manage without her for the next month.

In the end, she'd asked for her full four weeks' holidays, saying she was suffering from emotional stress after the sudden death of a dear aunt. The hotel management hadn't been thrilled with the short notice, but they hadn't been as difficult about her request as she'd imagined they'd be. Clearly, they valued her as an employee and didn't want to lose her.

Jessica was well aware she did a good job, but it had always faintly worried her that she'd won her present position more for her model-like looks than her qualifications. Not that she didn't have plenty of those, as well. A degree in hotel management and tourism, plus years of experience working in every facet of the hotel industry from housekeeping to reception to guest relations.

Jessica closed the door of her near-new North Sydney apartment—an airy two-bedroomed unit with a lovely view of the bridge and harbour. She'd bought it only four months previously, the deposit alone taking every cent she had saved during her working life.

But she'd craved her own place after sharing rented accommodation for years.

Funnily enough, whilst she adored the bathroom and bedroom privacy, she wasn't finding living alone quite as satisfying a way of life as she'd thought it would be. She missed not having anyone to talk to in the evenings. Lately, she'd felt awfully lonely, which was unfortunate. In the past, whenever her chronic loneliness reached these depths, she had launched into an affair with some highly unsuitable man.

Of course she never knew they were unsuitable at the time, since they always declared their undying love and devotion at first, to which she invariably responded.

It was only later, when she found out they were married, or an addict of some sort, or allergic to long-term commitment, that she recognised her own folly for what it was. Just desperation to feel loved and not be alone, and a deep desire to find the man of her dreams, marry him and have so many children she would never be alone again!

At that point the scales would fall from her eyes and she would see her great love for what he was—usually no more than a handsome and highly accomplished liar who was using her for what he could get and giving her very little in return, not even good sex!

Jessica knew from talking to girlfriends and reading women's magazines that she had always been short-changed in the bedroom department. Perhaps she should have complained at the time, but you just didn't when you imagined you were madly in love.

The thought of going that road again made her shudder. Better she remain alone than involved with one of those. Better she remain unmarried and childless than shackled to some selfish guy who would make a lousy father and who didn't even satisfy her in bed!

Which left *what* to cure her present loneliness?

'A flatmate!' she decided aloud. 'A female, of course,' she added dryly as she strode down the small hallway and into her bedroom, tossing her handbag onto the double bed and kicking off her shoes.

'Stuff men!' she muttered as she began to strip.

One particular man suddenly jumped into her mind.

Her Aunt Lucy's lover—the enigmatic Mr. Slade. She'd been going to ring him earlier at the office, but had kept putting it off. It irked her that she felt nervous about ringing him.

Ring him now, her pride demanded. *What's wrong with you? So he might give you the cold shoulder—you can't help that. Just be polite, anyway. You're used to being polite to some of the rudest and most arrogant men around. Your job has trained you for it. Use some of that training now!*

Jessica glared over at the telephone, which sat on the bedside table nearest the window. Lifting her chin, she moved over to snatch up her handbag from the bed, opened it and drew out the business card the solicitor had given her. She didn't delay once the number was in her hands. She sat down and dialled straight away before she procrastinated further.

'Hi there,' said a male voice at last. 'Seb here.'

Jessica frowned. If 'Seb here' was Mr. Slade, then he did indeed sound young. Far too young to be the lover of a woman in her fifties. Unless...

Her stomach contracted at the thought her aunt might have fallen into the clutches of the type of unconscionable young man who preyed on wealthy widows. Jessica was not unfamiliar with the species. They often hung around the bars in the hotel, waiting and watching for suitable prey. They were invariably handsome. And charming. And young.

If Mr. Slade turned out to be one of those, she thought crossly, he would get short shrift after the month was over. He would not get a cent from her. Not one single cent!

'This is Jessica Rawlins,' she said, simmering outrage giving her voice a sharp edge. 'Would I be speaking to Mr. Slade?'

'You sure are. Pleased to hear from you, Jessica. I presume Lucy's solicitor has been in touch. So when are you coming over?'

Jessica's eyebrows lifted. Well, he was certainly straight to the point, and not at all resentful sounding. If she hadn't been on her toes, she might have been totally disarmed by his casual charm.

'I'm catching the seven o'clock flight from Sydney on Sunday,' she said stiffly.

'I'll meet you then. Oops, no, I can't. I promised Mike I'd go fishing with him Sunday morning. Tell you what, I'll get Evie to meet you.'

'And who, pray tell, is Evie?' she asked archly.

'Evie? She was your aunt's chief cook and bottle washer. You'll like Evie,' he went on blithely. 'Everyone does. Now perhaps you'd better tell me what you look like, so she won't have any trouble recognising you on Sunday. Are you tall?'

'Reasonably,' Jessica bit out after smothering her frustration. She supposed she'd find out everything she wanted to know soon enough. And she could trust her eyes far more than a conversation on the telephone.

'Slim?' he went on.

'Yes.'

'What colour hair?'

'Black.'

'Long or short?'

'Shoulder-length, but I always wear it up.'

'How old are you? Approximately,' he added quickly with humour in his voice.

'Twenty-eight,' Jessica said, having no reason to hide her age.

'Really. You *sound* older.'

She tried not to take offence, and failed. 'Well, you don't,' she snapped.

'I don't what?'

'Sound as old as I thought you'd be. If I didn't know better, I'd say you were no more than thirty.'

His laughter might have been infectious under other circumstances. 'You've no idea how many people say that to me, Jessica,' he said. 'But it's some years since I saw thirty.'

Jessica wasn't sure if she was mollified by that statement or not. She should have been relieved to find he was respectably middle-aged, but she didn't feel relieved. She felt decidedly nettled. Mr. Slade was rubbing her the wrong way, for some reason.

'I *look* young for my age, too,' he volunteered. 'But I try not to worry about it.'

She could hear the smile in his voice and bristled some more.

'By the way, bring your swimmers and shorts with you,' he added. 'It's pretty warm here at the moment. How long will you be staying?'

'Just the month.'

'Ah,' he said with a long sigh. 'What a pity. Still, we can talk about that more when you get here. I'm glad you rang, Jessica. I'm really looking forward to meeting you. I'm just sorry I can't welcome you myself at the airport. I'll try to get back by the time you arrive at the house. Au revoir for now. Have a good flight.'

He hung up, leaving Jessica not sure what she thought about him now. Clearly, he *was* middle-aged. He'd been most amused at her saying he sounded thirty.

If she were honest, she had to admit he'd been very nice to her, and not at all resentful of her inheritance. She wondered what he wanted to talk to her about. Did he hope to persuade her to stay and run the guesthouse? If he did, then he'd be wasting his breath. She had no intention of doing any such thing.

But she did want to talk to *him*. She wanted to find out everything he knew about her aunt. Maybe this Evie would know things, as well, depending on how many years she'd been Aunt Lucy's cook.

Thinking of cooks reminded Jessica how hungry she was. Levering herself up from the bed, she headed for the door and the kitchen, dressed in nothing but her camisole and pantihose. She caught a glimpse of herself in the mirrored wardrobe as she passed and recalled the rather bland details she'd given Mr. Slade. Twenty-eight, tall, slim, black hair, worn up.

Not much of a description. Difficult to form a complete picture. But she could hardly have added she had a face that wouldn't have looked out of place on the cover of *Vogue*, and a body one of her lovers had said he'd kill for.

He had certainly *lied* for it, she thought tartly.

'And what do *you* look like, Mr. Slade?' she mused out loud as she continued on to the kitchen. 'Tall, I'll bet. And slim. Men who look young for their age are always slim. And you won't be bald. No way. You'll have a full head of hair with only a little grey. And you'll be handsome, won't you, Mr. Slade? In a middle-aged sort of way. And just a little bit of a ladies' man, I'll warrant.'

Jessica wondered anew if he'd really been her aunt's lover, or just a good friend. He'd said nothing to indicate either way. Really, she hadn't handled that call very well. She'd found out absolutely nothing! Mr. Slade's youthful voice and manner had sent her off on a cynical tangent, and by the time she'd realised her mistake, the call had been over.

Still, it was only three days till Sunday. Not long. In no time she'd be landing at Norfolk Island airport and be right on the doorstep of discovering all she wanted to know.

A nervous wave rippled down Jessica's spine, and she shivered. It had not escaped her logical mind that something pretty awful must have happened for her mother to lie like she had. Maybe she'd done something wicked and shameful, then run away from home. Or something wicked and shameful had been done to *her*, with the same result.

Jessica wasn't sure what that something could have been. Whatever had happened, she meant to find out the truth. Oh, yes, she meant to find out everything!

CHAPTER THREE

JESSICA'S flight on Sunday morning took two and a half hours. Two and a half long hours of butterflies in her stomach. Some due to her fear of flying; most to fear of the unknown that awaited her on Norfolk Island.

She stared through her window the whole way, despite high cloud preventing a view of the ocean below. Not that she was really looking. She was thinking, and speculating, and worrying. It was only when they began their descent that the sight of the island itself jolted her back to the physical reality of her destination.

Goodness, but it *was* picturesque, a dot of deep tropical green within a wide blue expanse of sea. But so *small*! Jessica knew from the travel brochures that the island only measured five kilometres by eight. This hadn't bothered her till she saw that the airstrip was even smaller. She hoped the plane could stop in time, that it wouldn't plunge off the end of the runway into the sea.

The plane began to bank steeply at that moment, a wing blocking Jessica's view of the island. All she could see was water—deep, deep water. Her insides started to churn. She did so hate flying, especially the landing part.

The plane landed without incident, thank heavens, quickly taxiing over to a collection of small terminal buildings. There was a short delay while everything was sprayed for God knows what and some lady with a foreign accent gave a brief talk over the intercom about the island and its rules and regulations.

Jessica rolled her eyes when she heard the speed limit was only fifty kilometres an hour around the island generally, and a crawling twenty-five kilometres an hour through the town and down on the foreshores at Kingston. Drivers were warned they had to give way to all livestock on the roads.

Lord, she thought with rueful amusement. This was as far removed from Sydney as one could get!

The formalities finally over, she hoisted her roomy tan handbag onto her shoulder and alighted, relieved to find that it wasn't all that hot outside, despite the sun beginning to peep through the parting clouds. She'd worn a summer-weight pants-suit for travelling, a tailored cream outfit that didn't crease. But it had a lined jacket and wasn't the coolest thing she owned.

Her hair was cool, though, slicked back into the tight chic knot she always wore for work. Her makeup was expertly done to highlight her big dark eyes and full mouth. Her jewellery was discreet and expensive. A gold chain around her neck. Gold studs in her lobes. A gold watch around her slender wrist.

She looked sleek and sophisticated, and a lot more composed than she was feeling.

The short walk across the tarmac to the small customs building was enough for Jessica to see that whilst the air temperature felt moderate, the humidity was high. As soon as she arrived at her aunt's house she'd change into something lighter.

In no time Jessica had secured her suitcase and was through customs. It seemed there *was* some advantage coming to tiny places like this. She'd barely walked into the terminal building when a funny little barrel-shaped woman with frizzy grey hair touched her on the arm.

'You'd have to be Jessica,' she said, smiling up at her.

'And you must be Evie,' Jessica responded, smiling back. Impossible not to. Mr. Slade had been right about that. Evie was the sort of person one liked on sight. She had a round face with twinkling grey eyes and a warm smile. She wore a shapeless floral tent dress and might have been sixty.

Jessica was given a brief but all-encompassing appraisal. 'You don't look much like your mother, do you?'

She certainly didn't. Her mother had been petite and fair with blue eyes.

Still, Jessica's heart leapt at Evie's observation.

'You *knew* my mother?'

'Well, of course I knew your mother, lovie! I've lived on this island for near nigh forty years now. Everyone knows everyone around here. You'll soon learn that. I knew your grandparents, too. Come on,' Evie urged, taking her arm. 'Let's get out of this crowd and into some fresh air.'

Jessica allowed herself to be led down some steps and out into a half-empty car park. Her thoughts were whirling. If Evie had known her grandparents, did that mean they'd lived here on this island, as well? Had her aunt and her mother been *born* here? Were her family *islanders*?

The desire to bombard Evie with questions was great, but something held Jessica back for the moment. Probably an instinctive reluctance to admit she was so ignorant about her own past.

Or was she afraid to find out the truth, now that it was within her grasp?

'The car's over here,' Evie said.

It was a Mazda. Small, white, dented and dusty. It was also unlocked, with the keys in the ignition.

Jessica could not believe her eyes. 'Er, don't you think you should have locked your car?' she said as she climbed into the passenger seat, not wanting to criticise but unable to keep silent.

Evie laughed. 'No one locks their car on Norfolk Island, lovie. You'll get used to it.'

'I doubt it,' Jessica muttered, shaking her head. Imagine doing such a silly thing in Sydney!

'Think about it,' Evie said, starting up the engine. 'Where are they going to go if they steal it?'

Jessica had to admit that was true, but she knew she'd still be locking the car doors, no matter what the locals did.

'It's not my car, actually,' Evie added as she angled her way out of the car park. 'It used to belong to Lucy, but she gave it to Sebastian before she died.'

Jessica frowned at this news. So Mr. Slade *had* been given something, after all. Okay, so it wasn't much of a car but maybe he'd been given other gifts, as well. For all she knew, her aunt might have handed over quite a degree of money to her loyal and loving companion before she died. It would explain why he'd received nothing in the will.

'This is the main street,' Evie piped up. 'A lot of the shops have duty-free goods, you know. It's one of the main pastimes for visitors. Shopping.'

There were, indeed, a lot of shops lining the road. Some of them were open but most looked pretty well deserted, as were the sidewalks. There was a young boy on a bike, plus a middle-aged couple wandering along, hand in hand. It looked as quiet and dead a place as Jessica had originally thought.

'It's pretty slow on a Sunday,' Evie said. 'Things will be hopping here tomorrow.'

Jessica decided Evie's idea of hopping might be a fraction different from her own.

'Sebastian seemed to think you might want me to come in and do the shopping and cooking while you're here, like I did for Lucy,' Evie rattled on. 'He's been looking after himself and the place since Lucy's death, though I do drop by occasionally to give the house a dust through. I only live next door and men never think of dusting.'

'That was kind of you, Evie. Yes, I think I would like you to do that. I'll pay you whatever Lucy did. Will that be all right?'

Evie waved her indifference to talking about payment. 'Whatever. I don't really need the money,' she said. 'My husband left me plenty when he died. I just like to keep busy. And I love cooking. Eating, too.' She grinned over at Jessica. 'So what do you like to eat? Do you have any favourite foods or dishes?'

'Not really. I'm not fussy at all. Cook whatever you like. I'll just enjoy being pampered for a change. Cooking is not one of my strong points.'

Actually, she could cook quite well, had had to when she was growing up to survive. If she'd waited for her mother to cook her a meal she would have starved. But she didn't fancy cooking for Mr. Slade. It had also crossed her mind that she'd be able to question Evie with more ease if she was around the house on a regular basis.

'That's fixed, then,' Evie said happily. 'I'll come in every morning around eleven-thirty and make lunch. Then I'll come back around five to cook dinner for seven-thirty. I don't do breakfast. Lucy always did that for herself. How does that sound?'

'Marvellous.' Jessica sighed her satisfaction with the arrangement and settled back to look around some more.

The wide streets of the shopping centre were quickly left behind and they moved onto a narrower road, with what looked like farms on either side. A few cows grazed lethargically along the common. The Mazda squeezed past a truck going the other way, then a car, then a utility, Jessica noting that Evie exchanged waves with all three drivers as they passed by.

She commented on this and was told it was a local custom, and that even the tourists got into the spirit of the Norfolk Island wave within a day of arrival. Jessica was quietly impressed with their friendliness, despite cynically thinking that if all Sydney drivers did that in city traffic, everyone would go barmy. Still, it was rather sweet, in a way.

'Here we are,' Evie announced, slowing down and turning into a gateway that had a cattle grid between its posts and an iron archway above, which said with proud simplicity, Lucy's Place.

The gravel driveway rose gradually, any view either side blocked with thickly wooded Norfolk pines. Finally, the pine borders ceased, and there in front of Jessica was the most beautiful old wooden house she had ever seen. Painted cream, with a green pitched iron roof and huge wooden verandas all round, it stood on the crest of the hill with a stately grandeur and dignity that were quite breathtaking.

Jessica was surprised, both by its elegant beauty and its effect on her. She'd heard of falling in love at first sight, but she'd always thought of that in connection with a man, not a house.

A sudden movement on the veranda snapped her out of her astonished admiration. Someone had been sitting there and was now standing up and moving towards the front steps. A man, dressed in shorts and nothing else, holding a tall glass in his hand. A young man with shoulder-length fair hair.

He stopped and leant against one of the posts at the top of the steps and watched as Evie brought the car round to a halt at the base of the front steps.

Jessica frowned at him through the passenger window. This couldn't be Mr. Slade, surely. She couldn't see the details of his face—it was in shadow—but that was not the body of a middle-aged man. Or the hair.

Maybe he was a workman. A gardener, perhaps. Or the man who mowed the lawns. There were plenty to mow, she'd noted, the house set in huge rolling lawns. There was quite a bit of garden, as well, beds of flowers underneath the verandas, backed by multicoloured hibiscus bushes.

'I see Sebastian made it back from fishing in time to greet you,' Evie said, shattering Jessica's delusion over the man's identity.

He straightened as the car braked to a halt, lifting the glass to his lips and at the same time taking a step forward out of the shadow of the veranda. Jessica sucked in a sharp breath as sunlight fell upon silky golden locks and smooth bronzed shoulders. He continued drinking as he walked slowly down the steps, taking deep swallows and seemingly unconscious of his quite extraordinary beauty.

A couple of drops of water fell from the base of the frosted glass onto his almost hairless chest, Jessica's fascinated eyes following them as they trickled down to pool in his navel, which was sinfully exposed above the low-slung white shorts.

Jessica found herself swallowing, her throat suddenly

dry. Her eyes dropped further as he continued his measured descent, taking in every inch of his leanly muscled legs. They lifted at last to once again encounter his face, no longer obscured by the glass.

It was as disturbingly attractive as the rest of him, with a strong straight nose, an elegantly sculptured jawline, bedroom blue eyes and a far too sexy mouth. As he drew nearer, Jessica's stunned fascination gradually turned to a simmering fury.

Hadn't seen thirty in many years, my foot! she thought angrily. Even if he did look young for his age, he could be no more than thirty-five. If that!

Before he reached the bottom step she'd flung open the car door and stepped out, drawing herself up to her full height and glaring scornfully into that now treacherously smiling face. No one had to tell Jessica what sort of man he was. She hadn't come down in the last shower.

His smile faltered, then faded, his narrowed blue gaze staring, first into her cold black eyes, then down over her stiffly held body and up again.

Was he taken aback by her obvious contempt for him? Had he imagined for one moment that he could fool her, too?

Jessica almost laughed. Sebastian Slade was everything she'd feared when she'd first heard of him. And possibly more.

Despite all this, she swiftly and sensibly decided to hide her feelings, smoothing the derision from her face and stepping forward with her hand politely stretched out. There was no need to be overtly rude to him. She knew the score now. Why make her stay more awkward than it would already be?

She would endure his undoubted hypocrisy for the next month then send him packing without anything to remember her by, except a few parting shots. Oh, yes, she would tell him what she thought of him on that final day. And she'd enjoy every word!

He hesitated to take her hand, staring at it for a few seconds before staring into her face. His expression reminded her of the way Aunt Lucy had stared at her that day. What was it about the way she looked that was so surprising? Okay, so she didn't look like her mother, but she was very like her father, who'd been tall, with dark eyes and hair.

Jessica was beginning to feel a little unnerved by his intense regard when Evie joined them, laughing.

'You should see the look on your face, Sebastian,' she said as she swept the empty glass out of his hand. 'Yes, Lucy's niece is a striking-looking woman, isn't she? Not exactly what you expected, eh what?'

'Not exactly,' he said, a rueful smile hovering about his sensually carved mouth.

She found herself glaring at that mouth and wondering caustically if it had pressed treacherous kisses to her aunt's lips. It would be naive of her to think that a woman in her fifties would not take a lover twenty years her junior. It happened a lot in the name of lust. Lust for a beautiful young male body on her aunt's part. Lust for money and material gain on Mr. Slade's.

'Welcome to Norfolk Island,' he said formally at last, taking her hand in his. 'And welcome to Lucy's Place. How do you like it?'

I'd like it a lot more, she thought crossly, *if you'd let go my hand. And if you'd go put some more clothes on.* Damn, but the man was breathtakingly attractive. On a rating of zero to ten, his sex appeal would measure twenty.

'It's lovely,' she said truthfully, but stiffly.

'Do you think you might change your mind about staying on and living here, then?'

'No, I can't see that happening,' she replied, despite feeling a definite tug at her heartstrings. Anyone would love to live in such a beautiful house. But a house did not make a home, and life on Norfolk Island was not for her, however sweet their customs.

Was that relief she glimpsed in his eyes, or disappointment? Actually, it looked more like frustration. Jessica's brain began to tick over. Did Mr. Slade have some secret agenda where she was concerned? Did he need more than a month to achieve his goal?

And what could that goal be? she puzzled. To move on to the next victim, perhaps? To seduce his dearly departed lover's heiress?

Jessica shuddered at the thought.

'She'll change her mind,' Evie said confidently, and moved up the steps. 'Her case is on the back seat, Sebastian,' she called over her shoulder. 'Flex your muscles and bring it inside. I'll go rustle up some lunch.'

At least he released her hand then. And moved away.

Jessica was annoyed with herself for letting him get under her skin, even a little. Still, she had to admit that his physical charisma was incredible. It was as well she was on her guard against him.

'I won't, you know,' she said tartly when he returned with her case.

'Won't what?'

'Stay on and live here. There's nothing you can say or do to change my mind.'

'What makes you think I'd *want* to change your mind?'

The coldness in his voice surprised her, as did the

scorn that flashed across his face. It was hardly the way
a man would act if he had seduction on his mind.

'I promised Lucy I would make your month's stay as
enjoyable as possible,' he went on, just as coldly, 'and
that I would show you what the island has to offer. But
I can see already you're not the sort of girl to appreciate
simple things or a simple lifestyle, so I won't overtax
myself playing persuader.'

'You're too kind,' she countered, matching his icy
tone.

His top lip lifted slightly, just short of a sneer. 'Tell
me, Miss Rawlins. What's the sum total of your reason
for coming here? Are you interested at all in finding out
about your heritage and your roots? Or is this simply a
matter of money?'

Jessica began quivering with suppressed rage. 'Don't
you dare presume to judge me, you…you *gigolo*!'

He actually dropped her case. It tumbled down the
steps, but he made no move to try to retrieve it. He simply stood there, staring wide-eyed into her flushed face.

'*Gigolo?*' he exclaimed.

His shock was echoed by her own. Whatever had possessed her to say such a stupid thing! As true as it might
be, it had been a tactless and very rude accusation. Still,
having voiced her private beliefs, Jessica was not about
to back down. Why should she when he'd virtually accused *her* of being a mercenary money-grabbing bitch?

'Are you saying you weren't my aunt's lover?' she
asked scornfully. 'That you haven't been hanging around
here for what you could get?'

'Good God. What a nasty piece of work you are!'

'Don't try to turn the tables on me, Mr. Slade,' she bit
out. '*You're* the one described in my aunt's will as her
loyal and loving companion, yet you must be twenty

years younger than she was. *You're* the one who's wangled it so that you're still living here free of charge. I've no doubt you always did! And *you're* the one who inherits everything if I don't comply with my aunt's peculiar wishes. Are you saying you never made love to her? That you didn't worm your way into her affections with sex? That she didn't give you her car, and God knows what else, for services rendered?'

Jessica reeled under the chilling contempt in his arctic blue eyes. 'I'm going to forget you said that, because if I don't, I might be tempted to break my word to the nicest woman I've ever known. You might be her niece, but I can see you don't have a single gene of hers. No doubt you take after your pathetic parents!'

Jessica's face went bright red. 'You didn't even know my parents! And you certainly don't know *me*!'

His mouth opened to say something, then closed again. He looked away from her, his hands lifting to rake through his hair before looking back, a shuddering sigh emptying his lungs.

'Let's stop this right now,' he said with cool firmness. 'I have no intention of spending the next month exchanging verbal darts with you. Neither will I defend the relationship I had with your aunt, other than to say I never sought anything from her but her friendship, which I hope I gave back in kind.'

'Are you saying that you weren't her lover?' Jessica challenged.

His top lip curled with more contempt as his gaze swept over her. 'Would you believe me if I said no?'

'Try me.'

His cold gaze swept over her quite insultingly.

'No, I don't think I will,' he said at last with a derisive glitter in his eyes.

Jessica stiffened. 'Very funny. If you won't deny it, then I will have to presume that you were.'

'Believe what you like,' he replied with cold indifference.

'Oh, I will, Mr. Slade,' she said tartly. 'I will. As to *your* accusation that I'm only here for the money... I won't be holier than thou and say money isn't important to me. It is. But not to the extent you've implied. Still, I, too, see no need to defend myself. I'm not sure if you know this, but I had no idea I even *had* an aunt till recently, when she showed up at the hotel where I work.'

'Yes, I *do* know about that,' he said, surprising her.

'But...but I thought you didn't know of my existence till the will showed up.'

'I didn't know your full name and address till the will showed up. But I did know Lucy had found she had a niece named Jessica working in a hotel in Sydney, and that she'd left everything to you in her will. Lucy only spoke of you by your first name. I naturally assumed I would know all the necessary details once the will was read, but when Lucy died, I couldn't find the damned thing. It had slipped behind a drawer, you see.'

'Yes, the solicitor told me.'

'Frankly, Lucy told me only the barest of details about you. She didn't seem to want to talk about your one meeting. I was about to ring every hotel in Sydney when I came across the will.'

'Are you saying you can't tell me *why* Aunt Lucy left the hotel that day without really speaking to me?' Jessica asked painfully. 'You know, she stared at me like I was a ghost at first. I was called away for a few minutes, and when I returned she was gone. She hadn't even told me *her* last name, either, which was why *I* wasn't able to trace *her.*'

'I see. That explains a few questions I had myself, but no... I'm afraid I can't tell you why Lucy ran away from you. God only knows. Perhaps she was having trouble coming to terms with the guilt of never having looked up her sister before and seeing if she was all right. I think the news that Joanne was dead came as a dreadful shock to her.'

Jessica was shaking her head, her eyes dropping wearily to the ground. 'I don't understand any of it.'

A surprisingly gentle hand on her arm jerked her head upright. She was stunned by the momentary compassion in those beautiful blue eyes of his, and the confusion it stirred in her heart. Compassion was not something she was familiar—or comfortable—with. On top of that, it was not at all what she was expecting from *this* man.

'Of course you can't understand any of it,' he said with surprising sympathy. 'It's hard enough to understand what goes on in our own lives. Much more difficult to work out the lives of others. But you have a month to find some answers for your questions. I'll help as much as I can. Not that I have all the answers. But for now, why don't you come inside? It's hot out here, and Evie will be wondering where we are.'

Jessica automatically pulled back when he went to take her arm, feeling flustered by his suddenly solicitous attitude towards her. Such an about-face had to be viewed with some suspicion.

His frown carried frustration. 'There's no need to act like that. I was only trying to be friendly.'

'Why?' she demanded. 'A few minutes ago, you were calling me a nasty bit of work.'

'That was a few minutes ago. Maybe I've changed my mind about you since then.'

And maybe pigs might fly, she thought cynically, one of her eyebrows lifting in a sceptical arch.

A wry smile curved his mouth to one side, bringing her attention to those sensually carved lips, and where they might have been. The thought that he might have changed his mind about seducing her held an insidiously exciting aspect, one she would find hard to ignore.

But ignore it she would. She hadn't come here to fall victim to the slick, shallow charms of a man like Sebastian Slade, no matter how sexy he was.

'I see you still don't trust me,' he said dryly. 'Funnily enough, I can see your point of view. I dare say there are others on this island who think the same as you. I've just never cared what they thought. I stopped caring about what people thought of me some years ago.'

'Lucky ol' you,' she retorted tartly. 'Would we could all have the same privilege. Unfortunately, most of us have to live in the real world and work at a real job, which means we do have to worry what others think.'

'But you *don't* have to, Jessica,' he pointed out in a silky soft voice, which rippled down her spine like a mink glove. 'You don't have to live in the real world any more, or work at a real job, if you don't want to. Neither do you have to give a damn what people think. You can do what you like from this day forward.'

It was a wickedly seductive thought, provocatively delivered by a wickedly seductive man. She looked at him, her face a bland mask, while she battled to stop her mind from its appalling flights of fancy.

He was technically right, of course. If she invested her inheritance wisely she would never have to work again for the rest of her life, or kowtow to a boss. He was also right about her not having to worry about what other people thought, especially during the next month. Out here on this island, in this isolated house, she could do exactly as she pleased, and there was no one to judge or condemn.

Why was he pointing that out to her? She puzzled over this. Was it part of his seduction technique, to corrupt his victim with thoughts of a lifestyle of totally selfish and hedonistic behaviour?

He would have to do better than that, she thought with bitter amusement. She'd been seduced before by good-looking liars and had no intention of going that route again, no matter how stunningly this particular liar was put together.

'Let me tell you something, Mr. Slade,' she said coolly. 'I happen to like the real world, not to mention my real job. But thank you for explaining that I don't have to worry about what other people think of me here. I hope that includes you.'

He stared at her, and she would have loved to know what he was thinking. 'Touché,' he said at last, the smallest of wry smiles playing around his mouth. 'By the way, call me Sebastian, would you? Or Seb, if you prefer.'

'I prefer Sebastian,' she said crisply.

Which she did, actually. It also suited him very well. It was a strong name, yet sensual—like its owner. Not a modern name. There was nothing modern about Sebastian's looks. If he'd been an actor, he would never be cast as a business executive. He would, however, make a magnificent Viking prince, or a knight in King Arthur's court, or one of the Three Musketeers, with a feathered hat atop his flowing locks.

'Sebastian it will be, then,' he agreed nonchalantly. 'I'll just get your case.' He turned and walked with indolent grace down the steps to where it had fallen, his bending over drawing his shorts tightly over his tantalisingly taut buttocks.

Jessica tried not to stare, but she was doomed to failure. Never had a man's body fascinated her so much before. There again…it was a gorgeous body.

He straightened and turned, their eyes meeting as he slowly mounted the steps. It wasn't just his body, she conceded ruefully. Those eyes were like blue magnets, drawing her, tempting her. And that mouth of his was made strictly for sin.

Damn, but she hoped nothing she was thinking was showing on her face.

Self-preservation had Jessica throwing him one of her coolest looks before whirling and walking up the steps and into her Aunt Lucy's beautiful home.

CHAPTER FOUR

THE house was even more beautiful inside than out. Over a hundred years old, Sebastian told her, but lovingly cared for and restored to retain its original old-world charm.

The use of Norfolk pine was extensive, from the polished timber floors to the stained wall panelling to the kitchen benches and cupboards. Very little of the furniture, however, was made from local wood.

Sebastian explained that most pieces had been shipped in from New Zealand and Australia and even England, and were made from a variety of woods. There were fine examples of oak and teak, mahogany and rosewood, walnut and cedar.

The bathrooms featured black marble from Devon, brought over in sailing boats a century before. The bedrooms were a delight to behold, with their carved four-poster beds and exquisitely delicate furnishings.

Everywhere Jessica looked there was lace in some form or other. Lace curtains and bedspreads, tablecloths and doilies. In pure whites and rich creams, the lace lent an old-world atmosphere and blended beautifully with the fine porcelain figurines that rested on the many ornamental side tables and shelves. Overhead, the light fittings were mainly brass. Underfoot, fine woven rugs in earthy colours took the chill off the floors.

It was a warm and wonderful home, with style and an air of contentment Jessica could only envy.

She felt guilty at the thought she might sell her aunt's property to someone who would not care for the home and its contents as her aunt obviously had. It would be a crime to disturb a single thing. Everything fitted together like a jigsaw puzzle. There wasn't a piece missing.

'What a perfect, perfect place,' she murmured as she wandered through one of the large living rooms, running an affectionate hand along the mantelpiece above the marble fireplace.

'It was Lucy's pride and joy,' Sebastian said.

Jessica's eyes moved reluctantly to where he'd stayed standing in the doorway, her suitcase at his feet.

She'd avoided looking at him too much during her grand tour of the house. Inside, he seemed even more naked than he had outside. And much sexier…if that were possible.

Jessica had been quite unnerved when they'd brushed shoulders once, a decidedly sexual quiver running through her at the physical contact. After that, she'd kept her distance. He seemed to keep his, too, for which she was grateful. She could think of nothing more embarrassing—or awkward—than his finding out she was in any way vulnerable to him.

'It's such a shame I have to sell it,' she said.

'Why do you have to sell it? Why not live here yourself?'

'It's not as easy as that, Sebastian,' she said stiffly. 'I have a life in Sydney. And a career.'

'You call slaving for someone else a career? You could make a real career out of running this place like Lucy did. She did very well yet she only opened the house for guests in the summer.'

'I wouldn't be very good at that type of thing.'

'Come now. The public relations manager of a big city hotel could run a place like this standing on her head. Now don't look so surprised. One of the things Lucy *did* tell me was what you did in Sydney, even if she didn't say where. She sounded very proud of you.'

'I see. Well it's not a matter of capability, Sebastian. It's a matter of what I enjoy doing. I enjoy being a public relations manager. I don't enjoy housekeeping.'

'Neither did Lucy. When she had guests, she had a girl come in every day to do the laundry and ironing, another to do the heavy cleaning and Evie to cook. Lucy's role was more of a hostess, though she did make breakfast in the mornings.'

'What did she do with herself all day?'

'She entertained her guests, in the main. Her friendly and relaxing style of companionship was one of the reasons the same people came back to stay here year after year. Lucy was a very calming person to be around. And then, of course, there was her garden. She spent a lot of time there, too. She loved her flowers. Do you like flowers, Jessica?'

'What woman doesn't like flowers? I can't say I'm much of a gardener, though. I've never had a garden.'

'You would here.'

'I didn't say I wanted one.'

'You didn't say you didn't, either.'

She sighed an exasperated sigh. 'Stop trying to change my mind, Sebastian. I don't want to run a guesthouse. I am not going to stay. I'm here for one month and one month only.'

He said nothing. Absolutely nothing. But his mouth tightened a little and she thought she saw scorn in his eyes.

Jessica bristled, resenting the feeling she was having to defend herself to this man all the time. She decided it was his turn to answer some questions.

'What else did Lucy tell you about me?' she demanded.

'Nothing much.' He shrugged. 'She said you looked and seemed very…efficient. That's about it. You must appreciate Lucy found out as little about you in your brief meeting as you did about her.'

He was lying. Aunt Lucy had told him something else, something that had made him stare at her when they'd first met. But it was clear he wasn't going to tell her. She felt quite frustrated with him. And totally frustrated with herself.

Dear God, it was as well he was on the other side of the room, for as she looked at him now, she felt the urge to reach out and touch, to see if his long golden hair was as silky as it seemed, to know if his bronzed skin was as satiny smooth as it looked.

The man was a menace! Why couldn't he have been rising sixty, with a paunch and a greying beard? she thought irritably. Why did he have to be a golden god with eyes one could drown in and a mouth to tempt even the most frigid virgin?

'Have you decided which bedroom you want to sleep in?' he asked abruptly.

Yours, came the wicked thought before she could stop it entering her mind.

Jessica took a deep, steadying breath. 'No,' she said. 'But not Lucy's. I wouldn't feel comfortable in Lucy's room.'

'Which leaves you four to choose from, since I have no intention of giving you mine.'

'It's hard to choose,' she said. 'From what I can remember they were all beautiful.'

'The view is better on the southern side,' he advised, 'and you get more breezes in the evening.'

'Which side is the southern side?'

'This side. *My* side. I'll put your case in the room next to mine, shall I?'

'Oh, er, all right.'

'Good.' He bent to pick up the heavy case, the movement highlighting the sleekly defined muscles in his chest and upper arms.

'I know you probably promised my aunt you would try to persuade me to stay, Sebastian,' she burst out, a type of panic invading her at the thought of spending a whole month in the bedroom next to his. 'But the truth is…I simply could not bear to live permanently on Norfolk Island.'

He straightened and looked at her with suppressed exasperation in his eyes. 'How do you know that? You haven't tried it.'

'You don't have to climb Mount Everest to know that it's freezing cold up there,' she said defensively.

'Meaning?'

'Life here is too slow for me. And far too quiet. I'd be bored in no time.'

His eyes locked with hers across the room, and she felt instantly breathless.

'You think so?' he said with a taunting softness.

'I *know* so.'

'You know nothing, Jessica,' he said with an almost weary sigh. 'Just as I knew nothing when I first came here. But I won't bore you by telling you about my experience. I can see Evie's quite wrong. You won't change your mind. Still, perhaps it's just as well. You really don't suit the island any more than it suits you.'

His eyes became cold again as they raked over her. 'No. You're much better suited to a career in Sydney. I dare say having to stay here for a whole month has inconvenienced you no end.'

Jessica resented the underlying contempt in his voice. Who was he to judge anyone? 'Yes, it has, actually,' she said curtly. 'I might have risked my job in dropping everything and coming at once.'

'Pardon me if my heart doesn't bleed for you. I'm sure your inheritance will more than compensate for any inconvenience. And if you lose your job, then what the hell? You'll survive till you get the next one.'

'You still believe all I care about is the money, don't you?'

'If the cap fits, wear it, Jessica.'

'I have not come just for the money!'

'Whatever you say.' His expression was distant, as though he didn't give a damn either way.

'Lunch in ten minutes!' Evie called from the depths of the house. 'I'll serve it out on the back veranda.'

'Fine, Evie,' Sebastian called down the hallway before turning to face Jessica. 'Let's get you along to your room,' he said briskly. 'You might like to shower and change before lunch. I know I do. I probably smell of fish. I threw away my T-shirt earlier because it was high as a kite, but I think I must still be on the nose a bit. I couldn't help but notice you run a mile every time I get too close.'

Jessica found some relief that this was what he thought. The last thing she wanted was for him to think she fancied him. My God, the last thing she'd wanted— or expected—was to fancy him at all!

She wasn't sure why she did, with the way he was treating her. Like she was a cold-hearted, ambitious bitch! Okay, so he was gorgeous looking, in a blond, bronzed surfie fashion, but she'd never been attracted to that type before, not even in her younger days. She'd always gone for dark, intensely passionate types, the ones who couldn't stop looking at you, who flattered you like mad and were always over you like a rash as soon as they got you alone.

Jessica's previous lovers had always rushed her into the bedroom before she could draw breath, and silly lonely love-struck fool that she was, she'd never thought to say no, even when the bells didn't ring and the stars didn't explode.

She'd long come to terms with the fact that while the men she'd fallen in love with had been passionate types, they hadn't been the most skilled lovers in the world. They had been impatient for their own pleasure, quick and selfish, takers, not givers.

She stared at Sebastian as she crossed the room and wondered what kind of lover *he* was. Which led her to the question of whether he had a girlfriend somewhere on the island.

She didn't like that idea. Not one bit. It was a perversely telling moment.

'I'll use the bathroom on the other side of the house,' he said, 'if that's what you're frowning about.'

Jessica frowned some more till she remembered none of the bedrooms had ensuites. Each side of the house had a bathroom and separate toilet, with a third powder room and toilet coming off the hallway near the living rooms.

'I think that's a good idea,' she said coolly. 'Perhaps you should always use that bathroom for the duration of my stay here. That way we won't have to worry about sharing, or running into each other accidentally in the bathroom.'

And I won't have to worry about drooling over you too much.

He stared at her for a moment, then shrugged. 'Okay. If that's what you want.'

'What I want, Sebastian,' she said as she followed him into the bedroom he'd chosen for her, 'is for you to tell me the truth.'

He placed her suitcase on the ottoman at the foot of her four-poster bed, then glanced at her, his face annoyingly bland. 'About what?'

'About everything.'

'Everything?'

'You know what I mean, so don't play dumb. It doesn't suit you.'

'What if I think you're not ready to know… everything?' he said with irritating calm.

'What gives you the right to make such a judgment?' she countered frustratedly. 'You know, you have a habit of making ill-founded judgments. You accused me earlier of not wanting to find out about my heritage. Then, just now, you virtually accused me for a second time of only coming here for the money. You were wrong on both counts. I would have survived quite well without Aunt Lucy's money. But I doubt I'll survive without knowing the facts surrounding my mother's flight from her family, and her pretending they didn't exist, and vice versa. So stop telling me what I think and what I feel! You don't know anything about me. Not the real me. You probably never will.'

His eyebrows shot ceilingwards. Jessica wasn't sure if he was impressed by her outburst, or taken aback. Frankly, she didn't care. She was too mad to care.

'I also want to know where you fit into all this,' she swept on heatedly. 'Okay, so you refuse to tell me if you and my aunt were lovers, but I still want to know who in hell you are, and how you came to live here, and why Aunt Lucy put you in her will in such a peculiar back-handed fashion?'

His smile was wry. 'Thems a lot of questions, Jess. It would take me all day and all night to answer them.'

His calling her Jess almost distracted her from her mission. For a few disarming seconds she took some perverse pleasure from the possibility that it meant he was beginning to believe her. Or perhaps even *like* her.

But just as swiftly she pushed such silly considerations aside and put her mind on why she was here. For it certainly wasn't to become involved with a man like Sebastian Slade, who was at best a bit of a beach bum, at worst, a gold-digging gigolo.

'I *have* all day and all night,' she said firmly. 'And so do you, by the look of things.'

'I work in the afternoons.'

'You...work?' Her face and voice must have shown her surprise.

'Yes. Did you think I just lazed around every day, doing nothing but fish?'

Pretty well, came the dryly cynical thought.

'What on earth do you do?' she asked. Maybe his idea of work and her idea of work were two different things.

'I write.'

'Write,' she repeated dully, as though she'd lost her brain power. But frankly, he looked about as far removed from a writer as one could get.

'What do you write?'

'I'm working on a novel.'

'You mean you're a novelist? You earn money from writing books?'

'I hope to. A publisher has already accepted my story on the first two hundred pages plus a synopsis. I've completed a further four hundred and have about fifty to go. Since my deadline is the end of this month, I'm sure you must appreciate I can't have an afternoon off at this stage.'

'What's it about, this novel of yours?'

His sigh was a little weary. 'Jessica, for pity's sake, you never open your mouth except to ask more questions. I could be here forever if I started answering them now. Have a quick shower and change into something cooler. You look hot. I'll tell you about my book over lunch. Then tonight at dinner, and afterwards, I'll try to answer all your other questions.'

'You won't hold anything back?' she asked. 'Promise?'

'I promise to put myself at your total disposal till you are well and truly satisfied. Fair enough?'

He could not possibly have meant any double entendre within that statement, but still, his words put perturbing pictures into her mind. Pictures of her staying all night in his bed, being made love to over and over, no sexual stone unturned till she lay exhausted and thoroughly sated in his arms.

Jessica swallowed, then struggled to find her voice. 'F-fair enough.'

He smiled at her then, an unconsciously sensual smile, which made her feel suddenly weak at the knees.

'See you at lunch,' he said. 'I'll tell Evie to hold the food for another five minutes, but don't be long.'

CHAPTER FIVE

JESSICA managed to find her way to the back veranda in just over ten minutes. Sebastian was already there, slightly more dressed than earlier in multicoloured board shorts and a bright blue singlet the same colour as his eyes. His hair hung darkly damp onto his shoulders in gentle waves.

He looked deliciously cool, hunkily handsome and irritatingly relaxed, leaning back in a deep cane chair, his bare feet up on the veranda railing.

'Great view, isn't it?' he said as she settled herself in an adjacent chair, a glass-topped cane table between them. He didn't even look her way.

Jessica's automatic pique was telling. She'd told herself she hadn't dressed to attract him, that she'd chosen to wear her white cheesecloth outfit simply because it didn't need ironing, and not because it was the most feminine thing she'd brought with her.

Now she gazed at her clothes with a rueful acceptance of the truth. The skirt flowed in sensually soft folds to mid-calf, the matching shirt falling loosely from her shoulders to her hips, its thin white material showing tantalising glimpses of the half-cup lace bra she was wearing underneath, one that pressed her breasts up and together. She'd deliberately left the top two of the mother-of-pearl buttons open at the neck, forming a deep

V neckline, which displayed a good inch or two of cleavage.

Jessica felt frustration at her own stupidity, and relief that the object of this unwanted sexual attraction was indifferent to her appearance. Still, she was thankful she hadn't had time to change her hair. Leaving her hair down might have delivered a none too subtle message.

With a small sigh she crossed her legs, noting as she did that her toenail polish was chipped. Embarrassed— she was a perfectionist about her personal grooming— she uncrossed her legs and swung them underneath her chair to hide her feet.

It was only then that she really took in the view Sebastian had remarked upon.

My God, but it *was* magnificent! Rolling green hills in the forefront, framed by stately Norfolk Island pines. The Pacific Ocean in the distance, a great expanse of blue-green water broken by two small craggy islands, which looked deserted. Above, cotton wool clouds were scattered across a deep aqua sky.

'There aren't any boats on the horizon,' she commented, surprised. In Sydney, you could rarely look out at the ocean and not see a boat on the horizon.

'We're not on any shipping line here,' Sebastian replied. 'The only boat you'll ever see other than local fishing boats is the occasional supply ship. It's quite an event when one shows up. Everyone goes down to the pier to watch the unloading.'

Wow, Jessica thought dryly, trying not to show what she felt about that on her face.

Sebastian laughed. 'You think that's about as interesting as watching grass grow, don't you?'

What was the point in lying to him?

She threw a rueful glance his way. 'Something like

that,' she admitted. 'But maybe I'm wrong. If a boat comes in while I'm here, take me down to watch for a while.'

'All right. I'll do that. Ah, here's Evie with some brain food.'

'It's nothing fancy,' Evie said as she carried a tray over and proceeded to put a plate each on the table between them. 'Just some club sandwiches, followed by banana cake and tea. Or coffee, if you'd prefer.' She directed the last remark towards Jessica.

'Tea would be just fine,' she said, smiling. The only time she liked coffee was first thing in the mornings and after dinner at night. 'This looks delicious.' Jessica picked up the long sesame-seed-covered roll filled with cold meat and salad and took a bite. 'Aren't you having one, Evie?'

'I already did, in the kitchen. Sebastian, you've let provisions really run down in the freezer. I'll have to do some shopping this afternoon before I can produce a decent meal tonight.'

'There's plenty of trumpeter in the fridge,' he said, and Jessica wondered what trumpeter was.

'We can't eat fish every night,' Evie told him, thereby solving the mystery. 'And I need some fresh vegetables.'

'Have you enough money to buy what you need, Evie?' Jessica asked. 'I'll pay you back tomorrow when I go to the bank. I didn't carry all that much cash with me on the plane.'

'I'll fix her up with some money,' Sebastian offered.

'Certainly not,' Jessica snapped. 'The will said you were to live here free of charge, and that's exactly what you'll do.'

'For pity's sake don't start arguing, you two,' Evie protested. 'That would be the last thing Lucy wanted. I'll pay for the food and Jessica can pay me back. Now eat up and I'll go get the banana cake and tea.'

'Forceful woman,' Sebastian said after Evie disappeared.

'She's a very nice lady,' Jessica defended.

'I was talking about you.'

'Oh.' Her head turned and their eyes met over their rolls.

He was looking at her now. *Really* looking at her, drinking her in, his eyes starting on hers and travelling slowly downwards, past her suddenly drying mouth, down the V neckline to where her swelling breasts were forming an even more impressive cleavage. Her nipples suddenly felt like hard pebbles, pressing against the lace confines of her bra. Her heart was thudding heavily behind her ribs.

Thank God I'm not given to blushing, she thought with growing irritation.

Her chin lifted instinctively in defiance of the effect he had on her. He wasn't even looking at her with desire in his eyes. If anything, there was a rueful edge to his appraisal, as though he recognised her physical attractiveness but was totally immune.

Not like you, came the voice of self-disgust. *He only has to look at you and your veins fill with a liquid heat.*

She looked away quickly and busied herself eating so that by the time Evie returned with a tray of tea and cake, she'd finished her roll and gathered her composure.

'That's what I like to see,' Evie said happily. 'An appreciative eater. Look, I might dash off to the shops now. Just stack the dirty things in the dishwasher after you've finished. Be back by five. Oh, and I don't want to hear you two have been squabbling while I'm gone.'

The atmosphere between them seemed to thicken appreciably with Evie's departure, though maybe it was Jessica's imagination. Perhaps it was simply because it was difficult to talk with mouthful after mouthful of banana cake. Truly, the square Evie had given her was enormous. The cake was delicious but quite heavy. One needed two cups of tea to wash it down.

'Having trouble with the cake?' Sebastian asked, breaking the awkward silence that had developed.

'A little. I'm not as hungry as I thought I was. My stomach must still be on Sydney time.' She'd had to put her watch forward two and a half hours before leaving the plane. On daylight saving time, it was only ten-thirty in the morning back home.

'You'll soon adjust. Well, do you want to start with the questions? I can give you half an hour before I have to get back to work.'

'That's not very long.'

'Then don't waste any of it,' he said quite sharply.

Surprise at his tone sent her eyebrows arching. 'Why are you angry at me?'

'I'm not,' he denied.

Oh, yes, you are, she decided. *You definitely are. I wonder why?*

'Get on with the questions, Jessica,' he drawled, his anger under control if his cold eyes were anything to go by.

'Very well,' she returned tersely. 'Why don't you tell me about yourself to begin with? Give me a brief autobiography.'

His laugh was disbelieving. 'Sorry. I'm not in the habit of telling a perfect stranger my entire life story.'

'But I'm not a perfect stranger!'

'Of course you are. I know as little about you as you know about me.'

'But...but...'

'Stop stammering. It doesn't suit you. Now do you want to know about my book or do you want to start giving me the third degree about your aunt and myself again?'

Jessica opened her mouth then snapped it shut. She eyed Sebastian closely, all her doubts about his relationship with her aunt resurfacing with a vengeance. She suspected she could ask questions till the cows came home, but that didn't mean he would tell her the truth. About anything. All she could do was ask away and watch his body language.

'How did you come to meet Aunt Lucy?' was her first question.

His shoulders visibly relaxed at the question, showing he had been a little tense over what she might ask. 'I came here for a holiday three years ago,' he said lightly, 'and I simply stayed on.'

'*You* came here for a holiday? To Lucy's Place?'

'Yes. What's so surprising about that?'

'Were you alone?'

'I certainly was.'

'But why?'

'Why was I alone?'

'No, why did you choose Norfolk Island, if you were alone? It's not the sort of place a good-looking young man would go for a holiday on his own.'

'Firstly, I wasn't all that young. I was thirty-five at the time.'

Jessica was startled. Thirty-five three years ago. That made him thirty-eight now. He didn't look a day over thirty, even if there were some lines around his eyes she hadn't noticed before.

'I wanted to get right away from the rat-race,' he went

on. 'I'd been working very hard for years and I was burnt out.'

'Working hard at what?'

'As a dealer in an American-owned bank in Sydney. If you know anything about dealing, and about American banks, you'll know how stressful such a job can be. On top of that, I was having personal problems.'

'What sort of personal problems?'

He flashed her a look that indicated that was not a question he wanted to answer. 'Money troubles,' he said brusquely. 'Amongst other things.'

'You still had enough for a fancy holiday,' she fired at him. 'This place wouldn't come cheap.'

He seemed taken aback for a second before smiling a slow smile. 'I managed,' he said.

'How long was the holiday for?'

'Three weeks.'

'At the end of which Aunt Lucy invited you to stay on, free of charge?'

'Not exactly. A couple of days after I arrived I fell ill with a virus. Apparently that happens sometimes when workaholics suddenly stop work. Perversely, their immune systems go down, instead of up, and they get sick. I was in bed for a week, then spent the rest of the three weeks recuperating. I had barely enough energy to do more than read a book. Lucy felt sorry for me and offered me another three weeks holiday, free of charge.'

'Which you jumped at.'

'Naturally. Wouldn't you?'

'I suppose so. So what happened at the end of that three weeks? Did Aunt Lucy invite you to stay on indefinitely, free of charge?'

'No, of course not. But by then I'd fallen in love with

Norfolk Island and wanted to stay, so I offered my services to your aunt in exchange for my bed and board.'

Jessica's eyebrows arched and Sebastian scowled.

'You have a dirty mind, do you know that?'

'I'm merely trying to imagine what kind of services a
big city banker could offer my aunt. Financial consultant
and adviser, perhaps?'

'No, a painter, Miss Suspicious.'

Her eyebrows shot up further. 'Painter? What do you
mean? Do you paint portraits?'

'No, walls. Your aunt happened to mention she was
going to hire someone to paint the house inside and out
during the winter break. She never had guests in the
house from the middle of May till the middle of
September. Since by then April was already fast drawing
to a close, I suggested she hire me to do it in exchange
for my board.'

He chuckled at the memory. 'I said I'd painted before.
Which I had…technically. I painted a bike once when I
was a kid. I figured it didn't take a genius to paint flat
surfaces and that I could learn on the job. I admit I was
a bit slow at first, but frankly, I think I did a better job
than a professional painter would have, simply because
I cared about the place so much.'

'You did a good job,' she had to admit. It was the first
thing she'd noticed about the place—the splendid paint-
work.

Sebastian gave her a look of mock shock. 'Careful
now, Miss Rawlins, that almost sounded like a compliment. Next thing you know, you'll start believing I had
no ulterior motive in staying on here.'

Her returning look was droll. 'As much as you'll start
believing I've come here for my health, and not my inheritance.'

This time, his laugh sounded almost amused. 'True, but perhaps, in the interests of Evie's peace of mind, we should at least agree to be polite to each other.'

'I *am* being polite, believe me.'

'God help me if you ever decide to get vicious.'

Jessica pulled a face at him. 'So how come you started writing a novel?'

'That was Lucy's idea. She said I should do something with my brain to stop it atrophying. She'd noticed how much I liked to read so she suggested I try my hand at writing a novel. I scoffed at the idea at first; said I was a typical male who only ever used the right side of his brain. Or is it the left?'

He frowned.

Damn, but he was even gorgeous-looking when he frowned.

'Whatever,' he continued, shrugging. 'The non-creative, non-communicating side. You know what I mean.'

'Indeed, I do,' she said dryly. Most of the men she'd ever known had lacked creativity and communication. They hadn't even been good liars!

She surveyed Sebastian's sexy face and body and thought *he'd* make a good liar. A woman would be too busy lusting after him to notice the bull he was feeding her. Poor Aunt Lucy would not have stood a chance!

'No one was more surprised than me to find I had a real knack for it,' he was saying. 'Moreover, I enjoyed it. That winter was marvellous. I used to paint every morning, write every afternoon and play games with Lucy every evening.'

Jessica barely had time to react before Sebastian laughed.

'Yes, I appreciate how that sounded. Sorry, but I still

can't satisfy your craving for decadence. Lucy was a game addict. Cards, board games, word puzzles, crosswords. I'm sure you've noticed there are no television sets at Lucy's Place. Lucy claimed people came here to get away from that sort of thing. She entertained herself and others with simpler, more old-fashioned pastimes.'

Jessica *hadn't* noted the lack of television. Now she was quietly appalled. Television had become her main backup for companionship and entertainment over the years. She could not imagine life without it!

'By the time I'd finished painting the house,' Sebastian went on, 'I'd told my story idea and received an advance, so I asked Lucy if I could stay on till I'd finished the book.'

'Free of charge still?' Jessica asked archly.

'Of course not. Lucy was kind, but no fool. Renting out rooms was her source of income. Though I admit she did give me a reduced rate for being a longstanding guest.'

'As well as her loyal and loving companion,' Jessica added dryly.

His glance was sharp. 'Back to that again, are we?'

'Not just now. Are you a good writer?'

'I think so.'

'Are you going to make a fortune out of your book?'

'Probably. It's a damned good book.'

She had to laugh. 'I see modesty is not one of your virtues.'

'Nor yours,' he said, his eyes dropping to her cleavage.

Jessica pulled another face at him.

'Don't take offence. There's nothing wrong with being proud of one's…achievements. You've obviously done very well for yourself. I take it your childhood was poor?'

Her astonishment showed in her face.

'Takes one to know one,' he drawled.

'You were poor as a child, too?'

'Dirt poor.'

Jessica digested that for a good minute or two. If he was anything like herself, then financial security would mean a lot to him. Perhaps that was why he was quick to think badly of her, because he himself put money above all else.

There was a time when Jessica had been ruthlessly ambitious in her aims to get ahead so that she would never be poor again. Now, she was content to do a good job and be paid well for it.

'What happened to all the money you earned as a dealer?' she asked. Jessica had dated a dealer once and knew the sort of salary they commanded, not to mention the bonuses they received.

'I invested it.'

'Badly, I presume.'

He chuckled. 'I could have done better.'

Which meant he'd lost it all. She could understand how that happened. Dealers were basically gamblers who usually only played with other people's money. It seemed Sebastian had started playing with his own, with dire results.

She was surprised that he wasn't more devastated. Maybe he had been, but selling his book had helped him pick up the pieces. Maybe that was one of the reasons he was so grateful to Aunt Lucy—because she'd put him on the road to a second fortune. And maybe that was why he wasn't concerned over not being left anything in her will. Because he believed he would soon be pretty rich himself.

And maybe I'm guessing all wrong, Jessica thought ruefully.

'What kind of investment was it?' she asked. 'The money market? Futures?'

His blue eyes flashed with sudden irritation. 'Must we talk about money?' he flung at her. 'If there's one thing I've learnt since coming to Norfolk Island it's that money doesn't make you happy. Far from it. Let's just say I invested in the property market in the wrong place at the wrong time. I wasn't the only optimistic idiot who got his fingers burnt, but I sure as hell can guarantee I'm the best adjusted to the consequences of my greed and stupidity. I haven't thought about those bad investments since coming here, and I don't want to now.'

Jessica raised her eyebrows. Hard to believe that a man who'd once been dirt poor could dismiss being broke so easily, or pretend he could be happy without any money at all! Maybe he was just saying that because he was on the verge of making a stack more with his book. Or maybe he'd already lined his pockets with cash gifts from Lucy over the past three years.

Jessica felt frustrated that she couldn't simply ask and know she'd get a straight answer. Still, she wasn't about to let him totally off the hook.

'Very well,' she said. 'We'll talk of other things. How would you describe your relationship with my aunt?'

His glare carried exasperation. 'I thought I'd already made myself clear on that score. We were friends. She helped me and I helped her. It was a give-and-take relationship. We enjoyed each other's company. We liked each other. It was as simple as that.'

He still hadn't denied he'd taken her to bed, she noted wryly. It seemed he wasn't going to, either. He was going to let her stew about it. Jessica decided to approach the question from a different angle.

'Why didn't she leave you something in her will, Sebastian? Why leave everything to me? She didn't even know me, whereas you and she were obviously very... close.'

'You were still her niece. Her flesh and blood. It was right that she leave everything to you.'

'You don't resent it?'

'Why should I?'

'You might be forgiven for expecting some kind of legacy yourself.'

'She did leave me a legacy.'

Jessica was taken aback. 'Surely you're not talking about the car!'

'No, I'm talking about my soul.'

'Your *soul*?'

'That's right. When I came here I'd totally lost mine. She gave it back to me.'

'But...but...'

'I can appreciate your confusion, Jessica. *And* your suspicion. But I strongly suggest you stop trying to make me fit the role you've selected for me in your city-cynical mind. You'll be much happier if you do. Now I think it's time for me to get to work,' he pronounced firmly.

'But you haven't told me anything about your book yet,' she blurted out, though her mind was still on his last remarks. Had she been misjudging him? Was she being cynical?

'There's not much to tell, really. It's an adventure action novel set partly on this island at the time of the convict settlement last century. When I take you sightseeing tomorrow morning, I'll take you down to the old gaol and explain the characters and the plot. Then it will make more sense.'

But nothing else is going to make sense, she thought bitterly as she watched him stand up and start stacking the plates. *Not my aunt's actions. Or yours. Or mine.*

Why did she have to be so attracted to him, against all the dictates of common sense? Why? Dear God, the thought of spending the whole morning with him tomorrow, alone, doing things lovers and honeymooners did on this island, was already sending her into a spin.

Once again, her eyes were drawn to the classical lines of his perfect face and perfect body, and the unconscious sensuality of his movements. His hands moved with a fluid grace, his fingers long and elegant, his fingernails spotlessly clean and neatly clipped.

Yet for all that, there was a primitive edge about him. A sense of the wild and untamed.

His lack of clothes, she supposed. Plus his long hair.

She watched it fall forward as he leaned over the table towards her, her eyes following his hands as they lifted to impatiently rake it from his face. The image came of her own hands sliding into his hair, of her drawing his mouth down to hers, then down to her breasts. Then lower...

Her stomach twisted with a raw jab of desire, and she almost moaned out loud.

God, but she had to get away from him, had to get him out of her sight.

'I'll finish that,' she offered as she jumped to her feet. 'You go back to your writing.'

She reached out to take the pile of plates, but in her haste their fingers brushed together, which was the last thing she wanted. It took all her willpower not to snatch her hand away. But the contact still sent a shudder rippling through her. The hair on the back of her neck and arms stood on end.

When her eyes flew to his face in panic, Jessica was stunned to catch a blazing blue gaze glaring at her.

It wasn't desire heating his eyes, however.

It was resentment, a bitter burning resentment.

He hid it quickly. But not quickly enough.

He said a brusque thank-you, turned and walked into the house before she could blink, leaving her staring after him.

So he *did* resent her over the will, she realised with a rush of…what? Disappointment? Dismay?

My God, that was telling, wasn't it? She'd almost begun to believe his assertion that he was an innocent party in all this, that he'd come here, shattered by some sort of personal crisis, then had the pieces put together by dear kind Aunt Lucy, after which he'd stayed on, stony-broke, yet wanting nothing from this lonely and very wealthy widow but friendship.

Silly Jessica. When was she going to learn that men lied when it came to sex and money? Of course Sebastian had been Aunt Lucy's lover. Only a fool would believe otherwise. And of course he'd received presents from her. But they hadn't been enough, had they? He'd wanted it all. But he hadn't got it all. A long-lost niece had popped up at the last minute to snatch his hard-won inheritance away from her.

It was no wonder he resented her.

So why had he bothered to lie to her? Why had he been so nice on the telephone, but not once she arrived? Perhaps he *had* been planning to seduce her, only she hadn't turned out to be quite so gullible as Aunt Lucy. He'd taken one look at her and known he had no chance in hell of conning such a city-smart broad.

Which was so ironic, it was almost funny!

Oh, if only he knew!

Jessica shuddered with self-disgust. How could she want a man to make love to her, suspecting he was nothing but a cold-blooded con man? She'd heard that everyone had a dark side, but this was the first time she'd encountered hers. In the past, she'd made love to assuage her loneliness or to feel loved. The feelings she had for Sebastian had little to do with loneliness or love, and everything to do with lust.

It was as well he wasn't out to seduce her, she realised ruefully. Lord knows what would happen if he made a pass at her. Jessica didn't like suffering from a case of unrequited lust—it was distracting and disturbing—but she was determined to ignore it. Maybe in a couple of days, it would wear off, once she got used to Sebastian's incredible sex appeal.

Meanwhile she would concentrate on the reason she was here. Finding out about her roots. She'd almost forgotten why she had come for a moment. Sebastian had made her forget. He was a menace, all right.

She wandered to her bedroom and began unpacking. She hoped Evie would come back a little earlier than five o'clock. Jessica was impatient to ask her some questions about her mother. Sebastian might know a few things Lucy had told him, but Evie had known Jessica's family for forty years!

God, but it would be good to finally find out what had happened all those years ago; good to have the jigsaw that had been jumbling in her mind fit together into a cohesive pattern.

She hoped Evie had most of the answers. Then she wouldn't have to spend too much time questioning Sebastian after dinner tonight. The less time she spent with him, the better!

CHAPTER SIX

EVIE arrived just after four-thirty, and Jessica trailed after her into the kitchen like a hungry puppy. She was hungry, all right, hungry for company and for answers for her ever-increasing curiosity.

It had been lonely lying on her bed all afternoon, unable to sleep, unable to do a damned thing. Her mind had been too active to read. If only there'd been a television to watch, to distract her growing agitation.

'I'm so glad you're back,' she said, and began helping Evie unpack the bags of groceries and other provisions.

'Hasn't Sebastian been keeping you company?'

'He disappeared into his room after lunch to write. I haven't seen hide nor hair of him since.'

Evie tut-tutted. 'He's a bit of a tiger where that book of his is concerned, but he could have put it aside on your first day here.'

'No matter,' Jessica said lightly. 'I unpacked and had a little lie-down. I've been up since four this morning. I had to be at the airport at five.'

'Goodness! It'll be early to bed for you tonight then, lovie.'

Jessica had to struggle to blank out another of those dark thoughts. 'Would you mind if I asked you a few things about my family while you work, Evie?' she said quickly.

'No, of course not. I've been wondering when you

were going to. I gather you didn't even know you had a family on Norfolk Island, am I right?'

'Yes. Mum always said she had no family, that she'd been dumped on a doorstep when she was a baby and had been brought up an orphan in a state institution.'

Evie shook her head. 'That was wicked of her,' she muttered. 'Just wicked.'

'She must have had her reasons,' Jessica defended. 'How old was she when she ran away from home, do you know?'

'Mmm. Must have been only seventeen. She hadn't long been home from school on the mainland after doing her higher school certificate. I remember Lucy toyed with the idea of her repeating because she'd been a year younger than most of her classmates.'

'Isn't there a high school here, on the island?' Jessica asked.

'Yes, right up to year twelve now. But in those days, kids could only attend school to year ten. If they wanted to go further, they were sent to boarding school, either over in Brisbane or Sydney. Joanne went to Sydney and came home with a real craving for a faster life than on Norfolk Island.'

Jessica could understand that. 'Do you think that's why she left home? Because she wanted to live in Sydney?'

'I really don't know. I only know she and Lucy had a big fight over something and Joanne took off, never to return. We all thought it was a rotten thing to do, because Lucy was getting married the following week and Joanne was supposed to be her bridesmaid. The wedding went ahead, but it was a pretty sombre affair.'

'I wonder what the fight was about?'

Evie shrugged. 'I dare say it was probably a teenager

rebellion thing, although I got the feeling she wasn't thrilled with Lucy getting married. Or maybe it was Bill she didn't like. I saw them arguing one day on the side of the road, and Joanne actually pushed Bill over. That's the sort of thing she would do. She had a temper and a half.'

Jessica could hardly believe what she was hearing. The woman she'd known had had no spirit. No fight at all. It was like she was hearing about a different person.

'No doubt she argued with Lucy over something and things were said that shouldn't have been said and pride prevented both of them from ever backing down later. Things like that can happen in families. Whatever it was, Lucy refused to speak of her.'

'As Mum refused to speak of Aunt Lucy. I wish I knew what they fought over.'

'I don't think we'll ever know that, now that Lucy's gone.'

'Maybe she told Sebastian.'

'I don't think so. He certainly never said anything to me about it, not even when he told me about you coming and all. And he would have, if he'd known something.'

Jessica wasn't too sure about that. A couple of times, she'd had the feeling Sebastian was keeping things from her.

'How much older was Lucy than my mother?' she asked.

'Let's see now. About five or six years, I think.'

'Five or six years…' Jessica mulled over the figures for a few moments. Her mother had been thirty-eight when she died eight years ago, which meant she would have been forty-six if she'd been alive today. Aunt Lucy, then, had only been fifty-two or fifty-three when they'd met a few weeks ago, younger than she'd looked. Of course, her illness would have made her look older.

'What did my grandmother die of, by the way?' she asked. 'She couldn't have been all that old.'

'She wasn't. It was tragic. Really tragic. She was flown over to Sydney for a simple operation and had a bad reaction to the anaesthetic.'

'And my grandfather? He's dead too, isn't he?'

Evie sighed. 'When his wife died, he promptly turned round and drank himself to death, as if that's what his poor daughters needed. Another dead parent.'

'That's how my *mother* died!' Jessica gasped. 'From drink.'

Evie's face was all sympathy. 'Oh, you poor love. I didn't realise. Lucy said she'd passed away from some disease. I just assumed it was cancer, too.'

'No, she died of liver and kidney failure. She'd been an alcoholic for years. You know, they say that runs in families,' she added, frowning, concerned that she might have inherited an addictive personality.

'What runs in families?' Sebastian said as he stalked into the kitchen and began filling up the kettle.

'Alcoholism,' Jessica admitted stiffly, wishing he'd stayed in his damned room. 'Both my grandfather and my mother drank themselves to death. Present thinking is that it's an inheritable disease.'

'What rot!' Sebastian snorted. 'Weak people just say that as an excuse. But you don't have to start worrying, Jessica. There's not a weak bone in your body.'

His sardonic tone suggested she'd just been criticised, not complimented. 'Another of your snap judgments, Sebastian?'

'An observation grounded in experience,' he retorted.

'Any woman of your age who's reached executive level in the hotel world in Sydney is made of steel.'

'Oh, good Lord!' Evie exclaimed crossly. 'I thought you two would get on like a house on fire. Instead, you keep sniping at each other. Heaven knows why!'

'Sebastian thinks all I'm interested in is Aunt Lucy's money,' Jessica said defensively. 'Just because I don't want to live here. Just because I'm going to sell.'

'Sell?' Evie repeated faintly. 'She's really going to sell?' She directed her question to Sebastian.

'As of this moment, yes,' he answered dryly.

'But…but this house has been in your family for over a hundred years!' Evie protested, her eyes swinging to Jessica. 'Your great-great-grandfather built it. He was one of the original Pitcairn Islanders who came here to settle the island after the convicts left. This land was a peppercorn grant given to your family by Queen Victoria herself, and you're just going to sell it?' She began shaking her head, her round shoulders sagging. 'Poor Lucy. She'd turn in her grave if she knew.'

'But…but…' Jessica struggled to say something. After all, this was the first she'd heard of any of this. She'd had no idea, no idea at all. Why hadn't she been told? Why had her mother kept her from knowing her family and learning to appreciate her heritage?

It was suddenly all too much. Tears filled her eyes, and she had to battle hard to control a wild mixture of feelings, not the least a deep dismay.

Sebastian's hands on her shoulders startled her out of her wretchedness. She'd had no idea he'd moved across the room to where she was standing.

'You shouldn't be so hard on her, Evie,' he said gently, turning her and cradling her against his chest. 'It's not her fault. She didn't know any of this. Lucy should have told her. Lucy should have told her a lot of things, I think, and not left it up to us. There, there, Jess, don't cry.'

Jessica wasn't crying any more, had stopped soon after he'd taken her in his arms. She wasn't thinking too clearly, or breathing, aware of nothing but Sebastian's hands, one cupping the back of her head, the other stroking rhythmically down her spine. Her face was turned so that her ear covered his deeply thudding heart.

Did it pick up its beat as he held her?

It seemed so, but probably didn't.

When he went to pull away, her arms snaked around his waist and held him close, wickedly revelling in the feel of his hard male body against hers. Her darker side had momentarily taken control, and the pleasure was mind-blowing.

But such pleasure always had a price. The price of peace. Jessica knew that she would pay for these moments of weakness. And pay dearly.

She could see herself now, lying awake at night, longing for more, longing to slip into his room, then slide between the sheets of his bed, longing to make love to him as she'd never made love to any man before....

The fantasy was so strong in her mind that her lips parted, sending a hot, shuddering breath across his thinly covered chest. He flinched under it, bringing Jessica back to the reality of what she was doing, hugging a man who didn't want to be hugged any longer.

She wrenched herself out of his arms with a strangled sob.

'I'm sorry,' she said gruffly, hoping and praying he took her flushed face for embarrassment. He was staring at her, but she had no idea what he was thinking. 'I...I'm not myself at the moment,' she stammered. 'I...I think

I'll go back to my room and lie down for a while. I'm terribly tired and I have a lot of thinking to do. Will…will you excuse me?'

Other than holding her by force, he really had no option but to let her blunder to her room. Jessica did just that, shutting the door behind her and leaning against it as she sucked in breath after ragged breath of much-needed air.

Dear God, what was happening to her? It wasn't as if she was the type of girl who'd ever been sex mad. Far from it. The way Sebastian kept affecting her was *way* outside her normal range of experience with men. When she'd been in his arms, she'd been consumed by a need so intense she could not begin to describe it.

It was insane! And very distressing.

Her head dropped to her hands and she wept, her tears almost despairing. She'd never felt so alone in all her life. Or so confused. Or so wretched.

There was a soft tap on her door. She whirled and stared at it, her heart racing madly as she dashed the tears from her cheeks.

'Jessica?'

It was Sebastian, his voice sounding concerned.

'Are you all right?'

'Yes…yes, thank you,' she replied croakily.

'Evie feels very badly over what happened in the kitchen just now. And so do I. She's made you a pot of tea, and I have it here with me. Can I bring it in?'

Jessica groaned and fled to sit on the side of the bed. 'All right,' she called, hoping she looked like she'd just sat up.

He came in with a small tray, which held two mugs and a teapot, which meant he intended to join her. Everything inside Jessica tightened at the prospect, but it seemed an inevitability so she vowed not to make a fool of herself again with him.

Luckily, all the bedrooms in Lucy's Place were huge, each having a large writing desk and a chair over in a far corner. Sebastian headed for this to set the tray on, which meant he was a nice safe distance from Jessica.

'You have milk with no sugar, isn't that right?' he asked, glancing over his shoulder as he poured.

'You…you've got a good memory.'

'Unfortunately.' His remark was oddly rueful.

He smiled at her, but she couldn't smile back. She kept thinking he knew…knew about what he could make her feel, what he could make her want. Their eyes met, but once again, his thoughts remained hidden from her. She could only hope her face was as unreadable.

His smile turned slightly wry, and she stiffened. 'Evie was going to send you another slice of cake but I vetoed that. Did I guess correctly?'

'That cake could fuel rockets to the moon,' she retorted, and he laughed, the relaxed sound defusing some of Jessica's tension. He couldn't possibly laugh like that if he knew she was secretly lusting after him.

'It's a traditional Norfolk Island recipe,' he explained. 'Cooking here is a mixture of English and Polynesian. Things can be a bit stodgy occasionally, and bananas are a very common ingredient. We don't import fruit and vegetables, you see, and although we have shortages of other fruits sometimes, bananas are always in plentiful supply, particularly overripe ones.'

Jessica frowned. He sounded like he considered himself an islander. Did that mean he meant to stay on Norfolk Island indefinitely? 'Tell me, Sebastian, after this next month is over, and you've finished your book, do you intend going back to Sydney to live?'

'God, no.' He sounded genuinely appalled.

Jessica was taken aback. How could a man who'd been a high-flying dealer settle for such a quiet lifestyle?

'Never?' she questioned.

'Never,' he affirmed.

'You love it here that much?'

'I do, indeed.'

'Where will you live?'

'I'll find somewhere.'

'What will you live on?'

'I have enough.'

Which meant either her aunt had given him plenty, or that book advance had been a corker.

Another thought came to her, and having thought it, she simply had to ask. 'Do you have a lady friend on the island?'

Their eyes locked as he handed her her tea, and Jessica hoped hers were as bland as his. His coming close to her again was revitalising all those involuntary sexual responses he effortlessly evoked. Her breath quickened. Her blood began to race through her veins. Her face was in danger of flushing.

Only by a sheer effort of will did she prevent this humiliation.

'Do you mean lady friend or lover?' he asked rather coldly.

Jessica swallowed and tried to look as though she didn't care either way. 'Lover, I guess.'

'You seem rather preoccupied with my sex life. Without being rude, might I point out it's really none of your business who I've slept with in the past, or who I'm sleeping with at the moment.'

Now Jessica did flush. With a very fierce embarrassment. For he was quite right, of course. It was none of her business. But it was a subject dear to her heart—that treacherous heart that was thudding painfully in her chest within a body that was wanting him more and more with each passing second!

'I think I was entitled to ask if you were intimate with my aunt,' she said in heated defence of her own silly self.

'Why?'

'Because I—because… Well, if you'd genuinely loved and cared for her, I was going to give you some money,' she blurted, twisting the truth in order to get out of the corner she'd backed herself into. 'I felt badly about your being left out of her will.'

He stared at her for a long moment. 'That's very generous of you, Jessica,' he said coolly, 'but I wouldn't accept, anyway.'

'Why? Because you didn't genuinely love her?'

'Because I don't have any need of more money. I told you, money doesn't make a person happy.'

Jessica blinked at this turn of events. A genuine fortune-hunter would have jumped at her offer. Maybe he really wasn't interested in money. Maybe all he wanted was to live on the island and do nothing but write adventure stories.

'Besides,' he went on. 'That was not what Lucy wanted. The only reason I'm even still here, in her house, is to try to make her last wish come true.'

'And what *was* my aunt's last wish?'

'That you live here, of course.'

A very real resentment welled up in Jessica. If that was what her aunt had wanted, then she should have stayed that day. She should have given Jessica a chance to know her. She should have supplied her with some answers. 'I'm sorry,' she bit out, 'but I simply can't do what Lucy wanted.'

'You're still going to go back to Sydney at the end of the month, then?'

'I have to.' *Especially now…knowing Norfolk Island will always hold you, Sebastian Slade.*

'And you'll sell?'

'I can't see any other sensible alternative.'

His eyes hardened as they moved over her. 'So be it, then. I'll leave you now to your rest. See you at dinner.'

CHAPTER SEVEN

DINNER was served in the main dining room, Sebastian and Jessica facing each other across one end of the long lace-covered table, a bowl of red hibiscus blooms between them. Once again, Evie chose to eat in the kitchen by herself, saying she felt more comfortable that way.

The main course was delicious—crumbed fish, which needed no sauce to enhance its sweet flavour, a creamy potato dish with a hint of banana in it, and a fresh green salad. A chilled chablis from New Zealand complemented the flavours and helped soothe Jessica's agitation.

Unfortunately, Sebastian had presented himself for dinner in scandalously tight blue jeans and a chest-hugging white T-shirt, both of which did nothing for her renewed resolve to try to ignore her unwanted feelings for him. She had discarded her white cheesecloth outfit in favour of a modest and very opaque pants-suit in pale green silk, though she had showered at length, shampooing the humidity from her hair, then blow-drying it thoroughly before leaving it down.

Sebastian was wearing a bright red bandanna high around his hair, probably to keep it from falling into his food when he bent forward. Jessica couldn't help but admire once again the natural wave in his hair, not to mention its glorious colour.

Hers was plain black and dead straight. Its only plus

was its thickness. She still had to spend a small fortune having its bulk regularly thinned then expertly cut so that it fell in a stylish curtain to her shoulders when down.

'You're staring at me,' Sebastian commented quietly, then lifted his glass to sip his wine and stare at her over the rim of the glass.

Pride demanded she not look away or blush with mortification.

She managed the former very well, and she hoped the dim light masked the latter.

'I was admiring your hair,' she confessed with a blunt ruefulness. 'Most women would give their eyeteeth for it.'

'Really?' he drawled. 'I was admiring your outfit. Just how many did you bring?'

'There's nothing about me you admire, Sebastian. You think I'm a hard-hearted, money-minded, insensitive bitch. Why not admit it?'

He laughed. It was a harsh, caustic sound. 'Am I so transparent?'

'You've made it perfectly obvious what you think of me.'

'As you have of me,' he countered smoothly. 'Which is a pity, really. I'm sure Lucy hoped we'd like each other.'

'And why would that be?'

'So that I could more easily persuade you to stay on here, of course. That's why Lucy put that condition in her will. She knew there would be no more convincing salesman for a cause than a convert.'

'She'll have to be disappointed then, won't she?'

'So you're still determined to sell? You won't even consider a compromise?'

'Such as what?'

'Such as keeping the house as a holiday home and visiting here occasionally. Maybe, in time, you'll get to love it so much you wouldn't want to go back. I could look after the place for you, if you'd like. Earlier, you offered me money. Offer me a house-sitting job, instead. I'll take that.'

He didn't understand, of course. It was his presence in the house that would keep her away, not any imagined dislike of the island.

'I'm sorry, Sebastian,' she said, 'but I find the idea of keeping a home this size for me to holiday in only four weeks a year totally impractical. I would prefer to lease it to someone to run as a guesthouse. Or pay someone to run it for me. Would you be interested in doing that?'

She could handle him from a distance, and on the end of a telephone. Just.

'No, I would not,' he snapped. 'That's not what Lucy wanted. She wanted *you*—her flesh and blood—living here and loving it as much as she did.'

'That's a very romantic notion.'

'Lucy *was* a romantic. Not like some other women I've known.' This with a meaningful glance Jessica's way.

She bristled and was about to bite when she decided not to give him that satisfaction.

'If Aunt Lucy wanted me to live in this house so much,' she pointed out, 'then she should have stayed that day in Sydney. She should have let me get to know her. And she should have explained what happened between her and my mother. I'm not at all sure I could ever live happily in this house not knowing what happened here. And now I'll never know, will I?'

Sebastian pursed his lips, then took a thoughtful sip of his wine. 'Did you ask Evie?'

'Yes, and she has no idea what was behind their falling out.'

'Well, if Evie doesn't know, then I can't imagine anyone else on the island knowing, either,' he muttered.

'That's what I thought. Unless Aunt Lucy told *you*, of course,' she said, locking eyes with him. 'Did she, Sebastian?'

'No,' he denied firmly. 'She did not.'

Jessica let out an exasperated sigh. 'I can't believe she didn't tell anyone. Or leave some clues to the truth.'

Sebastian said nothing, merely put the wineglass to his lips again and swallowed more deeply. There was something wearily dismissive about his gesture, as though he was already very tired of her and would be glad to see the back of her and her questions.

She felt personally rejected and perversely piqued. So much for her resolve to ignore her feelings for him.

'I know you'd like nothing better than for me to shut up about all this,' she snapped. 'But I have no intention of doing so. What peeves me most is why you all jump to the conclusion that Aunt Lucy was the injured innocent, yet she was the *older* sister. Maybe my mother was the wronged party. Maybe Aunt Lucy left everything to me out of guilt!'

Sebastian's right eyebrow lifted in a surprised arch. 'It's a remote possibility, I suppose. Though if you'd known Lucy personally, you'd know there wasn't a nasty bone in her body. Isn't that right, Evie?' he said as Evie bustled in.

'What's right?'

'Lucy would never have deliberately hurt a fly, would she?'

'Oh, no. She was a very gentle, good-hearted woman. I never knew her to tell a lie in her life, or to speak badly of anyone. She always believed the best of people. The only time I ever saw her really angry was on the one occasion when she was confronted with absolute proof of someone's wickedness and barefaced lies.'

Evie continued talking as she gathered their dirty plates. 'There was this girl whom Lucy used to employ to do the laundry. Her name was Marie. One day, a guest's blouse—a beautiful blue silk thing—went missing. The guest claimed she'd put it out to be washed and ironed, but Marie vowed she'd never seen it, let alone washed and ironed it.

'Three months later, after the guest had long gone, Lucy and I dropped in to the worker's club for morning tea and there was Marie, wearing the blue silk blouse. My God, you should have seen Lucy. I've never seen her so angry. She made sure everyone on the island knew the girl was a no-good thief, so much so that Marie had to go to the mainland because no one here would give her work.'

'Maybe that's what my mother did,' Jessica mused. 'Maybe she stole something, and Lucy found out about it and banished her.'

'Seems a bit harsh,' Sebastian put in.

'Certainly does,' Evie agreed. 'Joanne was family, and Lucy was big on family.'

'Yet she didn't have a family herself,' Jessica commented.

'It seemed she couldn't, the poor love,' Evie informed them. 'She was right cut up about it. Bill, her husband, didn't seem to mind so much. There again, he wouldn't have made much of a father. He was a man's man, always out playing golf and going fishing and the like. It was the fishing that did him in, in the end. He was washed overboard during a storm. Lucy was inconsolable for a long time. I don't mind saying it was me who got her on her feet. I gave her the idea of running this place as a guesthouse. Said I'd help her with the cooking and such. She perked up no end once there were people in the house. She always was good with people.'

Except her own sister and niece, Jessica thought rue-fully.

'You're right there, Evie,' Sebastian agreed. 'I think Lucy's greatest virtue was her ability to lend a sympa-thetic ear.'

Jessica said nothing, but privately she was getting heartily sick of feeling guilty just because she wasn't falling in with her aunt's last and probably guilt-ridden wishes. Jessica believed that no matter what her mother had done, her sister should have come after her much sooner. My God, she'd waited nearly thirty years! She wouldn't have come then, either, if she hadn't been dy-ing.

No, Jessica felt no deep obligation to fall in with her aunt's wishes. Her only regret was that she could not lift the whole of this lovely house and transfer it to a beach-side suburb in Sydney. She would have liked nothing better than to live in it and look after it, but not on Norfolk Island, and nowhere near Sebastian Slade.

'Both of you are having dessert, aren't you?' Evie asked.

Jessica thought of the banana cake and her figure. 'Er...'

'We definitely are,' Sebastian overrode her, bringing a sharp glance from Jessica.

'Worried about running to fat, city girl?' he taunted once they were alone. 'Won't your lover love you any more, if you deviate from your perfect size eight?'

'I don't have a lover,' she snapped. 'At the moment.'

'Poor Jess. Is that why you're so tetchy?'

Jessica had had enough. 'What is it with you? Why do you keep needling me like this? What have I ever done to *you*?'

'You were born,' came the bald and decidedly bitter-sounding announcement.

'Meaning if I hadn't been, you'd have inherited all this yourself?'

'Not at all. Meaning if you hadn't been, I might have been able to finish my book on time.'

'I won't stop you. I didn't ask you to take me sight-seeing tomorrow. I can get a map and take myself sight-seeing. I don't need you to do anything for me.'

'I realise that, dear Jess, but you wouldn't want me to break a deathbed promise, would you?'

Evie arrived at that moment with dessert, a huge help-ing of sherry trifle and jelly and cream.

She tutted as she placed their plates in front of them. 'I could hear you two out in the hall, bickering away like naughty children. I won't come cook for either of you if you don't start behaving yourselves. You *are* going to let Sebastian take you sight-seeing, my girl,' she said sternly to Jessica. 'And you're going to be very nice about it, aren't you, Sebastian?' She folded her arms and glared at him.

'You've shamed me into it,' he said dryly.

'I sincerely hope so.' Her hands moved to her hips. 'Now smile at her, me lad, and use some of that charm of yours to sell her this place and Norfolk Island. That's what Lucy wanted you to do, wasn't it? Why else would she have arranged for you to be here during Jessica's stay?'

'Why else, indeed?' he muttered.

Evie rolled her eyes and left the room.

Jessica went to say something, but her words died when those incredible blue eyes of his fastened onto hers. He lifted his wineglass in a toast, his mouth pulling into the most appallingly sensual smile.

It electrified every nerve ending she owned, tugged at her heart and turned over her stomach.

'To my new-found charm and your unlikely conversion,' he mocked softly.

Jessica was proud of herself when she scraped up a cool smile in return. She even raised her glass in a counter toast. 'You've got a snowball's chance in hell, Sebastian,' she said, not a quiver in her voice. 'But best of British luck to you.'

Jessica woke at three. Exhaustion had sent her to bed straight after dinner, and she'd quickly fallen asleep. But now she was wide awake, and there would be no more sleep for her that night.

She lay in the huge four-poster bed meant for a couple and watched the lace curtains blowing beside the French doors. Sebastian had told her to leave them open to let in the cooling night breezes.

Sebastian…

He was there, in the bedroom next to hers. Only one wall away. Less than twenty feet.

So near and yet so far.

Jessica groaned softly into her pillows. Why did she want him so much? It was perverse in the extreme when it was obvious he didn't even like her, let alone want her in any way, shape or form.

Could that be part of the reason? Was she challenged by his indifference? Jessica had to admit she wasn't used to men being indifferent to her. Even the ones who hadn't liked her professionally had found her physically attractive.

Sebastian, however, seemed immune to her looks. Or was it career women he was immune to? There was no doubt he was scornful of her ambition and drive. Scornful of her unwillingness to throw in her life in Sydney and move here to live.

Yet that was so unfair! Why should she abandon everything she'd worked for because an aunt she didn't know wanted her to? And why should she adopt a lifestyle that would not come naturally to her? It was all very well for Aunt Lucy to leave her everything now, then try to manipulate her from the grave, but where had she been when Jessica had really needed her, when her mother had needed her?

No. Aunt Lucy had a lot to answer for, in Jessica's opinion. If she'd been the wronged party in the feud between the two sisters, then why hadn't she told someone about it? Why keep silent?

'Because she was probably the guilty party, that's why,' Jessica muttered. 'She left me everything out of guilt!'

A creaking floorboard outside her door stopped Jessica's heart in its tracks. As she lay there, deathly still, her instantly alert ears made out the soft footfall of someone walking down the hallway. The sound of a door opening and shutting was more distinct.

Eventually, Jessica let out her long-held breath, though her heart was still racing. It seemed Sebastian was having trouble sleeping, too. Or hadn't he gone to bed yet? There was a dull light on the veranda, which she'd thought was moonlight, but which she now realised was coming from his room. Maybe he'd stayed up late, writing.

More sounds filtered through the door. Sebastian moving around somewhere, possibly in the living room across the hallway. What was he doing? Getting a book to read? Pouring himself a nightcap, perhaps? She'd noticed earlier that that room contained quite a library, plus a large rosewood sideboard with decanters full of whisky and sherry and port sitting in a row on lace doilies.

The thought of Sebastian awake and prowling around the house gradually began to unnerve Jessica. What was he doing? What was he wearing? Why didn't he go back to bed, damn it?

Time passed. Three-thirty came and went, then four. Finally, Sebastian returned to his room and switched off his light. She heard the squish of his mattress as he climbed into bed. Soon, the house was deathly silent.

Jessica couldn't go back to sleep. She lay there, thinking thoughts that unnerved her even more. She was becoming obsessed with the man, she realised. Totally obsessed.

Tomorrow was going to be a nightmare!

CHAPTER EIGHT

'IT'S beautiful, isn't it?' Sebastian said as he pulled the Mazda to a stop and cut the engine. They were less than a minute from Lucy's Place, halfway down the steep hill she had seen from the back veranda.

What she hadn't been able to see from the back veranda, however, was this magnificent view of the foreshore below, not to mention the collection of impressive Georgian buildings at the base of the hill.

'Captain Cook described the whole island as paradise when he first saw it,' Sebastian informed her, 'but this part is my favourite. That's Kingston down there, where the British first settled and built the convict gaol early last century. The gaol is in ruins now but the government buildings are all still in use. They're well worth a look, inside as well as out.'

'Not this morning, though,' Jessica vetoed, thinking that would take hours. And she didn't want to be with Sebastian for hours. Their brief moments at breakfast together had been trial enough.

Jessica had risen around seven, showered and dressed sensibly in fawn Bermuda shorts with a striped fawn and cream shirt, which was slightly baggy, revealing nothing of her figure. She'd wound her hair into a tight knot and applied no makeup except a coral-coloured lipstick and some mascara, emerging from the bathroom looking cool and composed while inside her stomach was a mass of butterflies.

Silence from Sebastian's room had assured her she'd be able to breakfast in peace, and she'd almost managed it, too. But he'd appeared as she lingered over a second cup of coffee, looking slightly bedraggled but appallingly sexy in black satin boxer shorts and nothing else.

Jessica had fled the room as quickly as politeness allowed, but there was no fleeing now, ensconced as they were in the small Mazda.

Thank goodness he'd put on a T-shirt to go with the white shorts he was wearing today. At least she could look at him and not want to touch him so much. But it was still difficult to sit so closely to him in a car and not be brutally aware of every living, breathing pore in his beautiful body.

'Why not this morning?' Sebastian asked.

'First, I really need to go to the bank before lunch,' she said, thinking up any excuse she could to shorten her torture. 'And I have a couple of personal items I simply *have* to buy. There's no rush for me to see everything this morning, is there? I can drive myself down here any time now that I know the way. It's not far.'

'It's not the same on your own,' he said. 'You need a proper guided tour. There's always this afternoon, I suppose.'

'Oh, no, you don't. You said you write every afternoon. Can't have you accusing me of holding up your writing, can I?' she finished, throwing him a false but very bright smile.

His laugh surprised her, for it had an odd note to it, as though she'd made a sick joke. 'I'll just give you a quick drive-by tour of the major points of interest, then. After all, we can't risk you actually soaking up any of the atmosphere of the place. You might find you like it, and then what would you do?'

Jessica declined to answer his sarcastic question because he didn't expect her to. But she did deliver a droll glance his way then turned to look through her window while he reengaged the engine and drove slowly down the hill.

After being whisked around Sydney a lot in taxis, it felt to Jessica as though they were crawling. When Sebastian slowed down to snail speed at the bottom of the hill, she sighed in exasperation. This was his idea of quick? At this rate their drive-by tour would take hours, as well.

'I thought you were allowed to do fifty around the island,' she pointed out tartly. 'Are you trying to annoy me on purpose?'

'Heaven forbid I'd do such a thing, or delay the time it will take to satisfy Evie that I've done the right thing by Lucy's wishes. Unfortunately, the speed limit through the town and down here in Kingston is only twenty-five. Didn't they tell you that when you arrived? Drivers also have to give way to all livestock,' he added when he pulled up abruptly.

One of the cows grazing on the common had done an unexpected right turn onto the road, followed by a flock of geese.

'Or are you so desperate to vacate my company that you would rather I ignore the rules and run them down?' he added.

Jessica decided enough was enough. Things were getting out of hand. She had two courses of action. She could return sarcasm for sarcasm, whereby the month ahead would quickly deteriorate from one of secret sexual frustration to a very nasty episode indeed. Or she could attempt to defuse the growing antagonism between them, thereby making the situation tolerable, at least.

Common sense and her own survival demanded the latter solution.

'Wherever did you get the idea I was desperate to vacate your company?' she asked lightly as they waited for the geese to complete their casual trek across the road.

'Oh, come now. Let's not pretend.'

'In the interest of civility and politeness, Sebastian, *let's*,' she said firmly. 'I understand your disappointment that Lucy's last wishes are not going to be fulfilled exactly as she planned. I fully understand I am everything you deplore in a woman. But let me assure you that—'

'That's not true,' he broke in brusquely, moving ahead slowly now that the road was clear. 'At least, that last bit you said isn't totally true.'

'Oh, come now,' Jessica drawled, echoing his earlier sarcasm. 'Let's not pretend.'

His laughter carried real amusement, as did his sidewards glance. 'Very well. I confess. Underneath, I deplore you. Or at least, the type of woman you project sometimes. But in the interests of civility and politeness, and Evie's possible punishment, I'm willing to pretend if you are.'

'Done!' she said, experiencing a weird stab of pleasure when he smiled at her. It had to be a sexual thing, she supposed, yet it didn't feel sexual. It was as though their secret conspiracy to feign friendship had sparked the beginnings of a very *real* friendship. For the first time since they'd met, they had agreed on something, and it felt surprisingly good.

She smiled at him.

Unfortunately, it had the opposite effect to the one she was looking for. His smile immediately faded, his eyes glittering with that old hostility. 'Don't pretend too well, Jess,' he said curtly. 'We don't want to give Evie false hopes, do we?'

'False hopes?'

'She's one of those romantic souls you despise. Smile at me like that too much and she might start thinking you've fallen in love with me, and Lord knows what complications that would bring.'

Jessica stiffened, her heart going cold under his rebuke. God, but he was a right bastard. She wished she hated his body as much as she hated his spitefully nasty tongue. And he called *her* cynical!

'Don't worry,' she retorted, pique firing her tongue. 'I don't think Evie will ever be under the misapprehension I've fallen in love with *you*, Sebastian. As much as you deplore my type of woman, I deplore your type of man. I like my men smooth and smart and sophisticated, both in their appearance and their lifestyle. I like them with ambition in their hearts, fire in their belly and passion in their eyes. For *me*!'

Jessica might have tossed her hair over her shoulder at that point, if it hadn't been slicked into a tightly controlled knot. Instead, she lifted her nose and chin in a disdainful gesture. 'I don't go for drop-outs who slop around in next to nothing, whose hair looks like it hasn't seen a barber in years, who think working for a living is dabbling at writing between labouring jobs. I especially don't like men who look at me like I was something nasty that had just crawled out from under a stone.'

Her tirade over, an electric silence fell on the car as it moved slowly across a small stone bridge then through a narrow wooden gateway. The ruins of the gaol squatted on their left—massive, bleak-looking stone walls behind which lay God knew what.

Not much, she realised when she peeked through an archway. It looked like everything inside had been stripped and largely levelled.

The outward shell of a smaller houselike building stood on a rise to their right, broken stone steps leading up to a gaping and empty doorway. A large stone monument of some sort stood in the middle of a sweep of lawn in front of them. Behind it were more old buildings, some in ruins and some not. The bay lay just beyond, a long concrete pier jutting out into the rough water.

'Have you finished?' he said coldly as he swung the car to the left and towards the gaol.

'Quite.'

'Good, then shut up and listen.'

She thought he was going to tear strips off her. Instead, he began a monotone commentary about the history of the gaol and the surrounding buildings.

Jessica didn't hear any of it. All she heard were her inner churnings. *What on earth possessed you to say all that, you idiot? He'll really hate you now. He'll certainly never look at you as you want him to look at you, with passion in his eyes.*

'Are you listening to me, damn it?' he suddenly snarled, and she jumped in her seat, the startled blankness in her face revealing her inattention to the history lesson.

He swore and accelerated down the narrow tarred road, the car jolting over a hump, which proved to be an ancient convict-built bridge.

'That's the old salt mill on the right,' he snapped, indicating a towerlike structure amidst some isolated pines on a grassy point. 'And this is Emily Bay.'

The road ran around the edge of the bay, with a thick forest of Norfolk pines behind it. Jessica lost sight of the water for a while till the car emerged on the other side on a bare rocky point, which boasted one rather straggly pine but a spectacular view.

Sebastian parked, facing towards Emily Bay, apparently to allow his passenger a few minutes to soak in the postcard scene. Or maybe to regain control of his temper. Jessica wisely decided not to ask which. She stared silently through the windscreen at the bay, searching for something to say.

Jessica's idea of beach heaven was Bondi, at home, with its high surfboard-riding waves and people-pounding promenade. She even liked the wall-to-wall bodies on the beach on hot summer days. Of course she didn't go there to swim. She went to feel the throb of life around her, to keep that awful feeling of loneliness at bay.

So when she looked at the small reef-protected cove with its calm blue-green waters, one single swimmer and an almost deserted sweep of sand, she could appreciate its quiet beauty, but not the sense of solitude it evoked. When she looked at it, she thought loneliness, not peace. Boredom, not relaxation.

But she knew to say as much would bring more scorn from Sebastian's lips.

'It's very beautiful,' she said at last.

She could feel his eyes upon her but refused to look over and see his scepticism.

'Do you like to swim?' he said. 'I come down here for a swim most nights during the week before dinner. It's usually deserted by then. You can come with me, if you like.'

The idea both terrified and fascinated her. To swim in that secluded cove in that warm-looking water with a near-naked Sebastian every evening. The scenario evoked erotic thoughts in her head and a fierce longing in her body.

'You don't have to take your pretence that far, Sebastian,' she said stiffly.

'Evie will suggest it,' he retorted. 'I was just getting in first. It's a large enough area. You don't have to swim anywhere near me.'

'All right, then,' she agreed tersely while thinking she was insane. What was she trying to do to herself? 'Now, do you think we might go up to the shopping centre and the bank?'

'No more sight-seeing this morning?'

'Not today. We don't have to do everything in one day, surely. I'm going to be here a whole month.'

'You could be here a year, Jess, and I doubt we'd do everything,' he said dryly.

Jessica suspected she'd just heard a snide double entendre, but she treated his words at face value. 'I had no idea Norfolk Island offered such a variety of entertainment.'

His expression remained bland, though the corner of his mouth twitched a little. 'I'm sure you didn't. Perhaps I'll be able to surprise you.'

'I'll look forward to it.'

He looked at her and laughed. 'I have to admire your capacity for pretence, Jess. I only hope I'll be able to keep up with you. So what are these personal items you are so desperate for?' he asked as he backed out of the parking spot and headed the way they'd come.

'Nail polish and remover,' she admitted, then cringed at how pathetic that sounded.

He glanced at her perfectly manicured and polished fingernails before lancing her with a questioning look.

'For my toenails,' she added. 'Their polish is chipped

and I didn't bring any red with me. I always wear red on my toes.'

'Chipped toenail polish,' he drawled. 'A true emergency, indeed.'

Jessica refused to let him niggle her, no matter what he said. 'So I don't like chipped toenail polish,' she answered lightly. 'Is there any real harm in that?'

'I guess not. To town then, and the shops. I might buy myself a decent hairbrush while I'm there. I do have one but most of the teeth are missing. Can't have you leaving me for dead in the grooming department, can I?'

'But what will Evie say,' Jessica mocked, 'if you come to lunch looking neat and tidy? She might think you'd fallen in love with me and are trying to impress me.'

'I don't much care what Evie thinks. You'll know the truth, Jess, and that's all that matters.'

'The truth?'

'That there isn't a chance in hell of my falling in love with you. You see, I don't like my women tough and hard and ambitious. I like them soft and sentimental and obliging. Most of all, I like them to like me. I'm funny that way.' He flashed her a patently false smile. 'But you can pretend, if you like.'

'Pretend what?'

'That you like me. You could even try soft and sentimental and obliging, for a change. And I could respond with pretend passion in my eyes. Evie would be delighted.'

Suddenly, Jessica felt like she wanted to cry. Couldn't he see she wasn't cold or hard at all? If she was, he wouldn't be able to hurt her like this with his cruel barbs.

'I'm not much of a one for pretending,' she said thickly. 'So just shut up and drive me to town. I'm suddenly very bored with this conversation and with this tour.'

'Oh, well, I wouldn't want to bore you.'

He sped up the hill, doing more than fifty, she noted ruefully. But wild horses wouldn't have dragged a remark from her. Or a protest.

Shopping was swift and silent. Lunch was swift and silent. The afternoon was not swift, nor silent.

'I hate him,' Jessica muttered as she paced noisily around her room. 'Hate him. Hate him. Hate him.'

'For pity's sake will you shut up in there?' Sebastian called through the walls. 'I can't concentrate with you prowling around like a caged lion, mumbling away to yourself. Go for a drive or something, will you? Just be back in time for us to go for our swim.'

Jessica stalked onto the veranda and along to his room. She stood in the doorway, hands on hips, glaring at him. The trouble was she was glaring at his back. He was seated at the writing desk in the corner, tapping away on the keyboard of a small PC. 'I don't know if you've noticed,' she snapped, 'but it's begun to rain.'

'So?' He swivelled round from his PC to look at her.

'I don't want to drive around into the rain. I also won't want to go swimming in the rain.'

'Why not? The water's lovely and warm when it rains.'

'To be honest, Sebastian, I don't much enjoy swimming.'

'Why not?'

'I'm not very good at it.'

'Practice makes perfect. Besides, you've nothing else to do except paint your nails.'

'Thank you for reminding me. That should take me all of ten minutes.'

'You could weed the garden, if you like.'

'In the rain, with freshly painted nails?'

'It won't rain for long. It never does. It's stopping as I speak. As for the nails, leave them till last.'

She sighed. 'This is going to be a long month.'

'Amen to that,' he agreed, and turned to stare at the screen of his PC. 'Just go and do something, Jess. Anything. But do it quietly.'

Jessica glared at his steadfastly turned back, then whirled and stalked to her room. In the end, she did weed the garden, angrily at first, snatching the weeds out and swearing under her breath. But gradually, she began to quite enjoy the feeling of satisfaction that came with seeing each bed become clear of the offending and highly unattractive weeds. She couldn't do the whole garden in one afternoon, of course. So she set herself goals, deciding to do so much each day till it was done.

After she'd finished her goal for that day she took her slightly aching but much happier body inside, where she showered at length to get the kinks out of her legs and shoulders, then lay down for a small rest before doing her nails.

They never did get done, for she promptly fell asleep, not waking for a couple of hours.

'Where's Sebastian?' she asked when she emerged, yawning, to find Evie preparing dinner in the kitchen. The clock on the wall said five-thirty. The delicious smell from the oven indicated a roast dinner.

'He's gone for a swim. He said not to wake you.'

'Oh.' Jessica wasn't sure if she was disappointed or relieved.

'You know, I'm surprised you two haven't taken to each other more. Two smart good-looking people like yourselves. I would have thought you'd get on like a house on fire. And I'd have thought Sebastian would be glad of your company, instead of avoiding it. He's been very lonely since Lucy's death.'

The thought of Sebastian being lonely, or missing her aunt, would never have occurred to Jessica. Yet it had occurred to Evie, who obviously knew Sebastian a lot better than she did, and had seen first-hand the nature of his relationship with Aunt Lucy.

Jessica could have kicked herself. There she'd been asking Evie all sorts of questions about her aunt and her mother, and she hadn't thought to ask her the one question she was dying to know the answer to.

'Tell me, Evie,' she began a little nervously. 'Were Lucy and Sebastian lovers?'

Evie shot her a startled look. 'Have you been listening to local gossip?'

'No. I just wondered. Has there been local gossip about them?'

'In a place as small as this? Yes, of course, there was. Heaps.'

'Well? *Were* they?'

Evie shrugged. 'I don't really know. If they were, they certainly hid it well. If you want my guess, I'd say not.'

'Wouldn't Lucy have told you?'

'Oh, no. Lucy and I were friends, but she never was one to confide personal details. Or even to gossip. Of course, there's always talk when a handsome young man is staying in the same house as a good-looking widow. And believe me, Lucy was a fine-looking woman when Sebastian first arrived. She looked many years younger than her age back then. It was the cancer that aged her.'

'I see,' Jessica said slowly, her disappointment acute. She'd been hoping Evie would clear up the matter one

way or another. 'What do you think of Sebastian, Evie?
Do you like him?'

'Yes, I do,' she said firmly. 'I didn't at first. But he's
changed a lot over the past three years. For the better, I
might add. He was very good to Lucy after she became
ill. Very kind and caring. Nothing was too much trouble.
Many's the time he sat with her all night when she was
in pain. I can't speak too highly of him. I'm only sorry
he hasn't chosen to show his good side to you. Perhaps
he's upset that you're going to sell,' she finished with a
reproachful glance.

Jessica didn't know what to think.

The sound of a car coming up the drive put paid to
any thinking at all.

'That will be Sebastian now,' Evie said. 'You could
always ask him yourself about his relationship with Lucy,
you know? Though on second thought, perhaps not. He
certainly hasn't taken to you, has he?'

Jessica had to laugh. 'You could say that.'

'Surprising. You're such a good-looking girl.'

'I'd better go freshen up for dinner,' Jessica said hurriedly when she heard the car door slam. The thought of
Sebastian joining them in nothing but a wet swimming
costume was unnerving in the extreme.

The white cheesecloth outfit made a reappearance for
dinner, not because she was trying to attract Sebastian
this time—difficult to attract a man who despised you—
but because she didn't want him to make some sarcastic
comment about her wearing a different outfit every day.
She waffled over leaving her hair down and in the end
put it up in a sleek French roll.

Sebastian presented himself at the dinner table wearing
those appalling jeans again and a navy blue sleeveless

T-shirt which darkened his eyes to midnight blue in the dimly lit dining room. Another bandanna—navy this time—kept his hair out of his eyes.

He looked utterly gorgeous. It was impossible for her to keep her eyes off him. His opinion of her appearance was not similarly admiring, if the curl of his top lip was anything to go by as he sat down.

'I see you managed not to come swimming with me after all,' he remarked sourly. 'I'd prefer you to say you don't want to come rather than pretend to be asleep every afternoon.'

'Very well,' she said with a weary sigh when she realised he was going to keep the antagonism going between them. Jessica fell unhappily silent and began playing idly with her cutlery.

'What's wrong with you tonight?' he snapped abruptly. 'Are you sick, or something?'

Jessica's chin lifted, her jaw clenching. 'Not at all.'

It was a struggle from that point to keep the conversation from deteriorating into a sniping match, though to control her temper, Jessica drank most of the claret Evie served with the roast beef and Yorkshire pudding. She toyed with the thought of apologising to him for all the rotten things she'd thought about him, but in the end abandoned the idea. What was the point? Come the end of the month she would be gone from here, never to return. Sebastian would be a thing of the past, nothing but a bad memory.

'At least your sleep seems to have done your earlier mood some good,' he drawled over dessert—another fat-producing pudding complete with custard.

'I wasn't in a mood earlier,' she denied.

His eyebrows lifted. 'You mean you're usually like a cat on a hot tin roof?'

Jessica stared at him across the bowl of pink hibiscus. Was she so obvious? Surely he hadn't guessed he'd reduced her to a state of acute sexual frustration the like of which she'd never known before.

The cold gleam in his eyes gave him away. He was just trying to stir her. It came to Jessica then that whilst Sebastian might not be a callous fortune hunter, he was still a bit of a bastard.

'It might have escaped you, Sebastian,' she said shortly, 'but all this hasn't been easy for me.'

'Really? I haven't seen you suffering in any way.'

The bitter laugh escaped Jessica's lips before she could stop it. She'd never known such suffering, such torment. Even looking at him across the table had become torture, she wanted him so much.

Evie bustled in with coffee and after-dinner mints, bringing Jessica a welcome moment of distraction from her escalating blood pressure.

'I'm off now, folks,' Evie said. 'I've cleared up everything except what's on the table. Just pop your dirty plates in the dishwasher, and I'll finish up in the morning. There's a show on telly I want to watch, which starts at nine. See you tomorrow.'

'Bye, Evie,' they both chorused.

'I'm glad to see television isn't banned on the island altogether,' Jessica said dryly once they were alone. 'At least I can go over to Evie's in the evenings if my withdrawal symptoms get too bad.'

'I seem to be suffering from some withdrawal symptoms myself,' Sebastian muttered darkly. 'I wish a few hours of television would cure mine, but I very much doubt it. A few more days of this and I'll be ready for the funny farm.'

'What on earth *are* you talking about?' she said impatiently.

He arched a sardonic eyebrow at her as he downed the last of the wine. 'You mean you don't know? You *honestly* don't know?'

'No, I honestly don't know!'

'Then I'll just have to tell you, won't I?'

'That might be a good idea.'

His laugh was bitter. 'I doubt it. But the fact of the matter is this. I can't sleep and I can't write.'

Jessica blinked her bewilderment. 'Are you blaming *me* for that?'

'I'm not *blaming* you. But you *are* responsible.'

'Would you kindly like to explain that remark?'

'No, but having come this far, I might as well continue. The awful truth is that from the moment I set eyes on you yesterday, Miss Jessica Rawlins, I was madly attracted to you.'

'A-attracted to me?' she repeated dazedly.

'Well, actually, the word attracted is a bit of an understatement,' he said dryly. 'It was more a case of lust at first sight. Quite embarrassing, really. Surely you must have noticed me gawking at you like an adolescent schoolboy. Evie certainly did.'

So that was why he'd stared at her! But...

She swallowed as her fluster receded and the reality of the situation sank in. He wanted her as much as she wanted him. More, perhaps. He was a man, after all. She tried to speak but couldn't. She didn't know what to say.

'Yes, I can appreciate your surprise over my confession,' he drawled. 'I'm pretty surprised myself that I made it. But I'm just not good at pretending, like some people. Also, as you have no doubt noted, I've been behaving like an absolute bastard to you without sufficient

cause. Let me offer my sincerest apologies. My only excuse is that I have obviously been celibate far too long.
Now laugh if you like. It really is rather funny, isn't it?'

Jessica didn't laugh. She didn't find it funny in the
least! All she could do was stare speechlessly over the
table at the man she'd been wanting more than any man
she'd ever met.

'For pity's sake, Jessica, don't make me feel any worse
than I already do,' Sebastian snarled into the electric silence. 'I'm sure you're quite used to members of the
opposite sex being smitten by your striking beauty. Not
to mention your body. So stop playing the offended virgin. I really have no patience with it tonight. You and I
both know you're not that.'

She might have been angered by this last barb if she
hadn't been so shocked.

Having vented his spleen, Sebastian sat there, playing
with his empty wineglass, twirling it round and round. It
was unnerving to watch. Not that Jessica needed unnerving. She was already totally rattled by his astonishing
admission and the thoughts it evoked.

Now there was nothing standing between herself and
what she secretly wanted. He would not reject her. He
would welcome any admission or advance on her part
with open arms.

But it would only be sex on his part. And sex in its
most base form. He not only didn't love her, he didn't
even *like* her. He merely wanted to...

'What if I threw myself on your mercy?' he suggested,
his tone coldly self-mocking. 'Begged you to alleviate
my pain.'

'Pain?'

'Yes, pain. Do you have any idea what it feels like for

a man to want a woman so badly that it's a physical ache? Have you ever wanted anyone like that?'

'Yes,' she said. *You,* she thought bitterly.

'Then you know what it's like. Have some compassion, woman. Come to bed with me tonight. I'm a good lover. I won't disappoint you.'

She could not speak. Her heart was thudding too wildly, her blood pounding through her head. All she had to do was say yes and he would be hers. All that stood between herself and possible ecstasy was her pride and self-respect.

But pride and self-respect were important to Jessica. She had a feeling the reason her mother had ended up a drunken wreck was a lack of both at some point in her life. Jessica had never liked the concept of casual or selfish sex. That was for sluts. And men.

She'd been a virgin till she was twenty-two, and even after that, she'd always believed herself in love with the few men she'd allowed to bed her.

'But I don't love you!' she blurted, voicing her inner dismay that she was on the brink of blindly saying yes to him, despite everything.

His mouth twisted in a wry smile. 'I'm not asking you to love me, Jess, just to let me make love to you. I find it hard to believe that a woman as intelligent and sophisticated as you thinks sex and love always have to go together. Haven't you ever been to bed with a man you didn't love before?'

'No!' she denied hotly.

His astonishment was very real. His eyes flared wide, then narrowed. 'No?'

Her blush was so fierce it had to be visible, even in the subdued light. 'I…at least…not consciously. I thought I was in love with them at the time.'

'Hm. Interesting. And did they hurt you in the end? These men you thought you loved?'

'You could say that,' she said stiffly.

He nodded slowly. 'Love can be cruel. It demands too much, expects too highly. One is inevitably disappointed. Sex, however, never disappoints, if that's all one wants.'

'That's a matter of opinion,' she snapped before she could snatch the words back.

His eyes moved over her heated face—watchful, knowing and intelligent eyes. 'You've found sex disappointing, Jess?' he asked with a gentle curiosity that was incredibly disarming.

'Sometimes,' she muttered, looking into her untouched coffee.

'Sometimes, or always?' he persisted.

Her eyes jerked angrily to his. 'Will you just drop this?'

'No. I won't. I think it's a crying shame that a woman as beautiful as you has not had a satisfying sex life. It's also a mystery to me. You've no idea how much sensuality you project, Jess. It leaps from your body and your eyes all the time. That's why I have been like a cat on a hot tin roof ever since you arrived, because my poor frustrated male flesh was besieged by the silent messages sent out by your highly sexually charged self. Frankly I'm stunned to find out you're unfulfilled in that regard. I can only think you've been very unlucky with your choice of lovers so far.'

'And you think you'd do better? A man I don't love?'

'I'd sure as hell like to try,' he said, a wickedly sardonic smile pulling at his mouth.

'I'll just bet you would!' she flung at him.

She glared at him, at his mouth, his hands, his body. And she wanted them all. On her, and inside her.

His words came back to haunt her, those words he'd said to her that very first day, about how she could do what she liked out here on this island in this isolated house, and no one would ever know or judge. He was offering himself to her for the night, and she would be an utter fool to refuse. For it was what she wanted more than anything else in the world. If she let this chance go by she knew she would regret it for the rest of her life.

But it was so hard to say the words, to voice her agreement. Her tongue felt thick in her mouth, and the palms of her hands had gone clammy.

Speak up, her dark side urged recklessly. *He's yours. Take him!*

'All right then,' she said at last. 'Try!'

His smile faded abruptly, and he was very still for several excruciatingly long moments. 'You don't mean that,' he said at last, clearly sceptical. He hadn't expected her surrender, had not bargained on it.

'Oh, yes, I do!'

Heat flooded all through her body. *Now you've done it,* that dark little voice crowed inside.

But it was not met with self-disgust this time. Or shame.

A strange satisfaction rose to squash any negative feelings. There was a sense of triumph. And excitement.

Her chin lifted. 'I definitely do,' she repeated, her voice steady and strong and sure.

CHAPTER NINE

JESSICA stood on the back veranda, her hands curled tightly over the wooden railing, her shoulders squared against the feelings rampaging through her.

Delayed shock warred with a very real dismay at what she had agreed to in the dining room. Yet both kept being overridden by that voice, that dark and insidious voice that kept whispering wickedly weakening things inside her head.

You can't change your mind now. You don't really want to. You want him to take you to bed. You want him more than you've ever wanted anything in your whole life!

Jessica gulped down the gathering lump in her throat, then glanced at the clear night sky, with its full moon and myriad stars.

It was a night for lovers, she conceded. A night for romance.

But Sebastian wasn't looking for romance. Or love. He wanted what most men had wanted from her over the years, the difference being that this time, she wanted the same thing.

Sex.

Jessica shivered as she thought of all that small word entailed. The nakedness. The intimacy. The act itself. It was an extraordinary thought that soon she would lie beneath a totally nude Sebastian while he fused his flesh with hers.

It was less than forty-eight hours since they'd met. It felt like a lifetime!

As did the fifteen minutes since she'd agreed to give him her body to do with as he willed.

Oh, God, she thought despairingly. *What have I done?*

'What are you doing out here?'

She whirled to find Sebastian standing in the doorway, frowning at her.

'Have...have you finished?' she asked shakily. He'd offered to clear the table while she fled to the bathroom, instant nerves bringing on a sudden call of nature. She hadn't been able to bring herself to go to her bedroom and change into something more comfortable, as he'd suggested. Nothing was going to make her feel more comfortable at this moment.

'Yes,' he said, still eyeing her warily. 'The dishwasher is busily chugging away.'

'Thank you.' Jessica wrapped her arms around herself, feeling not cold but suddenly shy before him. Or was it ashamed? Did he think her cheap for having agreed to sex without love?

Probably, she accepted unhappily. That old double standard still applied, no matter how much women tried to change the status quo. A man who slept around without caring and commitment gained kudos from his mates, and was chased after by women for his prowess. He was a stud, whereas a woman of similar morals was a slut.

'I want you to know that I don't usually do things like this,' she said defensively, her arms still wrapped tightly around her.

He came forward and slowly but firmly unwound her arms before placing them around his neck. 'I can see that,' he said, sliding his arms around her then pulling her against him. 'It makes me want you all the more.'

He kissed her softly on her nose, then her cheek, then the corner of her mouth. Her lips were parted and quivering by the time he covered them with his own. There was no barrier to his tongue as it slid deep into her mouth.

Jessica linked her fingers behind Sebastian's neck and clung on like grim death lest she fall down, for her knees had suddenly gone to jelly and her head was spinning. His arms tightened around her, and she was dimly aware of her breasts pressed painfully against his chest.

Her main focus, however, was on that sensually probing tongue and how it was making her feel, what it was making her want. *Him,* inside her, not his tongue. Him, all over her. Him, and only him, for ever and ever.

She moaned a tortured denial at this crazy notion. Anyone would think she loved the man.

This isn't love, Jessica reminded herself brutally. *It's lust. Sebastian's a man of the world and he spelled it out to you earlier. You're enjoying sex without love, the same as men and wanton women have for centuries.*

Jessica shivered in his arms. Did that make her wanton? She certainly *felt* wanton under his plundering mouth and welded to his appallingly aroused body.

Vivid images flashed into her mind, starkly explicit and shockingly erotic. Sebastian, undressing her here, where they stood, touching her all over, taking her on this veranda, in the moonlight, her cries of ecstasy sounding shamefully loud in the stillness of the night.

'Jess,' he groaned thickly into her swollen lips.

'Mmmm?' The dazed murmur was all she could manage. She was still off in another world, a world where there was no shame, only the darkest and deepest of pleasures.

'You shouldn't have rubbed yourself against me like that,' he muttered. 'But no matter. It was probably all for the best. But I'll have to leave you for a minute or two.'

He was gone a full thirty seconds before she could assemble her jumbled brain enough to make sense of his words. When she realised what had happened, she groaned her embarrassment and spun round to grip the railing with a white-knuckled intensity.

Dear God, she hadn't even realised she *had* been rubbing against him. Though she accepted it must have been so. She'd been beside herself with longing for him.

Even now, with her fantasy fast fading, her heart was still pounding urgently within her chest. She wanted Sebastian back, with his mouth on hers again, and the hard warmth of his body enveloping hers.

As though her mind had conjured him up, he was suddenly there, his arms winding like steel bands around her chest from behind, pinning her upper arms to her sides.

'I was as quick as I could be,' he murmured as he nuzzled her neck, brushing cool lips across her burning skin. His arms were cool, as well, droplets of water on his fine body hair showing that he had showered during his brief desertion. 'I didn't want to waste all that lovely mad passion.'

Jessica only heard the word *mad*.

I must be, she thought dizzily. *Quite mad. He only has to touch me and I turn into a different woman. A stranger with totally alien responses and desires. Never before have I felt such abandon or excitement. He has totally bewitched me.*

'Tell me what you were thinking about earlier,' he murmured seductively. 'When I was kissing you.'

She shook her head, then gasped when his lips opened and closed on her neck, sucking at the already fevered skin till the sensations went from pleasure to pain.

'Stop,' she gasped, and wriggled against him.

It was then that she realised he was naked, totally, stunningly naked.

'Then tell me,' he insisted. 'I won't be shocked.'

Again, she shook her head, her eyes wide with the mental image of his nude body pressed up against hers.

'You were wanting me,' he whispered in her ear. 'Weren't you?'

'Yes,' she confessed with a shudder.

One of his arms released its hold to start stroking her throat, tipping her neck up and her head back against his shoulder with each upward caress. Her eyes squeezed shut when his hand moved down her throat, down to caress her cleavage, to tease and torment her as yet untouched breasts.

'*How* were you wanting me, Jess?' he demanded, his voice remaining soft and almost dreamlike. '*Where* were you wanting me?'

'Here,' she choked out, as though impelled to answer by his sheer willpower. 'Here,' she repeated, her voice becoming more dazed as his fingers continued to trace the curves of her bra.

'Here and now?'

'Yes,' she rasped.

'Tell me more. Tell me what I did in your mind.'

'You…you undressed me,' came her thickened words. 'And touched me.'

'Where?' His hand had slipped inside a bra cup, and one of his fingertips began gently rolling the rocklike nipple.

'E-everywhere.'

'And then what happened?' he asked, his voice amazingly calm, whereas hers, hers was trembling violently. 'Did I make love to you? Here, against the railing? As we're standing now?'

'Oh.' Her face flamed, along with her body.

'I see I did. And did I satisfy you in your mind?'

'Yes,' she groaned. Dear Lord, why didn't he stop making her talk about it? It was turning her on like crazy. His hand in her bra was turning her on like crazy. She felt like she was going to explode!

'How many times?'

She moaned her dismay. 'I...I don't know.'

'Has that ever happened to you before?'

She had to laugh.

His hand stilled on her breast. 'Are you saying you've never been satisfied by a man before?'

'Only...afterwards.'

'What about before?'

'Before?' Her tone echoed her bewilderment at the concept.

He removed his hand from her bra then, and slowly started to undo the buttons of her shirt while he kept her pinned against the railing, her back to him. Oddly, panic immediately assailed her, which was as confusing as it was disappointing. She hadn't felt panic in her fantasy. She had been all wild and willing abandonment.

But it seemed a fantasy was just that. A fantasy. Reality was not going to be as cooperative.

'No,' she said, her hands flying to cover his. 'I can't. Not out here.'

'Trust me, Jess,' he said, holding her hands still with one of his while he touched her with the other. His fingers moved with deceptive tenderness over her chest, reawakening her breasts through her clothes. Soon panic was the last thing on her mind. All she could think about was that warm, strong hand and where it was wandering. It moved up to stroke her throat and then her face, tracing her eyebrows and eyelids, her nose and finally her mouth.

She moaned as his fingers rubbed lightly over her lips. When they fell softly apart he inserted one of his fingers, and she found herself sucking on it, the mindless response echoing the fever pitch of arousal he'd brought her to, arousal that could no longer lay claim to conscience, or control, or command over what she was doing.

Her arms fell limply to her sides when he released them. She made no protest when he eased her away a little and finished undoing the buttons on her shirt. The thin white shirt was soon peeled back from her shoulders and discarded, along with her bra.

His hands on her bare breasts brought Jessica to some kind of awareness of what was going on, but by then she was so excited, so driven, she didn't care.

Maybe if he'd started being rough with her she might have snapped out of it. But he was all exquisite gentleness, his touch a tantalisingly tender torment. His hands cupped her breasts like they were spun gold, and he whispered to her his admiration of their beauty. He teased the nipples to an exquisite sensitivity, rotating his thumb pads over them in gentle circles, so unlike her previous lovers, who had been rough with her breasts in their impatience for their own pleasure, thereby giving her next to none.

There was such sweet magic in Sebastian's gentle hands as they adored her female shape. She moaned into the still night air under his soft caresses, groaning her dismay when he stopped.

But any dismay was quickly forgotten once he started

peeling her skirt and her undies down over her hips. Anticipation of what was to come held her spellbound as he pushed her clothes past her hips to fall to her feet.

'Oh,' she gasped when he wrapped one arm solidly around her waist and hoisted her off her feet so her panties fell from her ankles to the floor. He kept her aloft, bending his back—and hers—while his free hand smoothed down over her quiveringly tense stomach. She tensed when his fingers slid towards the damp curls between her legs, fearful that she would explode straight away if he even so much as touched her there. She'd never felt so excited in all her life.

And she didn't want to let go. Not yet. Please, not yet.

But he seemed to know exactly where to touch and where not to, to tease without giving her release. Closing her eyes, she leaned her head against his shoulder and wallowed in his expert foreplay. He balanced her on a razor's edge for what felt like ages before he abruptly changed tactics and touched her directly on that bursting bud of exquisite sensitivity.

'No!' she cried out. 'No, I...'

Too late. She was already splintering apart, her flesh contracting wildly. He lowered her swiftly, still gasping, onto decidedly unsteady feet, his hands steadying her around the hips while she grasped the railing for support. She knew what he was going to do—and oh, how she wanted him to do it! She was wanting him even more than she had before. Her legs moved restlessly apart, and she thrust backward as her desire searched to meet his.

She moaned as she felt him slide into her still throbbing body. She moaned again when her flesh gripped his with an intensity that was as foreign to her as it was fantastic. With a blind and suddenly wild urgency, she began rocking backwards and forwards.

'Oh!' she gasped, when astonishingly, she spilled into a second climax even more electric than the first, and far more satisfying. For she knew he'd be able to feel it and draw pleasure from it. She wanted him to feel pleasure in her, wanted him to join her.

Her back arched voluptuously and her bottom lifted to press hard against him, seeking to engulf him totally.

'God, Jess,' he muttered.

His hands moved from her hips, not so gentle now, grazing roughly over her painfully erect nipples as they swept down the front of her bowed body and up again. They roved hotly from breast to throat to her face again, in her mouth before stroking over her hair and down her back.

As she spun back down to earth, she began to sag beneath him, but he gripped her hard around her waist again, holding her up while he surged deeply into her.

Jessica was stunned when she slowly began to meet each powerful thrust, at first as though by some reluctant instinct, then more eagerly, till she was lost in sensation, lost to everything but the rhythm of his flesh within hers. She forgot time and place. Her eyes remained shut, and she was swirling in an erotic sea where pleasure didn't end. It just ebbed and flowed, not so intense now, but just as sweet.

At last she heard him cry out, felt him shudder within her. She sighed his name with a satisfaction as deep as it was dazed. Her legs went to jelly when he withdrew, and she might have collapsed if he hadn't swept her exhausted body into his arms.

'Sebastian,' she murmured again, looping her limp arms around his neck and pressing her face against the heavily beating pulse in his throat. She'd never felt so content, or so loved.

She was already half asleep when he placed her in the cool of his bed and pulled the sheet over her. But she knew she didn't want it to end yet, this feeling of oneness, of completion.

'Don't leave me,' she mumbled when his hands began to slide out from under her.

He climbed in beside her.

'Kiss me,' she whispered, her arms searching for his neck again.

He kissed her.

'Hold me.'

He held her and she sighed. He kept holding her and kissing her till she fell into a deep and dark oblivion.

Her last and very fleeting conscious thought was a stab of dismay that his loving attention was only an illusion. Sebastian didn't love her. He only lusted after her. Any attractive woman would have done. As he'd said, he'd been celibate too long....

Yet it was not of lust that Jessica dreamt in her sleep, but love. And it wasn't just any man loving her. It was Sebastian. They were married in her dream, married with a baby, married with many babies. There were babies all round her. Babies smiling. Babies gurgling. Babies. Babies. Babies.

CHAPTER TEN

JESSICA shot bolt upright in the bed, the word *babies* flying from her lips in a shocked gasp.

It took a couple of seconds for her eyes to focus in the darkened bedroom and see that the other side of the four-poster bed was empty.

A movement across the gloom beyond the bed drew Jessica's eyes to the large silhouette of a man filling the doorway that led to the moonlit veranda.

'Is that you, Sebastian?' came her panicky demand.

The figure came into the room, looming larger as it approached. 'Who else?' he drawled, and climbed into bed with her, giving Jessica a brief glimpse of a body as naked as her own. 'What is it? Bad dream wake you up?'

'In a way.' She lay back on the pillows and pulled the sheet modestly over her bare breasts, her embarrassment acute.

Talk about the morning after! Yet it was still the middle of the night.

She groaned when she thought of all she'd allowed and all she'd enjoyed. Then moaned when she thought of her dream.

'What's wrong?' he asked, levering himself on his elbow to stare at her.

Now that her eyes had grown accustomed to the light, she could see him quite clearly. His hair was no longer confined by the blue bandanna. It spilled in abandoned sensuality around his equally sensual face, bringing to mind all that he represented.

Nothing more than the pleasures of the flesh. There was no future with Sebastian. No hope of love, or commitment, or marriage. A baby by him would be a disaster! He might be the best lover in the world, but that would not make him a good father. He was thirty-eight years old, for pity's sake! If he'd wanted marriage and a family he would have had both by now.

'Sebastian,' she began, her voice betraying her panicky fear.

His brows drew together and he reached out to lay the most gentle hand on her cheek. 'What is it, Jess?'

'Did you...I mean...I couldn't tell...but did you... protect me?'

His hand fell from her cheek and his eyes grew cold. He dropped onto the pillows and linked his arms behind his head. 'Of course,' he said in a bored tone. 'Do you take me for a fool? But perhaps it was *me* I was protecting the most.'

His implication stung her to the quick. 'Come now, Sebastian. You might have been celibate lately, but Aunt Lucy wasn't always indisposed. And who's to say you were her first lover? She'd been a merry widow for some time, after all.'

He moved so fast she was flat on her back with her wrists pinned savagely to the bed before she could blink. 'Talk like that about Lucy again,' he said angrily, his mouth only an inch from hers, 'and I'll—I'll...'

His defence of her aunt's character sparked a dark resentment within Jessica. Plus a stabbing jealousy. Perhaps he'd really loved her Aunt Lucy, whereas all he felt for *her* was lust.

Well, at least he felt that, she thought wildly. At least

she could stir his senses…against his will, it seemed. He didn't like her but he'd wanted her, wanted her with a want that knew no pride. That was a heady thought, to have such power over a man.

Jessica savoured it, then acted on it. Without conscience or qualm.

Her tongue seemed to snake out of her mouth all by itself and sweep in an erotic circle around his lips.

'Or you'll what?' she taunted huskily, lifting her head to take his bottom lip between her teeth and nip it, not at all gently.

He wrenched his head back, releasing her so that he could wipe the back of his hand across his mouth. When he saw blood on his skin, he glared at her with a fierce gaze that made her tremble with a mixture of fear and excitement.

'You little bitch,' he snarled. 'I'll make you pay for that.'

'Promises, promises,' she returned, aware she was being provocative in the extreme but unable to stop herself. All she wanted was for him to want her again. She would do anything to achieve that end. Anything. 'Tell me what you like,' she said huskily, running her tongue over her slightly swollen and quite parched lips. 'Tell me, Sebastian, and I'll do it…'

He glared at her expectant and quivering flesh for a long moment, then abruptly rose from the bed and stalked out of the room, banging the door with shuddering force behind him.

Jessica lay there, wide-eyed and stunned. He wasn't going to make love to her ever again. That was how he was going to make her pay.

The thought brought despair to her heart, as well as her body. She could not bear to never again feel what she'd felt with him on that veranda. With a strangled sob, she leapt from the bed and went in search of him, vowing to say anything, do anything, to bring him back to bed with her. Her nakedness meant nothing to her as she ran from the room, calling to him.

She found him in the living room across the hallway, drinking a glassful of what looked like straight whisky. He hadn't turned on the light, but the large windows let in enough moonlight for her to see him quite clearly.

She gulped as her gaze abruptly encountered a full frontal view of his magnificent male body.

'So there you are,' she choked out from the doorway, and he slanted her a savage glance.

'Come to gloat, have you?'

'Gloat?'

He laughed and filled the glass anew from the whisky decanter on the sideboard. 'You played me for a sucker, Jess, and I, stupid fool that I was...I fell for it. Do you play these erotic games often? Does it turn you on to have each new lover think you've never been really satisfied before, thereby challenging them on to greater heights of passion? I should have known that a twenty-eight-year-old city girl who looks like you would have done it all by now.'

His tirade stopped just long enough for him to drain the glass with one long swallow.

'So what else turns you on?' he asked derisively as he whirled to fill the glass a third time, slopping some onto the lace runner. 'Believe me when I tell you I won't knock you back on any score. Let me get a bit more of this into myself and I'll be ripe and ready for anything. I just need to wipe that stupid idea from my head that what happened between us tonight was special.

'God, I must be going soft in the head! Maybe I *have*

been on Norfolk Island too long. I need a dose of Sydney and some of its poisonously promiscuous women to get me back on track. Fancy thinking I could mean something to you, when in reality I was just another one-night stand!'

'No!' she denied hotly, tears welling up in her eyes. 'That's not true. Nothing you've said is true. I do not have one-night stands, and you *are* special to me, Sebastian. I've never experienced anything like what I experienced with you tonight. Never! I don't know what got into me just then. You…you seem to have released something in me…something a little bit wild and wicked and yes, wanton. But it's only for you, Sebastian. Only for you…'

The tears were streaming down her face, dripping from her nose and running into her mouth. She had never felt as devastated as she had under his scorn. Or as despairing. His good opinion of her was suddenly more valued than his lovemaking.

'Please believe me, Sebastian,' she said, sobbing. 'I'm not what you think. I'm not.' Her head dropped into her hands and she wept floods of tears.

His hands curving gently over her shaking shoulders sent her sagging against him in relief and joy. 'You believe me,' she cried as she hugged him. 'You believe me…'

He said nothing, however, and his lack of confirmation finally sank in. Eventually, Jessica lifted her tear-stained but dry-eyed face to his. 'You *do* believe me, don't you, Sebastian?'

His expression was disturbingly implacable.

She pulled out of his arms. 'You *don't* believe me,' she said, rather dazed.

'Does it matter? Tonight was a mistake. You and

I...we are a mistake. It won't work. Believe me when I say what happened tonight won't happen again.'

'You don't mean that!'

'I'm trying to,' he said, hard blue eyes raking over her nude body with rueful regard.

She saw his vulnerability and took bold advantage of it, moving to wind her arms around his neck and press herself against him. 'I won't let you go,' she said with all her natural stubbornness and new-found sexuality.

He held himself stiffly in her clinging embrace, but she could feel the effect she was having on him.

'What is it that you want of me, Jess?' he asked. 'Spell it out. And don't lie. I need to know the truth.'

'I...I want you to be my lover while I'm here,' she said truthfully. To want more was fantasy land.

'And when the month is over? What then?'

'What do you mean?'

'Will you be able to walk away from me and never look back? Never think of me or want me ever again?'

'I...I...'

'Swear to me now that you definitely won't fall in love with me!' he demanded fiercely, his hand grabbing her upper arms, his fingers digging into her flesh. 'That all you want from me is sex.'

She tried to say it. Her mouth actually opened, but she knew in her heart it would be a terrible lie. She was already half in love with him already.

'No,' she blurted, agonised by what she was admitting. 'I...I can't swear to that.'

A great shuddering sigh rushed from his lungs, and his bruising fingers gentled on her flesh. 'That's all right, then,' he said, and before she could blink, he swept her into his arms and kissed her.

'I've had my fill of hard bitches, Jess,' he told her. 'If

I'm to have a woman in my bed for the next month, then I want it to be a real woman, with a real woman's heart and feelings. God, for a minute there I thought you were going to so swear, and where would that have left me?'

He laughed, a sound mixed with self-mocking and delight. 'With a whole month of torment, that's where! Now…now I can make love to you as I want to make love to you, with no holding back, no reservations. Beautiful Jess,' he murmured, kissing her still startled mouth. 'Lovely Jess.' He kissed her again. 'Exquisite Jess.' And yet again.

Jessica was speechless as he carried her to his bed and laid her gently down. 'Tell me what you like, Jess,' he whispered. 'Tell me and I'll do it.'

Oh, God, she thought, and, sliding her shaking hands into his hair, she drew him down, first to her mouth, then to her breast.

He did her silent bidding, suckling at her erect nipple as though he were a hungry infant, greedy and demanding. Waves of pleasure flooded Jessica, tossing her this way and that. She moaned when he slid down her body to kiss and lick her stomach, then lower. Her legs seemed to open of their own accord, offering herself up to his lips with such trust she could hardly recognise herself.

And he did not betray that trust, showing her ecstasies she'd never known before. What fools her other lovers had been. What ignorant fools.

'No more,' she said at last with limp happiness.

He merely laughed and gathered her to him again, showing her that she still had no judgment over when her pleasure was done. He smiled triumphantly when his powerful possession made her feel that pleasure again, smiled and told her she was the most sensual, most beautiful, most wonderful woman in the world.

Jessica had never felt so happy. Or so tired. Sighing, she closed her eyes and was asleep in no time. If she dreamt, her dreams did not disturb her this time. She slept on and on, through the night and past the dawn. She might have slept till noon…if it hadn't been for Evie arriving to make lunch.

CHAPTER ELEVEN

'YOOHOO! Where is everyone? Anyone home?'

Jessica was instantly awake, recognition of the female voice hitting her simultaneously with the lateness of the hour. She wasn't sure exactly what time it was, but the sun was well up.

'Oh, my God,' she groaned. 'Evie!'

Sebastian's hand on her arm stopped her flight from the bed. 'She might as well know, Jess. There's no keeping it from her.'

Jessica stared at him as though he were mad, shrugged his hand off her arm and scrambled out of the bed. 'Don't you dare say a word,' she hissed, her heart beating madly. 'If you do, I'll kill you!'

He chuckled. 'If you do, it'll be Norfolk Island's first accredited murder.'

'Sebastian, don't joke,' she cried, embarrassment making her stomach curl. She could only imagine what Evie would think if she saw her with Sebastian like this, after they'd seemingly not even *liked* each other yesterday. 'Oh, my God, I just remembered my clothes. Will Evie see me if I creep out of here and round the back to my room via the veranda?' she whispered in desperation.

'Not if you're a quick creeper. She's sure to go into the kitchen first and make a cuppa. The kitchen window faces the front.'

'Thank God,' Jessica said with a ragged sigh.

'Aren't you going to kiss me before you go?' Sebastian said, smiling his amusement at her agitation.

'Don't be silly. Oh, all right.' But when she bent her mouth to his, he grabbed her and pulled her on top of him. She tried to smother her squeals as he tickled her mercilessly but feared she was very noisy in her struggles to free herself.

'I'll get you later,' she threatened as she pushed her hair from her face and stumbled across the room to the open doors. A warm breeze was wafting in, making her acutely aware of her nakedness.

'Promises, promises,' he drawled after her in a sardonic echo of what she'd said to him the previous night.

She didn't stop to spar with him this time, peeping up and down the veranda before running as quietly as she could around the corner.

The sight of her abandoned clothes brought her up with a jolt. They looked so...so *abandoned*!

Closing her mind to the memories that flooded in, she snatched them up and bolted to her room, expecting any moment to hear Evie's shocked voice behind her. But she made it inside without any humiliating encounters.

Her perfectly made and unslept-in bed seemed to stare at her, looking pure and pristine with its white lace quilt. Would she ever use it again during the next month? she wondered.

Not if I can help it, came the wicked thought.

No, not wicked, she denied. Wonderful. Being made love to properly was wonderful! She didn't aim to spoil it with any thought of blame or shame. She didn't know what the future would bring with Sebastian but she aimed to enjoy every single moment she had with him.

Let tomorrow worry about tomorrow! she decided with a recklessness new to her. She usually had a prosaic and pragmatic way of looking at life. She'd always been a planner, and so damned practical. To hell with that for the next month! To hell with everything except Sebastian.

Jessica carried a silly, fatuous smile into the shower with her. She was still carrying it when she made it to the kitchen some twenty minutes later.

'Well, if it isn't Miss Sleepyhead!' Evie said brightly from where she was chopping up vegetables at the sink. 'Sebastian told me he'd let you sleep in. He said he kept you up playing games till the wee small hours and that you were a bit wrecked. I had no idea you liked games. Lucy was quite an addict, too. Which one's your favourite?'

Jessica's whirling mind finally ground to a halt. She was going to kill Sebastian when she got him alone…amongst other things. 'Oh, I like them all,' she said swiftly, and tried desperately not to blush.

'That's good. It'll give you and Sebastian something to do in the evenings while you're here. You must be bored without a television. I must say your sleep-in seems to have done you good,' Evie rattled on. 'You look positively glowing this morning. Bright blue suits you, doesn't it?'

'What?' she said, distracted by her thoughts of the coming evenings. Boredom would no longer come into it, of that she was sure! 'Oh, yes. Blue. I suppose so, but I think blue looks good on just about anyone, don't you?'

Actually, she'd dragged on the blue shorts and matching singlet without much thought except for the heat. It was much warmer than it had been the previous day, the sun shining brightly. Her face was scrubbed free of makeup, and her hair was scooped up in a ponytail. She was a far cry from the sleek sophisticated number who'd stepped off the plane on Sunday, but she felt much more alive and incredibly relaxed.

'If you'd like a cuppa, I haven't long made a pot,' Evie offered. 'It should still be hot. You don't mind getting it yourself, do you?'

'Not at all,' Jessica said. She began humming as she did so.

'Pour Sebastian a mugful at the same time, will you?' Evie asked. 'He says he has a bit of a hangover this morning and hasn't been able to stomach any breakfast as yet. And I don't wonder why,' she added dryly. 'The whisky decanter's only half-full, I noticed. He said he had a touch of insomnia. Not that the drink seems to have done much good. You should have seen his bed. He must have tossed and turned all night. It was a right mess, with pillows on the floor and all.'

Jessica thought she did well not to look guilty, though she was relieved Evie's observations carried no noticeable insinuations. 'Insomnia's an awful thing,' she commented lightly as she poured the tea.

'I'll say,' Evie agreed. 'I'm making a simple grilled steak and salad for lunch, since Sebastian's stomach is feeling a bit fragile. Is that all right?'

'Perfect. I'll just take this tea along to him. Is he in his room?'

'Should be by now. He did pop along to the other bathroom for a shower and shave while you were showering. But I dare say he's back at his desk by now, writing away, trying to meet his deadline.'

He wasn't writing. He was standing on the veranda outside his room, dressed in nothing but shorts again.

Jessica swallowed as she walked through to join him, telling herself she would soon get used to his going around half-naked. Surely, she would not always look at him and feel an emptiness yawn in the pit of her stomach. Maybe, after he'd made love to her for a week or two, the intensity of her feelings would wear off.

'Here's the tea you wanted,' she said, smiling at him as she handed him the mug. She was glad that she'd thought to bring her own mug with her. It gave her an excuse to stay.

He gave her a strangely thoughtful look over the rim of the mug as he lifted it to his lips.

'What?' she asked.

'What what?'

'What are you thinking, silly?'

'That I'm going to be wicked and play hooky from my writing today.'

'Oh?' She was thrilled but tried not to show it. 'What happened to the hangover?'

'It's still there, hovering. But I can endure it provided I don't do any mental work. Not that I could. My creative ability seems to have still flown the coop. Actually, I'm feeling awfully basic this morning.'

'Hangovers *are* basic things,' she said.

'I wasn't thinking of the hangover,' he said dryly as his eyes washed over her. 'You could have worn a bra, Jess. What are you trying to do to me?'

She had to laugh. 'That's the pot calling the kettle black.'

'What on earth are you talking about?'

'Do you have any idea what *you* do to *me*, going around half-naked all the time? What you've done to me from the first moment I saw you?'

His eyebrows lifted, his expression going from surprise to a pleased speculation. 'No. What do I do?'

'You put indecent thoughts into my head.' And her eyes drifted over his bare chest and past his navel.

He groaned. 'God, don't look like at me like that, woman. It puts thoughts into places other than my head, and I'm just not capable of making love at the moment. Give me an hour or two.'

'Poor Sebastian.' She ran a teasing finger down the middle of his bare chest.

'I might have to have a little rest after lunch. Care to stroke my brow for me? And any other parts you fancy?'

'Only if I can brush your hair, as well.'

He seemed taken aback. 'Brush my hair? Why, is it that messy?' One hand reached up to rake through its tangled glory with an elegantly nonchalant grace.

'No,' she said. 'I just like the thought of brushing it.'

'Whatever you like.' He shrugged.

I'd like a lot of things, she thought as she looked at him and sipped her tea. *I'd like to touch you all over, kiss you all over. I'd like to massage sweet scented oils into your beautiful body and hear you groan with desire. I'd like to take you with me into the abyss you took me to last night, make you tremble and cry out with mindless joy.*

'Evie's making steak and salad for lunch,' she said, for all the world like lunch was the only thing on her mind.

He moaned. 'I can't think of food.'

'Don't think of it. Just eat it.'

He slanted her another of those thoughtful looks. 'You like giving orders, don't you?'

'No, but I'm disgustingly sensible.' *Most of the time,* she thought. 'Besides, someone has to give orders or nothing gets done.'

'Why should anything *have* to get done?' he said with a flash of irritation.

'Now don't start that with me, Sebastian. It won't

wash. You imagine you're a free spirit with your life here, but you still discipline yourself to write your book most days because if you don't, it won't get done.'

'That's different.'

'Why?'

'Because it's what I choose to do. No one orders me to do it.'

'How fortunate for you. Cast your mind back to when you were dirt poor and you'll find you didn't have that option. You had to work to live, and working usually involved someone giving and taking orders.'

'That's a smart mouth you have, Jess. Frankly, I'd prefer you to use it for other things than making me feel a fool.'

Her face flamed at the image of what he'd implied. He stared at her.

'Don't tell me you've never done that, either. That's stretching credulity too far.'

She looked away from his sceptical face, out at the view. 'Believe what you like,' she said, a painful constriction around her chest.

'Hey, don't get upset with me. I do believe you. Honest. It's just difficult getting used to your being so different to what I first thought.' He reached out to touch her face, stroking her cheek while everything inside her melted with longing for him. 'Not that I mind. I like the Jess I'm discovering.' The back of his hand grazed across her mouth. 'Such sexy lips, yet so innocent…'

They didn't feel at all innocent at that moment. They burnt to do all that his words evoked in her mind. Her eyes met his and she knew he saw her utter willingness to do anything for him. Sexually, anyway.

'Have you changed your mind yet?' he murmured, his hand drifting down to stroke her jawline.

'About what?' she asked, even though she knew what he was asking.

'About selling this place. I'll look after it free of charge…if it will keep you coming back to me.'

Despite her deciding earlier to throw caution to the winds, Jessica hesitated. 'No…I haven't changed my mind,' she said carefully. 'Look, let's not talk about that just now. If we do, we'll only end up arguing again, and I don't want to argue this morning.'

He snorted, then swept his mug of tea around in a panoramic wave. 'How can you possibly prefer the city to this?' he demanded.

Jessica looked at the deep valley, and while she saw its beauty and splendour, it was still just a view. See it every morning and you'd soon get used to it. 'It's very lovely,' she said. 'And I do appreciate it. It's very peaceful and relaxing.'

'Meaning it's a nice place to visit but you wouldn't want to live here,' he scoffed.

'I am not going to let you provoke me this morning, Sebastian. I'm too happy.'

He scowled for a moment, then smiled. It was a very sexy smile. 'What are you going to let me do, then?'

'Nothing you're not capable of, that's for sure,' she said, her eyes dancing with mischief as she lifted her mug of tea to her lips.

He took the mug out of her hands, balanced it with his on the top of the railing then drew her into his arms.

'I think this should wait till Evie leaves after lunch,' she said firmly. 'Much as *you* don't care if she finds out about us, I do!'

'Tough.' His kiss was as uncompromising as his attitude towards keeping their affair a secret.

'I thought you said you weren't capable,' she mocked

softly when his mouth finally lifted. There was nothing remotely incapable about what was pressing with undisguised urgency against her stomach.

He cupped the back of her head and kissed her again, quite savagely, his lips bruising as they reduced her supposed willpower to pulp. 'Now you know,' he muttered into her gasping lips.

She stared into wildly glittering blue eyes.

'Know what?' she whispered shakily.

'That I'm a liar.'

For a split second she didn't know what to think. There was something quite frightening in the way he was looking at her. But then he laughed, whirled her round and pushed her off with a smack on the bottom. 'Get thee behind me, Satan.'

Still slightly disoriented, she stopped and glanced over her shoulder at him, aware that she was suddenly holding her breath. But he was smiling at her so sweetly that her earlier momentary qualm seemed ridiculous. What possible reason would he have for lying to her? It wasn't as though he'd declared undying love, or proposed marriage, or anything like that. They were just having an affair. If Jessica secretly hoped for more than that, then it was her own silly female fault!

No, she had to stop hoping for too much and do what she'd vowed to do last night. Enjoy each moment for what it was and leave the future to fate.

With a surge of devil-may-care mischief, she whirled and walked towards Sebastian, enjoying the surprised flaring in his nostrils and eyes as she drew right up to him, her arms seemingly going round him in a tender embrace. When she drew back, laughing, with the empty mugs in her hand, his eyes narrowed and he pouted at her.

'I'm really going to make you pay for that one,' he warned darkly.

'Ooh. I'm petrified.'

'So you should be.'

'Before my punishment begins, would you be able to run me down to the shops again? I really must do my toenails this afternoon.'

'Let me guess. You bought the wrong colour nail polish?'

'No, I forgot the cotton wool balls. You have to separate your toes with cotton wool balls so that you don't smudge the polish.'

'How come I didn't think of that?' he scoffed.

'Because you're not a woman. As I said, I'm not going to bite today, Sebastian. Now, if you'd like to put a shirt on, we could get this little emergency fixed up before Evie serves lunch.'

'You're giving orders again.'

'You can punish me for it later,' she countered blithely, and swanned off to the kitchen before he could accuse her of wanting her bottom smacked, or some such other kinky thing.

'Sebastian's driving me down to the shops, Evie. We won't be long.'

'Better not be. Lunch in half an hour. Then I have to dash off. Monday's my craft afternoon. And I won't be back till five-thirty. What do you think you'll do all afternoon? You can bet Sebastian will get back to his book once he's got some food in his stomach.'

Jessica was amazed at her artfully nonchalant shrug. 'Oh, I don't know. I'm sure I'll find something to occupy my mind....'

CHAPTER TWELVE

'YOU two seem in bright spirits tonight,' Evie said as she served the evening meal.

Jessica swiftly forked some of the mouth-watering beef casserole into her mouth in an effort to hide her guilt from Evie. Though guilt was a bad word. She didn't believe she'd done anything *wrong* in spending all afternoon in bed with Sebastian. It had been a wonderful few hours, full of tenderness and pleasure, passion and fun.

Yes, fun!

Jessica smiled when she thought of Sebastian painting her toenails for her after she'd brushed his hair at length, then given him a long, deliciously sensual massage to get rid of the last vestiges of his hangover. He'd done an excellent job on her nails after a few practice runs, and while she'd giggled over his mistakes, it had been a surprisingly sensual experience, having a man paint her toenails.

Perhaps it had something to do with having him sit between her legs as she lay on the bed in spread-eagled nudity. Or the way his fingers kept brushing over the highly sensitive soles of her feet. By the time he'd finished, it had been hard to keep her bottom half still for five minutes while the polish dried. She'd wanted him so badly that she'd been easily seduced into accommodating him in more imaginative ways.

She'd never dreamt that her breasts could be used in

such a way. She couldn't claim to such an innocent mouth any more, either.

'Jess and I are great mates now, aren't we?' Sebastian said naughtily. 'I decided, in the end, to abandon my book for the day and do the right thing by our guest.'

'And high time, too, Sebastian. So, where did you take her? You had a lot to choose from since you only managed Kingston and Emily Bay yesterday.'

'Places the like of which she'd never been before.'

Jessica wanted to strangle him as an embarrassed heat started creeping up her neck and into her face.

'Well, of course she'd never been there before, you crazy man,' Evie pointed out impatiently. 'She's never been to Norfolk Island before, have you, Jessica?'

'No,' was all she could manage, averting her burning face while she picked up and ripped her bread roll asunder. She'd have liked to stuff it all into that mischievous mortifying mouth of his!

'Did you take her to Anson Bay?' Evie asked Sebastian.

'Not yet.'

'The top of Mount Pitt?'

'No.'

'Cascade Bay?'

'No.'

'Then where on earth *did* you take her?'

'I wanted to go to Kingston again,' Jessica lied in desperation to stop Evie jumping to the right conclusion. 'And I did some more shopping. Those duty-free prices are so tempting.'

'I promise I'll give her a more in-depth tour tomorrow, Evie.' Sebastian's glittering blue eyes were full of wicked promise as they locked onto Jessica's across the table. Dear God, just how more in-depth could her sexual education become!

She knew her cheeks had to be a fiery red by now, and this time, Evie noticed. Her eyes went from Jessica's face to Sebastian's before a decidedly wry smile appeared.

'I'm so glad to see you're getting along better than you were yesterday,' she said with deliberate understatement. 'Your Aunt Lucy would be pleased, I'm sure,' she said to Jessica.

Jessica bit her bottom lip as she realised she'd almost forgotten about Aunt Lucy, not to mention all those questions she'd been so eager to find answers to yesterday. Being in bed with Sebastian all afternoon had wiped everything from her mind but the present.

Now that she was reminded, her thoughts turned to her mother once more, and the mystery of her flight from her family and Norfolk Island.

'Speaking of Aunt Lucy, there's something I've been meaning to ask the both of you,' she said to Evie and Sebastian. 'Aunt Lucy must have left some personal papers and effects behind. Letters, photo albums and the like.'

Jessica frowned as she realised there were no photos around the house at all, either on the walls or sitting on shelves, which was unusual. 'Have they been packed away? I'd really like to look through them. There might be some clue to…you know…'

'There's a small boxful in the bottom of her wardrobe,' Sebastian said abruptly. 'She did throw quite a lot of things away when she knew she was dying, but you might find something in what's left. I doubt it, though.'

'Why's that?'

'I went through everything myself when I was looking

for her will. There's nothing relating to the falling-out Lucy had with your mother. Still, there are some photos you'd probably like to look at. I didn't think to give them to you. I'm sorry. It was remiss of me.'

She shook her head, knowing the blame was hers. 'I should have asked for them earlier. I don't know where my brains were.'

'There's no harm done,' Evie said kindly. 'You can look through them as soon as you've finished your tea.'

'I'll do that.' Already she was looking forward to doing so, hoping there might be something, *anything* to fill in those missing pieces.

'Don't go getting your hopes up,' Sebastian warned as soon as Evie left the room.

'I might see something you didn't,' she told him. 'A woman has a different perspective to a man.'

'True. Just don't go imagining things.'

'Such as what?'

He shrugged. 'God knows. Women have a capacity for complication and melodrama. They see problems where there are none. If there's only one simple and obvious answer to a question, they will still look for another. Alternatively, they would rather lie, to themselves and others, than accept an answer that is unpalatable to them.'

'I'm not like that. I'm a very clear and direct thinker. And I don't lie.'

'Want to put that to the test?'

'If you like.'

'How many lovers have you had before me?'

'Three.'

He was startled, but pleased. 'Three idiots, from what I can tell. You're well rid of them.'

'I fully agree, Sebastian. I much prefer you in my bed.'

'I hope you remember that when the end of the month comes.'

'I hope you do, too.'

His eyes narrowed on her. 'You think I'm going to come after you, don't you? I won't, you know. But I do want you, Jess. And not for just a miserable month. So be warned. When I want something I can be totally conscienceless.'

'I've been known to be pretty ruthless myself,' she countered blithely. 'So I suggest you reconsider your thoughts about living in Sydney, or at least visiting it more often.'

His eyes darkened to slate. 'God, but you're one stubborn woman!'

'So I've been told.'

'I won't play fair, you know.'

'This isn't a game, Sebastian. I don't play games with my life.'

'No. You're quite right. It's no game. It's deadly serious. You remember that.'

He glared at her, and she glimpsed a Sebastian she hadn't seen before. A ruthlessly determined Sebastian. The same Sebastian who'd once held a high-pressure job where only the bold and the brave survived for long.

Jessica quivered with a weird mixture of sexual arousal and fear. For she knew he meant to use her newly discovered sensuality against her. Use it quite mercilessly.

There was excitement in that idea. She would be a liar to deny it. He was so skilled at the art of lovemaking. And so much more experienced than she was. He could certainly take her to places where she'd never been before. Dark, alluring places.

But maybe some of them were places she should not

go. Surely there had to be danger in being so turned on that she lost all control!

'You…you wouldn't ever hurt me, would you, Sebastian?' she asked a little shakily.

Shock sent his eyes rounding. 'Good Lord, no! What did you think I was talking about?'

'I'm not sure. What were you talking about?'

'I only meant that I was going to be so damned impossibly good to you in every way that you would not be able to bear to leave me.'

Her heart flipped right over at his impassioned words, and she looked at her plate. Dear God, but she was in trouble here. Deep, deep trouble.

If she didn't watch it, she would end up doing what he wanted. Blindly. Mindlessly.

She could see herself not selling this house, not leaving Norfolk Island at the end of the month. She might even give up her career and her life in Sydney to stay here with him. Yet she knew in her heart it wouldn't work. It couldn't. He didn't love her. Besides, she didn't want to live here. Not forever.

'Say something, Jess,' he said, and she looked at him.

'What would you like me to say?'

'Tell me you want me as much as I want you.'

'You know I do,' she whispered huskily.

'You wouldn't lie, would you?'

'No.'

He smiled then, a smile that stirred her heart as no man's smile had ever done before.

Jessica knew then. Her feelings for Sebastian were no longer just lust. She was in love with him.

Oh, no…

She dropped her eyes and went back to eating her meal.

CHAPTER THIRTEEN

'YOU were right,' she said, looking up with a sigh from the shoe box. 'There's nothing. Not a mention of my mother. Not even an old photograph of her.'

Jessica was sitting cross-legged on Sebastian's bed while he was at his desk. He'd been writing while she sorted through everything.

He swivelled in his chair to face her. 'I did try to tell you, Jess,' he said gently. 'But seeing is believing.'

Jessica frowned. 'She must have burnt a lot of things. There's not much here. The only things I would want to even keep are these photographs of my grandparents, and Aunt Lucy as a child. Oh, and I suppose I can't throw out the one of her wedding. I must say that husband of hers was a very good-looking man. He could have been a movie star. I can see why she was besotted with him.'

'Handsome is as handsome does,' Sebastian said brusquely. 'He was a bastard.'

'I'm not saying he wasn't. I'm simply saying he was a looker. Tell me, Sebastian, do you know anything at all about his background or family?'

'No. Neither did Lucy, from what I can gather. He jumped ship onto the island when he was a young man, got a job on a fishing boat and married Lucy within a few short months. I might be cynical, but in view of what Lucy found out about him just before she died, I dare say he married her to ensure he could never be tossed off the island, not because he loved her. It's the surest and quickest way of making one's stay here permanent, by marrying an islander. You *can* earn permanent status by buying a business and working it for five years, but a man like Bill Hardcourt liked things quick and easy, I reckon.'

'Who was it that told Aunt Lucy about her husband being unfaithful?' Jessica asked.

'The doctor who diagnosed her cancer. Apparently, he'd known Lucy for eons. They were having a long heart-to-heart when he blurted that he'd always felt guilty about Lucy believing she was sterile, when he suspected her husband had had a vasectomy. It seems that shortly after Bill had been killed, the doc heard that Bill had been drinking heavily one night some years before and boasted that he'd had himself fixed up so he could tomcat around without consequences. He muttered something about having knocked up one girl too many.

'The doc remembered that round the time Lucy was engaged to Bill, he had a young girl patient who refused to name the father of her unborn baby because he was an engaged man and she didn't want to cause any trouble. She subsequently went to the mainland to have an abortion and never returned. Since Bill was dead by the time the doc worked all this out, he never said anything to Lucy. But it had played on his mind ever since.'

Sebastian scowled with displeasure at the story he'd just related. 'Personally, I think the old fool should have kept his stupid mouth shut. He eased *his* conscience whilst destroying Lucy's peace of mind.'

Jessica agreed with him. 'You're right, Sebastian. He shouldn't have told her. It must have been soul-destroying for Aunt Lucy, finding out the man she'd loved all these years was nothing but a low-down rat, and a filthy liar, to boot.'

'There again,' Sebastian sighed, 'I think down deep Lucy might have suspected the truth, but refused to believe it till confronted with evidence from someone she trusted and had faith in.'

'Yes, she must have heard rumours about her husband, living in a small community like this.'

'Evie said everyone knew about Bill's womanising. It's even said that he didn't fall overboard by accident, either. The man who owned the fishing boat had a pretty young wife.'

'Serve him right!'

'I couldn't agree more,' Sebastian said tersely. 'There's nothing worse than unfaithful husbands. And wives,' he added bitterly.

Jessica wasn't really listening to him, her thoughts on another tangent. Suddenly, her head jerked up, excitement coursing through her. 'That's it, Sebastian! That's it!'

'What's it?'

'That young girl. The one who became pregnant just before Lucy married that creep. I'll bet my mother found out about it and told Lucy, only Lucy wouldn't believe her. No doubt Bill made up a pack of lies to defend himself. He probably called my mother a troublemaker and a liar. Maybe he even made Lucy choose between him and his sister.'

Jessica was bouncing up and down on the bed with excitement at finding a logical solution to the puzzle. 'Well, what do you think?' she asked eagerly. 'Do you think I could be right?'

Sebastian was irritatingly unenthusiastic. 'You could be, I suppose.'

'You think I'm being melodramatic, don't you?'

'Lord, no,' he said dryly. 'I'm sure another woman could have come up with a much more torrid story.'

Jessica sighed with satisfaction. 'Oh, I feel so much better now. I just *know* that's how it happened. Evie told me she saw my mother and that disgusting Bill person arguing on the side of the road one day. My mother even pushed him over. That was very brave of her to do that, wasn't it? He was a big man.'

'Very brave.'

'What a shame Lucy didn't believe her.'

'It's difficult to believe badly of someone you genuinely love and trust.'

'I suppose so,' she said thoughtfully, before flashing Sebastian a speculative look. 'You're not trying to tell me something, are you? You're not a serial killer, or an international jewel thief, or an embezzler?'

'Not quite.'

'But there's something, isn't there? What haven't you told me, Sebastian?'

'Where would you like me to start?' he said ruefully.

'Wherever you'd like to start. I want to know everything about you.'

'Everything?'

'Yes, everything.'

His eyes went a cold steely blue. 'In that case, I suppose you'll want to know about my marriage.'

Jessica gaped at him. In all this time, this was one thing that had never occurred to her. Sebastian married! Oh, God, this was much worse than his perhaps having slept with Aunt Lucy. Much, much worse!

'Plus my divorce,' he added, and she almost burst into tears with relief.

But then another thought struck and she groaned.

'Don't tell me you've got children!'

He laughed. But it was not a happy sound. 'I thank God every day that Sandra refused to have any. She was waiting, supposedly, for me to make us both financially secure before she took such a big step as ruining her figure for a family.'

Suddenly, Jessica saw his very real pain and was moved by it. Her heart went out to him, and she wanted to touch him and comfort him. She put aside the shoe box and climbed from the bed, coming over to settle in his lap and wind her arms around his neck. 'She hurt you a lot, didn't she?' she said with soft sympathy.

'You could say that.'

'Was she very beautiful?'

'On the surface. It blinded me to her very ugly soul.'

'What did she do, Sebastian? Tell me.'

'I don't like talking about it.'

'But you must.'

He sighed and hugged her close. 'Yes, you're right. I must. Lucy always said she would not be erased properly from my mind till I talked her out of my system.'

'Did you talk to Lucy about her?'

'Not in great detail. She knew I'd been married at one time. And that it ended unhappily. That's all.'

Jessica couldn't help being pleased that Sebastian had left this confidence for her and her alone. 'Was your wife unfaithful?' she asked gently.

'Continuously.'

Jessica could hardly believe it. If she were married to Sebastian she would never ever even *look* at another man. 'But why didn't you leave her? Why did you put up with it?'

'Because I had no idea at the time. You know the adage. Love is blind. I only found out when she made the mistake of picking up someone who worked in the bank I was employed in. She'd met him in a bar and given him a false name to cover her tracks. She had no idea, of course, that this Casanova had a hidden video camera in his apartment. He brought some still shots in to work and was passing them round to his mates. When a close colleague of mine recognised the naked brunette who was being imaginatively serviced on a coffee table, he had the decency to take me quietly aside and tell me the situation. I was very grateful to him.'

'Oh, Sebastian, how appalling for you! What did you do?' Jessica asked.

'What did I do? I changed jobs and divorced my wife.'

'You're not telling the full story. Give me all the gruesome details.'

'Okay, so I punched Casanova's lights out, got fired, went home, packed my things, took a taxi to the advertising agency where Sandra worked, shoved the incriminating photo in her beautiful face and asked her why.'

Jessica wanted to know why, too.

'And do you know what she said?' Sebastian asked scornfully. 'She claimed it was all *my* fault, that I'd neglected her. She'd been bored, staying home so many evenings by herself while I worked late. Might I mention I was only working so bloody hard to give her everything she wanted. Sandra liked the good things in life. When I caustically asked her how long she'd been bored, she confessed since about a year after we were married.

'She assured me she hadn't been having affairs, only one-night stands. She imagined for some reason that that made a difference. She actually told me she still loved me.'

Jessica could not begin to appreciate the shock or the hurt Sebastian had suffered.

'That night I moved to Sydney, took the first of several medical tests, got myself a better job, worked my butt off, made pots of money, then, after a year of clear tests, started seducing every woman who so much as smiled at me. Believe me when I tell you it didn't take much to get them into bed.'

She believed him.

'What happened to all the money you made?'

'What?' he snapped, his body still tense with remembered distress.

'How come you lost your fortune?'

'I don't want to talk about money, Jess.'

'All right, then why did you decide to come to Norfolk Island?'

'I woke up one day and didn't like what I saw in the mirror.'

'What did you see?'

'A burnt-out wreck of a man who hated himself and everything around him. It felt like the air was crowding in on me, suffocating me. I had to get away somewhere I could breathe. So I drove to the airport and took the first small island destination that had a spare seat. The plane came here. I was a lucky man.'

'You're certainly not a burnt-out wreck any more, either,' she soothed, cupping his face and pressing feather-light kisses on each temple, his forehead, his eyelids. She drew back, and his eyelids fluttered open.

'What?' he asked, instinctively knowing there was something she wanted to ask him.

'I must know, Sebastian. Don't be angry with me. Did you sleep with my Aunt Lucy?' And she held her breath.

'Never,' he said firmly, and all the breath raced from her lungs. 'I told you…our relationship was a platonic one. I hadn't slept with a woman since I came to this island, till you came along.'

Jessica could hardly believe how wonderful that news made her feel. She'd thought she'd come to terms with his having slept with her aunt. But now she knew she hadn't. Not for a moment.

He cupped her face firmly between his hands and looked deep into her eyes. 'I love you, Jess. Surely you must know that by now.'

She found she could not speak, so great was her joy, so full her heart.

'I fell in love with you at first sight,' he went on thickly. 'I was furious with myself, of course. And with you. Because I feared you were another Sandra. By the time I realised my mistake I'd alienated you entirely. You've no idea how I felt that night when you took me up on my totally desperate offer. I made up my mind then and there that I was going to make love to you as no man had ever made love to you before. I thought, I'll *show* her how much I love her. I'll win her with the power of my desire, blind her with passion, seduce her with sex.'

'And you did, my darling. You did. I'm hopelessly, blindly, madly in love with you.'

She started kissing him all over his face, gently at first and then more passionately. When she finally kissed him on the mouth, he grabbed her and kissed her with a hunger that was as explosive as it was needy. He rose and carried her to the bed, drawing her down with him and making love to her with a savagery both primitive and satisfyingly simple. She held him for a long time afterwards, held him and stroked him and loved him till he fell asleep in her arms.

CHAPTER FOURTEEN

'ARE you going to do some writing this afternoon?' Jessica asked Sebastian as they washed up after lunch the following day. She'd spent most of the morning trying to clean the house while Sebastian made a total nuisance of himself, touching her all the time. And kissing her. And finally seducing her on the dining-room table. She'd just managed to drag her shorts on before Evie had arrived to make lunch.

He sighed with disgruntlement over the idea. 'I suppose I'd better. Do you mind?'

'Not at all. I've got some gardening to do.'

His eyebrows arched and she smiled. 'Yes, Mr. Smartypants, I discovered the other day that I do enjoy gardening. Now say I told you so and get it over with.'

He grinned. 'I told you so.'

'Don't get cocky. This still doesn't mean I'm not going to sell this place at the end of the month.'

His smile was distinctly smug. 'Wanna bet on that?'

Jessica laughed as she wiped her hands on the tea towel Sebastian was holding, then went outside to start weeding the garden beds. If she wasn't going to sell the place—and it seemed a likely possibility at this stage—she might as well keep it looking shipshape. Not that she was going to tell *him* that. Yet.

She was kneeling on the grass, about to attack the bed

near the front steps, when long brown legs suddenly appeared beside her.

'Hello,' the owner of the legs said when Jessica stood up, weeding fork in hand. 'You must be Lucy's long-lost niece. I'm Myra. I used to do the laundry for Lucy when she was running the place as a guesthouse. I was wondering, since you've hired Evie back to do the cooking, if you might want me to do your washing and ironing while you're here.'

Jessica looked Myra up and down with interest, her thoughts turning automatically to Sebastian.

The girl was about nineteen, very attractive, with a sultry mouth, a shapely figure and long straight honey-brown hair. A temptation, Jessica conceded, for any man, let alone a supposedly celibate one.

'I'm sorry,' she began, trying to be polite despite that automatic niggle of jealousy and suspicion. 'But I don't have that much washing and ironing. Not enough to hire someone.'

'But it's not just you, is it?' Myra countered, that sultry mouth turning slightly sulky. 'Sebastian's still living here, isn't he?'

'Yes, but he looks after himself pretty well.'

'Really? He never did when Lucy was alive. She waited on him hand and foot. Not that it did her any good,' the girl said, sneering. 'A man like that wasn't going to marry an old bird like her, no matter how much money she had. If Sebastian marries anyone on Norfolk Island,' she added, tossing her hair over her shoulder, 'it'll be someone young and pretty.'

Jessica found herself on the end of a sharp look.

'You're not staying long, are you?' Myra said. 'Word is you're going to sell and go back to Sydney.'

'I might,' Jessica said slowly. 'And I might not.'

The girl's eyes narrowed. They were not her best feature, her eyes, and narrowed, they looked sly. 'Is Sebastian in? I'd like to speak to him.'

'He's busy writing,' Jessica said firmly, 'and doesn't like to be disturbed. Can I give him a message perhaps?'

'He still writing that silly book of his? I thought he'd stop that once Lucy passed on. I reckon he only did it because it got him in good with her. He did lots of things to get in good with her, from what I could see. Not that it worked. She didn't leave him anything in her will, did she? Looks like he might have to get himself a real job now. Either that, or latch onto another rich woman quick smart.'

'I think you'd better go, don't you, Myra?' Jessica said coldly. 'You know, it's not a good idea to go around maligning people. You might find yourself in trouble one day.'

'I'm not maligning anyone,' the girl denied with a childish pout. 'I'm just saying it as it is. I suppose Sebastian claims he *wasn't* sleeping with your aunt. But he was. I know that for a fact. I'd watch yourself around him if I were you. You're much better-looking than your aunt.'

'I'll have you know,' Jessica said icily while trying to keep her temper, 'that Sebastian was *not* sleeping with my aunt, and if I hear you've spread this malicious gossip around the island, I am going to sue you for slander!'

'I don't need to spread what is already common knowledge. Everyone knows what went on here. If you're fool enough to be taken in by Sebastian's lies, then you're a bigger mug than your aunt. Just remember what I said when he professes love and asks you to marry him. It wouldn't be the first time a mainlander married an islander for reasons other than love.'

A few days ago, Jessica might have believed the girl's accusations, but now that she knew the man, she thought them quite ridiculous.

'If all Sebastian wanted was a marriage certificate to an islander, he'd have no trouble with silly little girls like you around,' Jessica pointed out crossly. 'Now go away and stop being a mischief-maker. I have better things to do than listen to jealous gossip.'

The girl huffed and puffed for a few seconds, then whirled on her bare feet and stalked off, her long hair blowing angrily behind her.

Jessica was standing there, staring after her disappearing figure, when Sebastian walked down the front steps.

'What did Myra want?' he asked.

'Her old job back,' Jessica told him.

He slanted her a horrified look. 'You didn't hire her, did you?'

'No.'

'Thank God. She's sex-mad,' he said. 'She made it perfectly obvious I could have her any time I wanted. No matter how rude I was to her she just didn't get the message. I was glad when Lucy closed the guesthouse after Christmas and Evie could get rid of her.'

'She said some pretty nice things about you, too.'

Sebastian laughed. 'I can imagine. Nothing worse than a woman scorned.'

'She suggested you might be out to marry me for reasons other than true love.'

'Did she now? And did you believe her?'

'No.'

'Why not?'

'Because it wasn't you.'

'Wasn't me,' he repeated, shaking his head in amusement.

'I figured if you'd wanted to marry an islander to wangle permanent status, or for tax reasons, you'd have done so by now. Myra would have been more than willing. Besides, you haven't asked me to marry you. Yet.'

'Do you want me to?'

'No. There is one thing I'd like to ask you, however,' Jessica added.

'Only one?' he mocked.

'Don't be facetious. I want to know how come you had such a supply of condoms on hand, if you were leading a celibate life?'

A decidedly guilty colour slashed across his cheekbones, and Jessica's stomach lurched. It seemed her faith in Sebastian wasn't quite total, after all. Or maybe the appearance of that sexy little woman had aroused more jealousy and suspicion than she'd realised. Myra *was* very attractive. And she'd been so sure Sebastian had been sleeping with Aunt Lucy.

'I bought them,' he confessed abruptly.

'But why? And when?'

'The day I took you to the chemist for your nail polish. Remember I bought myself a new hairbrush? Well, I picked up a couple of packets then.'

'A couple of packets,' she repeated numbly, aware that most packets contained a dozen. 'You bought two dozen condoms way back then, when you thought I hated you, and vice versa?'

'You can't blame a guy for hoping. Or for being prepared.'

Jessica's heart was thudding loudly in her chest. She wasn't sure if she was angry, suspicious or simply disbelieving. 'You were planning on seducing me even then?'

'Look, I had to do something, Jess! I was mad about

you, and so damned mad at myself for getting you off-side. I decided that afternoon to change my tactics some-what.'

'And you assumed I'd just come across?'

'I didn't assume, Jess. But I was hopeful.' He smiled a very sexy smile at her. 'I do have a pretty good strike rate with women...once I set my mind on one.'

She didn't know whether to feel admiration or exas-peration. 'You're an arrogant bastard, do you know that?'

'I try not to be,' he said, and, drawing her forcefully into his arms, he kissed her till she was melting against him in glorious submission. 'How about coming to bed and making mad passionate love to me for a while,' he suggested, 'and then reading my manuscript for me? As much as I've done, that is.'

'You'd let me?'

'Of course! My body is always at your complete dis-posal.'

'Don't be silly.' She thumped him playfully on the chest. 'That's not what I meant, and you know it. I mean about reading your manuscript.'

'I'm having trouble with the ending,' he admitted. 'I want you to read what I've written, then I'll tell you what I was going to do and you tell me what you think.'

'Reading what you've written could take hours.'

'Why do you think I suggested bed first?' He scooped her into his arms and carried her inside.

'You're a devious man.'

'And you're a wonderful woman.'

'That kind of flattery will get you nowhere.'

'You're also beautiful, clever and incredibly sexy.'

'Ah, now you're talking...'

'Enough talking,' he muttered, as he dumped her on his bed and began peeling off her shorts. 'The only sounds I want to hear from you for the next hour are mmm, and aah, and ooh.'

Late that afternoon, after they'd made love leisurely for hours and abandoned any idea of Jessica reading his manuscript that day, Sebastian took Jessica swimming in Emily Bay.

It was a milestone in her life.

For she loved it. Loved the isolation. Loved the warm, quiet waters. Loved the peace that flowed through her body as she floated, feeling nothing but the sweetest pleasure over the knowledge that no matter where she was, if Sebastian was with her, she'd never be lonely again.

He took her with him to the pontoon in the middle of the bay, where they lay together and kissed and touched, oblivious of everything but each other. The urgency to make love again quickly overtook them, and he pulled her into the water with him.

Stripping her in the water was not easy, especially since she was wearing a one-piece with straps. Sebastian's brief black trunks were much more easily disposed of. Once they were both naked, he seated her on a rung of the raft ladder and pushed deeply into her. Jessica wound her legs around his hips and her arms around his neck and was soon lost in pleasure.

An elderly man walking along the beach with his wife of fifty-five years nudged her and pointed to the entwined lovers in the distance. They smiled at each other, silently recalling their own passionate courtship. Then they kissed lightly and walked on.

Afterwards, an increasingly besotted Jessica insisted Sebastian drive her past the gaol and tell her its history again, the one she'd missed the first time around. She wanted to know so that she could do justice to reading his book. He wasn't prepared to just tell her, however. He wanted to show her, insisting she get out.

'But I'm still in my swimming costume!' she protested.

'Look around. There's no one to see. The place is deserted. It's beginning to get dark, as well.'

Which it was, the sun having set while they were in the water, making love. Jessica gave in gracefully and climbed out, tracing the steps of the convicts as Sebastian relayed their cruel and inhumane treatment at the hands of their gaolers.

Jessica was both moved and appalled by all the horrors that had transpired within those creepy old walls. She shuddered as she viewed the flogging wall and gallows gate, but was truly shocked when she saw how small the cells had been, cells in which up to three men had been incarcerated, unable to even stretch out properly in their rough hammocks.

'I can understand how this place could inspire you to write a book,' she told Sebastian after they finally climbed into the car. Great drama could come from human suffering, and there were all the ingredients down there in those ruins for a fantastic story.

'You still haven't told me about your plot, you know,' she reminded him. 'Or the characters.'

'I've decided not to. I'd rather you just read the manuscript.'

'Then you'd better get me home so that I can start.'

He stared at her, and she was moved by the look on his face. So full of love and happiness. 'What did I say?'

'You called it home, not Lucy's Place.'

A lump formed in Jessica's throat. 'So I did.'

'You won't sell it now, will you?' he asked with soft

insistence. 'You'll be staying here…on the island…with me.'

He bent to kiss her before she could answer. But her response told him all he needed to know.

'Is there something you'd like to tell me, lovie?' Evie asked Jessica the following day after lunch. Sebastian was in his room, trying to write, and Jessica was helping Evie clear, as had become her habit.

Jessica thought about playing dumb, then decided it was demeaning to Evie. The older woman was nobody's fool and would have to be deaf, dumb and blind not to notice what was going on.

'I suppose you mean about me and Sebastian becoming lovers.'

Evie nodded smugly. 'I suppose I do.'

'Do…do you think Aunt Lucy would be disappointed in me? Or annoyed?'

'Oh, no. She'd be pleased as punch.'

'Would she? I'm not so sure about that. I think Aunt Lucy was a bit in love with Sebastian herself.'

'Well, you're wrong there! She might have found him attractive, but what woman wouldn't? Sebastian's a sexy man. If I were twenty years younger I might have fluttered my eyelashes at him myself. No, Lucy only loved one man in her life, and that was Bill. But she certainly admired Sebastian and thought he had a lot of fine qualities. She'd be very pleased to see you married to him.'

'Why do you assume I'll marry him?'

Evie looked perplexed. 'You're in love with him, aren't you? Blind Freddie can see that. Call me old-fashioned, but the way I see it people in love usually get married, if there's no reason they shouldn't. Is there any reason you shouldn't, lovie? You got a boyfriend back in Sydney?'

'No…'

'Well, then. What's stopping you?'

'Yes, what's stopping you?' Sebastian asked her as soon as Evie left after lunch.

Jessica frowned at him till the penny dropped. Then she waggled her fingers. 'Eavesdroppers do not hear anything good of themselves.'

'I only heard that bit. I was on my way to the bathroom. Well? You are going to marry me, aren't you?'

'I don't want to talk about marriage for now, Sebastian. Call me careful, but I can't help it. I love you to death and I'm quite happy to come back and live here with you. But marriage is a very serious step, and I need more time.'

'What do you mean, come back? Why don't you just stay?'

'I have to go back to Sydney, at least for a while.'

'Why? You can quit your job over the phone.'

'I don't want to do that.'

'Why?'

'Because you never know when I might want it back again. Or another job just like it.'

'Don't you trust our relationship to last?'

'Don't you trust me to go back to Sydney, even for a little while?'

He pursed his lips and thought about that for a while. 'I suppose so.'

'Just as well.'

When he went to take her in his arms, she backed away. 'Oh, no, you don't. You get that body of yours back to your book for a few hours.'

He groaned. 'It's still not going well.'

'How can it, when you spend all your time finding other things to do?'

He pouted. 'I like doing those things better. Besides, I'm waiting for you to finish reading what I've written so I can hear your verdict.'

'I'll be finished by dinner tonight if you'll just leave me alone. Now get back to work!' she ordered, and pointed to the door.

'Spoilsport,' he muttered as he left. 'Slavedriver!' he called over his shoulder. 'You'd have made a good warden down in that gaol!'

CHAPTER FIFTEEN

JESSICA was sitting on the back veranda just over three weeks later and only two days before her departure when a guilty thought came to her. She hadn't written to any people she knew in Sydney since she'd been here, hadn't even sent a postcard!

She bit her bottom lip and remonstrated with herself for her thoughtlessness. It was as though since falling in love with Sebastian she'd forgotten everything outside of her life here.

She'd become a different person from the woman who'd stepped off that plane, there was no doubt about it. For one thing, she didn't lock her car any more! What's more, she could actually sit out on this back veranda for well over an hour doing absolutely nothing except enjoying the warm breezes, the beauty of the scenery and the general peace and quiet.

Yesterday, Sebastian had taken her down to the pier at Kingston, where they'd sat on a bench on a hilltop overlooking the bay for three solid hours, watching a ship being unloaded. It wasn't at all boring, as she'd once thought. It had been very interesting.

The Jessica of a month ago would have scorned such simple, supposedly boring pastimes. Slowly, she'd begun to appreciate she'd been frittering her life away in Sydney, doing things she didn't really enjoy doing just for the sake of keeping busy, a legacy perhaps from all those years of seeing her mother wasting her life. Or maybe it was because she used to be so terribly, terribly lonely.

She wasn't lonely any more. She was also beginning to understand what Sebastian saw in Norfolk Island and its laid-back lifestyle. She could not wait to finish up work in Sydney, put her flat on the market and get back here to live.

Sebastian still wasn't thrilled with her going to Sydney. But she'd remained firm, believing that a short separation would do them both good. Their relationship had been so sexually intense this past month, it was hard to see things clearly sometimes. Sebastian could do with some time alone, too, to finish his book, his deadline having been put back to the end of March.

But what a book it was going to be! She'd been more than impressed when she'd read it. As for his idea for the climax and ending of the book—it was exciting and satisfying, but demanded a sequel, she informed him excitedly.

Already Sebastian's imaginative mind was forming the first chapters of another book about his hero, the unforgettable Tristram Marlborough, a handsome English nobleman who'd been cruelly framed by his evil and envious younger brother, then deported to Australia where his intractability caused him to be sent on to the infamous gaol on Norfolk Island.

What befell Tristram there would make the readers' hair curl, but would also fascinate them as their hero was degraded and tortured, starved and flogged by his jealous and perverted gaolers.

Jessica had no doubt that readers would want to know what happened after Tristram sailed off to sea in a small stolen boat. The last pages would see him rescued during a storm by a passing trading ship captained by an infamous pirate. Tristram was to bargain with him to take him back to England in exchange for promised riches when he would regain his earldom. The captain agreed, and the stage was set for the sequel.

'I'm off,' Evie announced, startling Jessica out of her reverie. 'Daydreaming again, I see.'

Jessica smiled and settled once again into the comfortable cane chair. 'I was thinking about Sebastian's book.'

'Going to be a winner, is it?'

'I think so.'

'You sure love him a lot, don't you, lovie?'

'More than I can say.'

'He's a good man. Lucy would be thrilled.'

Jessica thought of her aunt much more fondly these days, without any resentment at all. She'd come to feel a type of bonding with the woman since doing her garden and living in her home. But she still had a niggling suspicion she didn't know the whole truth about what happened between her mother and her aunt.

And she never would.

'I wish I'd had a chance to know her personally,' Jessica said with a sigh. 'And look after her. Was she in much pain towards the end?'

'Terrible. The doctor used to give her morphine, but she claimed it made her lose her mind, and she didn't like that much. Still, there were times when she just had to have it.'

'Oh, I feel awful that I wasn't here to help.'

'That wasn't your fault, Jessica. Think how happy Lucy would be knowing you've decided not to sell. She wouldn't care about your not running Lucy's Place as a guesthouse as long as it stayed in the family and was looked after and loved. How long do you think it will be before you can come back?'

'I'm not exactly sure. No more than four weeks. Sebastian will stay and look after the place for me. But I'll be back, never fear.'

'I know you will. Must go. I have friends popping by shortly. See you tomorrow. Enjoy your dinner out with Sebastian tonight.'

It was their habit to go out to dinner a couple of times a week in one of the many restaurants around the island.

'I will. Bye, Evie. Thanks for the lovely lunch.'

'My pleasure.'

Talking to Evie about her imminent return to Sydney prompted another guilty thought. She hadn't rung work once during the last month, either. She could have at least called Mark to see how he was managing. It was very remiss of her.

Not that he would really care after he found out she was going to resign. He was a very ambitious young man and would make an excellent public relations manager. She would recommend him for the job and hope management could overcome their ridiculous bias against hiring a man for the job.

Perhaps she would give him a ring now, see how things had been going.

Jessica rose and made her way to the telephone in the living room, perched herself on the wide arm of the nearby sofa and dialled. Mark's answer was quick and crisp.

'Public relations. Mark Gosper speaking.'

'Mark, it's Jessica.'

'Jessica! Great to hear from you. Don't go telling me you won't be back on Monday. Things are hectic here. I *need* you.'

'You *need* me?' she repeated, laughing. 'That's a first. It's me who usually needs you.'

'I never knew how much work you did till you weren't here,' he groaned. 'I've missed you like mad.'

'Well, it's nice to be appreciated. And I've missed you, too. I haven't had anyone here to bring me my morning cup of coffee. I've had to get it myself.'

'Poor Jessica.'

'Oh, I wouldn't say that. My stay on Norfolk Island has been…interesting to say the least.' Jessica smiled at this huge understatement. But she'd never been one to tell her private life to people at work. Or anyone else, for that matter. Even Sebastian hadn't been able to coerce much from her as yet, though he'd tried several times.

'I'll bet you've been bored to death,' Mark stated confidently. 'I'll bet you can't wait to get back here and at it.'

'No, definitely not bored. Not at all! But I won't deny I'm keen to get back. Though I don't…'

At a sound behind her, Jessica turned her head. The sight of a stony-faced Sebastian glaring at her from the doorway confused, then worried her. Had he overheard her conversation with Mark and misunderstood it?

'Jessica, are you still there?' Mark called down the line. 'Hello! Hello!'

Still frowning, she returned her attention to the telephone. 'I'm still here, but I must go, Mark. Sorry to cut you off like this. I'll see you Monday, okay?' She hung up and stood to face a still glowering Sebastian.

'That was Mark,' she said. 'My secretary. I thought I'd better give him a call.'

'A male secretary?' he drawled in caustic tones. 'How modern of you.'

'Don't go imagining things, Sebastian.' She tried a

sweet smile as she walked towards him. 'You *do* have a vivid imagination, darling heart.'

'Don't try to con me, Jessica,' he snapped. 'I know what I heard. The one thing I didn't hear, however, was your telling him you were quitting.'

Dismay held Jessica silent for a few seconds. My God, but he was quick to condemn. Maybe her one-sided conversation with Mark could have been misinterpreted, but he wasn't even giving her a chance to explain.

She couldn't help remembering the day Myra had come, making all sorts of nasty accusations about Sebastian. But she hadn't believed them, not for a moment. Because she felt she knew Sebastian, knew the man he was, what he could do and what he couldn't do.

One thing he *could* do, she realised unhappily, was be blindly, blackly jealous. He'd told her once a relationship was based on trust. Where was his trust, then? Was it so thin that one slightly ambiguous conversation could blow it away?

'Are you sleeping with your secretary?' he demanded before she could explain or voice her concerns.

'No,' she denied, trying to stay calm. But it wasn't easy.

'Perhaps I phrased that badly. I dare say one doesn't *sleep* with one's secretary. Are you *screwing* your secretary, Jessica darling? Does he bring you your coffee in bed in the mornings, or just at your desk, afterwards?' he asked, sneering.

'You've got a dirty mind, do you know that?'

When Jessica went to brush past him, he grabbed her arm and twisted her quite cruelly. 'Don't play prude with me, sweetheart. I'm the man you've spent most of the last month in bed with, remember? You did a damned good job of pretending to be pretty inexperienced at first, but it was wise of you not to claim complete innocence. That way you could become amazingly accomplished at sex with a lot more speed than some simpering virgin. How about telling me the truth now, lover? Just how many men *have* there been before me? Or are you going to claim your darling Mark was only one of the lucky three?'

She tried to pull out of his hold but failed. 'You're hurting me!' she cried, her face twisting with pain as his fingers dug deep. 'Let me go!'

'I'll let you go, all right,' he snarled, releasing her with a savage twist so she staggered against the doorframe. 'Right back to where you came from.'

'And that's where I'll stay, too,' she flung back, rubbing the ache from her arm. 'There's no future with someone as warped and twisted as you are!'

'And there's no future with you, you lying, conniving, deceiving madam. You're your father's daughter, all right!'

The immediate grimace of pained regret on Sebastian's face betrayed more than his actual words.

'What…what do you mean?' she asked, her voice faltering. She grabbed his arm and shook it. 'Sebastian, what are you saying?'

'I'm not saying anything, damn it!'

'Yes, you are. You don't even know my father, and yet you said…you said… Oh, no,' she groaned. 'I don't believe it. Not my mother and Lucy's husband! That's too awful to be true. And it *can't* be true! My mother didn't have me till over a year after she left the island. Tell me it's not true!'

'I can't do that,' he groaned.

'But how? *How?*'

'He met up with her again on the mainland,' Sebastian

admitted tersely. 'I think it was your mother's pregnancy that finally convinced him to have a vasectomy, not that other unfortunate girl's.'

Jessica felt her heart was breaking, so tightly was it being squeezed within her chest. 'I don't believe you,' she choked out.

He grimaced. 'Do you honestly think I would make this up?'

'You…you said Aunt Lucy hadn't told you why my mother left the island. You *lied* to me.'

'No, I didn't. Not technically. Lucy didn't tell me. She used to rave on while under the influence of morphine. She had no idea she was talking out loud, or that anyone was listening. I eventually put two and two together and worked out what happened.'

'Well, go on!' Jessica raged when he fell silent. 'Tell me. I want to know it all, every last pathetic putrid detail!'

'No, you don't.'

'Tell me! No more lies, either. The whole truth and nothing but the truth!'

'Very well,' he said. 'Lucy's sister came to her just before the wedding and told her she was in love with Bill and he with her. She said they were sleeping with each other. Lucy didn't believe her and Bill denied it, called Joanne a jealous little troublemaker. Lucy said she never wanted to see her again and Joanne left, devastated by her sister's hatred and her lover's betrayal. But that wasn't the end of it. Bill often went to the mainland, apparently. He must have looked up your mother and talked her into having another affair with him.'

'Why must he?' Jessica wailed. 'Why must I be his child and not the daughter of the man my mother married?'

'Because you're the spitting image of Bill, damn it! You'd have seen the likeness if you'd been a male. You have his hair and his eyes and his mouth. Lucy knew it the moment she saw you. It so shocked her she ran away. Before that, she'd thought of you only as Joanne's daughter, not Bill's.'

Jessica could only stare at him, too appalled to speak. She didn't know who to feel sorriest for. Her mother, for being so weak as to love a man like that. Lucy, for being betrayed over and over again. Or herself, for being the offspring of so ghastly a man. She hadn't thought much of her supposed father, but her real one was even worse!

'Jessica...' Sebastian reached out as though to take her in his arms.

'Don't touch me!' she snapped, her nervous system in a very fragile state. 'Go away! I don't want to speak to you ever again. I don't want to *see* you ever again. You don't love me. You don't trust me. I dare say you never even liked me. You lied to me more times than I can count. For all I know, you probably *did* seduce my aunt, for the same rotten reasons you seduced me. For this house. Or money. Or tax reasons. Or all three! You're despicable, Sebastian Slade, and I hate you!'

She could not look him in the face, for of course she did not hate him. She loved him. But she didn't want to have anything to do with him ever again. He had hurt her terribly this day, and she would never forgive him.

'I'll be putting this place on the market before I leave,' she said, her eyes fixed on a spot on the far wall. 'I want you out of here today. Be damned with the will! And be damned with *you*!'

'Jessica, I...'

When her eyes flashed black fury at him, he closed his mouth again.

'Don't even *try* to talk your way out of this. You'd be wasting your breath. I've known men like you before. Now get out! I'm sick of the sight of you.'

He looked at her for a long moment with a stony face, then whirled and walked away.

For a split second, Jessica almost ran after him, but in the end, she ran to her room instead, threw herself down on the bed she had not spent one single night in since the first, and wept as she had never wept before. Her tears seared into her very soul, for she knew she would never love a man again as she had loved Sebastian. Never.

CHAPTER SIXTEEN

'BAD news?' Mark asked as Jessica put down the telephone.

'No,' she said. 'Just business. Now where were we?'

'We were discussing how best to entertain the group of American VIPs we have arriving next week. They're only going to be here three days. Darned hard to show them Sydney in three days.'

'I agree. But what they miss out on, they'll never know, as long as what they do see is memorable. Put down a harbour cruise on day one, dinner here in the hotel that night followed by whatever's on at the Capitol Theatre. We've still got plenty of seats for the show there, haven't we?'

'Not enough.'

'Pop off and see what you can rustle up at one of the other theatres, then come back. By then I'll have figured out what to do with them on days two and three.'

'Right, boss. You sure do make snap decisions. But I like it,' he grinned, and turned to leave.

Jessica watched him go, a very good-looking young man who was also gay. If only Sebastian had known *that* when he'd accused her of sleeping with her secretary, Jessica thought bitterly.

Her mind turned to the phone call she'd just taken. It had been the solicitor, informing her that the sale of

Lucy's Place had been finalised the day before, with contracts being exchanged.

Jessica found the news depressing in the extreme. But it was done now, and could not be undone.

The buyer had been a company called Futurecorp, who refused to divulge their plans for the property to the vendor, though the solicitor thought it would likely be developed into a larger resort.

In hindsight, Jessica wished she'd put a covenant on the sale not allowing the house to be torn down or changed. But she'd been so upset and emotional at the time she'd merely demanded it be sold as quickly as possible for the best reasonable offer.

The offer had been more than reasonable, as it turned out. It had been exceptional. Jessica had originally consoled herself with the thought that if she could not be happy, she could at least be rich. Now, she wondered what insanity had possessed her. She should have protected her aunt's home and her own heritage. She'd let Aunt Lucy and herself down, and she felt terrible.

Tears welled up in her eyes. She was just reaching for a tissue when the telephone rang.

'Jessica Rawlins,' she answered.

'Jessica, Michelle here, from the front desk. I'm afraid we have a problem with the gentleman who booked into the presidential suite this morning. He's just rung down and demanded to see the public relations manager. I'm sorry, but he hung up before I could find out what about.'

Jessica sighed. 'It's all right, Michelle. I'll go up and see him. What's his name?'

'Mr. Slade.'

Jessica's heart missed a beat. It was not such an uncommon name, she supposed, but it was still an awful coincidence. A part of her began to panic. 'Do you have a Christian name to go with the Slade part? Or an initial?'

'Sorry. He paid with a company credit card.'

Jessica sighed with relief. Sebastian would not have done that. Neither would he have been in the presidential suite. It was another Mr. Slade.

'All right, I'll pop straight up and sort out whatever the problem is.' No doubt some trivial little thing. These company executive types could be so arrogant and demanding, especially when they were spending their company's money.

Jessica gritted her teeth and rose reluctantly from her desk. Where once she'd relished the challenge of soothing the most difficult guests' ruffled feathers, now she found such daily tasks a grind. There was no pleasure or satisfaction in her job any more, or in her life in Sydney. What she had once loved, she now hated. The hustle and bustle, the noise, the pace, even the smell.

She longed for the salt-sea breezes that wafted over the back veranda at Lucy's Place in the afternoon. Longed for the rolling green hills, and the warm waters of Emily Bay. Longed for...

She dragged in a deep breath as she punched the lift button for the top floor of the hotel.

I must not think of him any more, she told herself. *If I do, I'll go mad!* The man was devious, and wicked, and a lying con man, prepared to use his undoubted sexual charms for material gain, not only with her but with Lucy before her! And she wasn't just guessing about that any more. She knew that for a fact.

She hadn't really believed he *had* slept with her aunt, not even when she'd accused him that awful day. She'd been upset and angry, and wasn't thinking straight. Afterwards, she'd worried for a while that she might

have possibly jumped to the wrong conclusions about
him again.

But she finally reasoned if he'd been so damned innocent and misjudged, then why had he left within the
hour? Why hadn't he stayed and fought for her love and
trust? Any lingering doubts she still had about him had
been obliterated the following Sunday when Evie had
driven her to the airport.

For one of the passengers waiting for a flight that day
had been none other than Myra, off to find work in
Brisbane.

When Evie had left momentarily to go the ladies,
Jessica had not been able to resist asking Myra exactly
how she'd known Sebastian was sleeping with Aunt
Lucy. And Myra had told her with blunt candour how
she used to get the house early in the morning to do the
laundry and how she'd seen Sebastian one morning, tip-
toeing from Lucy's bedroom out through the French
doors onto the veranda, wearing next to nothing, then
sneaking to his own room that way. And this had been
ages ago, well before Lucy became ill, when there were
still guests at Lucy's place.

Given the circumstances, Jessica could find no reason
for Myra to lie. It was Sebastian who was the liar, she
concluded with despairing finality, like most of the men
she'd ever known.

The lift doors opened and Jessica emerged, squaring
her shoulders as she made her way briskly along the
lushly carpeted corridor. The personal valet attached to
the presidential suite was just emerging when she arrived.
'What's the problem with Mr. Slade?' she asked, her curt
tone reflecting her mood.

'Problem?' The efficient young man's forehead wrinkled with a puzzled frown. 'He said nothing to me about a problem.'

'He probably wants me to fix up a squash partner for him,' she said tartly, 'or some such similar emergency. Don't you worry about it. If you could let him know I'm here before you go, I'd appreciate it.'

The valet nodded and disappeared for a few short seconds before reappearing.

'He's in the sitting room, having a drink,' Jessica was informed. 'He said to go right on in.'

Her first impression was of superbly suited shoulders and perfectly groomed brown hair. And that was only from the rear. Mr. Slade was standing at the plate-glass window, his back to her, his body silhouetted in the afternoon sunshine. Sydney's city skyline lay behind him, dominated by the Centrepoint Tower.

'How do you do, Mr. Slade,' she said crisply as she walked across the spacious room. 'I'm Jessica Rawlins, the public relations manager. How may I help you?'

He began to turn, the light catching gold streaks in his light brown hair as he did so. Jessica stopped breathing once his face came fully into view.

'Sebastian!' she gasped, shock coursing through her in a shivery wave. What on earth was he doing here? And why was he dressed like that? Surely he hadn't come after her, hoping to get her back?

He said nothing at first, penetrating blue eyes raking over her, perhaps taking in her pallor and her thinness. She hadn't had much appetite since her return from Norfolk seven weeks before.

'Hello, Jess,' he said at last.

'You…you've had your hair cut,' she blurted, thinking he looked incredibly handsome and suave, in a sleek, citified sort of way.

Yet she didn't like his new image. Or was it simply an old one? Had he reverted to the Sebastian prior to his stay in Norfolk Island? The ruthless and decadent dealer who made and lost fortunes for other people and played Don Juan with promiscuous aplomb.

Lord, but he looked incredibly cool and intimidating in that grey three-piece suit and with his hair totally under control, not at all like the casually relaxed Sebastian she had met and fallen in love with.

How ironic that when she'd first seen him on the veranda at Lucy's Place, she'd scorned the idea of his ever playing the part of a business executive. He didn't have to play the part. He *was* the part, for real.

She looked at him at felt…what? Distress, but still desire. Dear God, she still loved him, would always love him.

It was a bitter pill to swallow.

'What is it that you want, Sebastian?' she asked, her voice strained. 'Why did you trick me into coming up here?'

'I didn't trick you. I gave my name.'

'Half-truths again, Sebastian?' she asked scornfully. 'Slade is not an uncommon name. You didn't give your Christian name. How could I possibly know it was you?'

'You must have suspected when you saw my company name.'

'Why? I never knew where you worked before, and I don't know now!'

'I do not work for a company, Jess. I *own* a company. It's called Futurecorp. The name must be familiar to you after the call from your solicitor today.'

Her eyes rounded to saucers. '*You're* Futurecorp?'

'Yes.'

'But…for how long? I mean, when did you…? I mean…'

'I formed Futurecorp several years ago,' he finished for her in a matter-of-fact tone.

Jessica's confusion was growing. 'Are you saying you're rich? That you've always been rich?'

'Not always. But for some years, yes.'

'Then you didn't lose your fortune before going to Norfolk Island?'

'I did make some unwise property investments back then, but no, I did not lose my fortune. Perversely, those same investments have come good during my stay on Norfolk. Ironic, isn't it, that my neglect has made me a wealthier man?'

Jessica thought it very ironic. And even more confusing. He obviously hadn't wanted to marry her for money, then, though the tax reason was still a valid contender. But if so, then what was he doing here? Why wasn't he on Norfolk Island conning some other gullible female? A man of his looks and wealth wouldn't have any trouble finding a suitable candidate.

'Did Aunt Lucy know you were rich?' she asked, frowning as she tried to make sense of everything he was saying to her.

'Not for the first year,' he admitted. 'She assumed— as you did—that I was bankrupt. I have to admit I found it…refreshing to know I was liked for myself and not my money. I also liked being helped and advised and cosseted. It soothed my soul to feel worthy of being cared about. I confessed my financial status to her when it no longer made a difference in our relationship. Lucy wasn't even angry with me.'

Jessica still was, though. *Very* angry. And very rattled by these astonishing revelations. She paced across the

room, then round behind an armchair, gripping the back
while she glared at Sebastian.

'Well, she wouldn't be, would she? The woman was
probably besotted with all the sex you were giving her,
just like I was! And don't lie to me about that any more.
I know you were sleeping with her.'

'No, I wasn't, Jess,' he denied again. 'Look, I know
what Myra told you that day at the airport. Evie tackled
her about it after you'd left to get on your plane. She
saw you talking to her. Believe when I tell you, Jess, that
I didn't make love to Lucy. Ever. But I did sleep with
her one night. That I do admit.'

What was the damned difference? Make love…sleep
with… He was playing with words again!

'It was the day Lucy found out about her cancer and
her rat of a husband. She was terribly upset. She needed
to talk to someone. But there were guests in the house
and we went to her room to be alone. We stayed up late,
talking. She became very distressed at one stage and
started to cry. I went over to where she was sitting on
her bed, took her in my arms and just held her. She
begged me not to leave her, and I didn't. I lay down and
held her till she went to sleep. Then I fell asleep myself.
There was no sex. I swear it.'

She stared at him, knowing deep in her heart he was
telling her the truth. But she couldn't bring herself to say
she believed him.

'Why would I lie to you?' he asked in the pained silence. 'If I'd slept with Lucy I'd tell you. Frankly, I
would not have been ashamed of it if I had. She was a
lovely woman. But she didn't want that from me. She'd
only ever loved the one man in her life, and bastard
though he was, she remained faithful to his memory to
the day she died.'

'Then why did you keep *me* ignorant of your wealth?' she demanded, confusion and hurt making her voice sharp. 'Because you found it *refreshing* that I liked you for yourself? Or was it that you didn't trust me, as you've never trusted any woman?'

'I'm not going to try to whitewash my behaviour with you. I haven't come here for that.' He sipped his drink, a bleak bitterness clouding his eyes. When he looked at her again, his chin lifted and he squared his shoulders, the actions carrying a dignified nobility that moved Jessica despite everything. How could she possibly admire him after all he'd done?

'I did love you, Jess,' he said. 'But you're quite right. Down deep, I didn't trust you. Even I can see that now. The trouble was that I'd experienced too many examples in the past of the aphrodisiacal power of money. Amazing how many beautiful women drop their pants for rich men. Age and looks have nothing to do with it. That's just an added bonus for the ladies in question. My strike rate was second to none in the seduction game, as I combined the best of both worlds.'

Jessica listened to what he was saying with some understanding and a large measure of guilt, conceding she'd had similar cynical thoughts about the opposite sex and their response to money. How could she condemn him for keeping his wealth a secret when she'd planned to keep even a modest inheritance to herself for the very same reasons?

'What I failed to appreciate,' he went on, 'was that not all beautiful women are like that, or like my chronically unfaithful wife. Basically, I was still as warped and twisted as you said, Jess. I'd fooled myself into thinking that I'd changed, that I was capable of truly loving and trusting a woman again. And I was—while I lived in a cocoon, and while I kept you in there with me. But it only took one small test to crack open the thin veneer of my so-called recovery.'

Jessica could not stop staring at him and thinking how brave it was of him to come here and say all this. How many men could admit to being wrong or weak? Not that she thought of Sebastian as weak. Just wounded.

But wounds could heal eventually, couldn't they? Given the right treatment. All they needed was some tender loving care. What Lucy had started, she could finish!

Jessica saw then that her love, too, had cracked under its first real test. She should have hung in there, not cut and run. She should have had more faith in Sebastian's love for *her*.

And he did still love her. She could see it in his tense face and his strained shoulders, in his actions as well as his words. The realisation moved her unbearably. Tears stung her eyes, and she had to blink to control them.

'You really bought Lucy's Place?' She choked the words out.

'Yes.'

'Why?'

'For two reasons. The first was to keep faith with my promise to Lucy to make sure her home was always looked after. I could not see it fall into unscrupulous hands, could I?'

Jessica's heart contracted. 'I...I shouldn't have sold it. I regretted it afterwards. Today, when I realised what I'd done, I felt so rotten.'

'I thought you might. That's the other reason I bought it, and why I have gifted it over to you.' He drew some papers from his breast pocket and handed them to her. 'Lucy's Place is yours now, Jess, to do with as you will.'

Jessica's mouth dropped open. 'But…but you've already paid me an exorbitant amount of money for it!'

'Call it conscience money.'

She groaned as she saw what lay behind these touching and generous gestures. Not guilt, and not just an ordinary love, but a very great love!

Oh, yes, he had hurt her, but only during a burst of irrational jealousy, and not with coldly deliberate cruelty. His act in not telling her about her real father was not such an unforgivable thing, either, given her father's wicked reputation. He'd probably been trying to protect her.

Jessica had come to terms with her parentage over the past few weeks, especially after a phone call to her legal father revealed he'd found out shortly after her birth that he wasn't her real father. He'd confessed to her that her mother's sick obsession with her sister's husband had been at the core of everything she did.

Her marriage—it had been a mad attempt to make Bill jealous. Her divorce—she'd fantasised Bill would marry her then. And her breakdown after Bill was killed—she'd turned to drink once her reason for living no longer existed.

The truth had not been a pretty story, but there had been a strange comfort in knowing the indisputable facts. Jessica no longer thought about her real father. He wasn't worth thinking about.

As for her mother, she'd been a very weak and self-centred woman. But she'd suffered for her sins. Jessica would not judge her any longer, especially now that she understood the power of love and desire.

She looked at Sebastian and thought how much she loved him and how much she wanted him. But did he want her? Did he want to try again? She was afraid he didn't. There was nothing in his bearing or his manner to indicate this visit was an attempt at a reconciliation, just a monetary reparation.

'I don't *want* your conscience money,' she cried brokenly.

'Then what *do* you want, Jess?' Sebastian asked just as brokenly. 'Name it and I'll give it to you if I can. It's the least I can do after the way I've treated you.'

Hesitantly, she came round from behind the chair, her heart in her hands as she reached out to him. 'I…I want *you*, Sebastian,' she croaked. 'Only you.'

He gave a choked cry and gathered her to him, hugging her so tightly she thought she might snap in two.

'Oh, Jess…Jess,' he rasped. 'Do you mean this? You really want me back?'

'For ever and ever, my darling. Life without you has been unbearable. And I do not blame you totally for what happened. I overreacted to everything. I should have stayed and explained. For one thing, Mark, my secretary, is gay. And I should have told you more about myself and my past life, and the men I became involved with. If I'd done that you would have known me better, and you'd never have believed so badly of me. I—'

'Stop!' Sebastian broke in. 'You don't have to explain. Or take any of the blame. In my heart of hearts, I knew all along you weren't promiscuous or cheap. That was a madman talking. I'm not that madman any more, my darling. I swear to you. I'm so sorry for the things I said that day. Please forgive me.'

Her heart melted at his heartfelt apology. 'Of course, I forgive you.'

He shook his head slowly, in awe of her forgiveness. 'I don't deserve you. Dear God, I was in despair after you left, but never more so than when Evie looked at me and said, "Oh Sebastian, what have you done? She loved you. She truly loved you." I knew then what I'd done. I'd driven the woman *I* loved away. The only woman I'd ever loved. You made what I felt for Sandra nothing but a shallow sickness. I wanted to cut out my tongue for the things I'd said. I wanted to die rather than go on. I almost did die.'

'Oh, Sebastian, don't say such things. I can't bear it.'

'It's true. I stood on the cliffs at Rocky Point and would have cast myself into the sea below if I hadn't remembered something Lucy said to me once. True love doesn't die, Sebastian, she'd said. It can't. It lives, despite everything. It goes on and on and on. It was then that I decided to wait a while, then give myself one last chance of winning you back. I came here expecting nothing, Jess, but hoping…always hoping…'

'I'm so glad you came, Sebastian,' she said, hugging him. 'So very, very glad.'

'I love you, Jess. I love you so much. And to think you are going to give me another chance. I can't express how that makes me feel. So humble. So grateful. So happy. Kiss me, my darling. Kiss me.'

She kissed him and all the pain of the last weeks melted away. The loneliness lifted, and joy seeped in.

'Marry me, Jess,' he proposed. 'Have my children. Live with me for the rest of our lives.'

'I will.'

'You will? You really will?'

'I really will. Only…'

'Only what?' he said, instant worry in his eyes. 'You're not still afraid I want to marry you for tax reasons, are you? Let me assure I don't need to marry you for that. I never did. I bought a half share in a fishing boat and tourist business shortly after I arrived on

Norfolk. I'll soon have my own permanent permit, if that's what's worrying you.'

'It's not that, Sebastian.'

'Then what is it?'

Jessica gave him a sheepish look. 'Could you, um, please grow your hair again?'

'You don't like my hair this way?'

'Let's just say I prefer it long. And much as I quite like that suit,' she went on, 'it'll have to go, as well. I mean, if we're going to live on Norfolk Island, then this stuffy attire will never do.'

'You're prepared to give up your job and live on Norfolk Island? You won't be bored? Look, I'm quite prepared to move to Sydney if that's what it takes to make you happy, Jess.'

Jessica smiled. 'Sydney's a nice place to visit, but I wouldn't want to live here.'

His eyes shone as he pulled her to him again. 'I'll wind up Futurecorp,' he said, his voice strong and steady. 'And we'll go back to Norfolk to live.'

When he went to kiss her again, Jessica pressed her fingers against his mouth. 'Hold it there. What do you mean, wind up Futurecorp? What kind of company is it?'

'A family trust. I started it up donkey's years ago to help out the folks. It holds all my investments, from which I can disperse money to family members each year. Mum and Dad have now passed on, unfortunately, but I've been giving my three older sisters money each year. They seem to have married chronically unemployed men. I thought I might set up individual trust funds for each of them so that they'd be permanently secure, though that will substantially reduce my net worth. Does that bother you at all?'

Jessica pursed her lips. 'Not really. I have plenty of

money of my own after some fool paid me twice what Lucy's Place is worth. Still, much as I admire your generosity to your sisters, Sebastian, you seem surprisingly untroubled at giving up most of your fortune. For one who was once poor, that is. Don't forget, I've been there and I know *I* wouldn't give away most of my money, no matter what I wanted to prove. Is there something I don't know about?'

'Could be.'

'Tell me, you devil, or I'll throttle you.'

'I dare say you might.' He laughed. 'Well, these are the facts, ma'am. Yesterday in New York, my American agent auctioned off my sequel on a synopsis only for four million dollars. Of course, the winning publisher *had* seen a finished copy of my book. And now Hollywood's entered the fray. I'm sorry, Jess, but I'm destined to remain a rich man no matter what I do.'

For all his dry amusement, Jessica could see a small wariness remained. She reached up to lay a tender hand against his cheek. 'I think I can manage to love you rich as well as poor, my darling,' she said softly. 'I already did, didn't I? And what is money, when all is said and done? It cannot change what is in my heart. I'll love you for better or worse, for richer or poorer, in sickness and in health till death do us part.'

He covered her hand with his and looked deep into her love-filled eyes. 'Lucy was so right, wasn't she? True love doesn't die. It goes on and on and on. Let's not wait long to get married, Jess. I want to start having babies with you as soon as possible.'

Jessica's heart turned right over. Babies. Her own babies, with Sebastian as their father. It was her dream coming true.

'I see no reason to wait for a piece of paper to cement

our love, my darling,' she murmured, and, taking his hand, led him toward the bedroom.

'You know, Sebastian,' she said to him as they lay in each other's arms afterwards, 'I think this was what Aunt Lucy wanted when she put that clause in her will, throwing us together. She wanted us to fall in love and get married and fill her house with babies.'

'I think you could be right, my darling. She was a romantic, your Aunt Lucy.'

'And she was right. We did fall in love. And we are going to get married and fill her house with babies.'

'We certainly are, my darling. It's just a matter of time.'

Their son Tristram was born nine months later to the day. Their daughter Lucy followed fifteen months later. In all, Mr. and Mrs. Sebastian Slade increased the population of Norfolk Island by five. Sebastian's books went on to be international best-sellers. The movies based on his books broke all box-office records. They became very, very rich but it never changed their lifestyle, which remained simple and satisfying. They gave a lot of money away.

Jessica never worked again. At an official job, that is. She was more than fully occupied, with her husband, her children, her home and her garden. Evie continued to cook for them on a casual basis, though she was more friend than employee. They named their second daughter after her.

On their tenth wedding anniversary Sebastian took Jessica around the world. She enjoyed the trip but she was more than happy to come home. She loved Norfolk

Island more than any place on earth, though not as much as she loved her husband. Home, she realised, was wherever he was. He was her love and her life. He knew it, and treasured her accordingly.

Although born in England, **Sandra Field** has lived most of her life in Canada; she says the silence and emptiness of the north speaks to her particularly. While she enjoys travelling, and passing on her sense of a new place, she often chooses to write about the city which is now her home. Sandra says, 'I write out of my experience; I have learned that love with its joys and its pains is all-important. I hope this knowledge enriches my writing, and touches a chord in you, the reader.'

REMARRIED IN HASTE
by
Sandra Field

REMARRIED IN HASTE

by

Sandra Field

PROLOGUE

"IT'S time you go and see your wife, Brant."

The rounded beach stone Brant had been idly playing with slipped from his fingers and fell to the floor. The noise it made seemed disproportionately loud, jarring his nerves. He bent to pick it up and said coolly, "I don't have a wife."

Equally coolly, Gabrielle said, "Her name's Rowan."

"We're divorced. As well you know."

Gabrielle Doucette was leaning back in her seat, her legs slung carelessly over one arm of the chair; her bundled black hair and deep blue eyes were very familiar to him, as was her ability to look totally relaxed in tense situations. "Sometimes," she said, "a divorce is just a legal document, a piece of paper with printing on it. Nothing to do with the heart."

"I was legally separated for a year, and I've been divorced for fourteen months," Brant said tightly. "In all that time I've neither heard from Rowan nor seen her. Her lawyer sent back my first batch of support checks with a letter that told me, more or less politely, to get lost. The letter with the second batch was considerably less polite. All of which, to my mind, indicates something a little more significant than a mere legal document."

Gabrielle stared thoughtfully into her glass of wine; they had eaten bouillabaisse, which was her specialty, and had moved from the table to sit by the window of her Toronto condominium, which overlooked the constant traffic of the 401. "On her part, maybe."

5

"On mine, too." Brant tipped back his glass, draining it. "When are you going to produce the delectable dessert I know you've got hidden away somewhere in the refrigerator?"

"When I'm ready." She smiled at him, a smile of genuine affection. "You and I were thrown together for eight months under circumstances that were far from ordinary—"

"That's the understatement of the year," he said; the stinking cells, the oppressive heat, the inevitable illnesses to which they'd both succumbed had been quite extraordinarily unpleasant. Not to say life-threatening.

"—Yet you never fell in love with me."

He opted for a partial truth; he had no intention of telling her certain of the reasons why he hadn't fallen in love with her, they were entirely too personal. "I knew you weren't available," he said. "You still haven't gotten over Daniel's death." Daniel had been her husband of seven years, who'd died in a car accident before Brant had met Gabrielle.

"True enough."

He looked around the stark and ultramodern room. "Besides, I don't like your taste in furniture."

She chuckled. "That, also, is true. But I think there's another reason. You didn't fall in love with me because you still love Rowan."

Brant had seen this coming. Keeping his hands loose on the stem of his glass, he said, "You're missing out by being a labor negotiator, Gabrielle—you should be writing fiction."

"And how would you feel if you heard Rowan was about to remarry?"

His whole body went rigid; for a split second he was twenty-six years old again, back in Angola that sultry evening when a live grenade had arched gracefully through the air toward him and his feet had felt like lumps of concrete. He rasped, "*Is* she? Who told you?"

Gabrielle smiled again, a rather smug smile. "So you do care. I thought you did."

"Very clever," Brant said, making no attempt to mask his anger; he and Gabrielle had long ago passed the point of being polite to each other for the sake of outward appearances.

"It's bound to happen sooner or later," Gabrielle continued placidly. "Rowan is a beautiful and talented young woman."

"What she does with her life is nothing to do with me."

Quite suddenly Gabrielle snapped her glass down on the chrome-edged table beside her. "All right—I'll stop playing games. I've watched you the last two years. You've been acting like a man possessed. Like a man who couldn't care less if he got himself killed. Any ordinary person would have been dead five times over with some of the things you've done, the situations you've exposed yourself to since you and Rowan split up." Her voice broke very slightly. "I don't want to pick up the paper one day and find myself reading your obituary."

Brant said blankly, for it was a possibility that had never occurred to him before, "You're not in love with *me*, are you?"

He looked so horrified that genuine amusement lightened her features. "Of course not. Someday I'm sure I'll fall in love again, it would be an insult to Daniel's memory if I didn't. But it won't be with you, Brant."

"You had me worried for a moment."

"And if you're trying to change the subject," Gabrielle went on with considerable determination, "it won't work. I *know* you still love Rowan. After all, you and I virtually lived together for the eight months we were held for ransom, I had lots of opportunity to observe you. One of the things that kept you sane through that terrible time was the knowledge you'd be going home to Rowan. Your wife."

Through gritted teeth Brant said, "Your imagination's operating overtime."

Imperturbably Gabrielle went on, "And then we were released unexpectedly. When you got home she was leading a tour in Greenland, and when she got back from there her lawyer made it all too clear that Rowan wanted nothing to do with you because she thought you and I were a number. You wouldn't let me go and see her to try and explain— oh, no, you were much too proud for that. In fact, you made me swear I wouldn't get in touch with her at all, stiff- necked idiot that you are. So you lost her. And you've never stopped grieving that loss. I know you haven't. I'd swear it in court on a stack of Bibles as high as this build- ing."

"Dammit, I'm divorced! And that's the way I like it."

"Don't lie to me."

He surged to his feet. "I've had enough of this—I'm getting out of here."

"Can't take the heat? Afraid you might have to admit to emotions? You, Brant Curtis, feeling pain because a woman left you?" She swung her legs to the floor and stood up, too, with a touch of awkwardness that reminded him, sharply and painfully, of Rowan's sudden, coltlike move- ments. "I know you have feelings," Gabrielle announced, "even if I don't know why you've repressed them so dras- tically they don't have the slightest chance of escap- ing...sort of like us in that awful cell. You have them, though—and they're killing you."

"You've got a great touch with purple prose."

"So you're a coward," she said flatly.

Her words bit deep into a place Brant rarely acknowledged to himself and certainly never would to anyone else. Of course he wasn't a coward. If anything, he was the exact opposite, a man who continually took risks for the highs they gave him. He headed for the door, throwing the words over his shoulder. "Remind me the next time you invite me for dinner to say no."

"You need to see Rowan!"

"I don't know where she is and I'm not going looking for her!"

"I know where she is." Gabrielle turned and from a wrought-iron shelf picked up a folded brochure, waving it in the air. "In three days she'll be leading a small group of people through various islands in the West Indies looking for endemic birds. Which, in case you didn't know, means birds native to the area. I had to look it up."

In spite of himself, Brant's eyes had flown to the folded piece of paper and his feet had glued themselves to the parquet floor. Conquering the urge to snatch the brochure from her, he rapped, "So what?"

"There's a vacancy on that trip. My friend Sonia's husband—Rick Williams—was to have gone, but he's come down with a bad respiratory infection. You could take his place."

His mouth dry, Brant sneered, "Me? Looking for endemic birds on those cute little Caribbean islands? That's like telling a mercenary soldier he's going back to kindergarten."

"You'd be looking for your wife, Brant." Gabrielle's smile was ironic. "Looking for your life, Brant. You didn't know I was a poet, did you?"

"You've been watching too many soap operas."

"Kindly don't insult me!"

His lashes flickered. Gabrielle almost never lost her temper; unlike Rowan, who lost it frequently.

Rowan. He'd always loved her name. His first gift to her had been a pair of earrings he'd had designed especially for her, little enameled bunches of the deep orange berries of the rowan tree, berries as fiery-colored as her tumbled, shoulder-length hair. Spread on the pillow, her hair had had the glow of fire....

With an exclamation of disgust, because many months ago he'd rigorously trained himself to forget everything that had happened between him and Rowan in their big bed, he held out his hand. Gabrielle passed him the brochure. Brant flattened it; from long years of hiding anything remotely like fear, his hands were as steady as if he were unfolding the daily newspaper. "'Endemic Birds of the Eastern Caribbean,'" he read. "'Guided by Rowan Carter.'"

She'd kept her own name even when they'd been married. For business reasons, she'd said. Although afterward, when she'd left him, he'd wondered if it had been for other, more hidden and more complicated reasons.

He cleared his throat. "You're suggesting I phone the company Rowan works for and propose myself as a substitute for your friend's husband? Rowan, as I recall, has a fair bit of say about the trips she runs—the last person in the world she'd allow to go on one of them would be me."

"Don't tell her. Just turn up."

His jaw dropped. For the space of a full five seconds he looked at Gabrielle in silence. "Intrigue," he said, "that's what you should be writing."

"Rick can cancel easily enough—he bought insurance and he'll get his money back. Or you can pay him for the trip and go in his place. All you'd have to do is change the airline tickets to your name."

"So I'd turn up at the airport in—" he ran his eyes down the page "—Grenada, and say, 'Oh, by the way, Rowan, Rick couldn't make it so I thought I'd come instead.'" He gave an unamused bark of laughter. "She'd throw me on the first plane back to Toronto."

"Then it'll be up to you to convince her otherwise."

"You've never met her—you have no idea how stubborn she can be."

"Like calls to like?" Gabrielle asked gently.

"Oh, do shut up," he snapped. "Of course I'm not going, it's a crazy idea." Nevertheless, with a detached part of his brain, Brant noticed he hadn't put the brochure back on the shelf. Or—more appropriately—thrown it to the floor and trampled on it.

"I made tiramisu for dessert. And I'll put the coffee on."

Gabrielle vanished into the kitchen. Like a man who couldn't help himself, Brant started reading the description of the trip that would be leaving on Wednesday. Seven different islands, two nights on each except for the final island of Antigua, where a one-night stopover was scheduled. Hiking in rain forests and mangrove swamps, opportunities for swimming and snorkeling.

Opportunities for being with Rowan.

For two whole weeks.

He was mad to even consider it. Rowan didn't want anything to do with him, she'd made that abundantly clear. So why set himself up for another rejection when he was doing just fine as he was?

Because he *was* doing fine. Gabrielle's imagination was way out of line with all her talk of love and needs and repressions. He didn't need Rowan any more than Rowan needed him.

He'd hated it when his checks had been returned by that smooth-tongued bastard of a lawyer. Hated not knowing where she was living. Hated it most of all that she'd never wanted to see him again.

But he'd gotten over that. Gotten over it and gone on with his life, the only kind of life he thrived on.

The last thing he needed was to see Rowan again.

What he needed was a cup of strong black coffee and a bowl of tiramisu laden with marscapone. Brant tossed the brochure onto the dining room table and followed Gabrielle into the kitchen.

CHAPTER ONE

AT THIRTY-seven thousand feet the clouds looked solid enough to walk on, and the sky was a guileless blue. Brant stretched his legs into the comfortable amount of space his executive seat allowed him and gazed out of the window. He was flying due south, nonstop, from Toronto to Antigua; in Antigua he'd board a short hop to Grenada.

Where Rowan should be on hand to meet him.

Among the various documents Rick had given him had been a list of participants; he, Brant, was the only Canadian other than Rowan on the trip. Therefore, he'd presumably be the only one coming in on that particular flight; the rest of the group would fly via Puerto Rico or Miami.

It should be an interesting meeting.

Which didn't answer the question of why he was going to Grenada.

His dinner with Gabrielle had been last Sunday. On Monday he'd phoned Rick's wife Sonia and told her he'd take Rick's tickets. On Tuesday his boss—that enigmatic figure who owned and managed an international, prestigious and highly influential magazine of political commentary—had sent a fax requesting him to go to Myanmar, as Burma was now known, and write an article on the heroin trade. Whereupon Brant had almost phoned Sonia back. He liked going to Myanmar, it had that constant miasma of danger on which he flourished. His whole life revolved around places like that.

Grenada wouldn't make the list of the world's most dangerous places. Not by a long shot.

So why was he going to Grenada and not Myanmar?

To prove himself right, he thought promptly. To prove he no longer had any feelings for Rowan.

Yeah? He was spending one hell of a lot of money to prove something he'd told Gabrielle didn't need proving.

And why did he, right now, have that sensation of super-vigilance, of every nerve keyed to its highest pitch, the very same feeling that always accompanied him on his assignments?

Don't try and answer that one, Brant Curtis, he told himself ironically, watching a cloud drift by that had the hooked neck and forked tongue of a prehistoric sea monster. He'd told his boss he had plans for a well-earned vacation; and the only reason he'd phoned Sonia back was to borrow Rick's high-powered binoculars and a bird book about the West Indies. The book was now sitting in his lap, along with a list of the birds they were likely to see. He hadn't opened either one.

Why in God's name was he wasting two weeks of his precious time to go and see a woman who thought he was a liar and a cheat? A sexual cheat. How she'd laugh if she knew that somehow, in the eight months he and Gabrielle had been held for ransom in Colombia, Gabrielle had seemed more like the sister he'd never had, the mother he could only dimly remember, than a potential bed partner. This despite the fact that Gabrielle was a very attractive woman.

He'd never told Gabrielle that, and never would. Nor would he ever tell Rowan.

A man was entitled to his secrets.

Tension had pulled tight the muscles in Brant's neck and shoulders; he was aware of his heartbeat thin and high in his chest. But those weren't feelings, of course. They were just physiological reactions caused by adrenaline, fight or flight, a very useful mechanism that had gotten him out of trouble more times than he cared to count. The airplane was looking after the flight part, he thought semi-humorously. Which left fight.

Rowan would no doubt take care of that. She'd never been one to bite her tongue if she disagreed with him or disliked what he was doing; it was one of the reasons he'd married her, for the tilt of her chin and the defiant toss of her curly red hair.

Maybe she didn't care about him enough now to think him worth a good fight.

He didn't like that conclusion at all. With an impatient sigh Brant spread out the list of bird species and opened the book at page one, forcing himself to concentrate. After all, he didn't want to disgrace himself by not knowing one end of a bird from the other. Especially in front of his ex-wife.

Rowan could have done without the connecting flight from Antigua being four hours late. Rick Williams from Toronto was the last of her group to arrive: the only other Canadian besides herself on the trip. The delay seemed like a bad omen, because it was the second hitch of the day; she and the rest of the group had had an unexpected five hours of birding in Antigua already today when their Grenada flight had also been late.

Rick's flight should have landed in Grenada at six-thirty, in time for dinner with everyone else at the hotel. Instead it was now nearly ten forty-five and Rick still hadn't come through customs.

His luggage, she thought gloomily. They've lost his luggage.

She checked with the security guard and was allowed into the customs area. Four people were standing at the

desk which dealt with lost bags. The elderly woman she
discounted immediately, and ran her eyes over the three
men. The gray-haired gentleman was out; Rick Williams
was thirty-two years old. Which left…her heart sprang into
her throat like a grouse leaping from the undergrowth. The
man addressing the clerk was the image of Brant.

She swallowed hard and briefly closed her eyes. She was
tired, yes, but not that tired.

But when she looked again, the man had straightened to
his full height, his backpack pulling his blue cotton shirt
taut across his shoulders. His narrow hips and long legs
were clad in well-worn jeans. There was a dusting of gray
in the thick dark hair over his ears. That was new, she
thought numbly. He'd never had any gray in his hair when
they'd been married.

It wasn't Brant. It couldn't be.

But then the man turned to say something to the younger
man standing beside him, and she saw the imperious line
of his jaw, shadowed with a day's dark beard, and the jut
of his nose. It was Brant. Brant Curtis had turned up in the
Grenada airport just as she was supposed to meet a member
of one of her tours. Bad joke, she thought sickly, lousy
coincidence, and dragged her gaze to the younger man. He
must be Rick Williams.

Her eyes darted around the room. There was nowhere
she could hide in the hopes that Brant would leave before
Rick, and therefore wouldn't see her. She couldn't very
well scuttle back through customs; they'd think she was
losing her mind. Anyway, Rick was one of her clients, and
she owed him whatever help she could give him if his bags
were lost.

At least she'd had a bit of warning. She was exceedingly
grateful for that, because she'd hate Brant to have seen all
the shock and disbelief that must have been written large

on her face in the last few moments; the harsh fluorescent lighting would have hidden none of it. Taking a deep breath, schooling her features to impassivity, Rowan walked toward the desk.

As if he'd sensed her presence Brant turned around, and for the first time in months she saw the piercing blue of his eyes, the blue of a desert sky. As they fastened themselves on her, not even the slightest trace of emotion crossed his face. Of course not, she thought savagely. He'd always been a master at hiding his feelings. It was one of the many things that had driven them apart, although he would never have acknowledged the fact. Rowan forced a smile to her lips and was fiercely proud that she sounded as impassive as he looked, "Well...what a surprise. Hello, Brant."

"What the devil have you done to your hair?"

Nearly three years since he'd seen her and all he could talk about was her hair? "I had it cut."

"For Pete's sake, what for?"

A small part of her was wickedly pleased that she'd managed to disrupt his composure; it had never been easy to knock Brant off balance, his self-control was too formidable for that. Rowan ran her fingers through her short, ruffled curls. "Because I wanted to. And now you must excuse me...I'm supposed to be meeting someone."

She turned to the younger man and said pleasantly, "You must be Rick Williams?"

The man glanced up from the form he was filling in; he smelled rather strongly of rum. "Nope. Sorry." Doing a double take, he looked her up and down. "Extremely sorry."

Rowan gritted her teeth. She rarely bothered with makeup on her tours, and her jeans and sport shirt were quite unexceptional. Why did men think that she could possibly be complimented when they eyed her like a specimen laid out on a tray? And where the heck was Rick Williams? If he'd missed the plane, why hadn't he phoned her?

Brant said, "Rick couldn't come. So I came in his place."

"*What?*"

"Rick has a form of pneumonia and the doctors wouldn't let him come," Brant repeated patiently. "It was all rather at the last minute, so I didn't bother letting you know."

She sputtered, "You knew if you let me know I wouldn't have let you come!"

"That's true enough," he said.

So that was why he hadn't looked surprised to see her; he'd known all along she'd be there to meet him. Once again, he'd had the advantage of her. "Were you bored and thought you'd stir up a little trouble?" she spat. "From reading the newspapers, I'd have thought there were more than enough wars and famines in the world to get your attention without having to turn yourself into an ordinary tourist in the Caribbean."

So she did care enough to fight, thought Brant. Interesting. Very interesting. He said blandly, "If we're going to have a—er, disagreement, don't you think we should at least go outside where there's a semblance of privacy?"

Rowan looked around her. The young man who wasn't Rick Williams was leering at her heaving chest; the customs officer was grinning at her. Trying to smother another uprush of pure rage, she managed, with a huge effort, to modulate her voice. "Is your baggage missing?"

Brant nodded. "They figure it's gone on to Trinidad— should be here tomorrow. No big deal."

"Have you finished filling in the forms?"

Another nod. "I'm ready to go anytime you are."

"I'll phone the airlines on the way out," she said crisply,

"and get you on the first flight back to Toronto. A birding trip is definitely not your thing."

"No, you won't. I've paid my money and I'm staying."

She'd forgotten how much taller he was than her five feet nine. How big he was. "Brant, let's not—"

He jerked his head at the door. "Outside. Not in here."

He was right, of course. Her company would fire her on the spot if it could see how she was greeting a client. She pivoted, stalked through the glass doors into the open part of the terminal and then out into the dusky heat of a tropical night. The van was parked by the curb. She swung herself into the driver's seat and took the key from the pocket of her jeans, shoving it into the ignition. Brant had climbed into the passenger seat. Turning to face him, Rowan said tautly, "So what's going on here?"

Brant took his time to answer. He was still getting used to her haircut, to that moment of outrage by the baggage counter when he'd realized she'd changed something about herself that he'd loved, changed it without asking him— and if that wasn't the height of irrationality he didn't know what was. The new haircut, he decided reluctantly, suited her, emphasizing the slim line of her throat and the exquisite angles of her cheekbones. Her eyes, a rich brown in daylight, now matched the velvety darkness of the sky. Eyes to drown in...

He said equably, "I needed a vacation. Through the friend of a friend I heard about Rick's pneumonia and thought I'd take his place. Don't make such a big deal of it, Rowan."

"If it's no big deal, why don't you just go home? Where you belong."

You don't belong with me, that's what she was saying. A statement that truly riled him. "You used to say—fairly frequently, as I recall—that I never took time to smell the roses. Or, in this case, to watch the birds…you should be pleased I'm finally doing so."

"Brant, let's get something straight. What you do or don't do is no longer my concern. Go watch the birds by all means. But don't do it on my turf."

"You've lost weight."

Her exasperated hiss of breath sounded very loud in the confines of the van. Brant watched her fight for composure, her knuckles gripping the steering wheel as if she were throttling him, and discovered to his amazement that he was enjoying himself. Enjoying himself? Was that why he'd come to Grenada?

To Rowan's nostrils drifted the faint tang of aftershave, the same one Brant had used during the four tempestuous years they'd been married. It brought with it a host of memories she didn't dare bring to the surface; she'd be lost if she did. Nevertheless, she let her eyes wander with a lazy and reckless intimacy down his flat belly. "You've lost weight, as well," she said and saw that, briefly, she'd stopped him in his tracks. "Am I right?" she added sweetly.

Brant glared at her in impotent fury. He knew exactly what was wrong. He wanted to kiss her. So badly that he could taste the soft yielding of her lips and the silken slide of her cheek, and feel the first stirring of his groin. But kissing Rowan wasn't part of the plan.

Not that he'd had a plan. He'd acted on impulse in a way rare to him, and now he was faced—literally—with the consequences. Rowan. His ex-wife. His former wife. His divorced wife.

His wife.

He said levelly, knowing he was backing off from something he should have anticipated and hadn't, "Look, it's been a long day and I'm tired. Please, could we go to the hotel so I can catch up on some sleep?''

''Certainly,'' she said. ''But let me make something clear first. I'm doing my job in the next two weeks, Brant. A job I love and do well. You're just another client to me. Because I'm not going to allow you to be anything else—do you understand?''

''I haven't said I want to be anything else,'' he remarked, and watched her lips tighten.

''Good,'' she said viciously, and jammed the clutch into gear. The engine roared to life. She checked in the rearview mirror and pulled away from the curb.

Rowan was an excellent driver, and knew it; and she'd had the last twelve hours to get used to driving on the left. She whipped along the narrow streets, took the roundabout in fine style, and within fifteen minutes turned into the hotel, where she parked next to the rooms that were partway up the hill. ''This is the only place we stay that isn't in close vicinity of a beach,'' she said, breaking a silence that to her, at least, had swarmed with things unsaid. ''You're in Room Nine—Rick had requested a single room.'' She fished around in the little pack strapped to her waist. ''Here's your key.''

She was holding it in her fingertips. To test his immunity, Brant deliberately closed his hand over hers; and as soon as he'd done so, knew he'd made a very bad mistake. Her skin was warm and smooth, her fingers with that supple strength he'd never forgotten. But they were as still in his grip as a trapped bird, and when his glance flew to her face he saw in it a reflection of his own dismay. Dismay? Who was he kidding? It wasn't dismay. It was outright terror.

He snatched the key from her, its cool metal digging into his flesh. ''What time do we get going in the morning?''

''Breakfast at six on the patio,'' she babbled, ''but you

can sleep in if you want, there's a really nice beach about fifteen minutes from the hotel and you'd probably rather have a day to yourself to rest up.''

''I'll see you at six,'' he announced and got out of the van as fast as he could. Room Eight was in darkness. A small light shone from Room Ten. Then Rowan hurried past him, unlocked the patio door to Room Ten and shut it with rather more force than was necessary. He watched as she pulled the curtains tight over the glass.

Brant stood very still under the burgeoning yellow moon. Frogs chirped in the undergrowth; palm fronds were etched against the star-strewn night sky in a way that at any other time he might have found beautiful.

But palm trees weren't a priority right now. How could they be when his whole body was a raw ache of hunger? Sexual hunger. He wanted Rowan now, in his bed, in his arms, where she belonged…and to hell with the divorce. How was he going to get a minute's sleep, knowing she was on the other side of the wall from him?

He'd been a fool to come here, to let Gabrielle talk him into an escapade worthy of an adolescent. If he were smart he'd take Rowan's advice and get on the first plane home. Tomorrow.

Soft-footed, Brant walked over to his own door and inserted the key. The door opened smoothly. He closed it behind him, and heard the smallest of creaks from the room next to his. Rowan. Getting into bed. Did she still sleep naked?

He sat down on the wicker chair, banging his fists rhythmically on his knees. What kind of an idiot was he that he'd neglected to take into account the effect Rowan had had on him from the first time he'd ever seen her, arguing with a customs officer in the Toronto airport seven years ago? He'd engineered a conversation with her that day, had

touched her wrist and had seen the instant flare of awareness in her face, the primitive recognition of female to
male, of mate to mate. Would he ever forget how her pulse
had leaped beneath his fingertip? That all-revealing signal
had engraved itself on his flesh within five minutes of meeting her, and would probably remain with him as long as
he lived.

Two days later they'd fallen into bed in his condo; three
weeks later they were married. A month after that he'd left
for Rwanda, and the fights between them had started, fights
every bit as passionate as their ardent and imperative cou-
plings.

Another tiny creak came from the room next door. He
wanted to kick the wall in, gather her in his arms, make
love to her the whole night through.

But this wasn't Myanmar or Afghanistan or Liberia. He
couldn't bash his way into the next room. Rowan wasn't
an arms smuggler or a drug dealer; she was his ex-wife.

How he hated that word! Almost as much as he hated
the prospect, now almost a certainty, that he was in for one
of his nights of insomnia, nights when too many of the
nightmare images he usually kept at bay would crowd
through his defenses, attacking him from every angle like
an army of fanatic rebels.

Normally it took every bit of his strength and integrity
to hold himself together during those nights; which were,
fortunately, rare. Tonight he had the added, overwhelming
torment of Rowan's presence on the other side of the wall.
Would he ever forget the first time they'd made love? Her
entrancing mixture of shyness and boldness, her astonishing
generosity, her heart-catching beauty…he could remember
every detail of that afternoon, which had blended into a
night equally and wondrously passionate.

Brant buried his face in his hands, his back curved like
a bow, a host of memories stabbing him like arrows.

CHAPTER TWO

ROWAN lay ramrod still in her double bed. The numbers of the digital alarm clock on the night table announced that it was 2:06. If she moved at all, the springs creaked. If she tossed and turned, sooner or later her elbow or her head thumped the wall. The wall that lay between her and Brant.

Her eyes ached. Her body twitched. Her nerves were singing as loudly as the frogs. And all the while her brain seethed with the knowledge that Brant was lying less than a foot away from her, separated from her by a thin barrier of stucco and plaster.

Separated from her by too many fights, too many angry words, too many long months of worrying about him and waiting for him, all the while trying to keep her own life on track. That last departure for Colombia had been, classically, the straw to break the back of their marriage. That and the woman called Gabrielle Doucette.

She had no idea how she was going to get through the next two weeks. No idea whatsoever.

2:09. She had to get some sleep. Tomorrow was a full day, although thank goodness she'd hired a driver and wouldn't have to negotiate roads that could be hair-raising at the best of times. Why *had* Brant come here? What stupidity had impelled him to seek her out just when she was beginning to hope that one day soon she might heal, that hovering somewhere on the horizon there was the possibility, however faint, of putting the past behind her and looking for a new relationship? One that would give her everything Brant had refused her.

How dare he interfere with her life, he who had damaged it so badly? How *dare* he?

Somewhere between two-thirty and quarter to three Rowan fell asleep as suddenly as if she'd been hit on the head. She woke sharp at 5:20; during the years she'd spent guiding tours, she'd trained herself to beat the alarm by ten minutes to give herself that space to think over the day ahead. As so often happened, everything seemed crystal clear to her now that it was morning.

She'd overreacted last night. Big time. And why not? It had been late at night. Her ex-husband had appeared totally unexpectedly and had thrown her for a loop. And again, why not? In all her thirty-one years he was the only man she'd ever fallen in love with; so she'd fallen in a major way. No holding back. No keeping part of herself for herself. She'd thrown herself into their relationship with passion, enthusiasm and a deep joy; and when, all too soon, rifts had appeared, she'd worked with all her heart to mend them. In consequence, the final and utter failure of their marriage had devastated her.

But that was a long time ago.

The only thing she'd have to beware of was touching him. The physical bond between them had never ruptured, not even in the worst of times, and when he'd wrapped his fingers around hers last night as she'd passed him the key, all the old magic had instantly exploded to life, like fireworks glittering against the blackness of sky.

He'd seduced her—literally—from the beginning. She mustn't, for her own sake, allow him to do it again.

There were six other people in the group; she'd have lots of protection. Plus the itinerary would keep everyone busy. On which note, Rowan thought lightly, you'd better get moving. She scrambled out of bed, headed for the shower and left her room at ten to six.

Breakfast started at six on a charming open patio twined with scarlet hibiscus and the yellow trumpet-shaped flowers called Allamanda. The six other members of the group were tucking into slices of juicy papaya; Brant was nowhere to be seen. Maybe he'd decided to heed her advice and take the day off, thought Rowan; or, even better, fly back to Toronto. She beamed at everyone, inquired how they'd all slept, and heard Brant's deep voice say from behind her, "Good morning—sorry I missed seeing all of you last night."

Rowan said evenly, "This is Brant Curtis, from Toronto. He's taking Rick's place, because Rick's ill with pneumonia." Quickly she introduced the others to Brant, then said, "I'm sure you won't remember everyone's name. But you'll soon get to know each other. Coffee, Brant?"

"Shower first, coffee second," he said easily, "that's been my routine for a long time."

He was smiling at her. Often they'd showered together; and they'd both loved Viennese coffee ground fresh and sweetened with maple syrup. Willing herself not to snarl at him, Rowan said, "Personally I prefer herbal tea—can't take the caffeine anymore."

Peg and May, the two elderly sisters from Dakota who looked fluttery and sweet and knew more about birds than most encyclopedias, passed Brant the plate of papaya and the cream for his coffee; Sheldon and Karen, the newly-weds from Maine, gave him the bemused smiles they gave everything and everyone; Steve and Natalie, unmarried and so argumentative that Rowan sincerely hoped they weren't contemplating marriage, both eyed Brant speculatively. Steve no doubt saw Brant as a potential rival for Alpha male; whereas Natalie was probably wanting to haul him off to bed the minute Steve was looking the other way.

Brant was a big boy. Let Brant deal with Natalie.

Peg said, "You missed some wonderful shorebirds in Antigua yesterday, Brant. But you'll have lots of time to catch up...I'm sure you saw the mangrove cuckoo in the breadfruit tree?"

"And the black form of the bananaquit in the bougainvillea?" May added.

Brant took a deep draft of coffee; he was going to need it. He said cautiously, dredging his memory for the pictures in the bird book, "I thought a bananaquit was yellow?" and realized he'd said exactly the right thing. Peg and May launched into an enthusiastic and mystifying discussion about isolation and Darwinian theory, to which he nodded and looked as though he understood every word, munching all the while on a deliciously crumbly croissant smothered with jam.

Natalie, who was wearing a cotton shirt with rather a lot of buttons undone, smoothed her sleek black hair back from her face and pouted her fuschia-colored lips at him. "On the way back to our rooms, Brant, I'll have to show you where I saw the crested hummingbird."

"You can show me first," Steve said aggressively; he had the build of a wrestler and the buzzed haircut of a marine.

"Oh," piped Karen, who had fluffy blond curls and artless blue eyes, "what's that black bird with the long tail on the ledge of the patio?"

"A male Carib grackle," Rowan replied. "The equivalent of our starling, we'll be seeing a lot of them."

Sheldon, Karen's husband, said nothing; he was too busy gazing at Karen in adoration.

Everyone else, Brant saw, had brought binoculars to the table; he'd forgotten his. Rowan looked as though she hadn't had much more sleep than he'd had. Good, he thought meanly, and took another croissant. He was already beginning to realize that keeping up with this lot was going to take a fair bit of energy and that he probably should have read more of the bird book and thought less about Rowan on the long flight from Toronto.

Not that he was here to see birds.

He was here to see Rowan—right?

By the time they left the hotel, the sky had clouded over and rain was spattering the windshield. Their first stop was an unprepossessing stretch of scrubby forest on the side of a hillside, the residence of an endangered species called the Grenada dove. Brant trooped with the rest up the slope, thorns snatching at his shirt and bare wrists, rain dripping down his neck. Wasn't April supposed to be the dry season? Where was the famous sunshine of the Caribbean? Where were the white sand beaches? And why was Rowan way ahead of him and he last in line? Natalie, not to his surprise, was directly in front of him, an expensive camera looped over her shoulder, her hips undulating like a model's on a catwalk. He'd met plenty of Natalies over the years, and avoided them like the plague; especially when they were teamed with bruisers like Steve.

When they were all thoroughly enmeshed in the forest, Rowan took out a tape deck and played a recording of the dove, its mournful cooing not improving Brant's mood. She was intent on what she was doing, her eyes searching the forest floor, all her senses alert. Maybe if he blatted like a dove she'd notice he was here, he thought sourly.

They all trudged further up the hillside and she played the tape again; then moved to another spot, where there was a small clearing. Rowan replayed the tape. From higher up the slope a soft, plangent cooing came in reply. She whispered, "Hear that? Check out that patch of undergrowth by the gumbo-limbo tree."

Brant didn't know a gumbo-limbo tree from a coconut palm. Peg said, "Oh, there's the dove! Do you see it, May? Working its way between the thorn bushes."

"I can see it," Natalie remarked. "Not sure I can get a photo, though."

"Then why can't I find it?" Steve fumed.

"Come over here, Steve," Rowan said, "I've got it in the scope."

She'd been carrying a large telescope on a tripod; Brant watched Steve stoop to look in the eyepiece. Then Karen and Sheldon peered in. Rowan said, "Look for the white shoulders and the white patch on the head. Brant, have you seen it?"

He hadn't. Obediently he walked over and looked through the lens, seeing a dull brown pigeon with a crescent of white on its side. Natalie rubbed against him with her hip. "My turn, Brant," she murmured.

May—who had mauve-rinsed hair while Peg had blue— said to him, "Isn't that a *wonderful* bird?"

She was grinning from ear to ear; Brant couldn't possibly have spoiled her pleasure. "A terrific bird," he said solemnly.

Ten minutes later they emerged back into the cleared land at the base of the scrub forest, and Rowan swept the area with her binoculars. Then she gasped in amazement. "Look—near the papaya tree. A pair of them!"

Brant raised his binoculars. Two more doves were pecking at the earth, their white markings clearly visible. Peg and May sighed with deep satisfaction, Natalie adjusted her zoom lens for a picture and Rowan said exultantly, "This is one of the rarest birds of the whole trip and we've seen three of them! I can't believe it."

Instead of staring at the doves, Brant stared at Rowan. Her cheeks were flushed, her face alight with pleasure; she used to look that way when he'd walked in the door after a three-week absence, he thought painfully. Or after they'd made love.

She glanced up, caught his fixed gaze on her and narrowed her eyes, closing him out; her chin was raised, her damp curls like tiny flames. Steve snapped, "Hurry up and put the scope on them, Rowan."

Rowan gave a tiny start. "Sorry," she said, and lowered the tripod.

Don't you talk to my wife like that.

His own words, which had been entirely instinctive, played themselves in Brant's head like one of Rowan's tapes. She wasn't his wife. Not anymore. And why should it matter to him how a jerk like Steve behaved? Furious with himself, he raised his glasses and watched the two doves work their way along a clump of bushes.

Then Peg said, "A pair of blue-black grassquits at the edge of the sugarcane," and everyone's binoculars, with the exception of Brant's, swiveled to the left.

"How beautiful," May sighed.

"This is the only island we'll see them," Peg added.

"Take a look in the scope, Karen," Rowan offered.

They all lined up for a turn. Brant was last. "All I can see is sugarcane," he said.

Quickly Rowan edged him aside, adjusting the black levers. Her left hand was bare of rings, he saw with a nasty flick of pain, as if a knife had scored his bare skin. "There they are, they'd moved," she said, and backed away.

Into his vision leaped a small glossy bird and its much duller mate. A pair, he thought numbly, and suddenly wished with all his heart that he was back in his condo in Toronto, or striding along the bustling streets of Yangon, Myanmar's capital city. Anything would be better than having Rowan so close and yet so unutterably far away.

They tramped back to the van, adding several other birds to the list on the way, all of whose names Brant forgot as soon as they were mentioned. He couldn't sit beside Rowan; she was in the front with the driver. He took the jump seat next to Peg and tried to listen to the tale of habitat destruction that had made the dove such a rarity.

They drove north next, to the rain forests in the center of the island, where dutifully Brant took note of humming-birds, tanagers, swifts, flycatchers and more bananaquits. Not even the sight of a troop of Mona monkeys cavorting in a bamboo grove could raise his spirits. His mood was more allied to the thunderclouds hovering on the horizon, a mood as black-hearted as the black-feathered and omni-present grackles.

When they reached some picnic tables by a murky lake, Rowan busied herself laying out paper plates and cutlery, producing drinks and a delicious pasta salad from a cooler, as well as crusty rolls, fruit and cookies out of various bags. She did all this with a cheerful efficiency that grated on Brant's nerves. How could she be so happy when he felt like the pits? How could she joke with a macho idiot like Steve?

He sat a little apart from the rest of the group, feeding a fair bit of his lunch to a stray dog that hovered nearby. He had considerable fellow feeling for it; however, Rowan wasn't into throwing him anything, not even the smallest of scraps. To her he was just one more member of the group; she'd make sure he saw the birds and got fed and that was where her responsibility ended.

He felt like a little kid exiled from the playground. He felt like a grown man with a lump in his gut bigger than a crusty roll and ten times less digestible. He fed the last of his roll to the dog and buried his nose in the bird book, trying to sort out bananaquits from grassquits.

Their next destination was a mangrove swamp at the northern tip of the island. Although it had stopped raining, the sweep of beach and the crash of waves seemed to increase Brant's sense of alienation.

Rowan glanced around. "The trail circling the swamp is at the far end of those palm trees."

"I'm going to wait here," Brant said. "I can see the van, so I'll know when you get back."

"Suit yourself," she said with an indifferent shrug.

May protested, "But you might miss the egrets."

"Or the stilts," Peg said.

"I'm going for a swim," Brant said firmly.

May brightened. "Maybe you'll see a tropic bird."

He didn't know a tropic bird from a gull; but he didn't tell her that. "Maybe I will."

"I wish you'd told us this morning we'd be at a beach, Rowan," Natalie said crossly. "I'd love a swim."

"You came here to photograph birds," Steve announced, and grabbed her by the wrist. She glared at him and he glared right back.

"We'd better go," Rowan said quickly. "Once we've trekked around the swamp we have a long drive home."

Brant had put on his trunks under his jeans that morning; he left his gear with the driver of the van, shucked off his clothes and ran into the water, feeling the waves seize him in their rough embrace. He swam back and forth in the surf as fast as he could, blanking from his mind everything but the salt sting of the sea and the pull of his muscles. When he finally looked up, the group was trailing along the beach toward him.

He hauled himself out of the waves, picked up his clothes from the sand and swiped at his face with his towel. Rowan was first in line. He jogged over to her, draping his towel over his shoulder. "Did I miss the rarest egret in the world?"

Midafternoon had always been the low point of the day for Rowan; and the sight of Brant running across the sand toward her in the briefest of swim trunks wasn't calculated to improve her mood. She said coldly, staring straight ahead, "There was a white-tailed tropic bird flying right over your head."

"No kidding."

She hated the mockery in his voice, hated his closeness even more. Then his elbow bumped her arm. "Sorry," he said.

He wasn't sorry; she knew darn well he'd done it on purpose. But Peg and May were right behind her and she couldn't possibly let loose the flood of words that was crowding her tongue. She bit her lip, her eyes skidding sideways of their own accord. The sunlight was glinting on the water that trickled down Brant's ribs and through the dark hair that curled on his chest. His belly was as flat as a board, corded with muscle; she didn't dare look lower.

To her infinite relief a night heron flew over the trees. Grabbing her binoculars, Rowan blanked from her mind the image of Brant's sleek shoulders and taut ribs. He meant nothing to her now. Nothing. She had to hold to that thought or she'd be sunk.

The yellow-crowned night heron was obliging enough to settle itself in the treetops, where it wobbled rather endearingly in the wind. Karen had never seen one before. Quickly Rowan set up the scope, immersing herself in her job again, and when next she looked Brant was standing by the van fully clothed.

Thank God for small mercies, she thought, and shepherded her little flock back into the van. On the drive home along the coast she gave herself a stern lecture about keeping her cool when she was anywhere in Brant's vicinity, whether he was clothed or unclothed. She couldn't bear for him to know that the sight of his big rangy body had set her heart thumping in her breast like a partridge drumming on a tree stump in mating season.

It was none of his business. He'd lost any right to know her true feelings; he'd trampled on them far too often.

He was a client of the company she worked for, one more client on one more trip.

Maybe if she repeated this often enough, she'd start to believe it. Maybe.

CHAPTER THREE

AT DINNER Brant ate curried chicken and mango ice cream as though they were so much cardboard, and tried to talk to Karen, whose sole topic of conversation was Sheldon, rather than to Natalie, whose every topic was laced with sexual innuendo. Rowan was sitting at the other end of the table laughing and chatting with Steve, May and Peg; she looked carefree and confident. He had the beginnings of a headache.

Would he be a coward to fly back to Toronto? Or was it called common sense instead?

People dispersed after dinner; it was nine-fifty and they had to be up before six to leave for the airport, to fly to the next island on the itinerary. Rowan had already gone to her room. Brant found himself standing outside her patio doors, where, once again, the curtains were drawn tight. Without stopping to consider what he was doing, let alone why, he raised his fist, tapped on the glass, and in a voice that emulated Steve's gravelly bass he said, "Rowan? Steve here. Do you have any Tylenol? Natalie's got a headache."

"Just a second," she called.

Then the door opened and at the same instant that her eyes widened in shock, Brant shoved his foot in the gap and pushed it still wider, wide enough that he could step through. Rowan said in a furious whisper, "Brant, get out of here!"

He closed the door behind him. She had started undressing; her feet were bare and her shirt pulled out of her waist-

35

band, the top two buttons undone. In the soft lamplight her skin looked creamy and her hair glowed like a banked fire.

She spat, "Go away and leave me alone—you're good at doing that, you've had lots of practice."

"For God's sake, leave the past out of this!"

"I despise you for pulling a trick like that, pretending you were Steve. Although it's just what I should expect from someone so little in tune with his feelings, so removed from—"

Brant had had enough. With explosive energy he said, "I'm not leaving until you tell me how else I'm going to get five minutes alone with you."

"I don't want ten seconds alone with you!"

"We're not going to spend the next two weeks pretending I've come all this way just to see a bunch of dumpy old pigeons."

Rowan felt her body freeze to stillness; in the midst of that stillness she remembered the resolve she'd made in the van. To keep her cool, her feelings hidden. She wasn't doing very well in that department so far; she'd better see what she could do to improve matters. Forcing herself to lower her voice, she said, "So why not tell me why you've come here, Brant?"

He gaped at her. *Because Gabrielle told me to?* That would go over like a lead balloon. "I just wanted to see you," he said lamely.

"You've seen me," she replied without a trace of emotion. "Now you can go back to Toronto. Or to whatever benighted part of the globe you're writing about next. Either way, I want you to stay away from me."

"Don't I mean anything to you anymore?"

He hadn't meant to say that. Her lips thinned. She answered tersely, "If you're asking if I'll ever forget you, the answer's probably no—the damage went too deep for that.

If you're asking if I want to revive any kind of a relationship with you, the answer's absolutely no. And for the very same reason."

"You've changed."

"I would hope so."

"I didn't mean it as a compliment! You never used to be so cold. So hard."

"Then you can congratulate yourself on what you've accomplished."

"You never used to be bitchy, either," he retorted, his temper rising in direct proportion to his need to puncture her self-possession.

"I'd call it a good dose of the truth rather than bitchiness. But there's no reason we should agree on that, we never agreed on anything else." Suddenly Rowan ran her fingers through her cropped hair, her pent-up breath escaping in a long sigh. "This is really stupid, standing here trading insults with each other. It's been a long day and I've got to be up at five-thirty. So I'm just going to say one more thing, Brant, then I want you to leave. I made a mistake seven years ago when I married you. I've paid for that mistake— it cost me plenty. And now I'm moving on. For all kinds of obvious reasons I don't need your help to do that. Get yourself on the first plane back to Toronto and kindly stay out of my life."

Her fists were clenched at her sides and she was very pale. The woman Brant had been married to would have been yelling at him by now, passion exuding from every pore, her words pouring out as clamorously as a waterfall tumbles over a cliff. Had she really changed that much? Even worse, was he, as she'd said, responsible for that change?

Rowan picked up the receiver of the phone by her bed,

knowing she had to end this. "I'll give you ten seconds. Then I'm calling the front desk."

"Go right ahead," he drawled. "I'll make sure I tell them I'm your ex-husband. I'll tell Natalie, too—she'll spread the word to the group, I'm sure."

"You wouldn't!"

He bared his teeth in a smile. "I've never been known for fighting fair. Had you forgotten?"

She hadn't. One of his weapons had always been his body, of course; his body and the searing sexual bond between the two of them. Suddenly frightened, Rowan said, "Brant, don't do this. You're only making things worse between us."

"According to you, that's impossible."

She took another deep breath and said steadily, "I can only speak for myself here. I still have some good memories—some wonderful memories—of the time we spent together. But when you force your way into my room like this, and threaten to expose my private life to a group of strangers who happen to be my business clients, then I start to wonder if I'm kidding myself about those memories—I was deluded, I wasn't seeing the real man, he never existed. Don't do that to me, Brant. Please."

Some of the old intensity was back in her voice, and there was no doubting her sincerity. Shaken, in spite of himself, Brant blurted, "Is there someone else in your life, Rowan?"

"No," she said flatly. "But I want there to be."

Relief, rage and chagrin battled in his chest: he'd never meant to ask that question. Where the devil was his famous discretion, his ability to control a conversation and learn exactly what he wanted to know from someone who'd had no intention of revealing it? His boss would fire him if he could see him in action right now. Defeated by a woman? Brant Curtis?

He said thickly, "One kiss. For old time's sake."

Panic flared in her face. She grabbed the phone and cried, "You come one step nearer and I'll tell everyone in Grenada that you're the world-famous journalist, Michael Barton. So help me, I will."

Michael Barton was Brant's pseudonym, and only a very small handful of people knew that Brant Curtis and Michael Barton were one and the same man; it was this closely guarded secret that enabled him as Brant Curtis, civil engineer and skilled negotiator, to enter with impunity whichever country he was investigating. He felt an ill-timed flare of admiration for Rowan; it was quite clear that she'd do it, she whom he'd trusted for years with his double identity. "You sure don't want me to kiss you, do you?" he jeered. "Why not, Rowan? Afraid we'll end up in bed?"

"Look up divorce in the dictionary, why don't you? We're through, finished, kaput. I wouldn't go to bed with you if you were the last man on earth."

"Bad cliché, my darling."

With a huge effort Rowan prevented herself from throwing the telephone at him, cord and all. Keep your cool, Rowan. Keep your cool. She said evenly, "It happens to be true."

"But why so adamant? Who are you trying to convince?"

She said with a sudden, corrosive bitterness, "The one man in the world who never allowed himself to be convinced of anything I said."

She meant it, Brant thought blankly. Her bitterness was real, laden with a pain whose depths horrified him. He stood very still, at a total loss for words. He earned his living—an extraordinarily good living—by words. Yet right now he couldn't find anything to say to the woman who had been his lover and his wife. She looked exhausted, he realized with a pang of what could only be compassion, her shoulders slumped, her cheeks pale as the stuccoed walls.

As if she had read his mind, she said in a low voice, "Brant, I work fifteen-hour days for two weeks on this trip and I've got to get some sleep."

"Yeah…I'm sorry," he muttered, and headed for the door. Sorry for what? For bursting into her room? Or for killing the fieriness in her spirit all those months ago?

Was her accusation true? Had he never allowed her to change his mind about anything? If so, no wonder she wouldn't give him the time of day.

The door slid smoothly open and shut just as smoothly. He didn't once look back. Instead of going to his own room, he tramped down the driveway and left the hotel grounds. He'd noticed a bar not that far down the road. He'd order a double rum and hope it would make him sleep. Or six of them in a row. And he wouldn't allow his own good memories—of which there were many— to come to the surface.

He'd be done in if he did.

The patio door closed. As though she couldn't help herself, Rowan peered through the gap in the curtain and watched Brant's tall figure march down the driveway, until it blended with the darkness and disappeared. Shivering, she clicked the lock and pulled the curtain tightly shut. After dragging off the rest of her clothes, she pulled on silk pajamas and got into bed, yanking the covers over her head.

What would have happened if Brant had kissed her? Would he be lying beside her now, igniting her body to passion as only he could?

She slammed on her mental brakes, for to follow that

thought was to invite disaster. She hadn't let him kiss her. She'd kept some kind of control over herself and over him, in a way that was new. Dimly she felt rather proud of this.

Perhaps, she thought with a flare of hope, something good would come out of Brant's reappearance in her life. Perhaps there was a reason for it, after all. Inadvertently she'd been given an opportunity to lay the ghosts of the past to rest. If she could detach herself from him in the next two weeks, really detach herself, then when she went home she'd be free of him. Free to start over and find someone else.

She wanted children, and a man with a normal job. She wanted stability and continuity and a house in the country. She wanted to love and be loved.

By someone safe. Not by Brant with his restless spirit and his inexhaustible appetite for danger. Never again by a man like Brant.

Freedom, she thought, and closed her eyes. Freedom...

At the St. Vincent airport, while he was waiting to go through customs, Brant phoned three different airlines to see if he could get back to Toronto. It was nearing the end of the season, he was told; bookings were heavy. He could go standby. He could be rerouted in various complicated and extremely expensive ways. But he couldn't get on a plane today and end up in Toronto by nightfall.

He banged down the phone and took his passport out. When he rejoined the group he saw that he wasn't the only one to have left it. Natalie and Steve were standing to one side. Natalie was, very nearly, screaming; Steve was, unquestionably, yelling. Their language made Brant wince, their mutual fury made him glance at Rowan. She was talking to May and Peg, a fixed smile on her face.

Then Natalie stomped over to Rowan. Not bothering to

lower her voice, her catlike beauty distorted by rage, she announced, "Get me a single room for the rest of this trip! I'm not going anywhere near that—" and here her language, once again, achieved gutter level.

May said crisply, "Young woman, that's enough!"

Peg added, "This is a public place on a foreign island and you're disgracing our country."

Natalie's head swerved. "Who the hell do—"

"Be quiet," Peg ordered.

"This minute," her cohort seconded.

As Natalie's jaw dropped, Brant threw back his head and started to laugh, great bellows of laughter that released the tension in his chest and the ache in his belly that had been with him ever since he'd first seen Rowan in the airport at Grenada. Uncertainly Karen smiled and Sheldon joined her; a smile tugged at the corner of Rowan's mouth and Steve said vengefully, "Shut up, Natalie."

For a moment it looked as though Natalie was about to launch into another tirade. But then the custom's officer said, "Next, please," and Rowan said briskly, "Your turn, Natalie."

As Natalie stepped over the painted line and fumbled for her passport, Steve said, "Two single rooms, Rowan, and it's the last time I'll travel anywhere with that b—" he caught sight of May's clamped jaw and finished hastily "—broad."

"I'll do my best," Rowan said.

"You'd better," said Steve.

"There's a marvelous word in the English language, Steve, called please," Brant interposed softly. "You might try it sometime. Because I don't like it when you order Rowan around."

Steve took a step toward him, his fists bunched. Even

more softly, Brant said, "Don't do it. You'll end up flat on the floor seeing a lot more than birds."

This whole trip was getting away from her, Rowan thought wildly. A screaming match in the airport and now the threat of a brawl. But, try as she might, she couldn't take her eyes off Brant. Once, she remembered, she and he had been walking down Yonge Street and had been accosted by a couple of teenagers with knives; that evening Brant had had the same air of understated menace, of a lean and altogether dangerous confidence in his ability to defend both himself and her.

It wasn't his job to defend her. Not anymore. Besides which, dammit, it was time she asserted her own authority. "I've said I'll do my best, Steve, that's all I can do," she announced. "And you'll both have to pay extra money, you do realize that? Karen and Sheldon, why don't you go through customs next?" That, at least, would keep Natalie and Steve apart. She'd have to get on the phone at the hotel in St. Vincent and rearrange all the other hotels. And if Steve and Natalie had a reconciliation before the end of the trip, they could darn well sleep apart. It would be good for them.

Not entirely by coincidence, she glanced at Brant. He was watching her, laughter gleaming anew in his blue eyes. It's not funny, she told herself, and winked at him, her lips twitching; then suddenly remembered she was supposed to be keeping her cool. What a joke! How could she possibly keep her cool with Natalie and Steve fighting like alley cats, Peg and May acting like the imperious headmistresses of the very snootiest of private schools, and Karen and Sheldon looking superior because they knew they'd never do anything so crude as to argue?

Not to mention Brant. Handsome, sexy, irresistible Brant. She looked away, flustered and upset. Deep down she

could admit to herself that she was extremely gratified
Brant had sprung to her defense. And explain that one,
Rowan Carter.

The hotel in St. Vincent boasted enough bougainvillea and
palm trees for any postcard, as well as a dining room open
to a view of the beach and a bar with pleasant wicker furniture right at the edge of the beige-colored sand. Rowan
was able to get Steve and Natalie single rooms in separate
wings of the hotel, and suggested they all meet for an early
lunch. She then had the baggage delivered to all the right
rooms, got on the phone to the rest of the hotels, and did
some groceries for the picnic lunch the next day. By which
time she was supposed to be in the dining room.

Steve sat down on one side of her, Brant on the other.
Natalie, she saw with an unholy quiver of amusement, immediately seized the chair on Brant's far side. Okay,
Rowan, she told herself, this time you really are going to
keep your cool, and said brightly, "This afternoon we'll
head up to the rain forest, where we should see St. Vincent
parrots."

"Excellent," said May.

"Exciting," said Peg.

Steve nudged Rowan with something less than subtlety.
"I'll stand you a drink in the bar for every parrot we see."

Over my dead body, thought Brant.

"I don't think so," Rowan responded. "We saw well
over a dozen on our last trip here."

"Steve excels at drinking too much, it's his only talent,"
Natalie said sweetly. "I bet you can hold your liquor,
Brant."

"So much so that I have no need to prove it," Brant
replied. "Rowan, how long a drive to the forest?"

He was smiling at her, his irises the deep blue of the sea,

his dark hair ruffled by the breeze that came from the sea. We're divorced, Rowan thought frantically, we're finished, we're over and done with, and gulped, ''Oh, about an hour, depending if we stop on the way.''

''The St. Vincent parrots are the ones with yellow and blue on them.''

''That's right, although it's more like gold and bronze, along with blue, green and white.''

''You look tired,'' he said quietly.

She was tired. Her period was due soon, and she knew she'd have to dose herself with medication to get through the cramps on the first day. She said in a loud voice, ''Because they're such handsome birds, they've been poached a lot for the parrot trade.''

This launched Peg and May into a discussion about the complexities of economics and environmentalism, and thankfully Rowan focused on her conch salad. When they'd all finished eating, she asked everyone to meet in the lobby in fifteen minutes, and scurried off to ask the kitchen if they'd cook some tortellini for the picnic lunch the next day.

The others went to their rooms. Brant filled his canteen with water from the table, enjoying the breeze, remembering how the skin beneath Rowan's dark eyes was shadowed blue. He'd never before considered how hard she worked; her job had always seemed like a piece of cake compared to his. Not really worth his attention.

This wasn't a particularly comfortable thought. His eyes fell to her chair; she'd left her haversack there. When he bent to pick it up so he could return it to her, he discovered that it was astonishingly heavy. Without stopping to think, he slid the zipper open and looked inside.

What for? Photos of himself? That was a laugh. Photos of another man? That wouldn't be one bit funny.

She wasn't dating anyone else. She'd told him so. And in all the years he'd known Rowan, she'd never lied to him.

Brant was highly skilled at swift searches. The weight of the haversack was due to binoculars, a camera and a zoom lens. No photos turned up. But in a pocket deep in a back compartment he found something that made his pulses lurch, then thrum in his ears. His fingers were caressing the cool ceramic surface of the earrings he'd had designed for her, earrings fashioned like the berries of the rowan tree.

"*What* are you doing?"

Like a little boy caught with his hand in the cookie jar, Brant looked up. He fumbled for the earrings and held them up. "These were the first present I ever gave you."

She whispered ferociously, "You're on vacation, Brant—but you can't give it a rest, can you? You've always got to be the perfect investigator, the one who invades and violates the privacy of others for your own ends. Why don't you just lay off?"

"Why were these earrings buried in your haversack?"

"That's none of your damned business!"

She was swearing at him, he thought in deep relief; the ice-cold, controlled woman of last night was gone. In her place was a woman whose eyes blazed, whose cheeks were stained red with rage and whose breasts—those delectable breasts—were heaving. He retorted, "Just answer the question."

"Oh, because I'm dying with love for you," she stormed. "I'm obsessed with you, I think about you night and day, week in, week out. Hadn't you guessed that? Or could it just possibly be because I'd planned to wear them on this trip since they're kind of neat earrings and when you arrived I decided against it, in case I put any ideas in your head?" She snorted. "I don't need to put any ideas in your head, you can come up with more than enough all by yourself.''

''I didn't—''

''I'm actually starting to be pleased that you're here, Brant Curtis, and how do you feel about that? Do you know why?'' She didn't stop long enough for him to answer. ''You're confirming all the reasons I left you. Every last one of them. By the time you get on the plane in Antigua to go home, I'll be free as a—as a bird, and don't you dare tell me that's another cliché. I'm going to get on with my life. Without you. And I'm beginning to think I'll have you to thank for that.''

So angry he was beyond thought, Brant closed the distance between them in two long strides. Taking her furious face in his hands, the earrings digging into her cheek, he planted a kiss full on her open mouth.

Rowan kicked out at him; his tongue sought all the sweetness he'd missed so desperately for so long, and from behind them Peg gasped, ''Oh, my goodness!''

Brant dropped his hands as if they were clasping fire. Rowan, he noticed distantly, looked as though she might fall down. May said, ''Well, this is a surprise.''

Briefly Rowan closed her eyes in horror, wishing she could open them and find herself anywhere but in the dining room of the Beachside Hotel on the island of St. Vincent. Then she turned around. Peg and May were the only members of the group to be present, for which she thanked her lucky stars. Before she could think of what to say next, Brant said, ''We—er, we knew each other. From before. Rowan and I.''

He sounded as off balance as she felt. ''Yes,'' she faltered, ''that's right. From before. In—in Toronto.''

Somewhere she'd read that if you were going to lie, it

was best to stay as close to the truth as possible. "A couple of years ago," she added.

"We'd rather you didn't tell the rest of them," Brant said.

"Much rather," Rowan gulped. It was odd to feel herself allied with Brant, even temporarily like this. Very odd.

"Just so long as you behave yourself, young man," May said severely. "I've been on six different trips with Rowan and she's one of the best."

"Yes, ma'am," Brant said. He'd had a teacher in grade five of whom he'd been healthily in awe; May and Peg, separately and collectively, fostered in him much the same feeling.

"*The* best," Peg corroborated.

"I'd better get my binoculars," Brant said hastily, dropped the earrings into Rowan's palm and fled.

Fight or flight? If it was Peg and May, he'd choose flight any day, he thought, unlocking the door to his room. But if it was Rowan?

Rowan was glad he was here because it was enabling her to free herself from him.

He didn't like that one bit. In fact, he hated it with every fiber of his being. So what was he going to do about it? Fight? Or run away? The choice was his.

As he brushed his teeth, something else clicked into his brain. Normally, strategy was an integral part of his life. Before he left on any of his assignments, he researched the area exhaustively, planned his itinerary and tried to anticipate all the things that could go wrong. Quite often, his life had depended on this.

Ever since Gabrielle had shown him the brochure for this trip, he'd been acting like a stray bullet ricocheting between two cliffs. Fighting with Rowan at the Grenada airport.

Forcing his way into her room. Searching her bag. Kissing her in a public dining room.

Only a couple of months ago a reviewer, referring to one of his articles, had spoken of his cool, multifaceted intelligence. Maybe it was time he tried to resurrect that intelligence.

Maybe his life depended on it.

Startled, Brant stared at himself in the mirror over the sink. Did it? Is that why he was here?

Then he caught sight of his watch. He was going to be late. Grabbing his haversack and binoculars from the bed, he left the room. But one thing was clear to him. He needed to kiss Rowan again. In privacy and taking his time. He had to know if she'd respond to him. Because if she did, she couldn't very well move on to another man.

No, sirree.

CHAPTER FOUR

THE road to the St. Vincent rain forest grew narrower and narrower, winding along sharp drops without a trace of a guardrail, passing through little villages where goats and donkeys watched the van pass by, and uniformed school-children waved at its occupants. Finally they reached a small parking lot, and everyone clambered out.

Rowan loved this particular nature reserve. The volcanic mountains, green-clad, reared themselves against the sky. Puffy white clouds were sailing along in the wind, which hissed through the sabered fronds of palms and rattled the broad leaves of the banana trees. Cows grazed at the boundary of the reserve, accompanied by white-plumed cattle egrets. She led the way up the slope, passing the picnic area where they'd eat lunch the next day. She had lots of time to find the birds and she felt much better for having told Brant a few home truths.

Freedom to get on with her life. Not until she'd put that into words had she realized the extent to which she'd been on hold the last two years. She'd been a walking zombie. A woman uninterested in other men, bored or repelled by her few attempts at dating, her sexuality buried as deeply as her emotions.

Time for a change, she thought blithely, and when Steve offered to carry the scope, accepted with a smile that was perhaps more friendly than was wise.

Brant saw that smile. He clenched his jaw, feeling a primitive upsurge of male possessiveness; he'd long ago concluded that civilization could be a very thin skin over

instincts and urges that ran far more deeply and impera-
tively.

Which led to the one question he was very determinedly
ignoring. The question of whether he still loved Rowan.

She brought the group to a halt in an open area, and
within minutes they were rewarded by a pair of birds flap-
ping rapidly across their field of vision. Brant would never
have known them for parrots; they were too far away. But
parrots they apparently were.

Unimpressed, he brought up the rear as they entered the
dense shadows of the rain forest. A stream ran alongside
the trail; tree ferns waved their delicate fronds above his
head, and bamboos whispered gently in the breeze; the vertical strands of lianas dropped from the heights of balsa
trees to the ground, like the bars of a cage. He'd spent a
lot of time in rain forests over the years, in the golden
triangle of Thailand, in Myanmar and Borneo and Papua
New Guinea. He trudged along, answering Natalie's attempts at conversation with minimal politeness.

The first flurry of excitement was a cocoa thrush; they
hadn't sighted one in Grenada, so St. Vincent was their last
chance. It was a chubby brown bird of no particular dis-
tinction, in Brant's opinion nothing to get excited about.
The same was true of the next sighting, a whistling warbler
endemic to St. Vincent. He caught a glimpse high in the
canopy of a black and white bird, and in the scope saw the
dark band across its chest that the bird book depicted.
Rowan, Peg and May were beaming; although she couldn't
get a photo of the warbler, even Natalie temporarily forgot
him in its favor.

The pace was excruciatingly slow. He dropped back for
a while, not wanting to talk to anyone, watching the small
patches of sunlight waver through the trees, noticing how
everything green struggled toward that light. Every other

time he'd been in rain forests, his nerves had been stretched
tight, alert for dangers that ranged from drug gangs to rebel
guerrillas. There was no danger today. No reason why he
shouldn't stop to admire a fern's single-minded climb up
the trunk of a waterwood tree, or listen to the innocent
burble of the stream in its mossy bed. He began to pick out
individual birdcalls; he watched a black and scarlet ant lug
a scrap of leaf across the path.

A flicker of movement in the trees caught his attention.
When he raised his binoculars, he saw a most peculiar
brown and white bird that was fluttering its wings continually, a big, smooth-feathered bird with a predatory bill. A
trembler, he thought, remembering his reading on the plane,
and flicked through the bird book until he found it. Feeling
very pleased with himself for actually having identified
something, he caught up with the rest of them.

"You missed the brown trembler," Natalie chided.

"No, I didn't," he said, and grinned at Rowan.

"Have you seen the tanager?" she asked, pointing to the
scope. "Lesser Antillean tanager, St. Vincent race."

Brant gazed into the eyepiece. Into his field of vision
leaped a bird with jade wings, a bronze cap and a rich,
golden back, all its feathers gleaming as though they had
been polished especially for him. He raised his head, looked
straight at Rowan and said huskily, "It's very beautiful. Its
head's the same color as your hair."

She blushed fierily. Steve pushed him aside, growling,
"Let me have a look."

That remark hadn't been part of Brant's strategy. But it
had worked. If she was ready to move on to someone else,
why should a compliment from him so evidently discom-
pose her?

The next bird they sighted was a solitaire, a handsome
bird with gray, white and rufous plumage, whose clear,

chiming call sounded as ethereal as a boys' choir in a cathedral. Rowan then located a ruddy quail dove, followed by a purple-throated Carib. The Carib, so Brant discovered, was a hummingbird. At first he wasn't overly impressed by this small, dark bird. But then it darted into a patch of sunlight; its feathers flashed like amethysts and emeralds, brilliantly iridescent, fleetingly and gloriously beautiful.

"Pretty, isn't it?" Rowan said casually.

"Exquisite," he said, making no attempt to mask his delight.

Rowan frowned at him. The Brant of old would no more have spent time watching a hummingbird than he would have canceled one of his own trips for her sake. He looked relaxed, she thought. As though he were enjoying himself. And that, too, was new.

Feeling uneasy and on edge, she folded the scope. Five minutes further along the trail she found another Carib, this time perched on a tiny, cup-shaped nest in the shade. "Is it a male or a female?" Natalie asked, focusing her camera.

"Female." Rowan looked right at Brant. "The pair bond lasts two or three seconds and then the male's gone."

Her chin was tilted. *We went to bed together that last night,* she was saying. *But then you left, didn't you? You left me alone for eight months.*

He had. She'd begged him not to go to Colombia that last time and he'd paid her no attention. She was using female intuition, so he'd told her, as a ploy to try and get her own way. Three weeks into his stay he'd been abducted, along with Gabrielle; ironically, both he and Gabrielle had been hired as negotiators to obtain the release of some oil company engineers who'd been kidnapped by the same group of rebels.

His eyes fell from the blatant challenge in Rowan's gaze, his fragile sense of peace shattered. In the four years of their marriage, had he ever changed his plans for her? As he sought through his memories, he could only conclude that he hadn't. His job was much too important for that. He earned five times her salary; his articles helped mold opinion in high places around the globe, and exposed atrocities that dictators the world over didn't want to appear in print. Whereas all she did was find birds.

Birds that had made his soul exult with their beauty.

More confused than he'd ever been in his life, Brant saw Rowan check her watch. They turned back, wending their way to the van and then driving to the hotel. Dinner remained a blur in his mind; he listened as Rowan outlined the plans for tomorrow, and escaped as soon as he could. In his room he thumbed through the bird book for a while and read a couple of chapters in the very badly written espionage novel he'd picked up in Toronto's Terminal Two. Although the room felt too small to contain him, he had no desire to head for the nearest bar. In Grenada all that had gotten him was a hangover the next day.

He'd go for a swim. If he didn't soon burn off some energy, he'd go nuts.

The moon was three-quarters full and the lights from the hotel glimmered on the water. The repetitive slosh of waves on the sand sounded very soothing. He strode past the bar, where Steve was chatting up one of the other female guests and Natalie was sitting with Sheldon and Karen, drinking rum punch and looking thoroughly bored. Quickly he dropped his towel on the sand and ran into the water, heading straight out in a fast crawl.

Away from the lot of them. But mostly away from his own thoughts.

There were powerboats and yachts anchored offshore. Brant swam around them, glad to be out of sight of the hotel; then he set off for the rocky point to the south of the hotel, swimming more easily now, enjoying the splashing in his ears and the pull of his muscles against the water's resistance. The moonlight that dipped and swayed on the swell was a cold, luminous white. Rowan had been cold toward him, cold and distant. Wasn't it up to him to ignite her to the fire and heat of the sun? All alone like this, feeling oddly peaceful, that didn't seem so impossible a task.

He pulled himself up on the rocks and sat for a while, until he started to get cold. Needing to get his blood moving, he set off at a jog back down the beach toward the hotel.

Halfway along the sand, a figure stepped out of the bushes that edged the hotel grounds. A woman. For a wild moment Brant was sure it was Rowan; in crushing disappointment he realized it was Natalie. She flung herself at him, winding her arms around his waist and leaning all her weight on him. He staggered, put his own arms around her to keep his balance and said flatly, "Natalie, I don't need this."

She smelled strongly of rum. She said blearily, "Sure you do...I'll give you a good time, I've wanted to go to bed with you ever since I saw you at breakfast that first day, you're just the kind of guy who turns me on."

She rather spoiled this speech by ending it with a hiccup. Brant set her firmly on her feet and moved back two paces. She was wearing a minidress that left little to the imagination and she was smiling at him, running her tongue over her full lips. "Steve is the one who turns you on," he said, wondering if it was true. "You're only doing this to make him jealous."

She reached out one hand and ran it down his body from breastbone to navel. "Don't make me laugh. You've got a great body."

Her caress left him as cold as the moonlight. "I'm not available."

She sidled closer. "Oh, yes, you are…although you do take the cake for being uptight. Wound up tighter than a drum, what's your problem?"

He wouldn't have expected her to be so perceptive. "If I've got a problem," he said wryly, "it's not your job to solve it. Make up with Steve…that's what you really want to do."

Her lip quivered. She sagged against him, wailing, "I asked him to marry me a week ago and he says he's not ready to settle down, and look at him at the bar sucking up to that blonde, I hate him, I hate his guts…"

She was sobbing now, luxuriantly prolonged sobs that Brant was sure everyone at the hotel could hear. "Natalie," he said with all the force of his personality, "shove it! It's the rum that's crying, not you, and maybe you should sit down somewhere all by yourself and think about what you really want out of life." Advice it wouldn't hurt him to take himself, he thought ruefully.

"I want y-you," she snuffled.

"I'm not your type any more than you're mine."

Her head reared up. "Right," she said venomously, "I've watched you, you've only got eyes for Rowan. Well, you can have her, the stuck-up bitch—I'm going back to the bar."

She set off unsteadily across the sand. Brant ran his fingers through his wet hair. He'd tried.

Much good had it done him.

He'd give her five minutes and then he'd get his towel and go to bed. Did every other member of the group think he only had eyes for Rowan?

Peg and May sure did.

Hell, thought Brant. Hell and damnation.

A voice wafted across the water, a voice full of mockery. "You missed your chance there, Brant."

The hair rose on the back of his neck. He looked out to sea, and saw a dark head, dark as a seal's, swimming toward the shore. Rowan.

Great. So she'd been a witness to that little fiasco. He said nastily, "This whole trip is rapidly turning into farce—remember that play we saw in London, the one where people kept bursting through all those doors? All we need now is Steve to blunder his way down the beach."

"Oh, no," Rowan said, "you've got it wrong. All we need now is Gabrielle."

She was standing up in thigh-deep water, moonlight glinting on her wet skin and on a one-piece swimsuit that clung to her body. His heart was jouncing in his chest as though he were seventeen, not thirty-seven. Bluntly he stated the obvious. "I sure don't need Gabrielle here."

The air was cool on Rowan's skin; but she scarcely noticed. In an effort to settle her jangled nerves before bed, she'd swum out behind the nearest moored powerboats, and it was from there that she'd heard Natalie's proposition, and her subsequent sobs and wails. Infuriated that everyone in the group now seemed to be aware of the tension between her and Brant, she'd then made the mistake of alerting Brant to her presence.

So much for keeping her cool.

Distantly aware that the water was to her knees now, wavelets rippling on the shore, Rowan said with icy clarity, "Oh? So you've dumped Gabrielle, too? She only lasted three years to my four? Dear me."

Brant's jaw tightened, his throat muscles corded like rope. "How about a little reality check here? You can't dump someone you've never had."

"Oh, for God's sake!" Rowan exploded. "Why don't

you give up this fiction that you and Gabrielle weren't lovers? I *hate* it when you lie to me."

"I've never lied to you about Gabrielle!"

All the pain and rage of the last two years seized Rowan in their fangs. "I saw you, Brant," she seethed. "The day I went to the hospital, the same day I got back from Greenland."

"I don't have a clue what you're talking about."

"I stood in the doorway of your room and watched you for a full five seconds that felt as long as a lifetime. You had your arms around each other, you and Gabrielle, and your cheek was resting on her hair. You were whispering something to her, heaven knows what...but do you know what was the worst? The expression on your face." In spite of herself, Rowan heard her voice break. "You looked so—so tender. So loving. I thought I was the only woman who called that up in you. I was your wife, after all. But that was the day I realized I'd been supplanted." She scrubbed at her cheeks, where tears were mingling with drops of salt water. "So I left. And I never came back."

Feeling as though someone had hit him with a two-by-four, Brant said helplessly, "My God, Rowan..." and all the while he was searching his memory for the details of the scene that must have, he realized with a sick lurch of his gut, cost him his marriage. "I didn't even see you..."

"Of course you didn't, you only had eyes for her. That's the whole point," Rowan said bitterly.

By now she was standing a couple of feet away from him. She was crying. But some deep intuition warned Brant against reaching out for her, even though he craved to do so. "For the last two years I've thought you didn't care enough about me to come to the hospital," he said. "That you'd condemned me for infidelity without even giving me a chance to defend myself."

"Oh, I cared. More fool me."

"I remember that day now," he said slowly. "Gabrielle was on the same floor as me, she'd had dengue fever, as well. And they kept trying to foist psychiatrists on both of us, I remember that, too. She'd—"

"Brant, I don't even want to talk about it," Rowan snapped. "I know what I saw. No explanation that you can conjure up two years later is going to convince me otherwise."

He fought down an anger that if he gave it rein would ruin everything. "Tell me something," he said levelly. "Up until I went away that last time, had I ever lied to you?"

"No," she said unwillingly. "I know there was stuff you didn't tell me about your trips, even though I begged you to. A whole lot of stuff. To protect me. Or yourself. But I don't think you ever lied." Again she swiped at her wet cheeks. "Why should you? You hadn't met Gabrielle."

Brant said forcefully, "In the three years I've known Gabrielle, I've never once made love to her. Or wanted to."

Rowan flinched. "Don't! Don't do this to me, Brant. You wouldn't be the first man to be unfaithful to his wife and I'm sure you won't be the last. Just don't lie about it."

There was a band around his chest squeezing the air from his lungs and he had no idea what to say next. "Dammit, I'm not lying!"

"Let me tell you something else. I was in Greenland sledding across the sea ice when you were released. So I didn't know anything about it until I landed in Resolute Bay. There were newspapers there, full of how you and Gabrielle had been imprisoned together. Full of innuendos. The photos showed the two of you holding on to each other at the Miami airport, then arriving in Toronto together— you were holding her hand by the ambulance." She dragged air into her throat. "I saw all that. And, of course, I'd lived through eight months of knowing you and she were together. But I still trusted you. So as soon as I got back to Toronto, I went to the hospital to see you."

She ran her fingers through her cropped curls. "I saw you, all right. That's when I realized you loved her, not me. That I'd been a fool to trust you." She gulped in more air. "What would you have believed, Brant? If it had been you standing in the doorway of that hospital room, watching me and another man in each other's arms? A man I'd spent the last eight months with."

His tongue felt thick in his mouth. "I'd probably have believed the worst. Like you did."

Her shoulders sagged; somehow she'd needed to hear him say that. "Well. You know the rest. I got a lawyer and a year later we were divorced." It hadn't been quite as simple as that. There was one particular secret from the last three years that she'd never shared with anyone, a secret laced with pain and guilt; nor was she about to share it now. Not with Brant.

Natalie's loud sobs had left Brant unmoved. Rowan's silent weeping rended his heart. He said quietly, risking a step closer to her so he could wipe her wet cheek, "Rowan, you're cold and it's late. But I really need you to hear me out. To try and listen with an open mind."

"My towel's around here somewhere," she said vaguely.

He looked around, saw the dark shape lying on the sand a few feet away and picked it up. Taking another risk, he draped it over her shoulders and watched her tug it around her body. In a small voice she said, "Okay—I'll listen."

He'd been afraid she'd say no. His own throat was clogged with emotion. But of course he never cried; hadn't shed a tear since the year his mother had died when he'd been five and his father had come home to take over his upbringing. Which was, he thought grimly, nothing whatsoever to do with Rowan.

He cudgeled his brain, desperate to convince her of the truth. "Three things," he said. "First of all, that day in the hospital was the day Gabrielle broke. She'd been incredibly brave through the whole eight months, but that morning her doctor had ordered some resident in psychiatry to see her, a young pup who insisted she had to process and integrate, you know the kind of jargon they use. She fled to my room and started to cry...she's like you, she hardly ever cries. And yes, I was holding her, and yes, there'd have been tenderness, even love, in my face because she and I had been through a lot together..."

Rowan stood very still. She was shivering, although not altogether from cold, the scene in the hospital room etched as clearly in her mind as if it were yesterday. "Go on," she muttered.

He'd sworn he'd never tell anyone what he was about to tell Rowan. But if ever there was a time to break one of his own rules, this was it. "The second thing is this, and don't ask me to explain it because I can't. Somehow Gabrielle in that eight months became the mother I missed so badly when I was a little boy...the sister I never had. I couldn't have gone to bed with her. It would have been like incest. If I love Gabrielle, Rowan, I love her like a sister." His laugh was humorless. "That sounds so damned corny."

It did. It also sounded peculiarly convincing. Rowan buried her chin in her towel. "Number three?" she said neutrally.

"That's easy. I wouldn't be standing here if it wasn't for Gabrielle. You see, her best friend Sonia Williams is the wife of Rick Williams, the fellow with pneumonia." Quickly he described the scene in Gabrielle's apartment last

Sunday, marveling that it was less than a week ago when it felt like a lifetime. "Gabrielle's the one who told me—in no uncertain terms—that I needed to see you."

She also thinks I still love you. But that was number four and he'd only promised three. He clamped his mouth shut, waiting for Rowan's response.

For what seemed like forever she was silent, the waves splashing gently on the shore, the moon rocking on the water behind her. Brant said in a cracked voice, "Don't you believe a word I've said?"

Finally Rowan looked up. It was odd, she thought, that after everything he'd told her, all she could feel was a dull ache somewhere in the vicinity of her heart. "I don't know what to think," she mumbled. "I—I guess I believe you."

She didn't sound convinced and she looked unutterably sad. Brant wanted more from her than that halfhearted avowal, a great deal more. Trying to smother his disappointment, searching for a kind of wisdom and restraint he'd never felt the need for before, he said with a twisted smile, "I think it's past time you went to bed, Rowan. Sleep on it, and we'll talk again tomorrow."

She nodded like a marionette on a string. "Okay," she said again.

Brant put an arm lightly around her shoulders and steered her toward the path to the hotel, remembering to pick up his own towel on the way. Five people were left in the bar, one of them Steve, now minus both Natalie and the blonde. Steve got to his feet, staggered over to them and said truculently, "He bothering you, Rowan?"

"No," Rowan said coldly.

"You sure?"

"Back off," Brant said in a tone of voice he used rarely but always to good effect.

Steve blinked. "If she wants to be left alone, then that's

what you oughta do,'' he pronounced with an air of profundity.

Brant might have laughed had Steve's words not been so unpleasantly near the truth. "I'll remember that," he said, and continued along the concrete pathway between the mounds of bougainvillea. When he came to the door of Rowan's room, he kissed her lips, which were cold, and said, "Thanks for listening."

His big body was so close Rowan could have tangled her fingers in the dark pelt on his chest. She'd never forgotten a single detail of Brant's body, not how he looked or felt, nor how he used to move against her own body with a sensuality she'd adored. Even the scent of his skin, salty now from the sea, was utterly familiar to her.

A great wave of terror washed over her. Clumsily she tugged the room key from around her neck and unlocked the door. "Good night," she said, scurried through the opening and shut the door in his face. Her knees were trembling and every muscle she owned ached. She stumbled to the bathroom, put the plug in the tub and turned on the hot tap.

CHAPTER FIVE

ROWAN was dreaming.

She was playing basketball, an all-important championship game that would determine whether her team got into the finals. The crowd was screaming in the background. Then she saw that the member of the opposing team whom she'd been assigned to guard was Brant: angry, sweaty, and altogether too large. She dodged, she ducked, she darted back and forth on the floor, her legs aching, her stomach tied in knots, and knew in her heart it was hopeless. She couldn't possibly outwit him.

A piercing beep signaled time-out.

Rowan found herself sitting bolt upright in bed, and jammed down the button on her alarm clock to stop its insistent summons. Her ears were ringing with the feral roar of the crowd and her belly was clenched with remembered fear.

Except it wasn't fear that was clenching her belly. It was a cramp. Oh, no, she groaned inwardly, leaning forward to ease the pain. Not today.

Rapidly she ran her mind back over the calendar. She was two days early. Stress, so they said, could do that to you.

Today they had the longest hike of the whole trip, and she had a picnic lunch to organize. She had to keep Steve and Natalie from each other's throats, she had to find a perched parrot for May and Peg, and she had to deal with Brant.

Just a regular day, she thought wryly. Right off the bat

she'd take one of the pills her doctor had prescribed for the first day of her period. She didn't like taking pills. But this was one time her principles could fly out the window.

Brant. He'd been telling the truth about Gabrielle last night on the beach, she was almost sure of it. So where did that leave her? Aside from late for breakfast.

Totally confused, that's where.

Rowan scrambled out of bed, showered in the hottest water she could bear, letting it beat on her lower back, and got dressed, picking out her favorite tangerine shirt. The hot water had given her face a tinge of color; she brushed her hair, put on some lipstick and gave herself an encouraging grin in the steamy mirror. She'd go out there and she'd do her job. No arguments with Brant, and if Steve and Natalie stepped out of line, she'd cream them. Diplomatically, of course.

She laced up her boots and left the room, and it seemed a good omen that in the dining room Peg was seated on one side of Brant and May on the other, and that all three were embroiled in a discussion about agronomics.

What Rowan knew about agronomics could have been put on the blade of a hoe. She smiled brightly at Steve, who looked rather the worse for wear, and started asking him about the scuba diving business he owned in Boston.

So what if she'd had a ridiculous dream about basketball? Everything was going to be fine today.

Rowan's optimism lasted through breakfast and most of the drive to the rain forest. But as the van jounced and bounced over the potholes in the road, the effects of the pill she'd taken began to wear off. While it wasn't an overly strenuous hike to the parrot look-off, it was considerably further than they'd gone yesterday; and there were lots of stops along the way, all of which involved either standing as she searched the dense greenery with her binoculars, or else bending over the scope. Her backache got worse; she tried her best to breathe her way through the cramps without being too obvious about it.

When they finally reached the look-off, the whole group got to see the graceful soaring of a black hawk over the canopy of trees; this island was their only chance to see the hawk's elegant black and white plumage and hooked yellow bill, so Rowan was delighted that it had appeared so readily.

Brant saw her pleasure. He also noticed, because he knew her well, that some kind of strain underlay this pleasure and that she was avoiding eye contact with him.

Several parrots—always in pairs, Brant couldn't help noticing—flapped across the gap in the trees, the gold on their wings in striking contrast to the green slopes of the mountains, their raucous calls echoing in the deep valley. They left Brant feeling edgy and uncertain; nor had the rain forest brought him the transitory peace of yesterday.

Rowan looked terrible.

She might be deceiving the others; but because all his senses were attuned to her, he was acutely aware of the pallor in her cheeks and the shadows under her eyes. She didn't look like a woman who'd discovered the night before that her ex-husband hadn't been unfaithful to her. Or else the discovery had brought her no joy.

She looked so weighed down and exhausted that he longed to comfort her. He could cheerfully have throttled sweet-natured Karen who wanted help in seeing vireos, hummingbirds, and then the two parrots that were obliging enough to perch in a tree on the far side of the valley.

There was no faulting Rowan's patience, nor her genuine pleasure when Karen suddenly gasped, ''Oh, *that* tree! Now I see them—oh, aren't they beautiful!''

The rest of the group was focusing on the parrots. Brant

watched Rowan lean back against one of the vertical posts
that supported the roof of the look-off, and shut her eyes.
The slender line of her legs in their bush pants, the curve
of her hips and jut of her breasts all filled him with a frantic
longing. But overriding his rampant sexual needs was
something new. The desire to protect her. To cherish her
and look after her.

Was this really a new feeling? Surely not. He and Rowan
had lived as husband and wife for four years, it couldn't
be new. He'd been a good husband...hadn't he?

His hiking boots soundless on the grass, Brant stepped
closer. "Rowan..." he said softly.

Her eyes flew open to meet his, and she pushed away
from the post. She didn't say a word. She didn't need to.
He got the message anyway.

Get lost. Now.

Then her face constricted with pain and, as if she
couldn't help herself, she hunched forward over her belly.

Brant, you idiot, he thought in a great surge of relief.
This is physiological, not emotional. First day of the month.
Rowan always had cramps that day. He said in a fierce
whisper, "I'm carrying the scope on the way back, as well
as that bloody great camera in your haversack, and don't
you dare argue."

Slowly she straightened, trying to breathe deep to relieve
the pain. "I sure wish you'd mind your own business."

"I can't," he said with raw truth.

"Then try harder."

"Rowan, I—"

Through gritted teeth she said, "Brant, go take a hike."

Sheldon called, "The first one's just flown. There goes
the other one—can you find them in the scope again,
Rowan?"

"I'll give it a try," she said with a cheerfulness that irked the hell out of Brant. But that was her job, of course. To find birds and be nice to her clients.

She wasn't wasting many of her niceties on him.

He undid her haversack for the second time and put her camera in his own bag. When they were leaving the look-off half an hour later, he pushed past Steve and put his hand on the tripod just as Rowan did. "I'll carry it," he said loud enough for everyone to hear, and felt her fingers dig into his in impotent fury.

He grinned at her, daring her to make an issue of it. "Don't worry, I'll stick close to you," he added, "so you can use it whenever you need to."

"Thank you, Brant," Rowan said in a honeyed voice, "you're so thoughtful."

You're an arrogant bastard, was what she really meant. "You're welcome," he said with his very best smile.

He kept to her heels all the way back to the picnic site, ignoring the waves of antagonism coming from both Steve and Natalie. Not to mention Rowan. It started to rain, drops pattering on the leaves; when they emerged at the picnic site, the mountain crests were hidden in thick gray cloud and the grass was drenched.

Bent over under the small corrugated tin overhang of the park headquarters, which was tightly locked, Rowan mixed tortellini with artichoke halves, sun-dried tomatoes, Parmesan and an olive oil dressing, and cut up green onions and cucumber for the tabbouleh. The others were huddled against the wall. Her back was killing her.

The sun came out again as they were finishing eating. Rowan cleaned up the leftovers and reloaded the van, and they drove to the Botanic Gardens in Kingstown, making a couple of stops on the way for shorebirds. While the cramps didn't seem to be abating very much, she was reluctant to take a second pill because they made her drowsy and heavy-headed.

There was a captive breeding program for the parrots at the gardens; as the rest of the group milled around the big cages and took pictures of the birds and of the dramatic scarlet and yellow heliconia flowers, Brant saw that Rowan was standing by herself, staring into the farthest cage. He stationed himself beside her, watching the parrots cling to the metal wire. "Neither of us ever liked zoos," he ventured.

"No," she said, her gaze fixed on the birds. "I just have to hope this is doing some good, increasing their population so they won't get extinct."

He didn't want to talk about the population dynamics of parrots. "I'm sorry you're feeling lousy. That first day always was bad for you, wasn't it?"

She turned to face him, her brown eyes openly unfriendly. "I'm not asking you for sympathy. I'm not asking you for anything."

His lashes flickered. "So you didn't believe me last night."

"Yes, I did. But it doesn't make any difference, don't you see?"

"Can't say that I do," he retorted.

Her brow crinkled. "Well, actually that's not strictly true, it did sort of make a difference. I feel better knowing you didn't lie to me, that you weren't unfaithful with Gabrielle. It's very strange." Absorbedly, she ran her fingers down the small metal squares of the cage. "I haven't given it a lot of thought because I've been feeling so awful all day. But I'd have to say I feel looser. Freer. As though I can let you go more easily now, because I know you didn't cheat on me with another woman."

Brant suddenly felt like the one in the cage, a cage that

was shrinking fast, pressing in on him on every side. He said hoarsely, "Freer? *That's* how you feel?"

"I know it's not logical," she answered with a helpless shrug.

"Is that what you want?" he rapped, hearing each word fall like a stone from his lips. "To be free of me?"

She glanced around. The others had headed toward a jacaranda tree whose blooms were a mist of purple, and would be, she knew from past experience, alive with hummingbirds. She should be there with them; but they could wait for a few minutes. With passionate intensity she said, "Brant, I've been like a robot the last couple of years. Separated but not separated, free to date but not wanting to, alone in my bed and with no desire to put anyone else there in your place. I'm thirty-one years old. I've got to move on—and the sooner the better. We've both got to. I'm beginning to think Gabrielle was right, you did need to see me. Just as I needed to see you." She managed a smile. "Smart woman, that."

Brant was sweating in the ninety-degree heat, yet his hands felt like chunks of ice. He was the one who'd sworn to Gabrielle that he was through with Rowan. That they were divorced in all senses of the word. He was also the one who supposedly didn't tell lies.

So where did that leave him?

In bad trouble, that's where.

"Rowan," he stumbled, "Gabrielle being like a sister to me wasn't the only reason I didn't sleep with—"

"Sorry, I've got to go, Natalie's waving."

His feet felt like chunks of ice, too. Weighted to the spot, Brant watched her hurry around the corner of the cage toward the jacaranda tree. He hadn't slept with Gabrielle because he loved Rowan. Loved her? Past tense? Or, despite all his protestations to the contrary, did he still love her?

She wanted to move on. To another man and another life, one that didn't include him.

He'd kill the son of a bitch and ask questions afterward.

Sure, Brant, he jeered. You know damn well you won't do that. Because if Rowan really wants to be free, there's not one solitary thing in the whole wide world you can do to stop her. Not one. You'd have to let her go.

He realized he was gripping the cage so tightly that his knuckles were white as bone. Rage, sexual frustration, and a sense of utter powerlessness were part of that grip; and all these emotions were fueled by a stark and unrelenting fear.

A lot of his assignments had made him feel afraid, although never to this crippling level. But powerlessness was a new sensation. He wasn't used to that.

He rubbed his hands down the sides of his jeans. He had to pull himself together; the others would be wondering what the devil was wrong with him, cowering behind a cageful of parrots. Basically he didn't care if he ever saw another parrot. He had more important things on his mind. Like what his next strategy should be.

He'd told Rowan the truth about Gabrielle. She'd believed him. But all he'd accomplished was to drive her further away. It was going to be hard to top that for sheer incompetence, he thought acerbically. Come on, buddy, you're supposed to be the guy with brains, the expert at getting out of tight corners. Or so your boss thinks. So why don't you put some of your expertise to use as far as your ex-wife's concerned?

He trailed across the gardens between royal palms and cannonball trees, between billows of bougainvillea and the scarlet spikes of heliconia. Steve was carrying the scope, but not even this could shift Brant's brain into any gear other than reverse.

He quite literally didn't know what to do next. Was this why he was so frightened? Or was it the prospect of Rowan in another man's arms that was making his armpits run with sweat and his blood thrum in his ears?

He followed the rest of them back to the van; he had a shower in his room, then trailed to the dining room for dinner. Rowan had put on makeup along with a bright orange silk shirt; with a nasty tightening of his nerves he saw she was wearing earrings, ceramic earrings shaped like rowanberries that matched her shirt. Brant ordered smoked fish and tried to quell the anger roiling in his gut. How was he to interpret her gesture except as a supreme indifference toward him and his long-ago gift? Toward the love that had been behind that gift?

To hell with fancy strategies. He was going to find out if she was indifferent to him and he was going to do it soon. And he wasn't going to be fussy about his methods.

He didn't bother ordering coffee, left the table before her, and strode down the corridor toward her room, which was in the other wing from his. Tucking himself into an alcove along with a potted, spiky and extremely ugly cactus, he waited for her to arrive. He didn't know what he was going to say. But he sure knew what he was going to do.

It was ten years since he'd had a cigarette and he'd give his eyeteeth for one right now. Brant jammed his hands in his pockets and waited. Five minutes passed, another five, and then he heard the soft pad of steps along the brick walk that connected the rooms. The steps stopped at Rowan's door. Moving with calculated slowness, he risked peering around the edge of the alcove.

Rowan's back was half turned to him. She was searching her pockets for her key, finally locating it in her hip pocket. Then she dropped it. She said a very pithy word that brought an involuntary grin to his lips, and stooped to pick it up. Then she wearily rubbed the small of her back. If she'd been pale earlier, she looked like a ghost in the dusk.

She also looked like a woman at the end of her tether. Brant's heart constricted with compassion. He couldn't confront her now. No matter how angry and afraid he was.

As he eased back into the alcove, a cactus spike stabbed the back of his knee; although he managed to smother his instinctive yelp of pain, the heel of his hiking boot struck the side of the pot. Rowan called out sharply, "Who's there?"

Feeling utterly foolish, Brant stepped out into the open. "It's me. But I wasn't going to—"

"I should have known it would be you!"

"I'd changed my mind, I wasn't—"

She rolled right over him. "You never give up, do you? I suppose that's why you're such a good journalist—but it sure doesn't impress me right now."

"Oh, quit it, Rowan! You don't need to be so goddamned argumentative. What you need to do is stop talking, spend an hour in a Jacuzzi and then get three nights' sleep."

She thrust the key into the lock. "I know I look awful, I don't need you telling me."

He said rashly, "When we were married, this was the night I used to rub your back."

"On the rare occasions when you were home," she flashed. "Which was probably one month out of six."

Stung, Brant said, "I had a job to do."

"Yes, you did. Job first, Rowan second. Too bad you didn't explain that to me before we got married."

"You wouldn't have listened," he snarled. "You wanted to marry me just as much as I wanted to marry you."

"So here's another cliché you can add to your collection—marry in haste, repent at leisure."

In the dim light her eyes were like pools of lava. Brant seized her by the elbows, yanked her against the length of his body and kissed her hard on the mouth. That, at least, had been part of his strategy.

Her body was as rigid as a board and between one moment and the next all his anger collapsed. Rowan was in his arms again after an absence that felt like forever. The blood beating in his ears, Brant slid his hands up her arms to her shoulders, kneading them gently with his fingers, and softened his kiss, seeking to evoke the response that had always been there for him. With his tongue he stroked the soft curve of her lip. One hand drifted down her back to gather her closer, soothing the knotted muscles of her spine.

For Rowan it was as though time had gone backward. She could have been in their condo in Toronto, and Brant come home to her after one of his trips: the hard curve of his rib cage, the taut throat, the scent and heat of his skin all achingly familiar and horribly missed. She wound her arms around his neck, digging her nails into the thickness of his hair, and opened to the thrust of his tongue. Heaven, she thought dazedly. Sheer heaven.

Brant felt her surrender surge through his body. Exultant, he found the rise of her breast beneath the orange silk of her shirt, cupping its softness, fiercely hungry to taste the ivory of her skin and the dusky, hard-tipped nipple. She gasped with pleasure, her body arching to his touch in the way that had always made him feel both conqueror and conquered. Then her hand fumbled for the buttons on his shirt, thrusting itself against his belly.

Leaving a trail of kisses down her throat, Brant muttered, ''It's been so long...too long.''

Rowan's fingertips teased the tangle of his body hair and laved the tautness of muscle. She didn't want to talk. She didn't want to think. All she wanted to do was feel. Touch.

Caress. Stroke. Luxuriate in everything she'd been deprived of. She rubbed her hips against his, and in an explosion of hunger as scarlet as a hibiscus blossom felt the hardness of Brant's erection.

His kiss deepened. Rhythmically his thumb abraded her breast, back and forth, back and forth, until she was drowning in a sea of scarlet petals.

Then, like a knife clipping a blossom from the stem, a small voice pierced the red haze of desire that had enveloped her. *You mustn't make love with Brant. He's not your husband anymore. You're divorced. Remember?*

In a crazy counterpoint to her thoughts she heard him say, "Let me spend the night with you, sweetheart...I want to hold you in my arms and never let you go."

It was as though ice-cold water had been dashed in Rowan's face: pleasure vanished and hunger was eclipsed by a panic as elemental as a hurricane. She shoved against Brant's chest with all her strength. "Don't call me sweetheart, I'm not your sweetheart anymore," she cried; then watched as, with enormous effort, he brought himself back to the harsh reality of her words.

He said forcibly, "I don't tell lies."

"Neither do I!"

"Rowan, don't try and tell me we're through with each other. That kiss proves otherwise."

She said in a clipped voice, "I haven't been to bed with anyone since the night you left for Colombia. Which, as you may recall, was nearly three years ago. Of course I'm going to fall all over you, I'm only human and we always liked sex."

"*Liked* it? It was a lot more than liking."

"So what? You're not spending the night with me. Not now or ever again."

"You make it sound as though there was nothing between us but sex!"

"There were times when I wondered," she said with the same glacial precision.

He whispered, "You can't mean that."

Did she mean it, Rowan wondered, or was she guilty of distorting the truth just so he'd leave her alone? So she wouldn't have to remember the woman who a few moments ago had rediscovered the heaven that lay in Brant's arms? "I mean it," she said in a low voice, knowing if she didn't get rid of him soon she'd lose it, pour out all the frustrations and deprivations of her marriage to the man who'd been their cause yet who'd remained oblivious to them.

"For God's sake," Brant muttered, "how can you say something so untrue?"

He looked stricken. She wanted to weep, she wanted to scream out her rage at the top of her lungs; she did neither one. She did know she'd had enough. More than enough. "I told you in Grenada to fly right back to Toronto," she said tightly. "I don't want you here stirring up the past, Brant. It's an exercise in futility."

Like a robot repeating a learned phrase, he said, "Of course—you want to move on." Then all his bitterness spilled out. "To a better man than me."

His words were like a trigger; Rowan abandoned all her good intentions. "That's right," she seethed. "To a man who's there at night when my cramps are so bad I need a backrub to go to sleep. Someone I can depend on to be around when we've made vacation plans—"

"It was only once—that time I had to go to Pakistan—that we had to cancel our plans."

Furiously she ticked off her fingers. "What about the trip we planned to Fiji? And to Antarctica? Were you available? No, you'd gone to South Africa the first time and to

Indonesia the second, because your precious boss had phoned. Drop everything, scrap a silly little vacation with your wife, you've got more important things to do.'' To her fury her voice cracked. ''I want stability, Brant. I want someone safe, so I don't have to lie awake at nights worrying where you are and whose feathers you're ruffling and whether you've stepped on a land mine or got in the way of a submachine gun—and I don't think that's much to ask.''

''I always came back to you!''

''You spent eight months in the company of another woman and I don't give a sweet damn how platonic it was!''

''Maybe you've forgotten it was my job that paid for the fancy condo on the shores of the lake—we sure couldn't have afforded it on your salary.''

Rowan's breath hissed between her teeth. ''I've always known you looked down on my job, you never made any secret of that. And let me tell you something else—I live in the country now. In a cabin that's only big enough for me. And I like it just fine.''

Knowing he was behaving execrably, Brant grated, ''Then go find yourself a farmer whose biggest excitement of the week is spreading cow manure on the back pasture.''

''Don't tempt me.'' Her eyes narrowed. ''But first, why don't you tell me something, Brant? Where have your assignments taken you the last couple of years?''

He didn't even have to think. ''Sudan, Turkey, Cambodia, Peru. Why?''

As Rowan's temper fizzled out like a spent firecracker, tiredness settled on her shoulders. What had she hoped for? That he might say England? Switzerland? The Bahamas? Safe, ordinary places? This was Brant, for goodness' sake. ''You've got to have danger, haven't you?'' she said.

"You've got to have your fix. That's what really destroyed our marriage, Brant. Because it truly is over. Finished. I won't go through another eight months like that ever again. Not for any man."

She could hear the finality in her voice. Brant went very still, a stillness like paralysis, and suddenly Rowan knew she couldn't bear prolonging this confrontation any longer. She reached up on tiptoes, kissed him lightly on the lips and whispered, "Good night, Brant. And goodbye." Then she turned away so he couldn't see her face.

Her key turned smoothly in the lock and the door swung open. Rowan hurried into her room, closed the door behind her and snagged the lock on the inside, sliding the chain into its metal groove.

Not that there was any real need to rush. Or to lock the door so securely. Brant was still standing on the brick walkway, his eyes stunned, his face a mask of disbelief and pain. It was the wrong moment to be torn by an intuition that she was betraying something infinitely precious. That she should stay and fight for it, not run away.

She was tired of fighting. She'd done too much of it over the four years of their marriage.

Not even bothering to take off her clothes, Rowan threw herself across the bed and started to cry, bunching her pillow over her head so Brant wouldn't hear her. And if she'd been asked she couldn't have said whether she was crying for Brant, for herself, or for the frailty of all that had bound them together.

Or for the utter finality of that one small word, goodbye.

CHAPTER SIX

OUTSIDE, Brant tried to pull himself together. Another cliché, he thought distantly. But true. All too true. The reason he had to pull himself together was because he felt like he was falling apart. Walking slowly, like a much older man, he headed for the bar, taking the table that was nearest to the beach and the ripple of the sea.

The rum punch he ordered was altogether too sweet, while the fruit floating in it turned his stomach. For the better part of an hour he stared out at the yachts anchored offshore, something in his demeanor keeping the other vacationers and the waiter a safe distance away. What had Gabrielle said? All your feelings are buried, gone underground; or something to that effect. She should see him now. He was nothing but feeling, a mass of raw and extraordinarily unpleasant feeling.

Maybe this was why people kept their emotions buried. It would make sense, wouldn't it? Why would anyone want to submit themselves to this kind of pain if they had a choice?

The moon glistened on the sea. A perfect recipe for romance, he thought, especially when you added palm trees, hibiscus and pale sand. All he needed was a woman. But for him there was only one woman who could bring all those other ingredients to life. A red-haired woman with a turbulent temper and a body that ignited his own. Rowan.

He'd been royally kidding himself for the last two years; he was no more through with her than he was with breathing.

79

But she was through with him. She'd made that all too clear this evening. The marriage is over, she'd said. Finished. According to her, he'd destroyed it: partly by his unspoken but very real belittlement of her job; but much more so by his need to live with danger, to push to the limits his courage and his powers of endurance. Regardless of the cost to her.

He couldn't bear it.

The ice had melted in his rum punch. He left it sitting on the table and walked away from the bar, stumbling along the beach to the rocks where he'd swum last night. It felt like a lifetime ago. It was a lifetime ago. Because last night he'd still had the hope that somehow he'd win Rowan back. And now he had none.

Sitting down on a boulder, Brant buried his head in his hands.

Rowan managed to wake five minutes before the alarm the next morning. The cramps were gone until next month, she knew that from experience. If only Brant would disappear as easily.

Brant, and all her tangled feelings for him.

She got out of bed and went to the bathroom, where she started to brush her teeth. She looked exactly like a woman who'd cried herself to sleep and who'd had the worst fight of her whole life with a man who had only to kiss her and she'd melt in his arms.

Sex. she thought fiercely. It was only sex.

Still, she looked a great deal better right now than Brant had looked last night. Staring at the white foam on the brush as though she'd never seen toothpaste before, Rowan felt her belly contract. She'd never seen him look so desolate. So heartsick.

All his emotions right there on the surface.

She gaped at herself in the mirror. That was it. That was what was new. Brant, as well she knew, was a man who only showed his feelings when he was in bed with her: that had always been the pattern of their marriage. She'd been content with that pattern until the last year they'd lived together, when things had really begun to fall apart. Two months before he'd left on that last assignment, she'd accused him of being the inventor of male detachment and the stiff upper lip, and he hadn't bothered denying it. So what had changed him?

Not your concern, Rowan. Not anymore. You severed any lingering connections between you and Brant last night when you told him the marriage was over.

Tears brimmed in her eyes and overflowed down her cheeks, dripping into the sink along with the toothpaste. Oh, damn, she thought helplessly, oh, damn…

With vicious energy she finished cleaning her teeth and splashed her face with cold water. She was going to keep so busy today she wouldn't have the time to think about him. And if that was a form of avoidance, too bad.

She didn't know what else to do.

By ten that morning Rowan had gathered the luggage, checked out of the hotel, reconfirmed the next leg of their journey, exchanged American money for Caribbean dollars and paid the airport taxes, gotten all the boarding passes, and herded the group onto the plane to St. Lucia. Brant, she noticed, spent an inordinate amount of time on the phone at the airport. He was probably talking to his boss, she thought shrewishly, setting up his next trip into danger.

Well, it wouldn't be her worry.

The plane was a Twin Otter and they were jammed in like sardines. In St. Lucia when they went through customs, she discovered the bulk of their luggage had been left behind in St. Vincent. She got everyone to fill in the appropriate forms, then picked up the driver of their van and drove to the hotel.

"Some off time," she said pleasantly to the group. "Lunch at one, and we'll head out to a scrub forest afterward, with the opportunity to see another captive breeding program, this time for the St. Lucia parrots. In the meantime, have a swim in the pool, or snorkel at the beach—it's a five-minute walk from the hotel—and there are some craft shops down the road…enjoy."

"Can I speak to you for a moment, Rowan?" Brant said brusquely.

"Of course," she said with rather overdone politeness, and smiled at the rest of them as they dispersed to their rooms. Bracing herself, she turned to face him.

"When we leave here the day after tomorrow, I won't be going with you to Martinique. I got a flight home via Antigua that day."

His businesslike speech entered Rowan's body like the stab of a dagger. Why hadn't she anticipated this? And wasn't he, after all, merely taking her advice that first night in Grenada? Struggling for composure, she said weakly, "I see."

"I'm going to stay around the hotel this afternoon, too."

"Fine," she said with a mechanical smile.

He nodded, picked up his bag and headed down the path that led to his room; he'd been allotted one with a deck that was laced with vines and further shaded by a deliciously scented frangipani tree. She watched him go, the familiar rangy stride and wide shoulders of the only man she'd ever fallen in love with, and felt a glacial coldness settle on her heart.

This really was the end. When he got on the plane two days from now, she'd never see him again. He'd make sure of that.

She was getting what she wanted and she felt like she was being slowly and agonizingly torn apart.

When Brant went to the bar before dinner, he found Peg and May there before him. ''A male Adelaide's warbler,'' May announced, raising her tankard of local beer.

''And a Lesser Antillean saltator,'' Peg added, flourishing the little paper umbrella with which her rum punch had been decorated.

''Great,'' said Brant, who'd hoped for privacy.

''We missed you this afternoon,'' Peg said.

''You don't look too chipper,'' May observed. ''I hope you're not catching anything, you can't be too careful in the tropics, you know.''

Brant, an expert on the tropics, said, ''I'm fine.''

''Rowan doesn't look her best, either,'' Peg added.

It was three-quarters of an hour until dinner, there was no one else in the vicinity, and Brant liked both women very much. He said flatly, ''I'm Rowan's ex-husband.''

Although Peg sucked in her breath, May said, ''I'd wondered.''

''You had?'' Peg said. ''You didn't say anything.''

''It would have been pure conjecture.''

''Gossip,'' said Peg.

''A pernicious habit,'' May said loftily. ''So why did you come on this trip, Brant?''

She was as bright-eyed as any bird. He said gloomily, ''Because I didn't stop to think. Because I'm a prize jerk. Will that do for starters?''

''Were you hoping for a reconciliation?'' Peg asked.

''If so, I was what you might call deluded.''

''She doesn't want you back?'' May asked delicately, sipping her beer.

"She wants me on the first plane back to Toronto. Which I'm taking the day after tomorrow."

"You're leaving us?" Peg said, shocked. "But you won't see the Martinique oriole."

"He won't get back together with Rowan, either," May said sternly. "Is there anything we can do to help?"

Her eyes were kind and he was quite sure she could be discreet. Although he was, from long habit, careful to protect his double identity, he found himself pouring out the story of his marriage, describing his job, their fights, the abduction and Gabrielle, and Rowan's putative visit to the hospital. "I must be a jerk," he finished, waving to the bartender for a refill. "I figured once she knew I'd never been unfaithful, everything would be okay. Well, it's not. I've got as much chance of a reconciliation as you have of—of finding a Martinique oriole on St. Lucia."

"Now that would be a coup," said Peg.

"Peg, this isn't the time for birds," May scolded. "We've got to think." Thoughtfully she twirled a strand of her mauve hair. "Sex," she said.

"I beg your pardon?" said Brant.

"When a marriage goes wrong, sex is often the reason."

"We always had incendiary sex. Still would, given half a chance. Guess again."

"Money," Peg offered.

"Lots of it between our two salaries. Plus an inheritance from my father." Which he hadn't touched and never would. But he didn't have to tell them that.

"Children?" May asked.

"We never wanted them," Brant said confidently. "We both travel, it would be totally impossible to try and raise a family."

There was an awkward silence, during which May looked at Peg, who looked back at May. Then May said carefully, "I do hope we're not betraying a confidence here. But if we are, then I believe the situation calls for it—desperate times call for desperate measures. Would it have been four years ago, Peg?"

"It was the trip to Brazil, the day we saw the red-billed curassow," Peg said promptly.

"A little less than four years then. I don't remember how the conversation got around to the subject of pregnancies, but I do remember very clearly Rowan saying how much she wanted to have children, and that she didn't want to wait until her mid-thirties as so many women seem to be doing. That was the gist of it, wasn't it, Peg?"

Peg nodded. May fastened Brant with a gimlet gaze. "Perhaps Rowan never told you."

"Well," Brant said uncomfortably, feeling like a secretive bird suddenly exposed to a set of high-powered binoculars, "I guess we did talk about it. But neither of us wanted to give up our jobs."

"Yuppies," Peg said disapprovingly.

"Shush, Peg," said May.

Brant was an innately honest man. "We fought about it, actually," he muttered and took a long gulp of the smooth, dark rum he'd ordered. "Well, I suppose it wasn't really a fight, because I wouldn't even consider the prospect of having kids." He ran his fingers through his hair, thinking absently that he needed a haircut. "I told her she was being ridiculous...I even laughed at her," he finished with painful accuracy.

"There you go," said Peg, tossing back the last of her drink and plunking the glass on the counter.

May eyed him speculatively. "How old is Rowan?"

"Thirty-one."

"Time's running out."

"She wants to find someone else."

Peg said with a touch of malice, "That won't be a problem. The men will flock to her like eider ducks in springtime."

May ignored her sister. "You were away a lot during your marriage, Brant, and now you're planning to leave Rowan alone again. Tomorrow. Do you always run away from your problems?"

He felt as though she'd slapped him. "May, she told me last night the marriage is over. Over and done with. It takes two to keep a relationship going. Two, not one."

"Peg and I have known Rowan for nearly six years. She's not the kind of woman to give up so easily."

"She's had three years to do it," he growled, wishing he'd never come near the bar. Let alone the Eastern Caribbean.

"She loved you four years ago, that was very obvious to both of us. I'd be willing to bet you a trip to Borneo—which doesn't come cheap—that she still loves you."

"No takers," said Brant.

"She's like the parrots," Peg interjected. "She mates for life."

He was sick to death of all things feathered. "You're suggesting I should cancel my reservation to Toronto?"

"You've got four more islands and nine more days to win your wife back," May said vigorously.

"May," Peg remarked, "you should have been a columnist for Advice to the Lovelorn."

"Yeah," Brant said snidely, "you could set yourself up as a marriage counsellor if you ever get tired of parrots and pigeons."

"Rowan's worth any amount of advice," May retorted. "Even when it's not being asked for." And she shot Brant a sly grin.

He didn't smile back. "I've already told her I'm leaving!"

"Then tell her you're not."

"I'll see," he said tersely. Change his mind? He'd be a darned fool. Because fight or flight wasn't the real choice that was confronting him; it would more accurately be phrased as masochism versus a graceful acceptance of defeat. How could he possibly believe May's claim that Rowan still loved him? Rowan hadn't given the slightest hint of that. Instead she'd told him in no uncertain terms the marriage was over.

Could it be true he'd spent the last seven years, ever since he'd met Rowan, running away from all his problems?

If so, he wasn't much of a man. Or a husband.

May couldn't be right, not on either count. He'd been a good husband, to the very best of his ability, to a woman who had, he knew, loved him with all her heart.

So why were they divorced?

He scowled into his drink, feeling as though he were being pulled in two, and heard Peg say, "Brant Curtis, if you go back to Toronto, you're a wimp."

Her sister glared at Peg. "This is no time for insults. We have to—oh, bother, here come the rest of them. It goes without saying that we'll never breathe a word of this conversation to Rowan, Brant...I do hope they have roti on the menu. And those delicious pineapple spareribs." She added in a carrying voice, "Good evening, Karen, what a pretty dress."

Rowan was wearing shorts, Brant saw. Her legs were lightly tanned and smoothly muscled, and every bone in his body ached for her. Somehow he got through the meal by seating himself at the far end of the table from her, and through the rest of the evening by going to his room to read. The espionage novel he'd bought in Toronto didn't improve upon acquaintance. More to avoid his own thoughts than from any literary pretensions, he found himself criticizing it savagely, his pen jabbing the page of the notebook he carried with him everywhere as he annotated how he'd change plot, dialogue and character to make it a better book. Tighter. More suspense. And a lot closer to political reality.

In a sudden intuitive leap he found himself thinking about his months in Afghanistan some years ago; it'd be the perfect setting for a novel. His pen began to fly over the page as scene after scene ignited itself in his imagination, and characters leaped, seemingly fully formed, into his mind. When he finally glanced at his watch, it was one-thirty in the morning.

The opening scene of the book was so clear to him that he could hear the character's voices, smell the camel dung and feel the slide of sand under his feet. Not a bad evening's work, he thought. Not that he'd ever do anything with it. But at least it had kept him from thinking about Rowan for the better part of four hours.

As if May had indeed slapped him in the face, Brant sat straight up in his chair. Earlier this evening May had painted, in a few well-chosen words, a harsh and unflattering picture of him. All through his marriage, she'd said, he'd used his job as a way out. He'd run away from real issues. He'd laughed at them. He'd even laughed at Rowan.

He could remember the evening—only a few days after her return from Brazil, he thought sickly—when she'd raised, not for the first time, the subject of children. With a logical precision as sharp as a surgeon's scalpel he'd detailed how many times over the last year they'd both been away at the same time and how little they'd actually seen each other; he'd finished by chuckling at the absurdity of the two of them bringing a child into the world with their particular lifestyles; and then he'd taken her to bed and wooed her to compliance.

A week later he'd been assigned to check out tribal warfare in Papua New Guinea. Rowan, he realized now, had been very quiet all that week, which for her was new behavior. But he hadn't addressed her unusual constraint. Oh, no. At one level he'd been glad of it. At another he'd been too busy making meticulous preparations for his all-important job as the hot-shot, world-renowned investigative reporter, Michael Barton.

He stared at the opposite wall, where a bright band of moonlight lay, sharp-edged and cold as any scalpel. He'd been like that light. All hard edges. No give. No negotiating, he who was so skilled at negotiation in the business world. Not even any real communication, other than in bed.

His thoughts marched on. And what about this evening? He'd just spent well over four hours playing with plot, characters and dialogue, and congratulating himself because it had kept him from thinking about Rowan. Once again, he'd been running from his feelings. Different means, same end.

He realized he was cold, and got up to turn the air conditioner off. The image he'd always carried of himself as a good husband and provider was beginning to seem as shoddy and meretricious as the espionage book he'd just finished reading. He used to congratulate himself on his unswerving fidelity to Rowan, especially when he was overseas and exposed to the flagrant affairs of many of the other journalists. Despite any number of opportunities, he'd never been unfaithful to her. Never wanted to. But hadn't he cheated her in other ways?

He'd run away from conflict, and from treating her as a true equal. He'd run away from the very real commitment that a marriage requires. The only thing he hadn't run from had been sex.

Because sex had been easy.

Hastily Brant dragged the curtains shut, no longer able to tolerate that sheath of blinding light against the wall. But the darkness wasn't any better, for in it there was nowhere to hide. Tonight he'd been brought, by a series of circumstances, face to face with a man he didn't like at all, whom only a few hours ago he would vehemently have denied had anything to do with him.

A man he was starting to recognize as himself.

CHAPTER SEVEN

BRANT woke from something less than four hours sleep in a belligerent mood. He couldn't have been as oblivious to his wife's needs as May had suggested. He'd been a more than satisfactory lover to Rowan and an excellent provider. And after all, she'd known about his job before she married him.

Why did women always want to change men? Domesticate them. Turn them into tabby cats purring by the hearth instead of mountain lions prowling the high forests.

He was no tabby cat; and he was damned if he was going to cancel his flight to Toronto.

Instead he hauled on his clothes for the planned trip to the rain forest in the center of St. Lucia, and joined the others for breakfast on the patio by the limpid turquoise pool. Rowan had her back to him. He said loudly, "Good morning, Rowan. How did you sleep?"

Rowan had woken with her nerves pulled tight, like a suspension bridge over a very deep gorge. Taking her time, she looked around. "Fine, thank you, Brant," she said and let her eyes wander over his face, which showed the marks of a sleepless night. "And you?"

"Fine," he said heartily. "Going to find us a whole raft of parrots today?"

"That's my job. To find birds and keep everybody happy. Including you."

The sun gleamed in her hair like electricity and her chin was stubbornly lifted. He fought down the temptation to

91

kiss her full on the lips in front of all of them and said with lazy arrogance, "Oh, I don't think keeping me happy is part of your job description. Or ever was."

"Maybe that's just as well," she said softly. "Impossible tasks have never appealed to me."

Direct hit, he thought, and raised his glass of mango juice to her in a mocking toast. Steve said rudely, "Rowan, can you find out if there's any more papaya? Seems like they're rationing it."

"Sure," said Rowan. Brant scowled at Steve, who scowled back.

"Good morning, Brant," Peg said severely. "We should see a lot more than parrots today, as I'm sure you're aware."

He didn't have a clue what birds he was supposed to be seeing today. "I'm not always as aware as I should be," he rejoined, winking at her as he picked up a slippery slice of papaya in his fingers. "Tell me what else we're going to find."

She was now scowling at him just as Steve had, which didn't prevent her from rattling off a whole string of names just as Rowan came back from the kitchen with a new platter of papaya. He said craftily, "I'll sit next to Rowan in the van—I noticed the front had three seats. That way I can pick her brains. Okay, Rowan?"

Rowan produced a smile that felt more like the toothy grin of a shark than an expression of pleasure. "Lovely," she lied, "I'll look forward to that."

So half an hour later she was sandwiched in the front seat between the driver and Brant. She felt Brant's arm go around her shoulders; with anyone other than him she would have assumed this to be a natural enough gesture in the constricted space. As the engine roared into life she muttered, "You sure looked pleased with yourself now you know you're going back to Toronto."

He tweaked the curls on the back of her neck, his fingers lingering on her nape. "I kind of like that haircut... although it took a while to get used to it."

"Behave yourself!" she seethed. "Or are you trying to get me sent back to Toronto without a job?"

They were driving toward the capital city of Castries, the wind blowing through the open window. Brant knew he'd never see the driver again, and in the seat directly behind them Karen and Sheldon were, as usual, wrapped up in each other. He pitched his words for her ears alone. "Tell me something. Did you really want children, Rowan, that last year we were married?"

The shock ran through her body as though he had struck her, and what had started as a game with Brant suddenly changed into something of far greater significance. Her hands, he saw with a stab of compunction, were clenched in her lap where moments ago they had been loose; her cheeks had paled.

To Rowan's infinite relief a truck roared past them, and then the driver leaned out of the window to shout a greeting to two men on the side of the road. It gave her a moment's respite to recover from a question that had, in taking her by surprise, stripped her of her defenses. Her brain scurried around various answers, none of them polite, not all of them honest. Opting for at least a partial version of the truth, because Brant would be gone tomorrow, gone from her life forever, Rowan said, "Yes, I wanted children—I told you at the time that I did."

With an effort he kept his voice level. "Is that one reason you're in such an all-fired hurry to find someone else?"

"That's part of it."

"What if I told you I'd changed my mind?"

"If—it's always conditional with you, Brant. What a neat way that is to avoid commitment!"

Which, thought Brant, was basically a rephrasing of May's message, the one he'd been so busy denying ever since he'd got up this morning. He blundered on. "But what if I have changed my mind, and somehow we could work it out with our jobs so we could start a family?"

Against the arm that lay around her he felt another of those betraying shudders. She grated, "I see precious little evidence of any kind of change in you, and I'm not going to discuss this in a van full of my clients. There's no need to discuss it. You're leaving tomorrow."

"That's negotiable."

"You don't know the meaning of the word! With you, it's always been your way or the highway."

"I swear I'm not the same man who left for Colombia three years ago. I'm not just talking about having kids— I'm trying to tell you I've changed in other ways, as well."

"Then why have you been behaving like that man?" she snorted. "Stop this, Brant, I hate it." Leaning down, she pulled out her bird book. "Look up black finch, St. Lucia oriole, blue-hooded euphonia and gray trembler. That's what we're here for. This is a birding trip. Not a workshop for the repair of marriages that are beyond repair."

He couldn't pull her into his arms and kiss her until she yielded: not here. He couldn't even raise his voice to get his point across. He'd done it again, Brant realized with a sinking in his belly. Spoken without thought, chosen the worst of times and settings. He'd given more consideration to the characters who'd sprung into his imagination last night than he had to his ex-wife this morning. Why the devil did his brain cells dissolve to mush every time he came within six feet of Rowan?

He'd have to erase that word strategy from his vocabulary.

But he'd discovered one thing in the last few minutes. Rowan had indeed wanted children. She still did. She just didn't want him to be the father.

She'd changed, even if he hadn't.

The driver said amiably, "You want me to stop anywhere along the way, Rowan?"

Thankfully Rowan turned her attention to the map, pushing the backs of her hands against her knees so Brant couldn't see that her fingers were trembling. Rowan's trembler, she thought with a desperate attempt at humor, felt him remove his arm from around her shoulders and from the corner of her eye saw him open the bird book.

By tomorrow morning he'd be gone. Less than twenty-four hours. Surely she could survive one more day. She said calmly, "The only reason we might want to stop is if we pass any ponds, you never know when you're going to pick up a new shorebird."

Her voice sounded like a stranger's to her own ears, and her palms were clammy. Twenty-four hours couldn't last forever. Tomorrow, once Brant had gone, she'd be safe.

Out of danger.

As they trekked along the trail at the forest reserve Brant was rewarded by sightings of every one of the birds Rowan had mentioned. But even the euphonia, a delightful little bird feathered in green and yellow with a sky-blue topknot, didn't raise his spirits. This was the last day to be with Rowan. Like a knell, the words repeated themselves in his head. The last day, the last day...

Tomorrow he'd be back in Toronto. As soon as he landed he'd call his boss and see if the Myanmar assignment was still open. The thirty or so groups of rebels fighting it out in the forests of Burma ought to take his mind off one small group of birders on a safe little island in the Caribbean.

He'd fallen behind on the trail, not wanting the company of the others. Today, to his jaundiced eye the rain forest's dense growth epitomized nature's desperate struggle for survival: everything scrambling toward the scanty light by any means possible, like an army of guerrillas. As he came around a grove of graceful bamboo trees with their curved, hollow trunks and feathered leaves, he heard voices raised in anger, echoing his own mood, and stopped in his tracks. He couldn't deal with Steve and Natalie. Not this morning.

Then through the thicket of bamboos he heard Rowan say crisply, "I'm going to break one of my own rules here, Natalie, as well as the company's rules. It's called sticking my nose into my clients' private lives. I don't think you two would keep arguing so much if you didn't care about each other. For goodness' sake, get it together!"

"I don't—" Natalie began.

Steve said, "She isn't—"

"Shut *up!*" Rowan snapped. "Go out for dinner tonight away from the rest of us, and figure out what it is you really want from each other and how you're going to get it. That doesn't sound too difficult, does it?"

"He's a—"

"She wouldn't—"

An edge of desperation in her voice, Rowan interrupted them. "Life's too short to waste, don't you *see?* And love's not as common as you might suppose—trust me on that one. And now I'm the one who's going to shut up and not before time…isn't that a solitaire up there in that cecropia tree?"

"Oh—where's my camera?" Natalie exclaimed.

"Hanging from your shoulder," Steve said irritably. "You'd lose your head if it wasn't screwed on, Nat."

Even through the trees Brant could hear Rowan's sharp sigh of frustration. She said, "I'd better go and get Karen, she didn't see the solitaire very well the other day."

Brant stayed where he was. Rowan didn't know he'd been eavesdropping, he'd swear to it. Was she only trying to repair Steve and Natalie's relationship because her own marriage was beyond repair? Or was she trying to give them what she wanted for herself?

All thirty rebel tribes couldn't be more complicated than one red-haired woman.

For the rest of the day he watched Rowan like the proverbial hawk. She excelled at a job whose difficulties and problems she smoothed away with tact, knowledge and humor; she conjured birds out of the trees with an ease that amazed him, and she concocted another tasty picnic lunch with a minimum of fuss; she gave Steve and Natalie no more advice; and all day she treated Brant with the same unfailing courtesy with which she treated everyone else. A courtesy that made him feel about two inches tall.

This time Brant tried to plan in his mind exactly what he wanted to say to her, so he wouldn't blow it again. His first step, late in the afternoon, was to carry the cooler back to the van. Knowing he was taking a huge step into the unknown, he took Rowan by the wrist as she showed him where to stow the cooler behind the back seat. Stumbling a little, but with patent sincerity, he said, "I *have* changed, Rowan. I used to look down on your job, you're right. I'm sorry. More sorry than I can say. I'll never do that again. Because it's a very difficult job and you do it superbly."

A flash of gratification crossed her face. She stared down at the fingers clasped around her wrist, gulped, "Thank you," and then tugged herself free. "Steve," she called over her shoulder, "would you mind holding the scope while we drive? I don't want it loose in the back."

Brant found himself gawking at her back as she walked away from him. Was that it? He'd told her he was sorry and he'd complimented her on her skills, and all she could say was thank you and leave him standing here? Didn't she understand that he was changing in front of her eyes?

Didn't she care?

The day proceeded, far too quickly for Brant's liking. Natalie and Steve joined them for dinner, with May sitting between them, her mauve-haired and magisterial presence keeping them in order. Rowan was late and snagged the seat at the opposite end of the table from Brant. As coffee was being poured, the hotel manager brought her a fax; she read it, finished her coffee and disappeared. She didn't reappear.

Brant sat himself down at the bar and ordered orange juice. Time was running out. If he was going to get five minutes alone with Rowan, he'd have to do it tonight. Tomorrow morning she'd be too busy for him.

Which hurt. Hurt almost as much as her determination to ignore how he was doing his level best to change from the man he'd always been, to admit to his mistakes and make reparation.

More feelings, he thought morosely, and watched Steve sit down on the stool next to him. Under the full moon a small steel band was playing out on the patio, and several couples were dancing. Three young women who were traveling together were sitting at the other end of the bar, laughing among themselves. Steve said, "We should ask them to dance."

"Go right ahead," Brant said.

"Don't want to." Steve signaled to the bartender. "Double rum and Coke,'' he said, adding glumly, ''Never thought I'd turn down the chance to meet three new broads. They're not bad-looking, either. Especially the blonde.''

His gray eyes looked genuinely unhappy. ''Still at odds with Natalie?'' Brant asked.

''You said it.'' Steve paid for his drink and took a healthy slug. ''Do you know what she did a couple of days before we left for Grenada? Asked me to marry her.''

''What did you say?''

''I said no. That's *my* job—the guy's supposed to do the asking the way I look at it.'' He poked at an ice cube with one finger. ''She's been cranky as a dog with ticks ever since.''

Brant smothered a grin. ''Why didn't you do the asking?''

''Oh, man, what I know about marriage you could put on the back of a tick. Like nothing, you know what I mean?'' Steve took another big gulp of rum. ''You ever been married?''

''Married and divorced.''

''Hey, sorry, didn't mean to step on your toes.''

''That's okay.'' Brant hesitated fractionally. ''Rowan was my wife. We were married for four years.''

Steve's head jerked up. ''*Rowan* and you? No kidding?''

''No kidding.'' She'd kill him for telling. But after tomorrow morning, he wouldn't be here, would he?

''Jeez…so that's why there's so many vibes between the two of you. Nat picked 'em up, too. But I never figured you'd been married. What happened?''

''My job takes me all over the world at a moment's notice. Rowan travels a lot. She wanted kids. I didn't. Got so we were fighting most of the time we were together.'' Brant stirred his juice with a swizzle stick, watching the liquid swirl in the confines of the glass. "I'm starting to realize I'm a Neanderthal when it comes to feelings."

"Hey, couldn't all have been your fault."

"Well, Rowan's got a temper, for sure. As you may have noticed."

"Yeah…she doesn't fool around if she's got something on her mind." Steve looked straight at him. "You two going to get it together again?"

"Don't think so. I'm going back to Toronto tomorrow."

"Quitting?"

Steve looked so scandalized that Brant had to smile. "It takes two to tango," he said tritely. "You planning on fixing things up between you and Natalie?"

"She's gotta make the first move."

"So here we are, two guys sitting alone at the bar," Brant said dryly.

"Maybe I will ask one of 'em to dance…the blonde's sort of cute. You coming?"

Brant shook his head. "I'm too old to be putting the moves on women in a bar," he said. "Good luck."

Steve joined the three women, drinks were ordered all 'round, and Brant left the bar. The last day, he thought. The last day…

He walked back along the pathway to his room. The moon was hidden behind a cloud, blurring the shadows; the wind scythed through the leaves of the huge breadfruit tree in the center of the compound. His feet carried him past his own doorway to the room at the very end of the block, where Rowan was staying. It was in darkness. He tapped on the glass patio doors, hearing the heavy pound of his heartbeat in his ears.

Nothing happened. He tapped louder, and again got no response. Peering through the open curtains, he saw that the room was indeed empty. His disappointment was overwhelming; worse, it was laden with fear. What if he didn't get to see her before tomorrow morning? Then what would he do?

He marched to the lobby. Rowan wasn't there, or in the pool. Outside in the bar Steve was dancing with the blonde, holding her a respectable distance away from his body and looking bored to the back teeth. The beach, Brant thought. Rowan loved to swim.

If she'd gone to some of the bars and little boutiques that lined the road, he'd never find her.

He went back toward his room, through the shadows trying to find the dirt track that led to the beach. He finally located a winding pathway edged with oleander shrubs: shrubs that were deadly poisonous, he thought with a ripple of his nerves, and started along it. Then through the hiss of wind in the shrubbery he heard the crunch of footsteps coming toward him on the finely ground cinders and felt the hairs rise on the back of his neck. He stood still, waiting.

The woman who came around the corner, her shoulders brushing against the pink and white blossoms, was Rowan. She gave a gasp of shock when she saw him and he suddenly realized how threatening he must look, a black silhouette blocking the path, his height and breadth magnified by the shadows. He said quickly, "Rowan, it's me—Brant."

"B-Brant?" she quavered.

"I was looking for you, I didn't mean to scare you."

"Looking for me?"

"Yeah." Although he longed to approach her, he held his ground, all his senses on alert. "Are you okay?" he said uncertainly.

She walked right up to him, wrapped her arms around his waist and leaned all her weight on him, her head tucked under his chin, the softness of her breasts jammed against his chest. Her hair was wet; she'd obviously been swimming. With another of those judders along his nerves, Brant realized she was weeping, quietly and copiously, her tears soaking through his shirt. He put one arm around her and with his other hand lifted her face.

The moon had reappeared. In its blank white light he saw blood streaking the curve of her cheekbone. He said sharply, "Rowan—what happened?"

"I—I fell. Tripped over the curb on the way back from the beach. Oh Brant, d-don't go…"

"I'm not going anywhere—I'll take you back to your room." He held her away, running his eyes down her body; she was wearing a baggy T-shirt over a pair of shorts. "Sweetheart, your knees…"

"I don't mean now," she wailed, scrubbing at her wet cheeks and spreading more blood over her nose. "Don't go to Toronto, that's what I m-mean."

Every muscle in Brant's body went rigid. "Do you really mean that?"

"Just don't go! Please don't go…"

"If you don't want me to go to Toronto, I won't. I promise," he said forcefully. "Let me see your hands, Rowan."

Obediently she held out her palms, which were grazed and scored with dirt and blood. With a wordless exclamation Brant picked her up, holding her against his chest, and heard her falter, "Were you really looking for me?"

"Yes. I couldn't bear to leave tomorrow without one more of my jackassed attempts at reconciliation. And don't tell me I'm like a bull in a china shop when it comes to communication, I've been doing enough of a number on myself the last couple of days and yeah, I know I'm spouting clichés."

She said, the faintest thread of laughter in her voice, "In

Martinique they have these huge white bulls with long horns. One of those loose in a china shop would be a sight to behold.''

"Compared to me, it'd be a newborn calf." He emerged from the oleanders into the open, where luckily there was no one in sight. Swiftly he crossed the compound to her room. "Have you got your key?"

She pulled a cord from around her neck. Propping her against his raised knee, Brant unlocked the door and shoved it open, then carried her through, putting her down on the edge of the bed. All his movements economical, he closed the door, switched on the bedside lamp and drew the drapes shut. Only then did he really look at her.

The fieriness of temperament which had attracted him to Rowan from the start had abandoned her; she looked helpless and exhausted and very much alone. Pierced by compassion, he said with sudden insight, "Rowan, for all our fights and love-making, I don't think we were much good at showing each other our vulnerabilities. I wasn't, I do know that much."

She was shivering. "I can't even talk about it now, I'm too tired. Just don't go to Toronto tomorrow, that's all I ask."

He knelt in front of her. "I won't. I swear I won't. I also swear I'll do my very best to figure out where we go from here. But not right now. Right now I think you should have a shower, and then I'm going to clean up your hands and knees."

"I wasn't watching where I was going, I was s-so miserable, and where I tripped it was all cinders on the path."

Volcanic cinders, in Brant's opinion, were probably the very worst thing you could choose if you were going to fall flat on your face. He didn't share this conclusion with Rowan. "Where's your first-aid kit?"

"Bottom left of my duffel bag."

"I'll get it. Go shower, Rowan."

She said in a rush, "I haven't got the energy to get dressed again so I'm going to put on my pajamas but I'm not—"

"The last thing we need tonight is to end up in bed together, " Brant said grimly. "We're in enough of a mess as it is...I'll try and imagine I've been reincarnated as a monk."

"Now that would be stretching the universe's powers," Rowan said with a small smile, and pushed herself up from the bed. Flinching, she added, "Hot water's going to sting like crazy, you realize that?"

He didn't offer to shower with her. He didn't offer to help her undress. You deserve a medal, buddy, he told himself, and stood up, too. "It'll relax you—you look kind of uptight."

"I could say the same of you," she remarked with another of those tiny smiles, took her pajamas from under her pillow and hobbled off to the bathroom.

Brant took out the very comprehensive first-aid kit from her duffel bag and tried not to picture Rowan's sleek body under the stream of water. She was right. He wasn't cut out to be a monk.

When she came out of the bathroom a few minutes later, her hair was a cluster of damp curls the hue of rust chrysanthemums. Her pajamas, pale green silk, consisted of a long-sleeved top and boxer shorts edged with satin, and more than hinted at her cleavage; he'd always thought her legs were exquisite. His mouth dry, Brant went into the bathroom to scrub his hands. The scent of her powder hung in the steamy air; he remembered that scent from years ago.

Rowan sat down gingerly in the room's only chair. She'd already realized that the only other choice was the bed, which wasn't really a choice at all. Through her exhaustion she was aware of the slow upwelling of a profound relief. Brant had promised he wouldn't leave tomorrow.

They had time. For what, she didn't know yet, couldn't even begin to guess. But at least when tomorrow morning came, he'd still be with her.

Brant came back from the bathroom. He was wearing cotton trousers and an open-necked blue shirt. A lock of dark hair had fallen over his forehead; he could do with a haircut. She had no idea what he was thinking, much less feeling. Not that there was anything new in that: his motivations and his demons had always been a mystery to her. He spread out some of the contents of the first-aid kit on the bed, and knelt beside her chair.

She held out her hands. Using tweezers, he picked out the fragments of cinder in her palms first, then slathered on an antibiotic ointment. Her knees were in worse shape. Despite the care he took, she couldn't always suppress her little whimpers of pain; by the time he'd finished, there was a sheen of sweat on his forehead. He taped gauze pads over the worst of the scrapes and stood up, stretching out his back. "I'm glad that's over," he said flatly.

"Me, too."

She pushed herself up, feeling her knees wobble under her. Brant announced, "Steve and I'll carry everyone's baggage tomorrow."

"Okay," Rowan said meekly.

"I don't believe it, nary an argument?" The smile died from Brant's face. Very gently he stroked her hair back from her cheek. "I don't know what we're going to do, or what we need to say to each other in the next few days, Rowan. If you want the truth, whenever I'm around you I'm scared out of what few wits I seem to possess."

He didn't look scared. He looked tender and solicitous,

the way he'd looked with Gabrielle that awful day at the hospital. She bit her lip. "I don't know how to read you...I don't think I ever have."

He was slowly and rhythmically caressing her cheek-bone, not meeting her eyes; the lamplight gleamed in the dusting of gray in his hair, shadowing the new lines in his face. Her heart caught in her breast; he could so easily not have come back from Colombia. Oddly, there was nothing sexual in his caress, and Rowan was suddenly, fiercely glad of this. Over the years she'd come to distrust the way their bodies could fuse so ardently while the rest of their lives remained so far apart.

He said with the same slowness, "The fact that you want me to stay here and that I want to stay—it's like a huge weight's been lifted from my shoulders. As though I've been released from prison for the second time 'round. Whatever's going on, we're in it together." He lifted his blue eyes, which blazed with pent-up emotion. "You have no idea how good that feels."

Tears pricked at her lids. "Yes, I do," she said softly, and did what she'd been wanting to do ever since he'd knelt by her chair a few minutes ago. With a tenderness that felt as deep as the sea, she stroked the dark lock of hair back from his forehead and smiled up at him. "I've felt very much alone the last three years," she confessed. "And it's like a small miracle that I'm actually saying that to you."

Brant took her in his arms, holding her wordlessly while time seemed to stop and the tension that drove him so mer-cilessly and so constantly slackened its grip. Then, gradu-ally, he became aware of other, more earthy sensations: the warmth of her body, the lissome curve of her spine and the scent of her skin. He edged away from her. "I'd better go."

Rowan took her courage in her hands. "Do you know what I want to say?" she whispered. "Stay with me, Brant, sleep with me, hold me in your arms the night through so I won't be alone…I've been lonely for so long, it sometimes feels like forever. But I'm not going to say it. Maybe I'm scared to, scared that we'll just fall back into all the old patterns.''

Brant never cried. He couldn't start now. He said huskily, ''You're so wise and brave and beautiful…and, dammit, you're right, as well. We shouldn't get into bed together, not yet.'' He paused. ''Just as long as you know that I want to.''

She chuckled. ''Now that's one thing I've never doubted.''

He chucked her under the chin, knowing he could leave now that she was laughing. ''I'll see you in the morning. The flight's not that early for once.''

''We can sleep in until seven o'clock, how decadent that sounds…good night, Brant.'' Good night, she thought with deep thankfulness. Not goodbye.

He leaned over and brushed his mouth to hers, then left her room. The moon was now entangled in the tall branches of the breadfruit tree; the cool, luminous night enfolded Brant in its arms, as Rowan had enfolded him in hers.

He felt happy.

For the first time in years, he felt happy.

CHAPTER EIGHT

BRANT woke happy the next morning. Happy, and in a physical condition such that had Rowan been there, she'd have been in no doubt as to his intentions.

She'd be in his bed again, and soon. He knew it.

They'd figure out what had gone wrong with the marriage. If they made it a joint effort, it shouldn't be too difficult. Although the thought of raising children made him break into a cold sweat.

But he wasn't going to think about that today. They both needed a respite from the last few days, from the anger, confusion and unhappiness that had traveled with them ever since she'd walked up to him in the airport in Grenada.

He got out of bed and headed for the shower, whistling. On his way to breakfast he met up with Steve and said cheerfully, "Good morning."

Steve growled, "You think there'd be two seats on that flight to Toronto? Nat saw me dancing with the blonde."

"But you looked bored to tears."

"The woman I was dating before Nat was blonde. She thinks I've got a thing about 'em."

"You can have my seat. I'm not going."

Steve brightened minimally. "You're not? Hey, man, that's great. What happened?"

"Rowan didn't want me to leave any more than I wanted to. Luckily we discovered this before I got on the plane. But you don't really want to fly out of here, Steve—why don't you just tell Natalie you're sorry and see what happens?"

"In the mood she's in? No way."

If Steve hadn't looked so unhappy, Brant might have lost patience. But Brant knew what that kind of unhappiness felt like. "Hang in there," he said. "Not that I know what makes women tick any more than you do."

"Four years of marriage to a neat gal like Rowan and you still don't know?" Steve said tactlessly.

"I never gave my marriage priority," Brant admitted. "My job was always more important."

"Women don't like that."

"They've got a point, wouldn't you say?"

With a certain self-righteousness Steve replied, "I'd rather be windsurfing or scuba diving right now. But I'm trailing around the countryside looking at birds because Nat likes to photograph 'em. You can't say I'm not putting her first."

"Maybe you'd be better off windsurfing and letting her do the photography…then you'd both be doing what you want to do, and you could be together the rest of the time."

Steve looked unconvinced. "How am I going to suggest that to her when she won't even talk to me?"

"Just do it and see what happens…oh, good morning, Rowan."

Rowan said with an endearing touch of shyness, "Hi, Brant. Steve, how are you?"

"Going to grab me a couple of croissants before Sheldon hogs the lot," Steve said, and marched off toward the dining room.

"How are your knees?" Brant asked.

"They've been better. But we're not doing much hiking today."

"Sleep well?" He let his eyes wander over her face. "You look very beautiful, my darling."

She blushed, sneaked a quick look around and kissed him

full on the mouth, a kiss whose brevity didn't negate its passion. Then she gabbled, "We've got an awful lot of talking to do, we mustn't forget that."

"How about we give it a rest today? I'm just so god-damned glad I'm not getting on that plane to Toronto...let's not worry about the future or dig up the past, not today. *Carpe diem* and all that."

"Sounds like a plan."

He laughed, the carefree laugh of a much younger man. "It's probably just as well we'll be chaperoned all day by six eagle-eyed birders—I'm not feeling at all monkish."

"I'll take that as a compliment."

"So you should."

Rowan glanced past his shoulder. "Speaking of eagles...good morning, Peg. Good morning, May."

Brant turned. "I was just telling Rowan how much I'm looking forward to Martinique and Guadeloupe," he said easily; the last time he'd talked to them he'd been hell-bent on going back to Toronto. "It'll give me the chance to brush up on my French."

"The language of love," Peg said mistily.

"One of the Romance languages," May said.

"It never hurts to brush up on a language you haven't been using," Peg added with a touch of severity.

"One can always improve one's vocabulary and one's usage," said her sister. "Wouldn't you agree, Brant?"

"I'm sure you're right," Brant replied, wanting nothing more than to change the subject. "Shall we go to break-fast?"

"We'll get the white-breasted thrasher in Martinique," Peg said happily, striding toward the dining room.

"And the oriole, don't forget the oriole," May said.

"An early start tomorrow," her sister remarked. "I'm not much for all this sleeping in."

It was seven-twenty in the morning. "Positively sloth-ful," Brant said, and pulled out two chairs, one for Rowan and one for himself. Sheldon and Karen looked like a couple who'd spent the night making very satisfactory love, while Natalie, beneath a layer of makeup, looked as though she were simmering with things unsaid; Brant wouldn't have wanted to be Steve. The whole group showed such solicitude for Rowan's scraped hands that he was touched.

At the airport he canceled his flight to Toronto, and nabbed the seat next to Rowan on the plane. It was a small plane; he took great pleasure in the rub of her thigh against his and in watching the little vein pulse in the hollow of her wrist. He felt more than happy. He felt exuberant, as though he could have lifted the plane from the tarmac single-handedly.

They flew over a turquoise sea with its curved reefs and its white triangles of sailboats, and then over the red roofs and dry hills of Martinique. That afternoon they drove to a beach at the very south of the island, where Brant in his binoculars saw a yellow warbler whose feathers were brighter than the sun and whose confiding dark eyes seemed to look right at him; again he felt that unaccustomed rush of pleasure in the natural world.

A flock of tropic birds was circling overhead, with their arched wings and streamered tails, dazzlingly white against the sky. He gazed at them for a long time, long after the rest of the group had moved on, and knew he wanted for himself and for Rowan that grace and ease, that sense of being so much at home with each other and with the wild and constant winds of the sea.

All that afternoon Rowan found herself watching Brant. He looked like a different man today, she thought humbly, his face gentled and relaxed, happy in a way she could scarcely remember. Too happy? For after all, nothing was settled, nothing was dealt with, and underneath her own deep relief that he hadn't left for Toronto was a burgeoning fear.

Was Brant changing, as he claimed he was? Could they rebuild a marriage different in reality as well as in spirit from their previous one? She knew she was willing to work very hard to achieve that. But she couldn't do it alone. Furthermore, to do so, she would have to share with him that longtime secret which was hers alone, yet which concerned him at the deepest of levels; it was a prospect she dreaded.

"Least sandpiper!" Peg hollered, and hastily Rowan dragged her attention back to her job. When they returned to the hotel she was almost glad she and her driver had groceries and other errands to do. Afterward she showered, put on a calf-length sundress that hid the deplorable state of her knees, and wandered down to the beach.

Steve and Brant were windsurfing, both of them well offshore where the breeze skimmed their boards over the waves. Natalie was stretched out on a beach chair; she was wearing a shiny bronze bikini, her face inscrutable behind huge sunglasses. "Hi, Natalie," Rowan said, "do you mind if I join you?"

"Go right ahead. Rowan, why are men such creeps?"

Rowan sat down, careful not to bend her knees too much. "Men identify with their jobs, women with their relationships," she said promptly, and wondered from what magazine article she'd gleaned that gem of wisdom. It had, from her own experience, the ring of truth.

"Look at the two of them out there, happy as pigs in...well, happy. Steve'd much rather be surfing than birding. He only came along to keep me happy."

Natalie's red mouth was drooping. "He's not exactly succeeding, is he?" Rowan said gently.

"Are you and Brant a number?"

"No...yes...oh, I don't know," Rowan said in exasperation.

"See what I mean? They're dorks."

Both men were now racing at an angle toward the beach. The muscles of Brant's shoulders and thighs were sharply delineated, his whole body taut as an athlete's: strain gracefully borne, thought Rowan, all his strength and nerve focused on the task at hand. As he passed dangerously close to some rocks, she heard him laugh in exhilaration. His board was carving a bow wave from the blue water; perfectly balanced, he raced toward the sand, and at the last minute sank into the sea. Only then did he see her.

He waved, hauled his board partway on the beach and ran toward her, shaking the water from his hair. The sun gleamed on his wet body and she wanted him so badly she could scarcely breathe. He said, still laughing, "I won—right?"

She said primly, "A tie. Wasn't it, Natalie?"

"Nah...Steve won," Natalie said.

Steve had stayed in the water, and was towing his board around for another run. Brant yelled, "Be right there," and said awkwardly, "He misses you, Natalie."

"So let him tell me—he's got a big enough mouth."

Rowan sighed. "Dinner in half an hour, Brant."

He leaned down and gave her a very explicit kiss. "One more run. Save me the seat next to you."

As he jogged back down the sand, Rowan, left gaping like a stranded fish, sputtered, "They're not only creeps, they're arrogant and insufferable creeps and why can't we live without them?"

"You find the answer to that one, you'd be a rich woman," Natalie said. "Still, Brant seems an okay feller.

Maybe you should give him half a chance instead of freezing him out every time he comes near you.''

''This trip is more like a prolonged singles weekend than an ornithological field trip! I'm going to have a drink, I'll see you at dinner.'' And Rowan made good her escape.

But as she walked toward the dining room to check on their dinner reservation, she was thinking hard. There was no give with Natalie and Steve; each of them wanted the other to make the first move and was prepared to wait—and suffer—until that happened. Brant and I aren't like that, not anymore, thought Rowan with a tinge of smugness. We're meeting each other halfway. How else can we repair all the damage that our marriage caused? We haven't got the time for games.

After dinner, served late and with a bewildering array of courses, Brant escorted Rowan back to her room. In the shadow of some hibiscus shrubs he kissed her good night with evident restraint. Rowan, who wanted more, pulled his head down and ran her tongue along his upper lip. He then kissed her until their combined heartbeats sounded like a tattoo and her inability to stand had nothing to do with the scrapes on her knees. She gasped, ''I shouldn't have done that, Brant…encouraged you like that, I mean…I'm sorry.''

''I don't know how I can be around you for the rest of the week and not make love to you,'' he groaned, nuzzling her throat, his hands sliding down her bare arms to clasp her waist.

''We've got to talk first,'' she said frantically. What a hypocrite she was, when all she wanted to do was tear the clothes from his body and make love to him the night through.

Just as well it was still the wrong time of the month. Or she'd be in deep trouble.

''Tomorrow evening,'' he grated. ''We'll go for a walk along the beach away from the rest of them and try and figure out where we're going from here.''

Which gave her exactly twenty-four hours to work out what she had to say. How to tell him what had happened that dreadful day she got the news he'd been abducted.

It didn't sound like nearly long enough.

The next morning Brant watched Rowan locate three of the rare white-breasted thrashers in the scrub forest on Presqu'ile de la Caravelle; he had to commend her patience, strategy and persistence. Unfortunately she also located a disheartening number of the mongoose that preyed on the thrashers. They then drove to a rain forest trail for the oriole. Brant wasn't feeling nearly as relaxed today. Despite the lack of sex, yesterday had been like a honeymoon. But today he had to convince Rowan to come back to him; and once again, his much-vaunted intelligence seemed to have deserted him. The fact that he craved her body wouldn't do him any good. The thought of starting a family panicked him. And she hated his job. None of this did much for his confidence that he could undo the damage of their divorce.

As the group picnicked under some tall pines, he fed most of his lunch to a stray cat, who then curled up in the grass and went to sleep; he envied its ability to be so unconcerned about the future. Rowan, he noticed, had a tendency to avoid his gaze. Unless he was very much mistaken, she was in as much of a funk as he was. This didn't comfort him in the slightest.

He was sure of only one thing. He wanted her back.

After lunch they stopped along the shore a few times to check out mangrove swamps. At the last stop Brant wandered away from the rest of them, and was rewarded by the sight of a plumed night heron fishing in the brackish waters of the swamp. He watched it for a long time, its single-minded concentration on the matter of food somehow encouraging him that if he only wanted Rowan enough, everything would turn out for the best. He had to trust himself, he thought. Himself, and her.

The alternative, that they would remain forever alienated, was insupportable.

Rowan had seen Brant disappear down the shore; she would have liked to do the same, because under her surface efficiency and good manners she was a mass of jangled nerves. In less than five hours her whole future would be decided, and she still had no idea what she was going to say.

She knew what she wanted: the same man and a different marriage.

In the swamp they found two kinds of egrets and a handsome green heron, and she was about to lead the birders back to the van when Natalie said, "Just a sec. I haven't gotten a photo of a cattle egret sitting on a cow yet—there's a field full of neat white cows just beyond those trees."

She took off at a fast clip. The wind from the sea was hot, the humidity stifling, and even May and Peg looked a little wilted. Rowan said, "I'll follow her, I guess...I'd still love to find a little egret."

"We'll all go," Peg said stoutly.

"Karen's tired," Sheldon said, "we'll stay here."

"If Brant comes back, tell him where we are," Rowan said, and headed after Natalie, Steve right behind her.

The grass was crisp and brown underfoot. As they left the mangroves behind, to her left Rowan heard the plaintive lowing of a cow. Then, splitting the still air like the swish of a machete, Natalie screamed.

For an instant Rowan was frozen in her tracks, the sun beating on her bare arms. Steve said, "What the hell—"

and started to run through the last of the trees, brushing aside branches and leaping over roots.

Rowan dropped the scope, hauled off her heavy haversack and asked May to watch them. Then she took off after him, racing across the dusty ground, ignoring the pain in her knees as that terrified scream echoed in her ears. She reached the barbed-wire fence around the field in time to see Steve clamber over it and a flock of cattle egrets take to the air at the far end of the field where a herd of cows grazed peacefully; and then she saw why Natalie had screamed.

Her camera around her neck, Natalie was edging backward from a very large cream-colored bull, talking to it in a high-pitched voice that at any other time might have been funny. The bull looked more interested in her than aggressive; but bulls, in Rowan's opinion, were not the most trustworthy of creatures.

Steve said in a loud voice, "Nat, as soon as I distract it, head for the fence." Then he started jumping up and down, yelling obscenities at the top of his voice.

The bull swung its massive head around, pawing at the ground with one large hoof. Natalie looked back over her shoulder, her cheeks as white as the feathers of any egret, and speeded up her retreat. The bull took one step after her, and she whimpered with fear. Then Steve picked up a rock and fired it at the bull. As the rock bounced off its flank, it snorted and turned its full attention to Steve.

Natalie was only a few feet from the fence. Rowan parted the strands, saying urgently, "This way, Natalie, not much further."

With another hunted look over her shoulder, Natalie stumbled toward the fence and scrambled through it; when two wire spikes caught in her shirt, she gave an exclamation of sheer panic. "Hold still," Rowan ordered, and carefully pulled the sharp wire from the cotton fabric. "There, you're okay now," she said.

Natalie grabbed her, burying her face in Rowan's shoulder; she was quivering all over. "How was I to know it was a bull?" she stuttered. "I was b-brought up in Boston."

Rowan patted her soothingly on the shoulder, decided lessons on basic anatomy could wait for another time, and with a flare of fear saw that the bull was advancing on Steve. She shouted, "Steve, Natalie's safe…get back here. Fast!"

Natalie's head reared up. "Steve?" she croaked. "Omigod, Steve—"

As she lunged for the fence, Rowan held on to her with all her strength. "He'll be fine," she cried, "you can't go back in there," and saw Steve begin to run toward the fence.

The bull started after him, breaking into a graceless canter. From behind her Rowan heard the pound of steps through the grass, and as though it were happening in slow motion watched Brant shuck off his haversack, dump it on the ground and vault the fence in a single agile flow of movement. He stooped and flung a sharp-edged rock at the bull.

The bull bellowed in surprise and wheeled to this new threat. Brant tore at the buttons on his shirt and hauled it from his back, waving it provocatively to one side of his body. He was, Rowan saw with a sick lurch of her heart, laughing.

Steve had reached the barbed-wire fence. He shoved himself through it and stumbled over to Rowan, his eyes only on Natalie. "Are you okay, Nat?" he demanded.

Natalie threw herself from Rowan's arms into Steve's, grabbing on to him as though she'd never let go. "That was so brave of you,'' she wailed. ''Oh, Steve, I do love you.''

''I love you, too,'' Steve muttered. ''Sorry I've been such a jerk.''

''Not half as dumb as I've been,'' Natalie said with a beatific smile, wriggled her hips against his and kissed him very thoroughly.

Rowan tore her eyes away. The bull was charging Brant.

Her breath was stuck in her throat and every muscle was paralyzed with terror. The whole world had narrowed to a man and an animal. A man who meant more to her than all the world. Like a woman turned to stone she waited for the inevitable and unequal collision; for Brant to be broken like a doll, crushed and gored in front of her eyes.

Brant shook the shirt so it billowed in the sea breeze and at the very last moment threw himself sideways. The sleeve caught in the bull's horns and ripped free, the sound shockingly loud through the thud of its hooves and the crunch of dirt. The bull tossed its head, infuriated by the scrap of fabric that blocked its vision, and swerved to charge again.

Brant had taken those few precious seconds to get closer to the fence. But not close enough, Rowan saw with an ugly lurch of her heart. Then, in a surge of rage that momentarily dispelled fear and that horrified her with its primitive force, she saw that he was still laughing, his teeth gleaming in his tanned face, his chest slick with sweat.

He was enjoying himself.

It was what had driven them apart, this deep need of his for danger, this hunger to live on the edge. She'd never been able to compete with it. Never.

In a reckless and mocking parody of a bullfighter, Brant swirled the shirt through the air and pivoted to one side. The bull tried to snag the shirt on its horns, but mysteriously the shirt was somewhere else. The bull gave another deep bellow, its great hooves churning up the dust as it, like Brant, pivoted.

It's a dance, thought Rowan dizzily. A dance with danger. A dance with death. That's what drives Brant.

I can't stand to go through this again.

Her fists were bunched at her sides, her nails digging into her scraped palms; dimly she was aware that her knees were bleeding from her frantic run to get to the field. Once more the bull charged, and this time Brant, in a split-second move that was perfectly judged, wrapped his shirt over the wickedly pointed horns, temporarily blinding the animal.

Brant seized his chance, racing for the fence and again vaulting over it with a lithe grace. Snorting ferociously, the bull scraped its horns in the dirt, reducing the shirt to a tangle of shredded fabric.

It could have been Brant, Rowan thought, and wondered if she was going to be sick.

She couldn't be. Not in front of everyone.

Steve and Natalie disentangled themselves long enough for Natalie to gush, "That was wonderful, Brant," and for Steve to say, "Yeah…thanks, man—you got me out of a tight spot."

"You're welcome," Brant panted, wiping the sweat from his forehead with the back of his hand.

He felt great, all his senses alert, his whole body alive with the rush of adrenaline. Then he looked over at the red-haired woman standing stock-still by the fence. Her cheeks were ashen-pale and there was something in her face that instantly banished his euphoria. He took two quick strides toward her, grabbing her by the elbow. "Rowan, you okay?"

She couldn't tell him what she was feeling. Not now, not in front of Natalie, Steve, Peg and May; for the two elderly women had by now arrived on the scene. With a monumental effort Rowan swallowed a turmoil of emotion that would consume her should she give it voice, and said stonily, "I'm fine. Shall we go back to the van? Thanks for looking after the scope, Peg—and my haversack, May."

"Brant, we thought you were going to be killed," Peg exclaimed.

"Right in front of us," May shuddered.

"Not a chance," Brant said with a cheerfulness that grated on Rowan's nerves. "Here, Peg, let me carry the scope."

"You were *very* brave," Peg said. "Wasn't he, Rowan?"

"Very," Rowan said in the same stony voice, and pulled her elbow free as Peg passed Brant the scope.

After one look at Rowan's face, May tucked her arm in her sister's and urged her in the direction of the van; Steve and Natalie were already heading that way, their arms around each other. Brant fell into step beside Rowan. He said noncommittally, "What was Steve doing in a field with a bull?"

"Rescuing Natalie who was taking a photo of an egret and didn't seem to realize that the cow it was sitting on was a bull."

"What's up, Rowan?" he went on with menacing softness. "You look like you're going to explode."

She glared into his brilliant blue irises. "It'll keep," she snapped. "Until tonight. Seeing as how I'd like to hold on to my job, it wouldn't be smart of me to stage a screaming match in front of my clients. Plus I prefer to keep my private life private. Weird of me, but there you are."

He didn't think it was the time to tell her that May, Peg and Steve all knew that he and Rowan had been married. She'd cut his throat from ear to ear by the look of her.

"Well, at least Nat and Steve seem to have mended their differences," he said.

"Hurray for them."

"Bully for them," he grinned, raising one brow.

"Cute," she seethed. "Real cute. Put on a T-shirt or you'll get sunburn."

"Don't tell me what to do, my darling Rowan."

"Don't call me darling!"

"Why did I ever think the Caribbean would be dull?" Brant drawled, putting down the scope and his haversack on the grass and pulling out a T-shirt.

As he raised his arms to pull it over his head, Rowan dragged her eyes away from his lean rib cage, where sun and shadow played over sinew and bone. The van was in sight now, the driver patiently sitting in the shade waiting for them. Karen and Sheldon were cuddled together on the beach, as close as the two halves of a shell, while Natalie and Steve were in a Hollywood clinch against a tree. She'd like to chuck the whole bunch of them, scope and all, into the sea and drive off without them, Rowan thought vengefully.

She couldn't do that. She needed her salary. She called out, "Let's head back to the hotel, I'm sure everyone's ready for a swim and a cool drink after that bit of excitement."

Bit of excitement? Who was she kidding? Death knell to her hopes for a different marriage was more like it.

The wind stirred her hair as they left the beach and drove down the road past a field of sugarcanes; and belatedly Rowan realized why she'd been trying so hard to hold on to her rage.

Because beneath it lay despair. Brant hadn't changed. Couldn't change. So tonight she'd be defeated before she even opened her mouth.

CHAPTER NINE

AT NINE that night Brant crossed the quadrangle toward Rowan's room. He had on his best blue shirt and new cotton trousers, and he'd showered, shaved and brushed his hair: just as though he were an adolescent on his first date. But he didn't feel like an adolescent. He felt like a grown man on a hazardous assignment, who could be walking into an ambush over ground sown with land mines.

And his life depended on how he handled this particular assignment.

He raised his fist and tapped on the door of her room. Rowan opened it immediately, as if she'd been waiting on the other side. She was wearing the same sundress she'd worn for dinner, with a lacy shawl thrown over her shoulders, and she looked like a woman standing in front of a firing squad. Unsmilingly she said, "Where are we going?"

Like a good strategist, he'd already scouted out the territory. "There are some rocks at the far end of the beach beyond the pier, why don't we sit there?"

Side by side they walked down the path. Brant could think of nothing to say; just like a goddamned adolescent, he thought in exasperation. "How are your knees?" he asked.

"No sign of infection. Thanks," she added as an afterthought.

"Good." He racked his brains. "We go to Dominica tomorrow?"

"Yes. It's my favorite of all the islands, it's not developed very much and the birds are wonderful. We do a boat trip there, too, that's always fun.''

He asked a couple of questions, she answered them and by then they'd reached the beach. It was deserted; music from the disco drifted over the water, while the moon had shrunk a little, its pale light shimmering on the waves. Brant took Rowan's elbow as they started over the sand. She flinched from his touch, and his nerves tightened another notch. ''This isn't a seduction scene,'' he said.

''I never thought it was.''

Her voice was a cold as the moonlight. They walked past the stone jetty to the rocks that lay beyond it, where the dark fronds of a palm grove rustled to themselves. Rowan turned to face him, thrusting her hands in the pockets of her dress. Like an adversary, Brant thought. Not like a woman intent on reconciliation.

Instantly she went on the attack, her words falling over themselves. ''You *had* to do that this afternoon, didn't you? Play with that bull as though it were a stuffed teddy bear and not an animal that could have killed you.''

''I was never in any real danger.''

''If you'd tripped and fallen, it would have gored you the way it ripped your shirt to pieces.'' Her voice was shaking. ''You haven't changed. You can't, you don't know how.''

''What did you want me to do? Leave Steve in the field to be gored instead?''

''You enjoyed it!''

''So what?''

Rowan jammed her fists still deeper in her pockets, pulling her dress tight over her breasts, and said raggedly, ''I love you and I want to live with you again, but—''

''You *love* me?''

She said blankly, "Well, yes. Of course. Why else do you think I'm here?"

"Despite everything, you still love me?"

"Don't you love me?" she asked in a hostile voice.

"Sure I do," Brant answered in a dazed voice, and knew he'd spoken the literal truth. A truth he'd had to travel twenty-five hundred miles to discover. "That was one more reason why I wasn't even tempted to sleep with Gabrielle, how could I make love to her when I love you with all my heart?"

Love. Present tense.

If, after this declaration, Brant had expected Rowan to fall into his arms as easily as a ripe coconut falls from a palm tree, he was soon disillusioned. She said, "I want you to quit your job."

The breath hissed between his teeth. Twice in less than a minute she'd outflanked him. Taken him completely by surprise. You're losing your touch, Brant, old man. "Are you serious?" he said. She nodded. "Give it up altogether?"

"Yes."

"You don't ask much, do you? Why do you want me to quit my job, Rowan?"

"I can't imagine you even have to ask that question."

"I am asking it," he said, holding tight to his temper.

She tossed her head. "You've got a choice. You can live with me and have a different job or you can keep the one you've got and stay divorced."

"I never thought blackmail was one of your talents," he said unpleasantly.

Her head jerked up, her nostrils flared. "Maybe we should quit right here—the shortest reconciliation on record," she said bitterly. "Because I'm not going to budge on this one, Brant. I don't know how to get through to you the cost of your job to me. In loneliness. Constant anxiety. Outright terror when I pick up the newspaper and see that the latest coup is in the place you flew into three days ago. I can't do it anymore! I won't do it anymore.''

''But I—''

''You saw how I looked this afternoon by the time you got out of that field! Try stretching that out over two weeks, or a month, or six weeks…however long your assignment lasts. I can't take it anymore. Lying awake night after night worrying about you. Knowing there's nothing I can do to keep you safe. Knowing I'm not as important to you as your job.'' She scuffed at the sand with the toe of her sandal, her head downbent. ''I'm tired of being second on the list.''

''I always came back,'' he said forcefully. ''I never took unnecessary risks, and I always knew what I was doing.''

''Then why were you abducted?''

''That was sheer bad luck,'' he said impatiently.

''No, it wasn't! You're the one who'd put yourself in the situation to start with.''

''So once in eleven years at that job I got into trouble,'' he said furiously. ''I'd call that a pretty good record.''

The words tumbled from Rowan's lips. ''Perhaps it's my fault you've never understood how badly your job affected me. What you said a couple of days ago about not sharing our vulnerabilities— I was guilty of that, too. Before you left on an assignment I'd try not to show you how much I dreaded you going, I think I was afraid it might jinx you so you'd never come back.'' Her voice was shaking again. ''And then when you came back, we'd fall into bed and it would all be forgotten. Until next time.''

She suddenly gripped his bare forearm with one hand. ''At the end I tried to tell you, before you left for Colombia. But you weren't listening, were you? And let me tell you something else. That eight months was the worst time of my whole life. Eight months of wondering if I was already a widow. If I'd ever find out what had happened to you or if you'd just disappear without a trace. No news, no body, nothing. It was so horrible... Oh, Brant, don't you *see?* I can't live like that anymore.''

Staring down at her fingers, he said, ''Where's your wedding ring?''

''Home,'' she said shortly. ''In the drawer.''

''I'd be nothing without my job,'' he said with raw honesty. ''It's what I do.''

She said steadily, ''I don't believe that. You're much bigger than your job.''

''I've done a lot of good over the years.''

''Of course you have! Don't think I don't know that.'' Her smile was wry. ''I just need you to be a different kind of hero, that's all.''

He repeated the one thing he was sure of in this whole mess. ''You've never stopped loving me.''

''I don't know how.''

''And you were never unfaithful to me.''

''Not even an issue.''

Shaken to the depths of his being, Brant put his arms around her and rested his cheek on her hair. ''I love you, too, Rowan,'' he said hoarsely. ''We're bound together, you and I...''

Her voice smothered in his chest, she mumbled, ''I don't think we ever really were divorced.''

So Gabrielle had been right: some divorces weren't worth the paper they were written on. But Brant didn't want to think about Gabrielle. Rather, he wanted to savor the wonder of holding Rowan close again. Her body felt absolutely right in his arms; it was an embrace, he thought humbly, that went far beyond the sexual. He said, ''This is what I want. You. But I don't have a clue how to go about getting it.''

Her arms were snug around his waist; he could hear the small, steady thud of her heartbeat against his chest. She said so quietly he could barely hear her, ''When you were away, the loneliness was the worst. Waking in the night to an empty bed, coming home from one of my trips to an empty apartment, going to the market on Saturday morning on my own, going to the movies and seeing people in couples...oh, God, how I hated the loneliness.'' She lifted her head. ''I'm no saint, Brant. Now that I look back, I think I lost my temper all over the place and at the drop of a hat instead of trying to make you understand how difficult it was without you. In the long run, losing my cool didn't really accomplish very much.''

''Whereas I'd just go away on another assignment. Run away. Because that's what it was.''

Her smile was troubled. ''Hindsight's great stuff, isn't it?''

But where do we go from here? Brant said helplessly, ''I love my job, Rowan.'' As if a tape deck had been turned on, into his brain clicked Gabrielle's words the evening she'd told him about this trip. *I've watched you the last two years. You've been acting like a man demented. Like a man who couldn't care less if he got himself killed.* Was that the attitude of someone who loved his job? Or had he been using his job to kill the pain of Rowan's absence?

Rowan said trenchantly, ''Maybe you should try and figure out why you're in love with danger. Maybe she's been your real mistress all these years.''

He couldn't have stopped the tremor that ran through his body. *In love with danger...* That, he knew, went back to a five-year-old boy whose mother had died and whose father had taken over his upbringing. "You'll be recommending a therapist next," he said nastily.

"I hit home there, didn't I?"

Another nasty retort was on the tip of his tongue. Brant bit it back. The stakes were too high to indulge in name-calling. Much too high. His mouth dry, he said, "I've never talked much about my father...never wanted to."

"Perhaps it's time," she said.

His throat closed. "If I quit my job, what else would I do?"

She was frowning in thought. "All these years I wonder if somehow you've been living your father's life—instead of your own."

"I don't want to talk about him!"

"Sooner or later you'll have to."

With unwilling admiration Brant said, "You don't quit easy, do you?"

"Not where you're concerned," she said pertly. "But don't let it go to your head."

He kissed the tip of her nose. "Or to any other parts of my anatomy."

She nuzzled his breastbone in a gesture that tore at his heart, so familiar was it, and so deeply missed. "We shouldn't get into bed with each other, not yet," she said.

The words were dragged from him. "You want children."

This time it was she who quivered as though he'd struck her. "Yes," she whispered. "Your children, Brant."

He tried it out on his tongue. "Our children."

A single tear hung on her lashes. "I've got—" But then she broke off, biting her lip, her face anguished.

"Sweetheart, what's wrong?"

She shook her head; the muscles in her throat moved as

she swallowed. "I just don't want to wait any longer, I'm thirty-one years old," she said.

He knew in his gut that she'd been about to say something different. Later, he thought, one thing at a time; and again tried to be as honest as he knew how. "I'm scared to death of having kids."

"I think your father has a heck of a lot to answer for!"

She looked very militant. He'd like to have seen Rowan and his father face to face, it would have been a confrontation worth witnessing; Douglas Curtis, however, had died two years before Brant met Rowan. "Do you think I'd be any good as a father?"

"If you gave yourself half a chance, I think you'd be a wonderful father."

It was the third time she'd knocked him off balance. He had none of her certitude about himself in the role of father. None at all. Seeking refuge in practicalities, he asked, "What would I do if I quit my job?"

"I've thought about that quite a bit. You could make a list of all your skills, see what's marketable…you're a very smart man, there's lots you could do. You could even start your own company, taking people to out-of-the-way places." She looked at him through her lashes. "Just don't include Colombia."

He burst out, "If I quit my job and then it didn't work out between you and me—I'd have nothing left."

She winced. "If we both want it to work out, it will."

Brant was quite astute enough to pick up the undercurrent of doubt in her voice. "What about your job? You travel, too. You can't very well go careering around the rain forest if you're seven months pregnant."

"I'd cut back on the number of trips I take. And my company gives maternity leave."

Her head was held high. But in the pallid moonlight he

could see the lines of strain around her mouth and the shadows under her eyes. "Why don't you sit down for a minute?" he said. "You look tired out."

As she turned, Rowan stumbled over a rock. Losing her balance, she banged her knee against the jagged edge of a big boulder. She gave a yelp of pain, put out a hand to support herself, scraped her sore palm and gave another pained yelp. Brant reached her in one quick stride and eased her down on the boulder. "Let me see your knee."

She lifted her skirt. The blood trickling down her shin was black as ink. He said, "God, sweetheart, your knee's a mess."

"When Natalie screamed this afternoon, I took off like a bullet out of a gun. That kind of wrecked it."

"We'd better go back...I'll put some more ointment on."

Rowan took him by the wrist. "Are we going to be okay?" she blurted.

He lifted her to her feet, wondering how he'd existed for over three years without being able to touch her and hold her in his arms. "We've got to be," he said huskily. "Because I can't live without you. You were never second, Rowan. I just behaved as though you were, and for that I deserve to be horsewhipped through three counties."

"You really *are* sorry..."

"Sorry—that's one hell of a wishy-washy word for the way I'm feeling. But yeah, that's what I'm saying."

"You've got a lot of feelings, Brant Curtis," Rowan said in a small voice. "You've just got to learn to let them out more often."

"Plus find a new job and raise a passel of kids," Brant said wryly. "Anything else you can add to the list?"

She gave a sudden delightful laugh. "Maybe somewhere

in there you should marry me again. For the sake of the children, you understand.''

''For our sake,'' he said fiercely, and kissed her with all the love that had been locked inside him for so long. Too long. She kissed him back with all her old tempestuousness; they were both trembling when he finally released her. She whispered, ''I think I'd better look after my knee myself. If you come into my room, we both know what'll happen.''

''And it's too soon,'' he said in an agony of frustration.

''I hate it when you look like that!''

With his fingertips he smoothed the distress from her features. ''Hey, I'm a big boy, I've managed for three years, remember?''

''I don't even want to wait for three days,'' she announced with a violence that entranced him.

''Three hours?''

''Not three minutes!''

He laughed. ''Back to your room, Rowan. Morning comes early.''

She took three or four steps, limping awkwardly. Giving him a sly grin she said, ''This is all your fault. If I hadn't been so preoccupied with keeping you off that plane to Toronto, I wouldn't have tripped over the curb.'' Then, as if her own words were replaying in her head, she paled and all the laughter vanished from her face.

Brant took her by the arm. ''Rowan, there's something you're not telling me.''

She made a tiny gesture to ward him off. ''I can't,'' she said in an almost inaudible whisper. ''Not yet. I just can't.''

''You can trust me! I'm not getting on a plane to Toronto until the end of this tour, and when I do I hope to God you're sitting beside me.''

''Please...let's go back to my room.''

''One reason we divorced is that we're both as stubborn

as any of the donkeys we've seen on these islands," he said. "We've got to trust each other, Rowan. Not doing so is what's kept us apart."

"Are you going to tell me what your father was like?" she flashed.

He wasn't, no. "Stalemate," he said tautly.

"For now." Rowan ran her fingertips over the gray in his hair, her lip caught between her teeth. "We can't expect to fix seven years in half an hour. I guess."

"Trouble is, I was never known for patience." Brant swung her up into his arms, his one desire to remove that haunted look from her face. "You don't weigh as much as you used to. Or else I'm in better shape."

A tiny smile pulled at her mouth. She ran her finger down his chest and said, "Oh, you're in fine shape."

"All talk and no action," he grumbled, grinning at her.

"Most of the time I talk too much."

"While I don't talk enough."

"Tonight was a marked improvement on that score."

"How about we call time-out? I, for one, need to do some heavy-duty thinking…we'd be strapped for money if I quit my job."

She ticked off her fingers. "We could sell the condo—I sublet it when I moved to the country. We've got my salary. And there's your father's inheritance. We'd be fine."

"I suppose you're right…" For the first time Brant could see possibilities in the money his father had left him, money he'd vowed never to touch. He rather liked the idea of using it to set himself up in some kind of new career that had nothing to do with Douglas Curtis. The perfect revenge, he thought grimly, and heaved himself off the soft sand onto the path. Within minutes he was depositing Rowan at her door and she was turning the key in the lock. He said lamely, "You'll be all right?"

"I'll be fine. I'll put some ointment on my knee and go to bed." Almost shyly, as if he were a man she'd only just met, she cupped his jaw in her hands and kissed him softly on the lips. Before he could say anything, she slipped through the door and shut it behind her.

Brant scowled at the closed door, then walked to his own room, which was, of course, empty of anyone but himself. He sat down on the bed. He had a choice. Keep his job and stay divorced, or quit and be with Rowan.

But was it a choice? He had to have Rowan. He needed her. The last two years he had indeed been like a man possessed, doing his best—or his worst—to get himself killed. More than once he'd taken risks that had been plain foolishness, for which he'd have fired another man without a second thought. Even though he hadn't deserved to, he'd gotten away with them. But if he kept that up, sooner or later—and it'd probably be sooner—he'd step on a land mine or walk into an ambush and it'd be game over.

No choice at all. He wanted Rowan. In his arms. In his life. And to achieve that he'd give up a lot more than his job.

She'd never stopped loving him. Nor he her.

If he'd deceived himself so badly on that score, what else was he hiding from himself?

A five-year-old boy crying for his mother…

But Brant didn't want to go that way. He wasn't ready.

One thing at a time, he decided, and shifted gears. He'd miss certain aspects of his job, he knew that. The unpredictability. The excitement of marketplaces and dusty streets half a world away from home. The alertness to signals most other people wouldn't even see, the sense of living on the edge: he'd thrived on all that. Until the last two years.

Funny, he thought. Going to get Rowan this evening,

facing her on the beach like a man fighting for something incredibly precious, he'd had the same sense of living on the edge, of being in a country he'd never seen before. Rather startled by this similarity, he allowed his thoughts to carry him forward. He'd stifle in an office, and he was much too used to being his own boss to suffer anyone else ordering him around. An administrative job? Forget it.

He'd come up with something. Or—and again Brant smiled to himself—Rowan would.

He bent to unlace his sneakers, gratitude and a deep happiness welling through his whole body. Although he would have much preferred not to be alone right now, he was nevertheless content to wait. Because Rowan still loved him and he loved her.

His soul was in her keeping. He knew that beyond a doubt.

He was the most fortunate of men.

CHAPTER TEN

THE next morning at the ultramodern airport in Martinique, Brant went into the drugstore; he needed shaving cream. He also picked up a package of condoms, paying for both in American money and getting a fistful of francs as change. He had no idea if Rowan was still taking the pill, and he wasn't taking any chances.

She wanted children.

In the antiseptic cleanliness of the drugstore under its white fluorescent lights he was suddenly attacked by all the symptoms of danger: pounding heart and sweating palms and that knife-edge of alertness to all his senses. No job and a baby on the way. Was he crazy? Was the woman born who was worth that?

"Monsieur? Êtes-vous malade?"

"Non, non, merci," he said rapidly and walked back into the terminal. Rowan was standing in front of the machine that exchanged currencies, her face intent as she counted out the sheaf of bills in her hand. She was wearing bush pants and her dark green shirt, a slim, capable woman doing her job, a woman whom he loved body and soul.

He'd shortchanged her for the four years of their marriage. He'd given her money, possessions and a fancy condo. He given her all the gifts of his body. But he hadn't given her himself. He'd never given anyone that.

A five-year-old boy facing the big dark-browed stranger who was his father...

Was he totally out of his mind, or was he really embarking on the most difficult assignment of his whole life?

136

Brant shoved his purchases in his backpack and walked over to her. "Rowan..." he said.

A note in his voice brought her head around. "What's the matter?"

"Nothing," he stumbled. "I just needed to—hell, I don't know what I need."

"It'll be fine, Brant," she said vehemently.

"Do I look that bad?"

"I've seen you look better and I'm not asking you to do anything you can't do—I swear I'm not! Besides, I'll be with you every step of the way."

As if the man were still alive, Brant could hear his father's voice sneering at him. *Look at you—adventurer and world-famous reporter—leaning on a woman. Letting her put bars around you, cage you and coddle you, turn you into a momma's boy. You're done for, Brant. Finished.*

Rowan seized the front of his shirt. "Brant, don't look like that—I can't stand it!"

The voice had vanished. He was left with a distraught woman to whom he had nothing to say, and with Sheldon fast approaching them with a fixed smile on his face. He also saw how Peg and May were hanging back because they knew something was up, and how Natalie and Steve were giggling over some of the more risqué postcards in the newsstand.

Sheldon, who was oblivious to the possibility of any relationship other than his own, said, "We need help, Rowan, you know none of us can speak French."

"I'll look after it," Brant said curtly, and took off toward the newsstand, Sheldon in his wake. And if he was running away again, there were always times on assignment when retreat was the most prudent of strategies.

An hour later they boarded the short flight to Dominica. The plane was full; Rowan sat near the front and Brant

ended up at the very back. At the Dominica airport there
was a slight holdup with their van. About to wander outside
to examine the river on the other side of the road, Brant's
attention was caught by a small display of books in the
little kiosk by the entrance. He picked up a couple of espionage novels, both by a well-known author whose works
got rave reviews internationally. As he went to pay for
them, the woman at the register said pleasantly, "My husband, he loves those books. Takes him away from it all,
that's what he says." She laughed. "You can forget him
once he gets his hands on one, oh, yes."

"I'll probably be the same," Brant smiled. "Thanks."

The van had just pulled up; he went over to help load
the luggage. Rowan was doing the driving on this island.
They'd landed on the windward coast, where the ocean was
laced with white and where women were doing the wash
in the many small streams that ran into the sea. Banana
plantations and lush forest lined the narrow paved road as
they wound their way across the island to the west coast,
where their hotel was located. Rowan carried on an ani-
mated discussion with Peg, who was sitting beside her,
about warblers and parrots; Brant sat quietly, content to
watch the play of expression on her face and to let the
island's beauty soak into him.

The hotel was unpretentious and friendly, with its own
dark gray sand beach edged with tumbles of orange, cream
and magenta bougainvillea amidst swaying coconut palms.
Brant's room was at the very end, so he got the breeze
from two directions; his balcony overlooked the sea and he
felt instantly at home.

They all met at the beach for lunch. That afternoon they
drove north to the rain forest, where Rowan produced a
red-legged thrush out of the scrub on the way up the mountain, and then a charmingly plump gray and white warbler

at the forest edge. Parrots flew overhead, flycatchers darted up from the grapefruit trees, and again Brant was delighted to see the tiny Carib with its glittering purple throat.

They left just before dusk. The trail down the mountain boasted some of the biggest potholes Brant had ever seen. Rowan negotiated them with considerable skill; but he noticed she was limping when she came into the dining room for dinner. After they'd eaten, he got her to one side. "How are your knees?"

"Not bad. But it's weird, it's only nine-thirty and I feel totally wiped." Her brows knit in thought. "It was hard work, what we did last night by the rocks."

"High stakes."

"You said it. And we have to get up at five tomorrow, to see the other parrot."

"The Imperial parrot, otherwise known as the Sisserou," he supplied with a grin.

"I'll make a birder out of you yet."

"Now that, my darling, is pushing it."

She bit her lip. "When you smile at me like that, I turn into a puddle on the floor."

"When you say things like that," he riposted, "I want to carry you off to my room and make love to you until neither one of us has the strength to pick up a pair of binoculars. Let alone identify what's at the other end."

She widened her eyes. "You mean if we make love you won't be able to tell a hawk from a hummingbird?"

"Want to put it to the test?"

Her smile faded. "It still feels too soon, Brant—and I'm not being coy and I'm not playing hard to get."

It was the answer he'd expected and that, to some extent, he agreed with. At least, his head did. His groin was another matter. He said slowly, "Maybe I won't be convinced any of this is really happening until we go to bed together."

"I want to, oh, God, how I want to," she said helplessly. "But I'm so scared we'll do what we did so often—fall into bed as a way of escape."

"It doesn't help one bit to watch Steve and Natalie crawling all over each other."

"Or Sheldon and Karen necking on the beach," she added.

"Look at it this way—we're building character."

"We'd darn well better be building something."

He brushed her cheek with his lips. "Good night, my love."

She blurted, "Even though we don't really know where we're going from here, I want you to know how happy I am, Brant. Wonderfully happy and not lonely at all."

"Good," he said, patted her on the bottom, and got a drink from the bar before he went to his room. He stripped to his briefs and piled pillows against the bamboo head-board. Sipping on a rum as smooth as velvet, he opened one of the books he'd bought and started to read, doing his best to put Rowan out of his mind.

The next day was for Brant the most pleasurable so far. In the high Dominican rain forest they got incredible views of the rare Imperial parrot as it munched on fruit at the top of a tree by their picnic site; in the scope he could distinguish the individual feathers on the back of its neck, deep maroon feathers in startling contrast to its lime-green plumage. That afternoon he thoroughly enjoyed the boat trip to the cliffs at the northern tip of the island, stationing himself on the upper bridge along with the captain and Rowan. Back at the hotel, they ate callaloo soup and mountain chicken, and the sun set in pink and gold splendor over the sea.

He'd stayed up reading until midnight the night before; at eight-thirty he went to his room to pack for tomorrow's flip to Guadeloupe, and to try and finish his book. Rowan had driven Peg and May to visit birding friends who lived near the capital, Roseau; he wouldn't see her again until tomorrow.

Time was passing, he thought uneasily. Two more islands, and then he'd be heading back to Toronto. He didn't want to be alone in his room, he'd been alone in far too many hotel rooms the world over. He wanted Rowan with him. Now.

Besides, there was something she was keeping from him. A secret of some kind that was causing her distress. He couldn't imagine what it was; and knew it was adding to his sense of apprehension.

He needed to make love to her, to anchor their reconciliation in the body.

With an impatient sigh Brant headed for the shower. Afterward he went back into his bedroom, a towel wrapped around his waist. After uncapping a plastic bottle of guava juice, he picked up his book and his pen—because he'd been taking notes in the margin—and settled himself on the bed to read.

Rowan had delivered Peg and May to a bungalow high on the hillside overlooking the ocean, had met their friends and had enjoyed a piña colada made with local coconut. When the husband, a retired bank manager, offered to drive the two women back to the hotel later on, she accepted gratefully. She'd realized on the drive to the bungalow that she'd neglected to tell everyone what time breakfast was being served: a very simple and routine detail, the forgetting of which showed how preoccupied she was with Brant.

She got back to the hotel, gave the information to Steve and to Sheldon, and then walked down the path to the unit at the very end of the hotel. Her heart was thumping in her chest like a drum at a Christmas parade. Swiftly, before she could lose her nerve, she tapped on the door.

Brant opened it. When he saw her, his involuntary smile of pleasure went straight to her heart; hastily he snugged the towel he was wearing more tightly around his waist. "Rowan," he said, "I thought you were in Roseau."

Her eyes skidded from his bare chest to his long legs and then back to his face. "I forgot to tell you we're meeting for breakfast at six-thirty in the morning, the flight's at eight forty-five," she mumbled. "Sorry to disturb you."

His eyes gleamed with sudden purpose. "You didn't," he said, lifted her by the elbows, swung her over the threshold and kicked the door shut with one bare foot. Then he kissed her. Kissed her, she thought dazedly, as if there were no tomorrow.

Hadn't she, when she'd left him to the very last, hoped that something like this would happen?

She was tired of being cautious, of worrying about old patterns and of holding him at arm's length. There was nothing remotely at arm's length in his embrace, and she was going to make sure it stayed that way. Rowan threw her own arms around his waist, feeling the nub of the towel against her wrists, and kissed him back with a passion as instinctual as breathing.

Brant muttered her name under his breath, kissing her lips, her cheeks, her closed lids, roaming her face as though to memorize it. He smelled delicious, a tantalizing mixture of the familiar and the unknown, this man whom she'd lived with for four years, yet who'd become, in so many ways, a stranger to her. She dug her nails into his spine, loving the tightness of muscle and the knobbed bone, feeling his arms strengthen their hold as once again he sought her mouth.

Opening to him, Rowan let her tongue dance with his in

an intimacy that caused her heartbeat to spiral. She pressed into his body so that the heat of his skin penetrated her shirt, kindling a still greater heat. She toyed with his hair, traced the flat curves of his ears and the taut throat muscles, and all the while her certainty grew that this was where she belonged.

As though he'd read her mind, Brant raised his head. "Are you sure this is what you want to be doing?" he said roughly. "Because now's the time to stop if it isn't."

The pulse at the base of his throat was hammering against his skin; another drumbeat, she thought, rested her fingertip there. "I don't want to stop. Not if you don't want to."

"I don't have words to tell you what I want."

"Then show me," Rowan said with sudden urgency. "We've done enough talking for now."

He smiled into her eyes, dropping kisses light as raindrops on her face. "Not entirely. I love you, I need to say that."

"I love you, too." Giving him a radiant smile back, she said artlessly, "It's really quite amazing, isn't it?"

"Astonishing," he agreed solemnly. "I've got something else to say and it's very important, so you'd better pay attention."

She tweaked his chest hair. "You have my total attention."

"Good." He was laughing at her, she saw with a catch at her heart; he looked as young and carefree as he had on their wedding day and she wanted him as she'd never wanted any other man. "But you'd better hurry up," she added, swiveling her hips against his and widening her eyes mischievously as she felt the imperious hardness of his erection. "Or I'll be accusing you of being all talk and no action."

He lowered his hands to grasp her hips and gave a sudden thrust that made her gasp with a fierce and altogether unfeigned pleasure. "What did you say?"

"Skip it," she said faintly.

"You have altogether too many clothes on, that's all I was going to say. Particularly as the towel keeps slipping."

"You do have a way with words, my love." Rowan tugged at the towel, sliding one hand beneath to caress the jut of his pelvis and his taut buttock. "I'm all yours," she murmured. "Because do you know what I want?"

Again he laughed. "Me?" he said hopefully.

"Whatever gave you that idea?" Her cheeks flushed, she added, "I want you to undress me, Brant—the way you used to," and watched desire and wonderment chase themselves across his rugged features.

He reached for the top button of her shirt. One by one he undid them, his knuckles grazing her breasts, and all the while his eyes were trained on her face. She was still blushing, she knew. She also knew all her happiness must be written on her features for him to read. No barriers. No anger or bitterness. Only a deep joy that Brant and she were together again and that her world had righted itself.

He tugged her shirt out of her waistband and eased it from her shoulders, and only then did his gaze drop. Rowan stood very still as her shirt fell to the floor and he sought the clasp on her bra. It, too, slid to the floor. For a long moment he simply looked, his eyes stroking her flesh, lingering where her nipples had tightened like the seeds of ripe fruit. "I've never forgotten how beautiful you are," he whispered, and took her breasts in his hands, lowering his mouth to taste their ivory smoothness.

Her body quivered like an overstrung bow. Arching toward him, she began her own exploration, relearning the banded muscles of his belly, the hollowed collarbone and ridged rib cage, feeling in her bones as though she'd come home after a long and arduous absence. His towel joined her shirt on the floor. With a deliberation that was both sensual and wanton, she let her hands move lower down his body, following the dark arrow of hair to his navel, then wrapping her fingers around his shaft.

He groaned deep in his throat. Roughly he undid the zipper on her trousers and pushed them down her hips. His haste was contagious; Rowan kicked off her sandals, then yanked at the lacy underwear that she always wore on her trips as an antidote to the practicality of her outer garments. Hauling them down her thighs, she grimaced a little as she bent her knees.

"Easy, sweetheart," Brant said, "we've got all night."

"But I don't want to take all night. I want you now."

He pulled back the covers and drew her down on the bed. Hunched over her on one elbow, he ran one hand down her ribs, his face intent. She burst out, "I know you better than anyone in the world and yet you're a stranger to me."

"Maybe that's one reason I've craved to have you in my bed again—so you won't be a stranger anymore," Brant said.

Then she felt the slight roughness of his palm at waist, hip and thigh as he continued his exploration. For a few moments she closed her eyes, the better to savor pure sensation. Very gently he circled her knee; he clasped her ankle; he traced the arch of her foot where the blue veins lay close to the skin. Then, more slowly, Brant let his mouth do the journeying back from ankle to breast.

Shivering with delight, Rowan watched him, glorying in the intimacy with which he was traveling her body, knowing she wanted him to touch her everywhere there was to touch, so she could melt and yield, be filled and fulfilled. She whispered, "Oh, Brant, I do love you."

His lips had reached the peak of her breast. With exquisite sensitivity he played with it, until again she arched toward him in blatant arousal; only then, taking her head in his palms, did he kiss her lips with a deep and passionate hunger.

Rowan pressed herself to the length of his big frame, the same hunger encompassing her in its imperative and ancient demands; she ached and throbbed with that hunger. Suddenly, so suddenly that she cried out with an ardor as naked as her body, Brant parted her thighs and thrust between them. She surged to meet him, her whole being nothing but the frantic need to mate with this man who was her true and only lover.

He gasped, "Wait a minute, Rowan—are you still protected? If not, I can look after that."

As though he'd struck her, Rowan spiraled from a passion as scarlet as hibiscus, as searing as flame, into a very different place: an ice-cold place, a place of thick darkness. She pulled away from him in a single, graceless movement, her face stricken. "No, I'm not protected," she said.

Four words that brought with them a crushing load of guilt and sorrow. She shoved at his chest, as frantic to escape as only seconds ago she'd been frantic to join with him, tears crowding her eyes. As she fought them back, Brant said, aghast, "What did I say? Rowan, what's the matter?"

Her chest felt so tight that she could scarcely breathe. She tried to scramble off the bed and felt Brant anchor her there with a hand around her wrist. Like a manacle, she thought, tugging at it, a manacle of steel, and heard him say with genuine desperation, "You're not leaving—not until I know what's wrong. We can't run away from each other any longer, sweetheart, don't you see that? It's what we've done for years, me more than you, I know. But we've got to change, Rowan—or we're lost.''

He was right, of course. Certainly she'd been running from telling him a secret that had torn at her soul. She threw herself facedown on the bed as the first sob forced its way from her throat, and from a long way away felt his arms gather her to his chest. He said forcibly, ''I love you. No matter what, I love you. And I'm not going to go away. Never again.''

But would he still love her, Rowan wondered, when he knew? Often over the years Brant had praised her for her honesty, told her how much he depended on her capacity to stick to the truth. But once, three years ago, she'd lied to him, quite deliberately, with consequences she couldn't possibly have foreseen and that had torn her apart.

How would Brant feel when she told him? Would he ever trust her again?

CHAPTER ELEVEN

ROWAN began to weep in earnest, her body shuddering with the force of her emotion as she plunged into that dark place of loneliness that she knew so well. She cried for a long time; and it took her a long time to come back to herself, to the reality of Brant's embrace, and of his voice murmuring soothing bits of nonsense into her ears. Gradually she became aware of two things. She'd needed to cry her heart out like that. Had needed to ever since she'd seen Brant at the airport in Grenada. And, secondly, this time she hadn't been lonely. She'd been held and comforted within the circle of Brant's arms and by the strength of his love.

She quavered, wiping her cheeks with the back of her hand, "I've got s-something to tell you."

He reached over his shoulder and passed her a box of tissues. "Blow," he said. She did as she was told, scrubbing at her wet cheeks and wondering if she looked as awful as she felt. He added flatly, "You don't have to be frightened. Not of me."

She hadn't realized she looked frightened. She said in a rush, her words rattling like stones in a stream, "Two or three months before you left for Colombia, I went to the doctor. He suggested I come off the pill for a while, for medical reasons. So I did. But I didn't tell you. I wanted a child so badly, and I thought if I got pregnant you'd be okay with it. You'd have to be."

A quality in his silence made her glance up. He looked stunned, she thought, and felt terror close her throat. "I lied

148

to you,'' she said. ''Not directly, in so many words—but it was a lie, nevertheless. I deliberately deceived you. And then you went away, even though I begged you not to…by the time you left, my period was three days late, I didn't dare tell you that, how could I? As a way of keeping you home? I wasn't going to play that game.''

She blew her nose again, blinking her wet lashes. ''After you'd gone, I went back to the doctor and discovered I was pregnant. You and I talked a couple of times on the phone before the abduction, remember? But I didn't know how to tell you, the connections were always so dreadful and I was so afraid of what you'd say…so I thought I'd wait until you came back.''

''And then I got dumped behind bars for eight months,'' Brant said in an unreadable voice.

Because she was so frightened, Rowan spilled out the rest of the story without finesse. ''They phoned me. From New York, to tell me you'd been captured and hidden away somewhere, they weren't sure where, but they'd try and have some news for me in a day or so. A day or so,'' she repeated, gazing at her trembling hands. ''They might as well have said a lifetime.''

Even through her fear, she was aware of the rigidity of Brant's muscles as he held her, of a quietness that was like the quiet before the howl of a hurricane. Hurriedly she went on, ''I was upstairs because I'd been resting, I'd been having morning sickness and I was tired a lot of the time. As I put down the phone, the front doorbell rang, and I was instantly convinced it'd all been a hoax and it was you at the door, you'd come home, of course you had, I'd fallen asleep and dreamed that phone call from London. I ran for the stairs and I forgot about the carpet on the third step, it was rucked up, remember? I tripped over it and fell headlong down the stairs, and when I came to I was in hospital and I'd—I'd lost the baby.''

She was pleating the corner of the sheet with tiny, agitated movements, her lashes lowered. ''I never told you. It was seven months before I saw you again, in the hospital room with Gabrielle. I suppose the miscarriage was one more reason I didn't go into that room to see you. Why bother telling you I'd lost a child you hadn't wanted in the first place, when you were—so I thought—in love with another woman?''

''My God…'' said Brant.

She risked looking up at him. His face was haggard, his gaze turned inward; she had no idea what he was thinking. ''I cheated you,'' she said in a low voice. ''I'm so sorry, Brant.''

He rasped, ''I'm the one who was too busy to repair the carpet. You'd asked me to, and it would only have taken a few minutes. But I was too goddamned preoccupied with getting ready to go to South America to bother with something as mundane as a carpet.''

''It wasn't your fault!''

''You could have been killed.''

''Brant, I could have fixed the carpet—it wasn't exactly a difficult job. But I was too stubborn to, once I'd asked you to do it. Anyway,'' she finished with a flash of spirit, ''this isn't about carpets. It's about how I lied to you and tricked you.''

Harsh lines had carved themselves into his cheeks; she was suddenly achingly aware of the dusting of gray hair over his ears. ''It's about how you were alone when you fell down the stairs,'' he said in a bleak voice, ''and alone when you came to in the hospital. That's what it's about, Rowan. I wasn't much of a husband, was I?''

She couldn't bear to see him blame himself. ''You were

the only man I ever wanted to marry. Still are," she said with the smallest of smiles.

"I never paid any attention when you said you wanted a child. I was scared to death of having children, but I didn't tell you that, oh, no, I laughed at you instead."

"Brant," Rowan said vigorously, "we both made mistakes back then. Big ones. Are you saying you can forgive me for getting pregnant without telling you, and then..." her voice wavered "...losing the baby and not telling you that, either?"

He stroked her bare shoulder, his face as naked to her as his body. "Yes, I forgive you...although in all honesty I don't think there's much to forgive."

"I felt so guilty! You don't know how I've dreaded telling you, and yet I knew I couldn't have any secrets from you, not if we're going to try again...maybe that's one reason I was procrastinating going to bed with you."

"You nearly told me by the rocks in Martinique."

She nodded. "I was afraid you'd get on the first plane back to Toronto."

Brant pulled the sheet corner from her restless fingers and trapped them in his own. "No secrets," he said heavily. "In that case I'd better tell you that forgiving myself is a lot harder than forgiving you." He grimaced. "Can you ever forgive *me*, Rowan?"

She lifted his hand and kissed it, her lips lingering on his taut knuckles. "I already have."

Briefly, he felt the prick of tears. Blinking them back, he muttered, "You're very generous—more so than I deserve."

She said emphatically, "I've learned something the last little while, Brant...since we met in Grenada, I mean. It's you I really want. Yes, I want children. But if I can't have you, then nothing's worthwhile."

He pulled her close, burying his face in her hair. "Let's go back to Toronto and get married again," he said in a muffled voice. "I'll quit my job and we'll do our best to start a baby, and somehow or other it'll all work out."

Her heart gave a lurch of pure panic. Wasn't Brant giving her everything she'd longed for—marriage, a different job and a child? So why didn't it feel right? Why was she still scared? No secrets, she thought, and said, "You should really want to be a father, Brant. It shouldn't just happen and then you'll make the best of it."

"Perhaps when the baby's real, when it exists, I'll understand what fatherhood's all about."

He didn't look convinced. Rowan said, "For now, I think we should use protection." She ran her fingers through her tousled curls, adding in frustration, "I'm the one who so desperately wants children, and I'm saying that? I wish to heaven I knew what was going on."

"I'm as yellow-bellied as a chicken," Brant said bluntly, "that's what's going on. The thought of having a kid—of being a father—scares me more than all the rebels in Colombia."

"Oh," said Rowan.

"So I think we should just jump off the deep end and trust there's water in the pool."

Rowan felt exhaustion wash over her. Brant was finally agreeing to start a child and she was telling him now wasn't the time. It was like the plot of a very bad movie, she thought wildly, one where there was no sense to anything that happened. She said with a stubborn lift of her chin, "I don't think we should start anything tonight."

He drew back. "You don't want to make love to me anymore?"

She glared at him, knowing she didn't look the least bit loverlike and not caring one whit. "Yes, I want to make love to you. No, I don't want to make love without protection. So there!''

"You know what I think we should do?'' he said dryly. "Get some sleep…you look wiped, my darling, and five-thirty comes early.''

"I sound like an echo, I know I do, but don't you want to make love to *me?*''

Brant grinned, guided her hand downward and said, "Sure I do. But I also want it to be perfect—we've waited a long time.''

From a wisdom she hadn't known she possessed, Rowan said, "I don't think perfection is the aim here. I mean, look at us three years ago—a smart young couple with interesting jobs, two cars, an expensive condo—I bet we looked perfect from the outside. And guess what? We got divorced.''

Brant's fingertip followed a tearstain down her face. "Real,'' he said. "Not perfect.''

"Splotchy eyes, red nose and all.''

His voice roughened. "Hair like fire, eyes dark as velvet and a body to die for.''

"You know what?'' Rowan said jaggedly, "I'd do anything in the world for you.''

"Yeah? Then convince me you want me,'' he said, a gleam in his eye.

"No problem,'' said Rowan.

Her tiredness lifted as though it had never been, her smile combining mischief with provocation. Gracefully she rested her weight on him, feeling against her breasts and belly the abrasion of his body hair. She moved against him, slowly and with deliberate seduction, her hands roaming his thick hair, the width of his shoulders, the planes and angles of his torso. Passion flared in the blue of his irises; but he lay still, giving her the lead.

She slid lower, giving her fingers and her mouth full play, hearing him gasp in that mingling of pleasure and pain that she remembered so well. Then his control broke. Quickly he dealt with the foil envelope by the bed before lifting her to straddle him, guarding her sore knees; she sank down, filled with him, her face blurred with desire, her body melting with its heat.

What had been a game became an imperative. In quick fierce strokes Rowan rode him until suddenly Brant rolled over, carrying her with him, his big body covering her, his eyes glued to her face. "Now," he said. "Now, Rowan."

His deep thrusts had reached that place in her where only he had ever been. Her own rhythms surged to meet his until she was lost in the blue of his eyes, a blue like the blue at the base of a flame; consumed, she whispered his name over and again, like a mantra, and at her very core felt him pulse to his own release.

He pulled her to him, his heartbeat carrying her own with it in frantic duet. Then he said with the kind of honesty that's hard-earned and is consequently rare, "I'll never lose you again, Rowan, I swear…somehow we'll work it all out. We've got to. You're my life's blood, I can't live without you."

"I mustn't start crying again," she mumbled. "Not twice in one evening…oh, Brant, I do love you."

He kissed her, a kiss infused with loyalty and love. Rowan looped her arms around his neck, snuggled her face into his shoulder and gave a sigh of repletion. "I want to stay awake the whole night so I don't miss one single moment of us in bed together again, it's so lovely," she said, and within two minutes was fast asleep.

Brant didn't fall asleep right away. He settled himself more comfortably, enjoying the weight of Rowan's thigh over his own, listening to the small steady voice of her heart against his chest. He thought he might burst with happiness. Simultaneously, because he now knew how much he had to lose, he realized he was still deeply frightened.

Fatherhood.

Rowan was a child who'd been wanted from the time of conception, he was sure of that. He'd always liked her parents, two people of intelligence and strong will who'd accomplished that not so minor miracle of remaining in love through years of marriage and raising children. Rowan's sister Jane was a eye surgeon in a remote hospital in India; her brother was a biologist studying reindeer migrations in Siberia. Rowan's parents had loved all three children and had encouraged them to go free.

His mother had loved him. In his memory she was a pretty, frightened woman, nervous, edgy and overly protective; when he'd grown old enough to understand such matters, he'd wondered if she hadn't used up all her courage in leaving her husband when her only son was a baby.

His father had been very different. The several photos Brant had of Douglas Curtis showed a burly, dark-browed man scowling into the camera, surrounded by the corpses of whatever animals he'd just shot. Grizzly bears, mountain lions, Dall sheep, lions, tigers and elephants, the list was endless.

Douglas's house had been a taxidermist's heaven. Brant could remember all too well how terrified he'd been at the age of five of a polar bear that had been stuffed upright, its wickedly curved claws pawing the air, its gaping jaws set in a ferocious snarl. Not coincidentally, he'd done several articles in the last few years about poaching, big-game hunting, and the illegal trade in animal parts, a couple of them at some personal risk.

But he'd never exorcised his father.

He stroked the soft slope of Rowan's shoulder, awed, as always, by the silkiness of her skin. Her breath escaped in a little sigh, its warmth against his chest touching him to the heart. He'd protect her with the last of his strength from any danger, he knew that in his bones. So could he also confront the demons of his past for her sake?

He had no answer to that question.

It was late when Brant finally fell asleep; he woke to the beep of his alarm clock. Rowan reached over, slammed it off and yawned. Then she gaped at him. "Oh, my goodness," she said.

"A man in your bed," Brant said lazily.

As he gave her a hug, she slid her hips closer to his. "A man to whom bird-watching isn't a priority."

"Have we got time to make love?" he asked, kissing first one breast and then the other, his tongue laving her nipples; to his gratification she was already trembling to his touch. "I'm good, aren't I?" he said immodestly.

"Extraordinarily and magnificently good, and no, we don't have time, not unless you want the whole group to miss the plane and me to get fired for seducing a client."

"Wouldn't it be worth it?"

She gave a throaty chuckle. "It might be more than— Brant, stop that!"

"But I like it," he said, sliding his fingers deeper between her thighs and discovering she was only too ready to receive him. Swiftly he entered her, watching her eyes darken and lose their laughter in an ardor that inflamed him. Then she reached over and kissed him, stroking his lips with her tongue, her hips opening to gather him in, rocking to his rhythm.

Their surrender was fierce, quick and mutual. Panting, Brant said, "I swear tonight I'll show a little more subtlety."

"How am I going to face them at breakfast?" Rowan moaned, her hands to her flushed cheeks. "It'll be written all over me."

"They'll be too busy eating papaya to notice," Brant said, hoping he was right. He patted her on the hip. "You can have the shower first."

As she scrambled out of bed, she must have seen the torn foil envelope on the bedside table. She paled. "Brant, we didn't use any protection."

His swearword was unprintable, his dismay blatant. "It didn't occur to me—I was always used to you being on the pill."

"We've got to settle this whole business of having kids," she said violently. "We've got to!"

He swung his legs to the side of the bed and stood up. "What you mean is, I've got to."

"We've got to," she said stubbornly. "We're a couple now."

"It's a time in your cycle when you're not likely to get pregnant," he said in a level voice, "and we aren't going to settle it between now and the time we have to catch the next plane. Shower, Rowan."

She gave a sharp sigh of frustration. "Sometimes I hate my job!" she announced and stalked into the bathroom, shutting the door behind her. Brant took the torn envelope and buried it in the wastebasket.

When Brant arrived at breakfast, a discreet few minutes after Rowan, Rowan's gaze flew straight to his face. Her temper had vanished; he saw only love and anxiety in the dark pools of her eyes. He smiled at her, with neither the desire nor the ability to erase the love from that smile. Then he realized sheepishly that Steve was grinning at him, Sheldon looking puzzled, while Peg and May were exuding smugness. He stumbled, "Er—good morning. How did everyone sleep?"

Dumb question, Brant.

"Wonderfully well," said May. "How about you, Brant?"

He'd cut himself shaving because he'd been thinking about Rowan, and there were circles under his eyes. "Great," he said, and sat down. Rowan, he could see, was struggling with a reprehensible desire to laugh. He grabbed the coffee jug and filled his cup.

They all got to the airport on time, Brant sat next to Rowan on the plane, and at the Guadeloupe airport, a replica of the one at Martinique, the van was waiting. Their hotel was on the beach and his room was air-conditioned. As he dumped his haversack on the bed, the two espionage novels he'd bought in Dominica fell out of one of the pockets, along with the notebook in which he'd jotted his own plot.

Brant sat down on the bed, gazing at them, his brain racing. He was a writer by trade. Realistically, he also knew he was a very good writer: his boss wouldn't have tolerated him if he were anything other than first-rate. Furthermore, he needed a new job and he had enough money to tide him over a lag in earnings.

He'd write his own book. Heaven knows he had enough experiences to draw on for a dozen books. A whole series of books. He could even make a collection of some of his best essays and hawk that. The sky was the limit.

Excitement kindled inside him. If he could get a novel published, at least two of his problems would be solved: job plus income. Which only left fatherhood.

Leave the worst until the last, why don't you?

He glanced at his watch. They were meeting for an early lunch in half an hour. He'd stay in the hotel the rest of the day and tomorrow and get started. He'd have to do a lot more work around characters and plot; but he could do it, he knew he could.

Do it and enjoy it, he thought. Take a rest from constant tension and the seductive lure of danger.

Rowan was seduction enough for any man.

He locked his room and went to the main desk, where he found out he could rent a laptop computer from a company in Pointe-à-Pitre. In rapid-fire French he made all the arrangements to have it delivered to the hotel that afternoon. Then he bought a couple of pads of lined paper in the boutique, and went for lunch.

"Not coming with us?" Peg said, astounded. "But you'll miss the seabirds at Pointe des Châteaux."

"You'll come tomorrow, though," Meg said confidently, "for the bridled quail dove and the Guadeloupe woodpecker."

He said mildly, "I've got a writing project I want to start—I'll have to skip the dove."

"But it's a real coup to spot one," Peg protested. "They're notoriously difficult birds. And the woodpecker's an endemic."

"You can tell me all about it at supper tomorrow night."

"Dear me," said May, "are you sure you're feeling all right?"

"Never better," said Brant and grinned at Rowan. "A novel's hatching in my brain. Espionage, dictatorships and a good dollop of sex. The kind of novel that might just make a bit of money."

Her eyes widened. "What a good idea," she said.

"So good I can't imagine why I didn't think of it sooner."

"You've been distracted," Rowan said demurely. Then she began an entertaining story of how she'd dragged a whole group out of bed at four-thirty one morning expressly to see the dove, which hadn't deigned to appear until five hours later.

After lunch Steve grabbed Brant by the elbow and in a loud whisper said, "Congrats, man. Nothing like getting laid, is there?"

"You don't have to tell the whole world."

"I asked Nat to marry me last night and she said yes."

Brant clapped him on the shoulder. "That's great!"

"You going to hitch up with Rowan again?"

"That's the plan."

Steve nodded sagely. "We're not getting any younger. Time to settle down."

Steve was probably ten years Brant's junior. "True," said Brant. "Give my congratulations to Natalie, Steve...I want to catch Rowan before she leaves, excuse me, would you?"

Hurriedly he took the pathway to Rowan's room. As she let him in, he saw she was gathering her stuff for the afternoon hike. He said, "As soon as I get back to Toronto, I'll call my boss and tell him I'm quitting. I may have to go over to London to clear up some loose ends—but I won't go anywhere else, Rowan, I promise."

She clasped her binoculars to her chest. She was, he saw, on the verge of crying. "I don't know how to thank you," she gulped.

"I'm past due for a change," he said awkwardly.

"To be able to sleep at night without worrying about you, to wake up in the night and know you're there...it'll make a world of difference."

This wasn't an opportune time for Brant to hear his father's voice taunting him. *She's done you in, hasn't she? Emasculated you, tamed you, domesticated you...how long before you regret this wonderful decision, Brant? You know*

your boss well enough to know that when you quit, that's
it. No going back. Sure you're ready? Perhaps you should
reconsider…

He fought the voice down and said, "I feel as though
I've put in a thirty-six-hour day the last twelve and I'm not
referring to sex. Whoever said love was easy?"

"Maybe that's why not very many people do what we're
doing."

"When this is all over, I'll take you on a honeymoon.
A proper one. Unaccompanied by birders."

"Moonlight and roses," she said dreamily.

"Gondolas in Venice?"

"They smell. I'd rather have satin sheets and candle-
light."

"Black satin sheets," Brant said promptly.

She giggled. "You're on." Then she wrinkled her brow.
"You know, I've been thinking…we're both trying to
change. But there aren't any guarantees, so we don't know
where we'll end up. That's pretty scary."

"We'll end up together, Rowan," Brant said strongly.

She flung her arms around him and hugged him with rib-
cracking strength. "I could bawl my head off again, which
is kind of crazy when I'm so happy."

"Off you go and find some purple-winged storks."

She laughed and looped her haversack on her back.
"Even Karen and Sheldon might pay attention if I did."

Brant kissed her thoroughly and with enjoyment, and
then went to his room. It seemed very empty without her.
He took out his new pad of paper and his scribbled notes
and determinedly began to work.

CHAPTER TWELVE

BY THE next afternoon Brant was both excited by the directions his imagination was taking him, and appalled by the amount of work it was leading him into. At two-thirty he decided to take a break and go for a quick swim; he didn't expect the others back for another couple of hours. He hoped Rowan had been successful in locating the elusive quail dove.

Rowan...she'd slept with him again last night, and they'd made love with a passionate intensity after dinner and with a languorous sensuality at two in the morning. As he strode to the beach, he found himself wishing her wedding ring wasn't in Toronto; he wanted it back on her finger, his seal on her publicly, their commitment restated.

Patience, Brant, he told himself, and plunged headlong into the sea. He swam for twenty minutes, feeling his head clear; with any luck he'd get another hour or two of work before the group got back to the hotel.

He didn't like waiting for Rowan. Even for a day. How had she ever managed when he was gone for weeks at a time to places like Peru and Afghanistan?

He'd been a selfish bastard.

But not anymore. He'd learned his lesson.

He waded to shore. A little boy of perhaps four or five was playing in the sand right by his towel. As Brant picked up the towel and wiped the salt from his face, the boy piped in French, "I'm building a castle."

The heaps of sand were lopsided and one of the tunnels

was in danger of caving in. Speaking French, too, Brant said, "It's a fine castle."

"Want to help?"

The boy's hair was brown and his eyes blue. Brant's hair had been that light a brown when he'd been younger. "Sure," he said, and knelt down on the sand. The boy passed him a green plastic bucket, which Brant packed with damp sand to make a tower. Before long they'd constructed a new tunnel and an impressive series of battlements topped with shells and scraps of seaweed. The boy's name was Philippe, he was five years old and he lived in Alsace.

Brant said finally, "The tide's coming in and I have to go, Philippe, I've got some work to do."

A wave tickled the little boy's feet. "The sea's going to wash away our castle," he said, his face puckering.

"You can build another one higher up."

A bigger wave rushed toward them, swamping the lower row of towers and gurgling into the tunnel. Philippe frenziedly tried to shore it up, but the backwash collapsed the last of the roof, leaving only a waterlogged groove in the sand. He began to cry, a heartbroken wail of protest. Brant said, giving the boy a comforting pat on the shoulder, "It's okay—we had fun making it and I'll help you start another one if you like."

His novel could wait. A little boy's feelings were far more important.

Then, from behind them, a man's voice yelled, "Stop that crying, Philippe! This minute."

Philippe flinched, trying to swallow a sob and scrubbing at his cheeks. But as grains of sand caught in his eye, his tears overflowed again. Brant took the dry corner of his towel and wiped around the boy's eyes, saying pacifically to the man who'd stationed himself beside them, "He got sand in his eye, he'll be fine in a minute.'' Then he stood up.

The man was unquestionably Philippe's father; he had the same blue eyes and wide cheekbones, although his face was choleric and his jowls flabby. Ignoring Brant as if he didn't exist, he shouted, ''Be quiet—what are you, a sissy to cry for every little thing?''

''I got sand in my eye,'' Philippe snuffled.

''Sand in your eye, that's nothing—you'd think you nearly drowned. Quit your bawling or I'll give you something to cry for.''

Almost the same words had been thrown at Brant time and again many years ago, hurtful, belittling words that, at first, used to make him cry all the harder. Only later had he learned never to cry, that tears were like the red flag to the bull and that feelings were to be buried so deeply they were never in sight. Standing up, his voice like a steel blade, Brant said, ''You don't need to shout at the child— after all, he's only five.''

The man glared at him. ''This is none of your business— he's not your child. Stupid little crybaby, I thought I had a real son and I've got a mama's boy instead. But I'll make a man of him if it's the last thing I do.''

Brant clamped his fists at his side and made a huge effort to speak rationally. ''You're going about it the wrong way.''

''When I want your opinion I'll ask for it.''

''The way to teach your son courage isn't to shame him publicly,'' Brant said. ''It's to show him your own courage.''

Something his own father had never been able to do.

''Keep your nose out of the affairs of others,'' the man blustered, and grabbed Philippe by the hand. ''You can go to your room, Philippe, until you learn to behave like a real boy."

Philippe was still sniffling. But as he grabbed for his pail he said with a flare of defiance, "Thank you, Monsieur Brant. It was a good castle."

"It was a wonderful castle," Brant said, "I enjoyed building it with you." Then he watched the two of them leave the beach, Philippe running to keep up with his father's longer strides.

If he'd followed his instincts, he'd have knocked the man to the ground regardless of the consequences. But somehow he'd had enough sense to realize that in the long run it would have been Philippe who would have suffered from such an action.

That whole scene was a replay. It could have been himself. Himself and his own father thirty-two years ago.

He felt flayed, every nerve ending exposed to the merciless sunlight. Memories that were insupportable crowded his brain, threatening to submerge him as the waves had so easily submerged Philippe's castle. Clutching his towel, blind to everything but a desperate need for privacy, because at some level he felt as vulnerable as a five-year-old, Brant started up the beach toward his room.

And then he saw her. Rowan, sitting on a beach chair watching him, her limbs as rigid as a doll's.

She must have heard every word.

There was no avoiding her. It was a good thing, he thought savagely, that she'd chosen a patch of shade that was away from the crowds near the pier. He kept going and when his knee butted against her chair and the shadows struck cool on his bare shoulders, said in a guttural snarl, "Spying on me, Rowan?"

She stood up with that coltish grace of hers, putting a hand on his arm. "Don't, Brant."

He shook her off, suddenly aware that he had a splitting headache. "I'm going to my room. Just don't follow me, not if you value living."

"I don't know what happened there, but—"

"No, you don't. So why don't you butt out?"

"I was *not* spying on you! We got back early and I went looking for you in your room. When you weren't there, I thought I'd try the beach."

"Why didn't you join me and Philippe?"

"I was enjoying watching the two of you—"

"Yeah...spying, like I said."

Rowan grated, "We're in this together, don't you understand that? That little boy was you, wasn't he? You and *your* father."

Brant's forehead was throbbing like a pneumatic hammer and he should never have eaten curried shrimp for lunch. "When I need your diagnosis, I'll ask for it. In the meantime, stay out of my life. Because it's *my* life, Rowan. Not yours."

The color drained from her face. "You're running away again."

With surgical precision he said, "Don't exaggerate. I'm only going to my room—not to Afghanistan."

"It doesn't matter, surely you can see that," she cried. "Please let me come with you, Brant. I won't say anything, I won't bother you—I only need for us to be together."

"No."

Behind Brant's eyes the hammer had reached bone, and he wasn't sure how much longer he'd be able to keep to his feet. He had to be alone; he craved solitude as a lover craves a mistress. But Rowan was speaking again, and through a haze of pain he heard her say, "You don't mean no. Tell me you don't!"

"I'm not cut out for spilling my guts all over the map. Some things are private, and best kept that way."

"Not if you want to be married to me," Rowan said, clipping off the words one by one.

"Your problem is you want to own me, body and soul."

"It's not about owning—it's about sharing!"

"Now you sound like that pup of a psychiatrist they foisted on Gabrielle," Brant sneered. Dimly he realized he was behaving unforgivably; and also knew he'd say anything to get Rowan off his back so he could be by himself. Anything at all.

For a long moment Rowan stood very still, staring at him, the shadows of the palm fronds slicing her throat and face. Then she said in a dead voice, "All this has been for nothing, then...our reconciliation, our plans to live together again. If you won't share your feelings or allow yourself to need me—we're done for."

And what was he supposed to say to that? "Just don't come looking for me. Not tonight."

"I won't," Rowan said, her chin high and her eyes like stones. "You don't have a worry in the world on that score."

"Good," Brant said, and somehow managed to steer a course around her chair and up the path to his room. He'd put the key around his neck. It was as much as he could manage to yank the string over his head and unlock the door. Slamming it shut behind him, he ran for the bathroom and lost what felt like every meal he'd eaten in Guadeloupe. Then, his knees feeling like rubber, he doused his head in cold water, took a painkiller and fell facedown on the bed.

Left alone on the beach, Rowan eventually got up from her chair and went for a swim. She felt as shaky as if she were recovering from the flu, as lethargic and dull-witted as she'd been after the miscarriage. Wincing away from that thought—from thinking at all—she swam back and forth parallel to the beach, her slow, rhythmic strokes gradually calming her. Only then did she go back to her room, shower, dress for dinner and make a couple of business calls. Finally she sat down on the bed.

She wouldn't be sleeping with Brant tonight. She was sure of that. But when she tried to whip up a rage that would sustain her through a dinner she didn't want and a night that would be crushingly lonely, she failed miserably. She didn't feel angry. She felt frightened and defeated and very much alone.

Brant had never, in the years of their marriage, talked about his father. It was a taboo subject, she'd learned that during their brief, tumultuous courtship when her innocent questions about his family had met with minimal information about his mother, and none at all about his father other than that the man was dead. At the time, she'd been so madly in love it hadn't seemed important. Now she was convinced that Douglas Curtis, killer of animals, had also killed something in his son's spirit.

His father was the one who'd driven Brant's feelings underground; had he also been the one who'd caused Brant to spend his adult life playing with danger?

Had his father shamed him as that horrible man on the beach had shamed the little boy called Philippe?

She couldn't answer these questions, questions that she knew were crucial. The only one who could was Brant. And he wasn't talking.

If he wouldn't talk to her, they were finished.

Around and around her thoughts carried her until, thankfully, she saw it was time for dinner. Brant didn't show up for the meal. She made some kind of an excuse for him and valiantly chatted with the group as if she didn't have a care in the world. Then May said, "We've been talking about our stay in Antigua tomorrow night. We saw all the birds on the list in our stopover the first day...the concensus of the group seems to be that we could go home a day earlier."

"I was wondering about that," Rowan replied. "I made a couple of calls, and I should be able to reschedule all of you out of Antigua in the morning. Should I go ahead?"

As everyone nodded, Peg said hastily, "It's not because we haven't had a wonderful time."

"You've done a brilliant job," May seconded, and again everyone nodded.

"Thanks," Rowan smiled. "I'll get on the phone after supper and see what I can arrange."

But what would she do herself? And what about Brant?

Rowan spent well over an hour on the phone, at the end of which she'd got flights for everyone tomorrow except herself and Brant, the only two Canadians. Great, she thought, just great. She and Brant now had an overnight stay on Antigua all by themselves and they weren't even on speaking terms. Top that one for irony.

As the leader of the group, she had a duty to let him know what was happening. As an estranged wife, she didn't want to go near him. The wife won, hands down. She fell into bed at ten o'clock and slept like the dead until the alarm the next morning.

Brant didn't show up for breakfast. Rowan waited until everyone else was tucking into fruit and deliciously flaky pastries before excusing herself to go and find him. Anxiety pooled in her throat, she tapped on his door.

Silence from the other side, and yet she was sure he was there. Was he playing games with her, refusing even to speak to her? Emboldened by a rush of temper, she knocked louder.

Woken from a nightmare in which he was being chased by a polar bear through a rain forest, Brant surged to his feet. The bed was rumpled, the bottle of pills still sitting on the glass table beside it. The digital clock said six forty-five. No way, he thought, it can't be that late, and flung the door open.

It was Rowan. She looked cool, crisp and capable. She also looked angry. But when she saw him, her face changed. "Brant—you look terrible."

To keep himself upright, Brant had grabbed at the door frame. He'd taken one painkiller too many through the night and was now paying for it, his brain fuzzy and his balance out of whack. Fingering his unshaven jaw, knowing his hair must be as rumpled as the bed and that his eyes were probably bloodshot, he said, "What are you doing here?"

Even to his own ears, he sounded far from friendly. He watched concern vanish from her face, to be replaced by a frosty reserve. "Breakfast," she said in a staccato voice. "There's been a change of plans. Because the rest of the group saw the birds in Antigua the first day, they're all going home this morning. But I couldn't get any seats to Toronto."

He rubbed at his forehead, wondering if he'd ever felt at such a disadvantage in his life. "Play that by me again," he said. "One fact at a time."

"Have you got a hangover?" she demanded.

"Painkillers. I had headache last night." Although headache was too mild a word by far.

"I see," she said noncommittally, and relayed the information again.

"So what are you going to do?" he asked.

She tossed her red curls. "I'll probably fly to Puerto Rico

with the rest of them and do some birding. You can do what you like.''

He was going to lose her, Brant thought in cold terror. Right now, standing here in his briefs looking like death warmed over, he was losing the one person who could give his life meaning. He said harshly, "Stay in Antigua. With me.''

"Why? So you can tell me one more time to stay out of your life? No thanks! Some of us know when to quit.''

His words came out without conscious thought. "I only got drunk out of my mind once in my life—the day I got home from the hospital in Toronto. The condo was empty, all your things were gone, and in the pile of mail was a letter from your lawyer saying you were filing for divorce.''

He moved his shoulders restlessly, wondering where he was going with this, knowing he had to keep talking. Although stray memories of what had happened last night were plucking at his brain cells, they refused to clarify themselves into any kind of coherence. God knows what he'd said to her. By the look on her face, plenty and none of it good. He labored on with painful exactitude. "The way I felt the next morning in the condo and the way I feel right now are about on a par...don't ask me what I said last night because I can't remember, but—''

"How convenient—now you've got amnesia.''

"I told you, I had a headache!''

Her gaze roamed past him to explore the untidy bedroom. "How many of those pills did you take?''

"I don't know—four or five.''

Her voice rose, her eyes blazing into his, "Maybe you don't remember what you said. But I sure do—and it's making Puerto Rico look pretty darn good.''

In a flash of insight that came from nowhere Brant said,

"Whenever my dad would yell at me, I'd try and hide. Run away like an animal to lick my wounds."

There was a small, charged silence. "Are you saying that's what you were doing yesterday?" Rowan asked.

Brant's knuckles whitened as he gripped the frame. "Yeah...I was running away. Trouble is, in those days there was nowhere to run. And no one else to keep me safe. Only my father." He looked right at her. "But now there's you."

In true anguish Rowan cried, "You've got to learn to stop running! It's too painful, Brant, when we're together as we've been the last couple of days and then suddenly you go away. Close me out. I can't bear it!"

He said roughly, knowing it was a moment of commitment that meant more than any wedding band, "I'll try my best never to do that again, Rowan. I promise."

She was staring at him, and this time the silence seemed to last forever, playing on all his nerves. If he'd lost her, he thought sickly, he had only himself to blame.

She whispered, "I've got to go back. The others will be wondering where I am."

"I've got a journalist friend from Antigua who owns a villa that he said I could use anytime. Let me see if it's available tonight, and go there with me. If it's not, we'll find a hotel."

"It was you and your father on the beach yesterday," she said, not very sensibly.

"Of course."

She was twisting her hands in front of her. "I'm like one of those boxers who never knows when to lie down. All right, I'll go."

"Thanks," he said hoarsely.

Rowan nodded, her face full of uncertainty. "You'd better get ready, the van's coming in three-quarters of an hour to pick us up…at least I only have to get through one more morning without all of them realizing about us.''

''Steve, Natalie, Peg and May already know. Karen and Sheldon don't care.''

''*What?*''

Rather pleased that she looked more like herself, Brant said, ''I told them.''

''You've got a nerve!''

''I must have, to be contemplating living with you again,'' he said with a smile that felt almost normal. ''Rowan, if I've only got forty-five minutes, I'd better get moving. I'll meet you in the lobby.''

''Bring your room key,'' she said faintly, and turned away. Brant watched her walk down the pathway, her hands thrust in her pockets. Then he went into his room, closed the door and picked up the phone.

CHAPTER THIRTEEN

THE flight from Guadeloupe was uneventful. In Antigua there were a couple of hitches in the new bookings Rowan had made; sorting them out required persistence and patience on her part. As for Brant, he was doing his best to contain a raging level of impatience. Much as he liked May, Peg, Natalie and Steve, he couldn't wait to see the last of them.

Eventually, however, the six other birders were called to go through security for the American Airlines flight to Puerto Rico, which would connect to their various destinations in the States. Natalie hugged Brant. "We'll send you an invitation to the wedding and we expect Rowan to come with you." Then Steve shook his hand, giving him a man-to-man bang on the shoulder.

Peg and May hugged him more sedately. "If you sight a little egret, don't tell me," Peg said.

"They're not going to be birding," May said and gave him an innocent smile.

"You could time your next wedding for the Point Pelee migration," Peg suggested. "Then we'd come, wouldn't we, May?"

"We'd come anyway, Peg."

The migration, for which Ontario was famed, was in mid-May if Brant remembered rightly. "Plan on it," he said, and wondered if he was tempting the gods.

Karen and Sheldon smiled at him and politely shook Rowan's hand. Finally, to his great relief, they all headed for the security area. Steve was the last. He gave Brant a thumbs-up signal, draped his arm around Natalie's hips and disappeared behind the frosted glass.

Brant turned to face Rowan. As he stood on the sunlit pavement, surrounded by travelers and airport employees, he realized that, paradoxically, he'd achieved his aim. He was alone with her. Finally. He said abruptly, "The villa's available—Keith's away. The housekeeper said she could have it all set up within the hour, food in, the works. Then she'll vamoose." He hesitated. "You look tired out and I'm still woozy from those bloody pills. But that doesn't matter, not really. This is about us, about our marriage— even if we aren't married right now. It isn't about a perfect romance in a perfect setting, like an ad in a glossy magazine."

"Us," Rowan said uncertainly.

"About good times and bad—those vows I made so lightly seven years ago without having any inkling what they meant."

"I suppose you're right."

The smart thing for him to do would be to take her straight to the villa; it was a setting he remembered as idyllic, by far the best place to end the long silence about his childhood and to convince Rowan to marry him for the second time. His heart thudding in his chest, his throat dry, Brant grabbed her by the elbow. "I've got to tell you about my father," he said jaggedly, "it won't keep any longer."

"Here?" she said, glancing around her. *"Now?"*

"I've waited too long—seven years too long. I can't wait anymore, Rowan."

She looked, Brant saw distantly, extremely frightened, and somehow that strengthened his resolve. When he'd rehearsed this in his mind, he'd planned to give her a dry-as-dust psychological portrait of Douglas Curtis as a father figure, keeping himself safely in the background. But as he pulled Rowan back in the shade of a pillar, other words fell

from his lips as though a floodgate had opened, an irresistible rush of words he couldn't have dammed up to save
his soul. "My father arrived five days after my mother
died," he said hoarsely. "I was crying when he walked in
the room. Bad beginning. He had three rules. Don't show
your feelings, never show you're afraid, and always push
yourself to the limit." Brant leaned his spine against the
rough pillar. "It didn't matter that I was only five and had
just lost my mother, whom I loved. He had no use for tears,
especially in his own son whom he was convinced his ex-
wife had ruined. So he set out to educate me."

A plane took off behind them in a roar of exhaust.
Beneath the noise Brant's voice sounded as rough-edged as
an engine in need of a tune-up. "He lived in a barn of a
house, full of stuffed game trophies, horns, antlers, tusks,
you name it. Along with an arsenal of guns. He sent me to
a private day school, where I had to learn to defend myself
against the bullies. Defend and go on the attack. If I cried,
I got shut up in the attic, which was gloomy and full of
shadows and spiderwebs, and held all the animals that
weren't in good enough condition to be downstairs—there
was a boa constrictor that used to give me nightmares. If I
defied him, I was locked in a dark cupboard—oh, hell,
Rowan, I hate talking about it! It all sounds so trivial."

"Keep going," she said.

Her dark brown eyes were fastened on his face. Puzzled,
he asked, "Are you angry with me?"

"Not with you. With him. And nothing you've told me
so far is the least bit trivial."

"Oh...well, I soon learned not to cry. I also learned to
hide my feelings, to bury my real self so deep he couldn't
reach me...I never showed him anything that could be con-
strued as weakness. He used to slap me around quite a bit—
called it toughening me up, making a man of me. He
couldn't keep that up indefinitely, though, because I had a

growth spurt at thirteen and started getting a lot stronger…I moved out as soon as I turned sixteen and legally could be on my own.''

Restlessly Brant rubbed at the back of his neck. ''He taught me some good stuff, I suppose. I learned to be a dare-devil skier, a rock climber, a surfer. Whenever I mastered one thing, he pushed me to the next, always upping the ante…I guess somewhere in all that I got hooked on danger. On living on the edge as a way of life—that was the one feeling he did allow. Hence my job.'' He gave the woman facing him a mirthless smile. ''It has a certain logic, wouldn't you agree?''

''Oh, yes,'' said Rowan.

''But do you see why I'm so afraid of becoming a father? What if I turn out like him? I couldn't bear to subject another little boy to that!''

''Brant, you won't. I watched you on the beach with Philippe, the way the two of you played together. The way you stood up to his father.'' Her voice shook with the depth of her feelings. ''I think you'd be a wonderful father because you'd be so aware of all the pitfalls.'' With a sudden grin she added, ''Anyway, you think I'd put up with the kind of garbage your dad handed out? No way.''

A little of the tension loosened in Brant's body. But he hadn't finished. Not yet. ''I think I married you knowing you'd be my salvation,'' he said harshly. ''That you'd give me intimacy, comfort, companionship, everything I'd missed out on. And then I blew it. I acted like a carbon copy of my father, tearing around the globe proving what a macho man I was.''

Rowan stood taller, her curls bouncing with energy. ''But you were always so tender and loving to me in bed. That side of you didn't atrophy. Your father didn't— couldn't—kill it, no matter what he did.''

"But I could only be tender in bed. Sexually. Not the rest of the time."

"That's changing," she said forcibly. "Besides, if it was only sex, anyone would do. Gabrielle, for instance. But it has to be me, doesn't it?"

She was right, of course. He'd known from the first moment he'd seen Rowan that no other woman existed for him. He wiped his damp palms down the sides of his jeans, noticing absently that the pavement was eddying with new arrivals, brightly dressed tourists, laughing and talking; they could have been a million miles away. Then Rowan put her arms around his waist and rested her cheek on his chest. "Thank you for telling me," she whispered.

Automatically Brant held her to him, staring blankly over her shoulder into the brilliant sunlight where an Antiguan family was milling around a pile of luggage. He'd done it. He'd broken all the rules his father had drilled into him, and described things he'd expected to carry to the grave unsaid. But instead of jubilation or release, Brant felt naked and exposed, as though he'd been staked out under a sun that had burned the skin from his body.

He said without a trace of emotion, "I arranged for a rented car. I'll get it so we can go to the villa."

Rowan looked up. Tears were glimmering on her lashes. "Brant, I can't—"

"Stay with the luggage, will you?" he interrupted in a clipped voice and pulled free of her, striding across the pavement into the glare of light. He was running away again. But he couldn't face Rowan's tears, the intensity of her gaze. Enough, he thought. Enough. He'd made a fool of himself, yammering on about spiderwebs and boa constrictors. A total fool. He should never have opened his mouth.

The clerk at the rental agency looked after him right away. He filled out the forms at the counter and couldn't have said two minutes later what he'd written. Then he walked outside, crossing the road, not even glancing in Rowan's direction. Some children were throwing a ball back and forth in the grass that surrounded the parking lot, their parents perched on white-painted rocks in the shade. He'd rented a red sedan; but when he tried to fit the key he'd been given into the lock, it wouldn't fit, and when he checked the licence number on the tag against the number on the car, they didn't match.

His fingers tightened around the key in a flare of pure rage. What had Rowan said on the beach in Guadeloupe? *You've got to share your feelings.* Well, he'd shared them, all right. And it had left him feeling worse that he'd ever felt in Colombia. Ten times worse. A thousand times worse. Passionately he wished that he and Rowan were like that perfect couple in all the ads, heading for a lighthearted romantic tryst by a tropic sea. No undercurrents, no battles. No past.

But they weren't. They were two real people instead. Two real people who loved each other, he thought, minimally heartened, and headed back across the lot toward the road. The children were now playing tag. He'd like to have half their energy.

Rowan had moved the luggage out into the sun. Her shoulders were drooping, her hair an aureole like a miniature sunrise. She was a woman of many contradictions, he knew that, for she could be fiery and gentle, capable and vulnerable. Yet ever since he'd met her, she'd fought him wholeheartedly with all the passion in her nature, because she believed in him and loved him.

Fight or flight. By telling her about his father, he'd chosen the very opposite of flight.

He waved the key at her, indicating the general direction of the rental agency, and was about to step off the curb when he heard a vehicle rounding the corner in a squeal of tires. A battered yellow van careened toward him, traveling much too fast. And then, to his horror, he saw one of the children, a little boy in a bright blue shirt, dash from the grass onto the road.

In a split second that was out of time thoughts tumbled through Brant's brain. Rowan was watching him. Once again she'd see him opt for risk, for danger: the very trait in him that she abhorred. She'd forgiven him the episode with the bull. But would she forgive him one more time?

He was risking all that he valued and longed to possess. Endangering his future with Rowan, the woman he loved enough to have bared his soul to her.

He moved like greased lightning, and even then, from the corner of his eye, saw fear transfix Rowan to the pavement, her hands flying up in the air as though to ward off what she was about to witness. In silence and in utter desperation Brant threw words across the space that separated them: *Forgive me, I've got to do this…I couldn't live with myself if I didn't.*

Then he lunged for the bright blue shirt, seeing a streak of yellow so close that in sheer terror he thought he was too late. Tires screeched. The stink of burning rubber filled his nostrils. He flung the little boy onto the grass, felt a glancing blow to his hip and struck the tarmac, from long practice protecting his head as he rolled into the ditch.

Silence fell, an instant of eerie and total silence. For a moment, crazily, Brant wondered if he were dead, because all the breath seemed to have been driven from his chest. Then the child started to wail, the mother screamed her son's name, the van door creaked open and footsteps raced toward him.

Rowan fell on her knees beside him, her hands roaming his body with desperate haste, then cradling his head. "*Brant*—Brant, are you hurt?"

He fought for air so he could answer her, the spiked grass

rough against his cheek. More people had joined her and a police whistle was blowing with excruciating loudness right in his ear. As though the jolting his body had suffered had also jolted his brain, Brant felt his mind suddenly open to a moment of blazing insight. Intimacy, he thought. That's the real danger, the one thing I'm afraid of. I have been for years, I was just too stupid to see it. It's intimacy that I always run away from.

It seemed truly ironic that—literally—he couldn't find his voice to share this insight with the one woman who deserved to know about it. Pushing against the ground with his elbow, Brant sat up, his head spinning. Swiftly Rowan lowered his forehead to his knees, her hands clutching his shoulders, and he took the first painful heave of oxygen into his lungs.

"The boy?" he gasped.

"Screaming his head off and not a scratch on him."

A babble of voices was surrounding them. Through it Brant muttered, "Sorry…"

"What do you mean?"

He managed to look up. "I did it again. Went for risk."

Rowan, who in the last five minutes felt as though she'd lived through a lifetime, said unsteadily, "I thought you were going to be killed in front of my eyes. The policeman wants to know if you can stand up or should he send for an ambulance?"

Brant had a horror of melodrama. "No ambulance," he said, and with the policeman on one side and Rowan on the other, staggered to his feet.

Rowan kept an arm around his waist, her eyes roving over him. He was swaying as if he were drunk, his face pale under his tan, his shirt smeared with grass stains and dirt. Wishing her heart would return to its proper place in her breast, she said with assumed calm, "How's your hip?"

He took a couple of experimental steps. "Nothing broken or sprained. For Pete's sake let's get out of here."

But first he had to endure the tearful thanks of the boy's parents, the voluble apologies of the driver of the yellow van, and the official questions of the policeman. It seemed an age before Rowan was finally settling him in the passenger seat of a red sedan, their luggage loaded in the trunk. Brant told her how to get to the villa and leaned back in his seat. The roadway was spinning in his vision, so he closed his eyes. She said succinctly, "You don't look so hot."

"Feel as though a whole herd of bulls has run over me. Rowan, I—"

"We're not going to talk about one single thing until we're settled in the villa and you've soaked in a hot bath for at least an hour," she announced.

"You sound like May."

"Be quiet, Brant."

Brant may not have been an expert on women, but he knew when to shut up. He drifted off into an uneasy doze, waking when Rowan turned down the driveway to Keith's villa. With crisp efficiency she escorted him inside and, against his protests, carried in their luggage.

The villa was nestled in a small cove; it had a red-tiled roof and white stucco walls, and was shaded by two tall African tulip trees. Trumpet vines and the pale blue flowers of plumbago clustered around the balcony, which opened onto a white sand beach and the jade green sea so typical of Antigua. The interior was cool, spotlessly clean and pleasantly furnished. As Rowan disappeared into the bathroom, Brant turned on the ceiling fan.

His hip ached and he still felt unpleasantly dizzy; various sharp twinges marked the parts of his anatomy that had connected with the ditch. But these were minor ailments, he thought, compared to the way he felt inside. Scared didn't begin to describe it.

He found shaving gear and some clean clothes in his pack and heard the water turn off. Rowan called briskly, "It's ready, Brant. I'll be in the kitchen checking out the food situation."

She didn't sound scared. She sounded as efficient and impersonal as if he were one of her clients, a conclusion that didn't help one bit. Although the hot water felt wonderful, easing the tightness of his joints, Brant soaked for much less than the hour that she'd prescribed. Wearing only a pair of shorts, he went in search of her.

The kitchen was empty. She was sitting on the balcony, staring out to sea, a bright red hibiscus tucked over one ear. "Rowan," he said, "come here." And wondered if she would.

Without a word she got up and walked into his arms. As he pulled her to his body, she whispered, "Your heart sounds like you've just run a marathon."

"I'm running scared—that's why."

Her head jerked up. "Scared? Of me?"

"Of us. Whatever that two-letter word means." Abruptly he let go of her, stationing himself with his back to the wall, his hands in the pockets of his shorts. "I had to rescue that little boy—are you upset because I opted for danger again?"

"Oh, Brant—of course not! How could you live with yourself if you turned your back on children in danger, or little boys like Philippe whose fathers mistreat them? That's utterly different from going off to Peru for two months at a time." Rowan riffled her fingers through her disordered curls. "I was proud of you. Truly proud."

Some of the tightness in Brant's chest eased itself. "I was afraid I'd blown it. For the umpteenth time."

"No way! Besides, even though no one ever rescued

you, this morning you were able to save one particular little boy from a terrible accident…because of you, he's alive and well. You could do a lot worse in this world.''

His throat tight, Brant mumbled, ''I hadn't thought of that.'' Looking straight at her, he spoke the simple truth. ''You're my rescue, Rowan. Only and always you.''

Rowan was rarely speechless; but for once, Brant saw that she was bereft of words. Without finesse he added, ''I want to go to bed with you. Now.''

Her grin was as lopsided as the hibiscus in her hair. ''I thought you'd never ask.''

''You still want me?''

''Why on earth wouldn't I?''

''After all I told you about my father…after the way I've behaved for so many years.''

''Brant,'' Rowan said, taking him by the hands, ''of course I want you. Don't you see? You're becoming just the kind of hero I've always wanted.''

''Huh?''

''You're hauling your feelings out of the closet to the light of day. You're letting me see you're less than perfect. That you're vulnerable. Don't you think that takes courage? Plus I'm finally starting to understand what's driven you all those years.''

''I've got another confession to make,'' Brant said roughly. ''All along the real danger's been intimacy—I figured that out while I was lying half-stunned on the grass and you were holding my head in your lap. Don't ask why it took me so long—some of us are slow learners, I guess. But intimacy's the one thing I've always run from.''

Rowan's eyes were suddenly swimming in tears. ''Little wonder, given your father.''

''So I haven't given up a life of risk, after all.'' He traced the softness of her lips with his finger, smiling at her. ''Not if I'm going to live with you.''

She was laughing through her tears. "And you have to ask if I still want you? You come with me and I'll show you how much I want you." Taking him by the hand, she led the way into the bedroom, where she pulled back the sea-green coverlet. Then she stood still, looking flustered and suddenly at a loss. "I didn't bring any sexy night-gowns. Didn't think I'd need them."

"You don't," Brant said. "Cotton sheets on the bed, though."

"White ones at that."

"Boring."

"Let's see what we can do to liven them up," said Rowan with a charmingly shy smile.

"Good idea," Brant replied, and took a deep breath. "If it's okay with you, we'll skip the protection."

This time two tears dripped from Rowan's lashes to run down her cheeks. "Oh, yes," she said fervently, "that's all right with me. Brant, I do love you so much."

Brant reached out for her just as she fell forward into his arms. "I love you, too," he muttered. "Oh, God, how I love you. It'll take me until I'm a grouchy old guy of a hundred and nine to tell you how much I love you."

"I don't want to wait that long," Rowan said pertly. "So you could show me. Right now." As she began unbuttoning the top of her shirt, the hibiscus tumbled from her ear onto the white cotton sheets. Brant picked it up, and when she had bared her breasts, he let the tissue-thin scarlet petals brush her flesh, his eyes holding hers captive.

In a low voice Rowan said, "Make love to me, Brant."

"Now and forever, I'll make love to you," he said, and with all the skills of his body and imagination, and with all the love in his heart, set out to do just that.

EPILOGUE

FIVE weeks later, as the first wave of warblers arrived at Point Pelee, Brant and Rowan were remarried in Toronto.

Rowan wore a simple linen suit with her rowanberry earrings, and carried a rather motley bouquet of orange and yellow lilies that made Brant laugh, so typical was it of his tempestuous and beautiful Rowan. Steve, Natalie, Peg and May were among the small group of friends and relatives who'd gathered for the ceremony. To his great pleasure his former boss had flown in from New York; he'd brought with him an offer from a well-known publisher for a compilation of Brant's best essays. Adding to that pleasure, Gabrielle was in attendance, as well. When she and Rowan had met the night before, they'd liked each other immediately.

The sun was shining. Brant felt extraordinarily happy. This time as he repeated the simply worded vows he understood something of their complexities and their demands, as well as their incredible rewards; and this time he knew he'd keep them.

At the end of the ceremony he kissed Rowan with all his fealty to her naked in his face, and heard Peg give a gratified sigh from the nearest pew. Afterward, as they drank champagne, he said to the two sisters, "I'm enormously flattered that you're here and not out at Point Pelee glued to your binoculars."

"We have a hired car picking us up after the reception," Peg said primly.

"We wouldn't have missed your wedding for the world," May added.

"Not even for a Bachman's warbler," Peg said.

Rowan twined her fingers with her husband's. "That, dearest Brant, in case you didn't know it, is North America's rarest warbler. We should indeed be flattered."

"Great party," Natalie put in, rubbing her hip against Steve's. She was wearing a fuchsia pink dress; Steve was having trouble looking anywhere but at her cleavage.

"Yeah," Steve said. "Kind of a rehearsal for us, eh, Nat?"

"By the way," Rowan said, "I'm afraid I won't be leading the trip to Trinidad and Tobago at the end of December—the one you've all signed up for."

"You won't?" May said in disappointment.

"Why ever not?" asked Peg.

Rowan smiled up at Brant. "I suppose the wedding reception isn't exactly the time to make this announcement—but by then I'll be eight and a half months pregnant."

"We just found out last week," Brant added, putting his arm around her shoulders and feeling her body curve into his. "So we've bought a house in the country—we don't want our children growing up in the city."

There was a flurry of congratulations. Then Peg said, "Of course you shouldn't go to Trinidad. Not with the baby due."

"Absolutely not," May said.

"There's no danger of that happening," Brant said. "She'll be here with me."

"The three of us," Rowan chimed in. "Home together."

On sale 3rd September 2004

Available at most branches of WHSmith, Tesco, Martins, Borders, Eason, Sainsbury's and all good paperback bookshops.

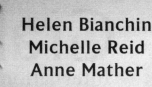

MILLS & BOON

**Volume 3
on sale from
3rd September
2004**

Lynne
Graham
International Playboys
*The Desert
Bride*

*Available at most branches of WHSmith, Tesco, Martins, Borders,
Eason, Sainsbury's and all good paperback bookshops.*

0804/02

MILLS & BOON®

Live the emotion

Tender romance™

HIS HEIRESS WIFE by **Margaret Way** *(The Australians)*

Olivia Linfield was the beautiful heiress; Jason Corey was the bad-boy made good. It should have been the wedding of the decade – except it never took place. Seven years later Olivia returns to discover Jason installed as estate manager. Will he persuade Olivia how much he still wants her, and always has...?

THE HUSBAND SWEEPSTAKE by **Leigh Michaels**

(What Women Want!)

Erika Forrester has fought hard to get where she is, and is used to living her life free from the stresses of relationships. But now she needs help – she needs a husband, fast! There's only one candidate she'll consider – Amos Abernathy, the best husband Manhattan has to offer!

HER SECRET, HIS SON by **Barbara Hannay**

When Mary Cameron left Australia she was carrying a secret – a secret she's kept to herself for years. But now Tom Pirelli is back, and she's forced to confront the choices she made. It's Mary's chance to tell Tom the real reason she left him – and that he's the father of her child...

MARRIAGE MAKE-OVER by **Ally Blake**

(To Have and To Hold)

Kelly loves every minute of being single – she even writes a column about it! But she harbours a secret she can never tell her readers: she's married! She hasn't seen her husband in five years, but now her famed column has brought Simon hotfooting it back to Melbourne...

On sale 3rd September 2004

Available at most branches of WHSmith, Tesco, Martins, Borders, Eason, Sainsbury's and all good paperback bookshops.

MILLS & BOON®   0804/03b

Live the emotion

Medical
romance™

THE ITALIAN SURGEON'S SECRET
by Margaret Barker

(Roman Hospital)

By leaving England to work in the A&E department of a
Roman hospital Dr Lucy Montgomery hopes to focus
on her career. But with handsome consultant Vittorio
Vincenzi she discovers a bond that soon turns to desire.
Vittorio wants to persuade Lucy to marry him, but he
can't – not yet...

EMERGENCY MARRIAGE *by Olivia Gates*

Dr Laura Burnside was pregnant, single and alone. Her
dream job had been snatched out of her hands by the
arrogant Dr Armando Salazar, and she had nowhere to
go. And then Armando made a proposal that turned her
world upside down: marry him, give her child a father –
and give in to the passion raging between them...

DR CHRISTIE'S BRIDE *by Leah Martyn*

Charming, handsome, a kind and talented doctor –
Jude Christie seems the perfect man. And Dr Kellah
Beaumont finds it impossible to resist when their
growing attraction results in a passionate kiss. But as
she comes to know Jude she realises that he has a
secret standing in the way of their happiness...

On sale 3rd September 2004

*Available at most branches of WHSmith, Tesco, Martins, Borders,
Eason, Sainsbury's and all good paperback bookshops.*